CHEROKEE NIGHTS

"I have wanted to do this since the first moment I saw you," King whispered.

He took the first pin from her hair, then the next, slowly, deliberately, all the while gazing into her eyes with that heavy-lidded look. Celina held her breath.

The train rolled on, rocking her up into the heated enchantment of his body, then back down. His hands weren't touching her anyplace but her hair. How could he do this when the most sensitive parts of her body were crying out for him? "King," she murmured. "King."

He smiled, spreading her hair out around her head. A cloud of glossy black framed the most perfect face he had ever seen. He hesitated, his hand no longer touching her. "Celina," he said. "Do you know what you're doing?"

Avon Books are available at special quantity discounts for bulk
purchases for sales promotions, premiums, fund raising or edu-
cational use. Special books, or book excerpts, can also be created
to fit specific needs.

For details write or telephone the office of the Director of Special
Markets, Avon Books, Dept. FP, 105 Madison Avenue, New
York, New York 10016, 212-481-5653.

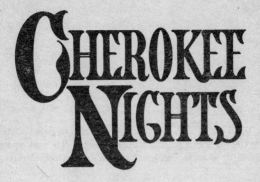

CHEROKEE NIGHTS

GENELL DELLIN

AVON BOOKS ◆ NEW YORK

AVON BOOKS
A division of
The Hearst Corporation
105 Madison Avenue
New York, New York 10016

Copyright © 1991 by Genell Smith Dellin
Inside cover author photograph copyright © 1989 by Bill Walker
Ms. Dellin's hair and makeup by Charlotte Simon
Published by arrangement with the author
Library of Congress Catalog Card Number: 90-93417
ISBN: 0-380-76014-2

First Avon Books Printing: April 1991

AVON TRADEMARK REG. U.S. PAT. OFF. AND IN OTHER COUNTRIES, MARCA REGISTRADA, HECHO EN U.S.A.

Printed in the U.S.A.

RA 10 9 8 7 6 5 4 3 2 1

For Nancy Yost,
Editor Extraordinaire

Ha! I am the White Kingbird!
Very quickly when you and I conjure
My soul wings down upon your body
Like the fire panther pierces the night.

—Inspired by traditional
Cherokee incantations

Chapter 1

Father could ruin the Fourth of July. Or Christmas. Without even trying.

And today he was trying. He was wearing his vindictive, self-satisfied, I-told-you-so look and he would, no doubt, completely demolish this beautiful summer afternoon the minute he spoke. Celina Hawthorne took a deep breath and tried to steel herself.

She stared at him, standing tall and gaunt in the doorway between their rooms in the law office, and he stared back, his eyes so hard behind his glasses it made her blood stop cold in her veins. He didn't come in, and she didn't get up from her seat on the window ledge.

Noises from the crowd outside in Spring Street floated through the open window behind her. "Right over here, folks!" the professional boomer cried. "Have some lemonade while we wait—made from lemons from the very land we're taking you to see. Buy two lots and have your own lemon grove in your own backyard—biggest bargain in all of Los Angeles, in all of California, in all of the U.S.A., in the entire year of 1887!"

The brass band began to tune up, drowning out the next lines of the spiel.

With movements so exaggerated they belonged in a melodrama, Eli opened his coat, reached into his pocket, and pulled out a folded piece of paper. What was he doing? Was he going to give her a note?

He *had* sworn never to speak to her again when she'd moved out of the house six months ago, but he had broken that vow almost immediately. Surely, at this late date, he hadn't started *writing down* orders for her to follow!

Maybe he had, though. If he'd found out that she was secretly trying to get some clients of her own, so she'd have an income that would free her from him completely, he would definitely be too angry to talk to her.

Celina wanted to run away from the paper, whatever it was, and from him. She could gather up her skirts, swing her legs over the ledge, and drop into the bougainvillea bushes below. She could join the crowd of newcomers and spend the afternoon on an excursion to that developer's new town.

Yes! She could talk to people, try to drum up business for herself, ask if anyone needed her services as an attorney—the whole town was humming with business deals. Maybe someone among all those people would not be averse to having a woman lawyer who was starting a practice of her own.

But she would always have to face Father later.

So she straightened her spine and stood up. ''Can I help you, Father?''

''You can.''

So. At least he was talking to her. He stalked into the room. Celina forced herself to walk to the other side of her desk.

Eli unfolded the page once, then again, and, with a contemptuous twist of his wrist, threw it down onto the polished walnut surface. ''You can help me by paying your own debts and not expecting me to pay them.''

''What?'' Celina hardly had enough breath to utter the one word. Dumb with shock that he knew about the desperate plight she'd tried so hard to keep secret, she read the black, spidery scrawl on the bill from her landlady, Mrs. Moncrief. It demanded that Eli pay the rent, "two months overdue" for the room of "Celina Esperanza Hawthorne, your daughter and charge."

"Or," Eli said, "since the look on your face tells me that the pathetic pittance your Grandfather Martinez managed to leave to you has run out and you cannot possibly pay your own rent, you can help me by returning to that hovel and packing up your things. I'll send Martin and Henry to move them back home."

"No!" The word came out sounding more like a plea than she had intended. It was still hard for her to openly defy him when for years and years she'd done so only in her heart. But it would never do to let Father know that, so she forced the supplication from her voice. "I'll hawk real estate in the streets like that man outside my window before I'll ever live at home again," she said coolly.

Disgust flickered in his eyes behind the shield of his spectacles. "You'll be hawking your *body* in the streets, if you take that attitude," he snapped. "But what else can one expect from a woman shameless enough to live alone in a rented room?"

Fury flamed in the pit of Celina's stomach. She fought it down—if she ever unleashed it she would wreck the world. She searched for her composed, noncommittal tone again and found it. "Mrs. Moncrief's is a perfectly respectable boardinghouse."

"I don't give a care if it's a nunnery! Your living there is a wanton disgrace when you've a father who provides you a home filled with luxury."

"And with tyranny." The word was out before she thought. Good. She was becoming more courageous with every confrontation.

It didn't faze him, however. "Martin and Henry

will come to move you this evening at six o'clock sharp. Be ready."

As recently as last January she'd have crumbled beneath the iron wheel of his will, but not now! Not after these six months of lonely misery invested in trying to gain her freedom; not with the threat of an arranged marriage hanging over her head, waiting for the moment Eli gained the slightest leverage.

"I will not! You have no right!"

"I most certainly do have the right. You are my charge, as Mrs. Whoever has reminded me, and I won't let you give me a reputation of not paying my debts; you've made me a laughingstock as it is. You'll come right back home where you belong."

Celina took a long, shuddering breath. "I won't. And if you don't stop trying to take over my personal life I won't work for you, either."

"Then you won't practice law at all, will you? Haven't you noticed that, in spite of all your secretive maneuverings, you have no clients?"

Celina's hands gripped the back of her chair. He knew! Oh, dear goodness, he must've known all along. How could she ever have hoped that his all-seeing eyes wouldn't be watching her every move?

Those narrow, dark eyes gleamed at her. "My dear, I have enough influence in Southern California to see to it that you have not and will never have a solitary piece of work in the law unless you are acting as my assistant."

That sudden explanation of her many rejections glued Celina's tongue to the roof of her mouth. All the confusing, contradictory feelings that she had for her father surged to life inside her.

How could he do this to her? Did he not love her at all?

She wished she could cry the question out to him—let it loose from the awful, burning spot where it lived in her heart. But twenty-one years of hiding

her real feelings from him had formed too strong a
habit to break.

"It seems a waste," she said calmly. "You sent
me to school and now you won't let me use my education."

"You can use your education by acting as my right
arm . . . someday," he hissed. "For the next year,
however, you won't see the inside of a courtroom.
You'll do research only—your punishment for going
behind my back and trying to steal my clients
away."

"I didn't! I didn't approach even *one* of your clients!"

"Aha! Then you admit you tried! You're an un-
grateful, deceitful daughter."

His words hurt like a grievous wound. *Papa!* she
wanted to cry, although she hadn't used that childhood term since her bitter leavetaking from his
house. *Have you no mercy in you at all?*

His gaze grew even sterner. Oh, why couldn't he
be kind to her, the way he used to be when she was
a little girl?

"You can't practice law unless you present yourself decently," he said coldly. "You must have the
sponsorship of a male relative—me or, seeing that
you have no brother, a husband."

His head thrust forward and he glared down into
her face. "If you don't care to work with me, Celina,
then cooperate the next time I arrange a marriage
for you. I can find you an open-minded attorney
who will share a practice with his wife, if that's what
you want."

"What I want is to practice on my own!" Her
hands curled into fists. "And I will *not* get married!"

"What you want is your own willful way! Why
can't you be biddable and sweet like a woman is
supposed to be?"

"Oh? All women should be just alike—obedient

to the dictates of a man? Is that what you're telling me?"

He ignored her challenge. "My big mistake was sending you away to school," he said. "And letting you live with Professor and Mrs. Tolliver was another."

Eli tapped his fingertips against the top of the desk with every word as if he were ticking off items on a list. "She filled your head full of suffragette nonsense so now you stubbornly refuse to see that she's nothing but a meddling do-good fanatic who doesn't know her place."

"She is not! How dare you criticize her!"

"Not meddling? Marching in temperance parades, going into the alleys of Chinatown to free slave girls who are none of her concern! The professor should've locked her in the house a long time ago."

"As you've done to Mother?"

His eyes glinted with pure anger. "Young lady . . ."

Behind Eli, someone cleared his throat. His secretary, Martin Ponder, had materialized in the doorway.

"Mr. Hawthorne, sir," he said. "Mr. Collingsworth is waiting to speak with you, sir."

Eli turned, hesitated, then took a step toward his rotund employee. "Tell him I'm coming."

Over his shoulder, to Celina, he said, "Go to that wretched hole-in-the-wall of yours and start packing."

Kingfisher Chekote pulled out his watch and checked it against the large, round clock of the Southern Pacific's Los Angeles depot. The two timepieces agreed: seventeen minutes after three.

Where was Jacobs?

King began to pace the platform again. He tightened his grip on his well-worn leather bag, keeping one eye on the depot doors and the other on the northbound 3:15, chugging away on the track in front of him.

" 'Board!'' the conductor shouted for the third time. "All's going north, come aboard this train!"

It would be pulling out at any minute. If they missed it because of the garrulous lawyer's socializing, he would skin the man alive.

"Mr. Chekote!"

King spun around to see Terrill Jacobs, hat and satchel in one hand, thin blond hair flying, racing toward him. "Jacobs! The train's about to leave. Where've you been?"

King took hold of the lawyer's thin arm and tried to hurry him toward the door of the nearest car, but Jacobs dug in his heels.

"I've gotten a new position, sir. I'm sorry, Mr. Chekote, but I'll be leaving your employ."

King stared at him.

"I've just met a professional developer," Jacobs continued, gasping for breath. "Named Larsen. He's come out here from Iowa because he says Southern California is the biggest boom of all time. He's offered to make me a full partner and I can't afford to turn that down." He fixed King with an innocent blue gaze.

The conductor cried " 'Board!'' again. His voice seemed to King to come from a far distance.

An old fruit peddler hurriedly climbed down the steps of the train, and the smell of ripe pears floated in a cloud to King's nostrils. He inhaled it as if it were smelling salts—God knew he needed something to clear his brain. Had Jacobs really said what he thought he said?

"A new position," King said, forcing the muscles of his jaw to loosen so he could talk. "And exactly when do you start?"

"Immediately."

The train's noise grew louder. It began to chuff in earnest, building up steam for the power to pull out of the station.

King shouted, "You ingrate! You're leaving me *immediately*, with an important land contract unsigned and a title trial coming up that'll decide whether my railroad lives or dies?" He shook the man. "Is that what you're telling me?"

Jacobs squirmed, trying to retreat from the force of King's anger, but as he stepped backward King advanced, holding him fast, thrusting his face ever closer to his employee's rapidly whitening one. The man twisted his whole body and tried to pull his arm free.

King let him go. Jacobs staggered backward.

"I'm sorry, sir." Jacobs shifted his hat to his other hand and offered King the satchel. "I've brought the papers pertaining to the Donathan purchase and to the title case, sir. They include all my preparations."

The train's puffing built to a crescendo. Kingfisher glared down into the pale blue eyes struggling to stay locked with his.

"I hoped you'd be happy for me, Mr. Chekote."

"I don't give a damn about your happiness!" King shouted. "What about my railroad?"

"I can't help the timing! It's now or never, Larsen says."

"It sure as hell is. Get out of my sight now or you'll never be able to."

Jacobs's eyes widened. He held out the satchel.

King ignored it. He took a step forward, fists clenched.

"Get out of my sight, I said."

"Y-yes, sir," Jacobs stammered. He dropped the satchel at King's feet, backing away with short, quick steps. "I . . . I'll see Marcus about my pay."

He turned and rushed away across the platform, bumping into a late passenger racing for the train.

Its high, shrill whistle tore the air and the wheels bit into the tracks. Kingfisher whirled and got a glimpse of the conductor's hat through one gleaming window, then it was moving too fast to distinguish anything or anyone. In less than a minute he was looking at the rear of the caboose, growing smaller by the second as it sped toward the Tehachapi Mountains and the title dispute that could destroy his dreams.

"Damn it!" King turned and hit a post with his fist so hard that its sign, "Check your baggage here," shook and clanged as if in a high wind. He wished it were Jacobs's pale, anxious face.

He threw his bag onto a bench and his hat after it. Now what was he supposed to do?

It wouldn't have made any difference if he had caught the train. Not without an attorney, because there were none living anywhere near Haileyville, where the title case would be tried—he had no choice but to take one with him.

There were plenty of lawyers here in Los Angeles, no doubt, but what good did that do him? How could he possibly find one who would jump onto a train—they'd have to catch the 6:05 tomorrow morning at the very latest—and leave all his other business to take care of itself?

He couldn't think of a single soul in Los Angeles he could call on to help him find someone.

Well, that's what he got for coming out here into a country full of strangers, he thought, his lips twisting in a wry smile. He could almost hear his mother lecturing him now; she'd say if he were home in the Nation he'd have a hundred people he could turn to any time he needed help.

He ran his hand through his hair. Then, slowly,

he drew it out and re-formed it into a fist. He hit the post again, but gently this time.

There *was* somebody here! Somebody from the Nation who was almost like family!

King closed his eyes and tried to visualize the letter from Aunt Felicity that had found him all those long months ago, when he had first come to California. Two years ago, in fact. Now, what was it she had said?

Her brother in Los Angeles was a lawyer who did a lot of work for different railroad companies. Yes. That was it.

And if King ever had need of legal help he should look him up. She had even sent a street address, but King had never bothered to find it; had never given the whole thing a second thought, if the truth be known. He had already hired Jacobs by then and the man had seemed to know his business right enough.

What would he give for that address now? It *had* been in Los Angeles, he was sure of that. . . . Well, maybe he didn't need to know more. Aunt Fee's brother's name would be Hawthorne, of course. But what Christian name?

Nothing came to him, but he strode across the plank platform to the ticket agent's window anyway.

"I'm looking for a lawyer named Hawthorne," King told him. "Can you direct me to his office or his home?"

"I'll check with the station master, sir," the man replied, touching the tips of his fingers to the shiny bill of his cap. "One moment, please."

King stood in the heat of the afternoon sunlight while he waited, his heartbeat slowing, his desperation melting away. This was going to work, he could just feel it. He would find Hawthorne, and the man would either go north with him or he'd refer him to someone who would.

When the knock came at the outside door, Celina didn't answer. She didn't even swivel her chair around to look. She had no idea why Eli had gone around through the hallway to enter, but she did know he'd never respected a closed door in his life; he would come in soon. And find that she had shut both her doors because she wasn't going to argue with him anymore.

She would just finish choosing the books that belonged to her, pull them out of the glass-fronted bookcase, and stack them on the desk in front of her. Then she would tell him she was selling them to pay her rent and he could stop worrying about his financial reputation.

But what would she do when next month rolled around?

She pushed the thought away and tried to pretend that these books would bring enough for several months' rent, knowing all the while that it'd be a miracle if she could get enough to keep the room another two weeks. Rents were skyrocketing all over town with the real estate boom and the steady influx of new people.

The knock sounded again, then she heard the door fly open as she had known it would.

"I'm looking for Lawyer Hawthorne."

The deep voice was that of a stranger. Celina whirled her chair around. One massive tome of the law thudded to the floor at her feet, another flew out of her hand and slid to a stop in the middle of her desk.

"Y-you . . . are?" she stammered.

The man, who most definitely was *not* her father, was already halfway across the room.

"Yes. I need an attorney. Now. This minute."

He strode straight to her. Clad in pale tan breeches and a coat obviously cut just for him, he was so resplendently handsome that he shone.

Celina couldn't take her eyes off him.

He towered over her desk. He was tall, at least as tall as Father's six feet, three inches; maybe taller: it was hard to tell exactly—he was so thickly built compared to Eli's reed thinness. He seemed huge enough to fill the entire room. He was so close she could smell his spicy, masculine fragrance, and feel the warmth of him.

He carried a hat, a finely woven Panama straw, which he tapped impatiently against his leg. His hair was long, tied back at the neck. The unusual style set off the stark Indianness of his face: high, sharp cheekbones and chiseled jaw, a slight hook to his nose that gave him an air of unassailable authority.

But his coloring was uncommon for an Indian. That thick club of shining hair was a dark amber brown, and his eyes matched it like an artist's dream.

His eyes. They riveted her to her chair. They didn't leave hers for an instant.

"I need Lawyer Hawthorne because my company attorney quit me an hour ago." A muscle along his jaw tightened. "In spite of the fact that we have a townsite title case coming before a judge up in Wheeler County and a pressing land deal in the works."

Celina forced herself to think about what he was saying instead of the way his wide, expressive mouth looked exactly right with his strong nose and high cheekbones. "What is the name of your company?"

"C and G Land Development. It's a subsidiary of the C and G Short Line Railroad owned by me and my partner, Travis Gardner. I am Kingfisher Chekote."

She wanted to know more, but she couldn't seem to form another question. And she couldn't stop now to ponder either his unusual name or his appealing looks. He wanted to hire an attorney this minute. She had to keep her wits about her, for here, by some miracle, was one final chance! Here, if the miracle would continue, was a client whom Father wouldn't know about until after she'd taken him for herself.

"Hawthorne's the name for railroad legal work," she said cagily, thinking she might as well get *something* out of being related to Eli. "You couldn't make a wiser choice."

"So I've heard. This'll involve some hard traveling, though. And we'll have to start by morning."

He began to pace back and forth as if he'd like to leave that instant, tapping the hat against his leg in a steady rhythm. His dark-lashed eyes demanded that she say something, do something.

To go and get Father, no doubt. Most people, on their first visit to the office, assumed that she was the secretary. She glanced at the connecting door; it was still closed. But the one to the hallway still stood open and the sign etched into its glass read: "C. E. Hawthorne, Lawyer." The words gave her courage.

Tricking this man into hiring her wouldn't matter. Hard traveling wouldn't matter. *Anything* would be better than moving back home. She could stand anything except letting Father run and ruin her life.

"I know it's short notice and I'm willing to pay well for that. I'll pay very well."

"And what do you mean by very well?"

He stopped pacing and gave her a quick, hard look as if the question were impertinent. As, indeed, it would have been coming from a secretary. Celina looked straight back at him.

He made a dismissive gesture, as if to say he had no time to lose arguing, and said, "You can tell him three thousand dollars a year and five hundred shares of stock, split between the development company and the railroad if he can stay. If he does only this one job I'll pay seven hundred dollars.''

So much money! Every single one of those amounts sounded like untold riches to Celina. But the handsome stranger had said "You can tell him." Just as she suspected, it was *Father* to whom he was offering the work.

"Well?" he said. "What's your opinion? Think he'll take it?''

She reached out for the thick book on her desk, drawing it to her with both hands, clasping it hard so they wouldn't shake. Oh, Dear Lord, don't let him be one of those people who would never consider hiring a woman attorney. Not now. Not when this was her very last chance.

"Yes,'' she said, standing up and holding out her hand. "I am Lawyer Celina Hawthorne and I will take it. The full-time job, I mean. At three thousand dollars a year and five hundred shares of stock. Terms to be renegotiated on July 7, 1888, one year from today.''

Struck dumb, he took her hand.

It was trembling. But her gaze was perfectly steady. Her eyes were the darkest, most enormous eyes King had ever seen, yet the most expressive. They were telling him that she was very pleased.

"Well, then, we have a bargain, Mr. Chekote,'' she said, in a voice as firm as her gaze. She was a pretty little thing. Beautiful, really.

He'd been too wrought up to actually look at her before, but now he saw that her looks, her appeal, were enough to take a man's breath. She had hair that made his hands want to feel it, shiny and black, twisted into a chignon so heavy on her slender neck that it tilted her chin in an alluring angle. King had a sudden sensation that she was holding her gorgeous, full mouth up to his for a kiss.

"Uh . . . no," he began. "I didn't . . ." He tried to let go of her hand. With a quick, desperate grip, she closed it around his fingers and shook his hand.

A door to King's left burst open and a thin older man hurried in. "Celina, I've instructed Martin and Henry—"

He stopped dead in his tracks and stared at King, then his eyes went to the girl and dropped instantly to their clasped hands.

Celina faced the man down, but something, fear or dread, came into her eyes. Instinctively, King closed his hand firmly around hers.

"Celina?" the skinny man said again. Then he straightened to his full height, glared at King, and demanded, "What is the meaning of this? And who, sir, are you?"

"I'm Kingfisher Chekote," King replied. "Who are you?"

"Chekote!" The man actually recoiled, as if King had slapped him.

"Mr. Chekote," the girl said, letting go of his hand to gesture gracefully, "This is my father, Eli Hawthorne."

Eli stared at King with a sudden, hard coldness in his eyes, as he might look at an importunate beggar. "What's your father's given name?" he demanded.

For an instant King thought he had not heard him right. What earthly difference did it make who *his* father was? "His name is Ridge Chekote."

"I thought as much!" Eli screeched. "Ridge Chekote." He spat on the floor.

He raised one long, thin arm and shook his fist at King. "What are *you* doing here?" He took a step toward him.

King planted his feet firmly apart. Would the old man actually attack him? Why, for God's sake?

"Father!" Celina came around from behind the desk to get between them. "Father, please!"

Eli ignored her. His eyes were on King's face, rushing over it as if he were reading something written there. "How did you ever find us, anyway?"

"Your sister, Felicity Battles, told me to look you up if I ever needed legal help," King said, wondering as he spoke why he was standing there talking to a deranged man. Aunt Fee must not know what kind of shape her brother was in. "I grew up in the Cherokee Nation."

"Well, good for you," Eli sneered. "So did I. And so did my meddling, bossy, interfering sister. She probably plans for us to become fast friends and partners; then all the bad blood between the Hawthornes and the Chekotes will be washed away."

"What are you talking about?"

"You don't know?"

"No."

"I don't know, either, Father. Please explain—you owe both Mr. Chekote and me an explanation and an apology."

"I don't owe this young whelp one word," Eli roared. "Except for this one: Leave! Get out! Get away from my daughter!"

"No!" Celina said.

She whirled around and gazed up into King's face with those huge, trusting eyes. Pleading eyes. How could any man resist her?

"Please, Mr. Chekote," she begged. "Don't listen to him."

"He'd *better* listen to me! If he wants to save his skin, he'll get out of this office."

Celina drew herself up very straight. The top of her head didn't reach past the middle of King's chest.

"This is *my* office," she said clearly. "*I* am the only one who can order someone from this room."

That drew Eli's hate-filled gaze from King's face to hers. Her perfect, peach-colored skin blanched, but she held her ground.

"I pay the rent here," the man snapped.

"I pay my part!" she protested.

Eli's tone turned nasty and sarcastic. "In the past, yes. But remember, Daughter, now you can't even pay for the place where you live, much less the one where you pretend to work."

"Oh, but I *can* pay my rent!"

Eli's beady eyes widened. His disdainful look called the girl a liar, but her steady return gaze told him he was wrong. He swallowed hard. "How? How can you possibly pay it?"

"With the advance Mr. Chekote is giving me. He has engaged me to work for him."

Eli's jaw dropped. The look of surprise on his face was so comical that King wanted to laugh.

The small, dark eyes darted back to his. "Is this true?"

"As a matter of fact," King drawled, flashing his most insolent grin, "it is. With the fee we've agreed on, Miss Hawthorne will be capable of paying any number of rents."

"Then you're a bigger fool than the bastard who sired you. This child couldn't do enough work to earn a two-bit fee without me telling her what to do."

Celina gave a strangled cry and took a step toward him. He put out one bony hand as if to hold her away.

"She's never been in court but twice and that was under my direction. She's got no experience except in research and preparation work. She's nothing but an apprentice, an assistant, and that's all she ever can be!"

Neither King nor Celina answered.

Eli's whole body went completely still.

"Go on," he said, speaking so softly that the sound was eerie. "See what happens." The words dropped like stones into the tense air of the room. "You both deserve the consequences of such a damn-fool agreement. Evidently you're two of a kind."

He turned and strode out of the room as fast as he had come in, flapping his long, black-clad arms as if he were washing his hands of them.

Celina stared after him.

King gazed at her. Her profile was still and perfect as a sculpture of the Madonna, her chin tilted even higher in a stubborn, courageous slant. But her lips were trembling.

She turned back to King. "I'm sorry," she said.

Then she gave him a smile that hit him like a fist in the solar plexus. "And I'm sorry that I mentioned an advance before we had discussed it—however, it will be necessary. Is fifty dollars acceptable as a retainer, Mr. Chekote?"

The sunlight caught on one of her tiny gold hoop earrings. They seemed an exotic touch to her conservative dress: fine white linen shirtwaist and impeccable gray skirt. A ribbon around her collar was tied in a bow at her throat.

"Mr. Chekote?"

He realized what she had just said. My God, what had he done? He couldn't take a woman to Caliente Crossing: she'd have to camp out in the wilderness. And he certainly couldn't risk his railroad in the hands of someone with no reputation, no experience.

"You surely can't think that we have a deal, Miss Hawthorne," he said. "The living conditions where I'm going wouldn't be at all suitable for a lady."

Her delicate face froze, except for a pulse that throbbed hard in her temple. "You told my father that we have an agreement."

"Well, yes, but . . . you must realize that I was just helping you out. I was only saying that for his benefit. He seems to be rather domineering, and you obviously . . ."

"You shook my hand when I agreed."

"But I wasn't offering the deal to *you*. You deceived me."

"I did not! You came into my office—"

"Look, Miss Hawthorne . . ."

"Which has my name and profession written on the door—"

King interrupted. "I'll be happy to lend you fifty dollars if it will help you right now." He opened his coat and removed his wallet. "But there is no way that I can take you to Caliente Crossing as my lawyer."

She was desperate. And he was sorry. Very sorry.

"I have to have an attorney who knows the business," he said firmly. "The fate of my railroad—of my entire career, in fact—turns on this case. I simply can't take a chance on you, inexperienced as you are."

Celina continued to stare at him, her incredible eyes accusing him of betraying her, begging him to say it wasn't true, demanding justice.

"Here," he said, thrusting a fifty-dollar gold piece at her. "I have to go now."

She let the money fall to the floor. It rang against the wood, spun, and began to roll.

King slapped his hat onto his head and left without waiting to see where the coin landed.

Chapter 2

Celina stood transfixed, half turned to the empty doorway. Were they all alike then? Was even this magnificently different man as patronizing as her father and every other man on the face of the earth?

The fifty-dollar gold piece rolled to a stop against the brass cuspidor and fell flat with a definite clink. She watched it, her eyes burning. She desperately needed that money, but she'd die before she'd touch it unless the job he had promised her came with it.

That renegade! That lying blackguard! He had held out this one last chance to her like a glass of water to someone dying in the desert and then he'd snatched it away again. No legitimate businessman could expect to do such a thing and retain his reputation. He *couldn't* do that!

A fury took her. She picked up her skirts and rushed out of the building and down the steps straight into the noisy crowd of new-home seekers. The street was filled—how would she ever find him among all these people?

She stood on tiptoe, using her hand to shade her eyes from the sun, and looked for his broad, tan-clad shoulders. He couldn't have gone far in those few seconds!

"Over here, Little Lady!"

The obnoxious organizer was waving at her,

pointing to the lemonade stand, trying to draw her near enough to hear his exhortation.

Celina turned away and continued to search the crowd. Every second person in it was wearing tan clothes.

Yet, in the next instant, in the middle of the throng, Kingfisher Chekote caught her eye. Because he was so tall, yes, but mostly because no other man walked with such overweening assurance!

She dashed after him, past the lemonade stand and the knot of people gathered around it. The brass band was playing in earnest now; she'd never be able to yell loud enough for him to hear her.

A hawker stood squarely in her way, shouting, "Over here! Get your umbrellas here to shade you from the sun." She swerved around him, watching that she didn't catch her skirt on the handle of one of his wares; when she looked up again, she could've shouted with relief. Kingfisher Chekote had come to a stop!

His way was blocked by a red-and-yellow wheeled animal cage with "Circus of Southern California" in fancy black letters across the top. Two Chinese men were pulling it to the middle of the street; half a dozen monkeys climbed and chattered inside it.

"Mr. Chekote!" Celina gasped, as she ran up behind him. He didn't turn, so she caught his arm.

He whirled, raising his other hand as if to defend himself. When he saw her, he lowered it to grasp her shoulder.

"Miss Hawthorne!"

His shocked gaze locked with hers. She tried to look formidably determined. "We didn't finish our discussion, Mr. Chekote. You offered me a position with your firm and I intend to claim it."

His hand was still cupping her shoulder. It warmed her skin faster than the much-touted California sun on her back. The warmth went all through her.

"Miss Hawthorne, I assure you . . ."

Another animal cage rumbled out of the alley, drowning out his words. It held a young tiger, wary and alert, bracing himself in the lurching cage, standing as completely still as the monkeys were restive.

"Oh, look, Mattie!" a nearby child squealed in a piercing voice. "It's the circus parade! Let's go see!"

A dozen or so children swarmed around them, brushing Celina's skirts, pushing against King's legs. He stood as motionless as the big cat.

Celina couldn't move, either. His fingers burned through her blouse. Why didn't he take his hand away? His keeping it there was a terrible liberty. To be fair, however, she *had* surprised him.

With her other hand she pushed back some tendrils of her hair that had come loose during the chase.

"You assure me . . . ?" she prompted.

Good heavens! She still had *her* hand on *his* arm! But really, she couldn't just let go of him. He might turn and walk away from her with his long, fast stride.

The crowd pressed in on them, drifting toward the children and the animals; the band stepped up the tempo. Still, the man didn't speak to her.

His muscles flexed beneath her fingers. She could feel them, hard and alive, even through the fabric of his sleeve.

Finally he said, "You surprised me, Miss Hawthorne."

"No more than you surprised me when you went back on your word."

His fingers tightened on her shoulder.

"I never *gave* you my word! I thought you were the secretary. I offered that job to your father."

"You offered that job to a lawyer by the name of Hawthorne with experience in railroad work, a lawyer who can be ready to travel with you by morning. I am that lawyer."

Damn! Why wouldn't she just let it drop? What kind of trouble could she be in that fifty dollars wasn't enough?

The band drew nearer, blaring out an uneven rendition of the Star-Spangled Banner. King bent closer to her and said, "You are a pretty little thing. You are, in fact, a beautiful woman. That, Miss Hawthorne, is what you are. And for that reason, you are *not* the lawyer to travel with me."

His breath was hot in her ear. A thrill raced through her, so sharp and fast it was scary. She dropped her hand from his arm and jerked her shoulder out of his grasp in the same quick, backward movement. "And why not?" she demanded.

"You'd have to live under the most primitive conditions for weeks; you'd have to convince other lawyers and a hidebound old judge to take you seriously in a case that's all-important to me. How can you do that when you have no experience?"

"Don't insult me!" she stormed up at him. "And don't believe everything my father told you! I've had experience in dozens of railroad litigations working for him—I'm the one who's prepared every case from start to finish. *And* I've been to school, which is more than you can say for half the self-taught attorneys in the state of California!"

The band blared louder than ever. The two of them were fast becoming an island in the melee of people and animals. Celina was shouting as she finished, "How many will you find who have a certificate earned at California College, as I do?"

"Schooling means nothing! All that matters is the skill to win this one case—I'm not going to gamble with my railroad, no matter what promises you think I've made."

That only made her chin lift in an even more stubborn slant. King sighed.

Another animal cage rumbled out of the alley, raising the dust, cutting close to them as it turned. He took her elbow and moved them out of the street. She tried to twist her arm free, but he didn't let go until they reached an arched doorway, where they could talk without shouting. Then he took a deep breath and smiled down at her.

He could talk her out of this, he knew he could. All he had to do was stay in control and speak to her calmly. She was a lawyer: she should respond to an appeal to reason.

King leaned over her, backing her against the wall of the building, propping his hands on the bricks on either side of her head. "Let's stop and think about this for a minute," he suggested.

"I *am* thinking! I've thought about nothing but getting work for the last six months! I can endure any amount of hard living conditions if that will give me a career of my own."

"But you can't go off alone with me and camp out for three weeks. That would ruin your reputation."

"I most certainly can. The only reputation that I'm worried about is my reputation as a lawyer."

"You don't mean that."

"I do mean that. What someone might think of my moral behavior is immaterial to me."

"But your . . . suitors . . . surely . . ." He shook his head. "A pretty little thing like you must have a half dozen beaus. They wouldn't stand for such an arrangement, now, would they?"

"Mr. Chekote, I have no suitors. I never intend to marry. I have more important things to do."

"What!"

"It's possible," she said coolly. "Are you married, Mr. Chekote?"

"No."

"Well, then. There'll be no objections from a jealous wife to our traveling together."

This woman was mad. Beautiful as a summer moonrise, but mad. He removed his hat and put it right back on in one swift irate gesture. Lawyer or no, she obviously was not going to listen to reason. Nothing was going to work with her except a bald declaration of his intentions.

That same muscle knotted along his jaw; his face grew hard as the bricks behind Celina's head. He was furious. As furious as her father had ever been. But she was past being scared of mere anger.

"Dammit, don't you understand? We aren't traveling together, Miss Hawthorne." He was grinding out each word from between his teeth now. "Wife or no wife, suitors or no suitors."

"Then why did you ever say that I could have the job?"

"I never *did* say it!"

"Oh, but you did! You told my father that I had a job and a salary that could pay any number of rents!"

"How could you possibly try to hold me to that? I was only helping you defy an impossible, dictatorial old man and you know it."

"How can you say that? Then you tricked me!"

"I can say that because *you* deliberately tricked *me*. You said, 'Hawthorne's the name,' when you should have said: 'My name is Hawthorne. I am a lawyer and so is my father in the next room; perhaps he's the one you want.' "

"I had no reason to go into such detail! And you shook hands on the deal! You did that before my father ever came into my office!"

"No! *You* shook on it. You took my fingers and shook them."

She raised her chin. "I did notice that you didn't have too much of a grip," she said. "But then, some men don't. I didn't realize that you meant it to be no handshake at all."

He glared at her.

"You have to admit," she taunted, "that such a weak handshake is strange in a big, handsome man."

"All right," he snapped. "You've made your point."

They glared at each other while the band finally let the anthem grind to a halt. The children's laughter pealed and the brightly colored birds went wild in their cage. The circus train rolled into motion.

Why couldn't he stare her down? Such a small, delicate body shouldn't hold a spirit this tough.

Softly, trying diplomacy one last time, he said, "It seems we've each deceived the other without actually intending to do so, Miss Hawthorne. Let's forgive each other and part friends. I'm sure that I'll find another attorney now and you'll find another client. What do you say?"

Tears stung her eyelids. She looked away; the cage holding the lion was just passing by. His eyes, the exact same color as Kingfisher Chekote's, met Celina's.

You might as well give in, he seemed to say. You're caught, just as I am.

Celina nodded to him, then her gaze returned to the man she had thought would be her savior.

He couldn't be this way, he just couldn't. Not when he had first been so splendid, siding with her against Father.

She was desperate. The raw truth was in her face, and she knew it, but she didn't have the strength left to conceal it.

"On the contrary," she said stubbornly, though every word hurt her throat. "I did intend to deceive you. I knew all the time you were trying to hire . . . Father."

Just saying the word made her want to cry, but she forced her eyes and her voice to stay steady. "However, I had no choice. You were my last chance, Kingfisher Chekote, my very last chance in this world to build my own career—my father has kept, and will keep, all other clients away from me."

He said nothing. The last circus cart rumbled by, the children racing behind.

"He wants to rule my life," she said, "but I have to prove to him that I can do what *I* want and succeed. Otherwise, I can't live."

Kingfisher Chekote went totally still. Those words could have come from his own mouth. He looked into the depths of Celina Hawthorne's dark eyes, no longer mysterious, open now into her very soul.

He took off his hat and tapped it against his leg once, then again. Finally he raised both arms and placed the broad-brimmed straw on his head, tugging it down, front and back.

"You don't know what you're begging for," he said gruffly. "But if you haven't changed your mind by morning, meet me at the Southern Pacific station. We'll be catching the six-oh-five."

Celina pushed open the oak-and-wrought-iron door of her parents' house. She stepped inside and closed it behind her, then stood still, listening.

Muted voices reached her from the direction of the kitchen. The softer one was her mother's. Good. Mama was supervising the dinner preparations as usual.

She tiptoed toward the stairs, feeling as guilty as a sneak thief. Maybe she could finish her errand and be gone without seeing her mother at all.

Not telling Mama good-bye gave her a lonesome feeling, she admitted, running her hand along the familiar, polished curves of the banister. But it couldn't be helped: Mama would faint if she knew Celina had taken a position traveling with a male employer—and without a chaperone! After all, Mama still cried every time she saw Celina, just because she was so unladylike as to live alone in a rented room.

Celina took light, careful steps even though the thick Oriental runner in the middle of the stairs silenced her feet. She reached the top of the stairs and ran, on her tiptoes, for the sanctuary of her mother's bedroom.

Celina closed the door behind her and hurried to the armoire, throwing it open to rummage through the dresses hanging there. The one she wanted was at the very back. Closing her hand on it, she pulled it out and held its dark folds up against her, turning to the long, oval mirror in the same quick motion. A knock at the door froze her there.

"Celina?"

Mama! Celina's eyes fastened on their own reflection in the beveled glass. Then they moved to the opening door and Dolores, sweeping into the room with her old-fashioned skirts dragging behind her on the shining oak floor. She was holding out her arms for a hug.

"*Mi corazon!*" she said in her soft, lilting voice. "Maria told me she saw you come in."

Celina dropped the dress. "*Mamacita!*"

They hugged and kissed. As always, Mama smelled like lemon verbena. And she felt wonderful; like the safe haven she'd been when Celina was a little girl.

Celina lingered in her mother's arms for just a moment, then she slipped away and bent to pick up the garment she'd dropped. She was a woman now, beginning her own career in a way Mama would deplore; she could no longer be a child running to her for protection.

" 'Lina, what are you doing? Why did you slip into the house?"

"I wanted to borrow your dress, Mama, and the veiled hat that matches it. And a pair of your reading spectacles, if you don't mind."

"But you're welcome to a dozen dresses! You didn't think you had to steal them, surely?"

"No." Celina took the dress to the bed and spread it out.

"Then why so secret?"

"Because I didn't want to tell you now," Celina burst out, whirling around to face her mother's worried look. "I was going to leave you a note."

"Which would say . . . ?"

"That I'm going north to Wheeler County to try a case. Mama, I've got a client! I'm starting my own practice at last!"

"But surely you can find such work in Los Angeles? You can come back and live in your old room and let Emilio drive you to the courthouse for this . . . case?"

"Father won't permit it. He told me so today."

"Won't permit it?" Dolores came to Celina and took her hand, pulling her to sit down beside her on the edge of the bed. "But, Celina, love, he's been begging you to come back home."

"Only if I work for him, Mama! And only if I marry Charles or somebody else he chooses."

"No, *niña*," Dolores said. "He gave that up. He knows Charles is too old for you."

"But I don't want to marry anyone, Mama. I want to practice law."

"So you can. Move back home and—"

"No, Mama," Celina said quietly. "Papa says he'll

keep all clients in Southern California away from me.
Here, I must work for him or not at all.''

Dolores made a sharp sound deep in her throat.
''He sent you far from me to San Francisco for all
those months and months so you could go to school?
To be a lawyer? And now he is forbidding you to be
one?''

Her hand tightened around Celina's and she
reached to take the other, also, turning so they
would be face-to-face.

''Yes,'' Celina said. ''Because he must control me
every minute. It's been a thousand times worse,
Mama, every since I refused to marry Charles.''

Celina saw tears starting in her mother's dark eyes
and felt the answering sting in her own.

Dolores dropped Celina's hands and lifted both of
her own to caress her daughter's face. ''It will be all
right,'' she whispered, wiping away the tear trembling at the corner of Celina's eye.

That was Mama's standard saying. She always denied unpleasant reality and pushed it to the back of
her mind while she insisted that the man of the
house, no matter what his behavior, should have all
due respect.

But then her face hardened into an expression
Celina had never seen before. ''Don't fret,'' she said,
''you're a grown woman and a smart one. Now,
then, tell me who is this who has hired you to go to
Wheeler County.''

''His name is Kingfisher Chekote,'' Celina said,
loving the way the words rolled off her tongue. ''He
owns a railroad and a land development company.''

Dolores's dark eyes softened. ''And he is a *muy*
handsome, *hermoso hombre.*''

''How do you know?''

''By the look on your face when you say his
name.''

''No!'' Celina cried. ''No, Mama. It is nothing like

that. This is a business arrangement only. Kingfisher Chekote is no different from any other man."

Except for his open honesty. His forthrightness that somehow had called to her own deepest feelings and forced her to spill them out into words.

It was still too scary to believe she had done such a thing. This *must* be a business arrangement only.

"Ah," said Dolores, nodding at her daughter. "I see."

Celina smiled. "You *will* believe me, Mama. When I win this case and become a famous attorney."

"You are very brave, 'Lina, *mi hija*," Dolores said, "braver than I ever was. So I am not going to tell you that you should not travel with a man or ask if you will have a chaperone."

She rose from her seat on the side of the bed with a brisk sweep of her skirts. "Instead, I say, tell me what you want with this black dress while I find the hat and the veil to go with it."

The summer sun washed the depot and the empty tracks with a glowing, rosy light. Even so early in the morning, it illuminated every one of the passengers waiting for the train. King paced up and down the platform and looked at them all. Miss Hawthorne was not there.

He clamped his jaw so hard that it made his head hurt. Where the hell was she, anyway?

And why, why, had he been so foolish as to give her this job? That one piece of folly could bring everything he'd built—railroad, development company, reputation, and all—crashing to the ground. He knew nothing about her, really. What if her obnoxious father had been right when he said she was incapable of preparing a case on her own?

All night he'd worried that she wouldn't be skilled enough to win the all-important title case. Never once had it occurred to him to be anxious about her catching the *train*, for God's sake! She had certainly seemed to want the job enough to be there on time.

What if she never showed up? He couldn't go into court with no attorney at all. Then defeat would be absolutely certain.

The depot door swung open and he glanced at it. A large family party. No black-haired, hourglass-shaped, doe-eyed young woman among them.

He compared his watch with the clock. This was like a bad dream. In his sleep he'd had the same nightmare two nights running, but never before in broad daylight when he was wide awake. What was wrong with all the lawyers, anyhow? This wild, boomtown mentality must be driving them crazy—it was driving everybody crazy.

Even the bankers! He still couldn't believe that Holleman had told him to wait a week for a decision on the loan King had requested. Didn't the money men know that small railroads had to survive and expand if they wanted the boom to last?

He spun on his heel, strode across the platform to the tracks, and looked down them to the south. No sign of the train yet, but it wouldn't be long. And still no sign of the lady lawyer who so desperately wanted a career. He resumed his pacing.

Likely story. That and the claim she never would marry. She'd had all night to think about it and had, no doubt, decided to go back to that obnoxious father of hers and let him find her a husband.

Damn! After losing half a night's sleep worrying about money and bankers and the other half calling himself forty kinds of a fool for hiring a woman lawyer with no experience, now she wasn't even going to show up! That took a lot of brass—and not even to send him a message, on top of it! Why, the next time he was in Los Angeles he would walk right into her office, grab her by those slender shoulders, and shake some sense into her. He would look her right in the eye and . . .

Kiss that gorgeous full mouth of hers until she gasped for mercy. Take the pins out of that softly swirled chignon on the back of that long, slender neck and run his fingers into the shiny, black, black, silk of her hair. . . .

He stopped in his tracks abruptly: What was he thinking? He would *wring* that long, slender neck of hers! He turned and started pacing back the other way.

Had it all been a fakery, a trick of some kind? Did one or more of his competitors, the other three fledgling short line railroads coming into the state, have something to do with this?

From far down the track came the blast of the whistle. A Southern Pacific employee pushed a tall cart full of baggage away from the wall and toward the tracks. Another ran to follow.

"Six-oh-five Northbound!" The ticket agent shouted from his window. "Comin' in!"

Celina rose from the platform bench where she'd been sitting quietly for nearly an hour. Now was the time. Mr. Chekote wasn't yet angry enough to do something rash (like refuse to take her with him out of sheer fury), but he was worried enough about having no lawyer at all to welcome even a woman attorney who had never argued a case alone.

He was getting more frustrated by the minute, she could tell. He was unlike any man she'd ever known: his body and his face, especially his clear, tawny eyes, fairly shouted his emotions to the world. Whatever he was feeling, he didn't care who knew it.

Whereas Papa always hid his emotions until they overcame him and then he would strike out like a snake.

An even louder blast of the train's whistle assaulted her ears, and then the gigantic machine swept into the station. The turbulence in its wake blew Celina's skirts up above her ankles. She waited for them to fall calm again, then she went to meet Kingfisher Chekote.

He was standing at the foot of the steps put in place by the conductor, chatting with the man while he waited for the others to board. While he waited for her. His amber eyes flicked over her head to scan the crowd.

"Mr. Chekote?"

Celina lifted her veil to the brim of her hat and smiled sweetly up at him.

He stopped talking and stared down into her face, searching its every feature as if he weren't sure of her identity. She bit her lip to keep from laughing.

"Miss Hawthorne!"

King closed his eyes, then dragged them open again. They must be deceiving him. "What is this? What kind of charade is this?"

He couldn't think of anything else to say. The small woman in a black mourning dress and veiled bonnet who had been sitting on the bench nearest the tracks appeared to be Miss Hawthorne.

"But wh-why?" he stammered. "Do you mean to say that you've been here all the time and didn't speak to me?"

The tiny gold hoops were gone from her ears. And not one ribbon nor one strand of her gleaming black hair could he see. Worst of all, over her astounding dark eyes she wore small, round spectacles.

A woman and man with three small children began crowding up to board the car. King and Celina stepped back.

"I wanted you to be glad to see me," she said.

"Glad!" he roared.

Celina was thankful for the noise of the train and the other people. Even so, one or two of them turned to look. Mr. Chekote glared, and they looked quickly away again.

"How do you figure that?" he demanded. "Making me think you aren't coming is supposed to make me glad?"

"Of course! At the very last minute before the train pulls out your fears of having to go into court without an attorney have been laid to rest. Doesn't that make you glad?"

He clamped his jaws together and she saw the muscle jump along the bone.

Well, he had to hand it to her, he thought grudgingly: she knew something about strategy. Because, on top of his anger and worry, glad was exactly how he did feel at this instant.

"You could've hidden around the corner of the depot," he growled. "Or behind a baggage cart. You didn't have to dress like your own grandmother or as if your best friend had died or . . ." He made a sound of pure frustration.

"All aboard!" the conductor called, practically in their ears.

Mr. Chekote took her by the arm, none too gently, and rushed her up the steps and into the car.

Inside, the aisle was crowded with travelers bumping into each other, stowing belongings in the overhead rack and settling children into their seats. He pushed her through them while she murmured apologies here and there and tried not to step on anyone's toes.

She had been right! He wasn't angry enough to leave her in Los Angeles. She had the job! She, Celina Esperanza Hawthorne, had begun her career at last!

King kept that same, hard grip on the Hawthorne girl's arm and propelled her toward the few seats still available in the middle of the car. If he had to put up with her, if he were responsible for her (which he was), then he'd make sure he knew where she was every minute. No more tricks.

Only two of the empty places were side by side—directly across the aisle from an elderly woman in an enormous, flower-trimmed hat. King guided Miss Hawthorne into one of them.

He asked whether she had checked her bag, she assured him that she had, he helped her remove her shawl, and they sat down. Then she immediately turned away from him to look out the window, her face shadowed by that stupid black bonnet.

He bent toward her.

"Why *did* you have to wear that ridiculous getup, anyway?"

She bristled. "It isn't ridiculous. I'm trying to please you, that's all."

"Please me?!" He glowered at her.

"First you hide from me to make me glad, then you dress like an old blackbird to please me! If this is an example of how you think as a lawyer, we're both in a lot of trouble."

"That remark was totally uncalled for!"

"It's the truth!"

Celina glared up at him through the tiny, round pieces of glass in those insane spectacles she wore.

He wished he could rip them away. She didn't need them—she certainly hadn't worn them yesterday.

"Well?" he demanded.

"You said I was a 'pretty little thing,' " she stated coldly. "And 'a beautiful lady. Therefore,' you said, I 'could not be the lawyer to travel with you' to argue this case. You seemed to think that people would be more aware of the fact that I was a woman than that I was an attorney."

She shrugged and with one graceful gesture indicated her appearance from her veiled hat to her feet.

"So. To please you, since I *am* traveling with you to argue this case, Mr. Chekote, I have made myself look as businesslike and unattractive as possible."

King let the unexpected explanation soak in while he stared down into those marvelous, mysterious eyes, shining from beneath the brim of her bonnet. Even in that shadow, and even behind the round metal frames that were far too small to contain them, they were the most incredible eyes he had ever seen.

"No one could *not* be aware of the fact that you are a woman," he said, very low. The angry cadence of his words slowed to a thoughtful drawl. "You are, in fact, the most beautiful woman I have ever seen."

That was the last thing on earth either one of them had expected him to say. They held each other's startled gaze while the humming wheels rolled on beneath them.

Chapter 3

He thought she was beautiful!

Celina dropped her eyes. Many men had said that, ever since she was fourteen or so—her father's associates had told him (in front of her, with their greedy eyes on hers to gauge her reaction); the young men who attended California College had sometimes been so bold as to tell her directly (on a group picnic or during a visit in Professor and Mrs. Tolliver's home)—but never, ever, had those words caused this sensation of spinning in the pit of her stomach, or this heady feeling that her body was suspended in air.

It was scary, but wonderful, too. She could learn to like it. And that would never do. "Mr. Chekote," she said firmly, forcing her eyes up to meet his, "I do hope I haven't misled you."

His eyes studied her face. "In what way, Miss Hawthorne?"

"In the fact that I . . . shall we say . . . foisted myself upon you," she said, and hastened to add, "as an employee. I hope that you don't have the impression that I am doing so in any other capacity."

"What are you talking about?"

She felt the heat flush harder into her cheeks.

"What I'm trying to say, Mr. Chekote, is that our relationship is to be strictly business."

He smiled. "It is?"

Celina's fingers gripped the handle of her reticule. He seemed perfectly at ease with this conversation. Did he have something besides business in mind?

"We need to get this settled definitely from the very outset," she said, speaking faster. "Since we are to be traveling together."

"Do we?"

"Absolutely." She waited. He said nothing, but the corners of his mouth lifted even more and a spark flared, deep in his eyes.

Was it one of amusement? Was he laughing at her?

She bristled. "Mr. Chekote, there is no need for personal remarks of any kind between us. I want you to treat me exactly as you would if I were a man who was your attorney."

His sensual mouth twisted into an unmistakable grin. "That's a situation I'd have a little trouble imagining," he drawled. "You'll have to give me a minute to try to picture you in breeches and boots instead of a mourning bonnet and your grandma's spectacles."

"You know what I mean!" she said, taking off the offending glasses and thrusting them into the bag on her lap. "And you needn't make fun of me! All I'm saying is that you should treat me like a man."

His smiling eyes traveled over her. " 'All you're saying,' huh? Treat you like a man? Sounds like a pretty tall order to me."

She refused to smile back. "I'm sure it's an order you can fill," she said coldly. "If you'll concentrate on your behavior rather than my mode of dress."

The amused look in his eyes changed to a purposeful glint. "I have every right to object to your running around California in some insane, lugubrious costume," he said, his voice as hard as his gaze. "After all, your appearance reflects directly on my—"

"Well! Hello there, Chekote! Is that you?"

King's head jerked around. "Holleman!" he said. His charming smile instantly returned, full-force.

A short, portly man had stopped in the aisle. His pale blue eyes, lively with curiosity, snapped from King to Celina and back again.

"Nice to see you, sir," King said heartily, rising to shake the man's hand. "I certainly never expected us to meet again so soon."

"Have to get out of that bank building once in a while," Mr. Holleman replied. "Thought I'd run up to Citrus Grove and look at a prospective investment."

"Wise man," King approved, still in that genial tone. "A trip to the country always does a person good."

He certainly could turn on the charm in a hurry, Celina thought. In the space of one second, with no effort at all, he had switched from stern boss to flattering *compadre*. Did he want something from this man?

"Going out to your townsite?" Holleman asked.

"Yes, indeed," King replied. "I'm eager to get back up there."

"I'm sure you are." The man looked past King to gaze at Celina again.

"Can we find you a seat, Mr. Holleman?" King asked, glancing around for one of the few scattered seats left empty.

"No, no," Holleman answered. "I'm sitting in the next car with a friend of mine. But before I go, I'd like to offer my sympathies to your wife."

He bent toward her in an unctuous way. "My condolences, Mrs. Chekote," he said, touching his hat brim as he spoke. "I'm sorry about your loss, ma'am."

"I appreciate your concern, sir," she said clearly. "However, I am not in mourning."

King moved restlessly, touching her knee with his

as if signaling her to be silent. She jerked away as if he'd burned her, flashed him an angry glance, and leaned forward to look the banker in the eye.

"And neither am I Mrs. Chekote," she said, in a firm tone. "I am Celina Hawthorne, Mr. Chekote's attorney."

Holleman's gaze widened; he stared at her, then at King.

"Well!" he boomed. "Lawyering must run in the Hawthorne family. You're Eli Hawthorne's daughter?"

"Yes."

The man let out a short bark of a laugh, but there was no mirth in it.

"You surprise me, Chekote," he said, his jovial manner vanishing as his glossy eyes shifted back to King. "I'd have expected you to be shrewd enough to hire old Eli instead of this slip of a girl."

Celina clamped both hands around the handle of her reticule.

"After all," Holleman went on, "you're gonna need the best legal help in California to get that townsite sewed up."

The words jerked her straight up in her seat, as sharply as if he had slapped her face. Here it was again: the old prejudice that always followed her.

"I know that," King said smoothly. "And I have no doubt that Miss Hawthorne is the best."

But he didn't sound as if he meant it. And he didn't. He hadn't really hired her—she had forced him, and herself, into this. He said no more in her defense and shot her a hard glance as if to tell her not to speak, either.

But she couldn't keep still. Holleman's narrow-minded attitude was one she'd encountered before, many times, beginning on her very first day of college: a male student had asked her to trade her front-row seat for his, which was behind a post. She would only be in school until she found a husband, he had remarked, so she shouldn't mind if she couldn't see the professor during the lecture.

"You speak of sewing up the townsite, Mr. Holleman," she said, smiling sweetly. "Mr. Chekote could not have found anyone else as equally proficient with a needle and with an argument as I."

The man's blue eyes shifted back to her, widening with surprise.

"I have had professional training and years of practice in both skills," she said. "Do you think any other attorney in California can say the same?"

The man gave a true, chuckling laugh and wagged his head until his jaws wobbled. His eyes flicked back to King. "Well, she's got spunk, Chekote," he said. "Can't deny that. And a sense of humor, too."

Then he sobered. "But money's no laughing matter," he said. "Just remember, son, it's my bank's money you're wanting to gamble out there."

"I remember," King said. "Don't worry, Mr. Holleman. I have everything under control."

Mercifully, the train's whistle screeched once, then twice, louder. The engine's puffing and huffing grew deafening.

Holleman gave Celina a little salute of good-bye, then said something unintelligible to King, who offered his hand again in a smiling farewell. The man stepped around him and continued on his way. King dropped back into his seat.

They moved forward a few feet, jerked back, then chugged ahead again, picking up speed. The train pulled out of the station. As always, immediately upon departure, the conductor materialized in the doorway and began making his way down the aisle, taking tickets.

King glared at Celina; his smile had departed with Mr. Holleman. "What *is* this, anyway?" he demanded. "One minute you're crying to be treated like a man and the next you're bragging about your proficiency with a needle."

"So?" she said. "One minute you're frowning and fussing at me in a voice full of vinegar and the next you're all honey and syrup, flattering that man. What do you want from him, anyway?"

"A loan," he snapped. "The money to make my plans for the C and G actually work. And I wasn't flattering him!"

"My mistake," she said dryly.

King said, "Before Holleman stopped by, I was saying—"

"That you didn't like my dress," she interrupted coldly. "And I was saying that we should make sure our association is entirely a business one."

His gaze went to her mouth and lingered there; by the time she had finished speaking the flinty hardness in his expression had vanished again. He didn't reply.

"Mr. Chekote!" she persisted. "Do we have an agreement?"

"You tell me, Miss Hawthorne," he said, and now his amber eyes told her that he was half teasing, half serious. "We had one yesterday and I didn't know it."

She caught her breath. "Please! Let's not refer to that again. If you still believe I tricked you, I apologize."

"I know you tricked me," he said comfortably. "And so do you."

"That doesn't answer my question."

He faced forward and shifted in his seat to cross his legs so that one ankle rested on the other knee. He unbuttoned his coat and pushed his hat onto the back of his head. Then he glanced at her sideways— a hot, quick look that sent thrills chasing up and down her arms.

"I'll tell you what," he said slowly. "I'll make

you a deal, Miss Hawthorne. We'll keep it all business in a personally friendly way. I'll do my best to keep my opinions about your looks to myself if you'll consent to call me King. I'll call you Celina, of course."

She stared into his open, innocent gaze.

"That seems to me a step in the wrong direction, Mr. Chekote."

"King," he corrected gently. "No, actually, it's a step in the right direction—a proposal based purely on practical considerations."

"I'm afraid I don't understand."

"It takes much less time and energy to say 'King' instead of 'Mr. Chekote' and 'Celina' instead of 'Miss Hawthorne'—so if we use our Christian names our discussions will move right along."

He picked up a leather portmanteau he'd left in the aisle beside his seat and said in a deep-strung tone, "What d'you say, Celina? Have we got a deal?"

Warm, prickly excitement danced over her skin at the sound of his voice. Every place it touched it melted the ice of her anger. Celina. All right. He would call a male attorney by his first name. And he was ready to get down to business. He had accepted her.

"We have," she said. "Now show me what I've gotten myself into . . . King."

He nodded, and shuffled through the pages, sorting them into separate stacks.

"I'm eager to start these preparations," she said. "I can't wait for you to wire your banker friend that this 'slip of a girl' has won the title case."

King shot her a covert glance. So. Holleman *had* upset her. She had certainly hidden it well. And, in spite of what he had said to her, he had to admit that she had handled the man well. She might make a good appearance in court, after all.

"The C and G Development Company bought land for a townsite, Caliente Crossing, at the junction of the C and G Short Line Railroad and the Caliente River," he began, continuing to sort pages as he talked. "And I sold a dozen lots or so almost immediately. Then I got an order to cease and desist because my title to the land was in question."

"According to whom?"

"The businessmen of Haileyville, the county seat—it's fifteen, twenty miles from Caliente Crossing."

"Why do they care whether your title is good or not?"

"They'll do anything to keep a town from springing up right on the railroad for fear it'll take business, maybe even the county seat, away from them. They tried to bully and bribe me to bring the tracks through Haileyville, but it wasn't the best route through the mountains."

"Why don't they move the town to the railroad? Plenty of others have done that."

"There's a copper mine right there. Its owner, a man named Rudisill, has built a little fiefdom, mostly in brick and native stone. Too much trouble to move, plus his attitude has always been that the world should come to him."

"So now he wants revenge on you."

"Right."

"Mmn."

She took the stack of papers he held out and her eyes flew over the pages, skimming, stopping here and there to read a line or two.

"How much time do we have to get ready?" she asked, without looking up.

"Three weeks."

She dropped the papers into her lap and fixed him with her dark eyes. "Three weeks! I thought it was more like three days; from the very beginning you talked about how urgent it was."

"It is."

"But not so urgent that we had to get up at five o'clock and catch this early train! Why was it the very last one we could take?"

"I've got a land contract in my pocket that's likely to win the case for us and I can't risk a delay in getting it signed—so far, all I have is an oral agreement to sell."

"From whom?"

"An old man named Donathan with vast holdings just across the river from our townsite. He's promised to sell me about seventy-five percent of it."

"So if the contract is signed you'll own both sides of the river and full water rights for miles along the Caliente."

Her insight brought him up straight in his seat. She was quick, he thought. He'd have to hand her that. "Right."

"And you can attract farmers by the dozens to live along your railroad because you can include those full water rights when you sell them their land."

"Right. In fact, I have a deal going right now to bring in a hundred Italian grape growers." King's heart lifted. Maybe they had a chance after all, if she could go straight to the heart of every matter as she had this one.

She stared at him, through him, obviously thinking fast, putting the pieces together in her mind. "Where does borrowing money from Mr. Holleman fit in?" she asked.

"There's a balloon note due on the townsite deal. I won't have the cash to pay it if I buy the Donathan land. I've borrowed about half of that purchase price, too, but from another bank."

"These must be enormous sums of money."

"They are. But that's what it takes to get the trains running on the C and G."

His eyes lit up, looking into the near distance as if he could actually see the cars moving on the road he had built. "It'll be the best short-line network in the country," he said. "I'm determined that it will."

His voice held the same blazing fervor as the day before when he'd said, "I'm not going to gamble with my railroad."

They were alike, she thought suddenly, at least in one way. He felt as passionately about his work as she did about hers.

"Does it frighten you to take such risks?" she asked. "Yesterday you said you weren't going to gamble with your railroad."

He gave her a long look. "This is hardly the same thing. When the C and G is finished and I sell land to farmers and start shipping their produce, when the country is settled with towns and we're hauling in freight by the trainload, then I'll be making huge sums of money. Far more than it'll take to pay my debts. All I need is a couple of years."

He had nerve, she thought. A tremendous amount of nerve. And confidence in himself. She admired that. He was making debts and deals that had to run into the millions of dollars and he could sit there and calmly say, "All I need is a couple of years."

"You also need to win this title case."

The horrifying words were out the instant she thought them, sending a sickening sense of their truth thudding into her heart. She turned away before he could see the panic in her eyes, and looked out the window into space that fell empty for thousands of feet. Her stomach seemed to be dropping fast all that way, down and down to the curve of shining track so far below that it looked as if it were made for a toy train.

Oh, Dear Lord, why had this been the case that

she finally got for herself? It wasn't just one case at all. And it wasn't only her future that hinged on its outcome. She had talked and tricked herself into a situation where she held in her hands not only her entire future but King's as well.

Her eyes followed the tortuous route of the silver track they'd just traveled, loop after loop doubling back on itself until the last curve she could see, where the caboose of their own train moved directly below. Then they shot into another tunnel, one of the eighteen that comprised the famous Tehachapi Loop, and darkness swallowed them.

Celina grasped the smooth, wooden arms of her seat with both hands and clung as tightly as if she were falling into an abyss. It was too late now. There'd be no going back.

Too late, no going back. The words repeated in her head in rhythm with the click of the wheels on the rails. But she didn't want to go back, no matter how scared she was that she'd fail.

She would simply have to win.

The train burst out of the darkness and into the sunlight again. King was watching her as steadily as if he'd had his eyes already fixed on her in the dark.

"I know I need to win this title case," he said. "That's what I meant about gambling with my railroad."

"Well," she said, lifting her chin to show a confidence that she didn't feel. "You won't be sorry you gambled, King."

He smiled and she saw doubt mingled with what might be respect in his eyes.

King reached into the inside pocket of his coat. "Here's the Donathan contract," he said, putting it on top of the stack of papers in Celina's lap. "Look through everything and then tell me what you think."

They worked on the title case for hours. King

picked up every page as soon as Celina had finished with it and worked through it again, thinking aloud, commenting on various important points if she had not done so.

The train stopped at Citrus Grove and Holleman got off after bidding them a brief farewell. It stopped at other towns, too, but instead of going into one of the station restaurants for lunch, they bought apples and cheese from the news butcher and ate while they worked. At last they'd gone through it all.

"Well?" he asked, his eyes fired to the color of topaz. "Do you think we can win it?"

She leaned back and stretched a little, rubbing the tired muscles in the back of her neck beneath the chignon. "Considering the ways that most Americans took land from the Californios, this is a moot question," she said. "It isn't open-and-shut by any means; everything will depend on the attitudes of the judge." And on her ability to sway him. What if he disapproved of women lawyers?

She handed the last of the papers back to King. "Let me assimilate all this and I'll start to get a feel for the best approach to take."

"Oh, that's obvious," he said, stacking the pages and slipping them back into the bag. "We'll emphasize the development angle. Judge Sullivan is a real gung ho California drumbeater, so the rapid settlement of the Caliente River Valley is what will appeal to him."

"Not necessarily," she said.

"Of course it is! As soon as I get this secret deal with Donathan all signed and sealed, that'll be the whole foundation of our case."

An alarm bell went off in her head. He was no lawyer; his was not the best judgment here. This case was too crucial to them both to let him control it. But he was so strong and so definite! What would she ever do?

''*I* will decide what is the whole foundation of our case,'' she said, coolly. ''That's what you're paying me for, remember?''

He shot her a fast glance as he finished putting the papers away. ''*You* remember that I'm the one who's paying. You work for me.''

Just like Father, she thought. And she'd do well to remember that when King's eyes warmed her skin and his fingers brushing against hers made her nerves start to tingle. All men were stubborn and dictatorial and would trample a woman into the ground if she'd let them. And King was more dangerous than most: his powerful charm made him just that much more likely to get his way.

His knee touched hers as he shifted to put the portmanteau aside; even through all their clothes she could feel the heat of him. Immediately she slid to the far side of her seat.

He shot her a look, one eyebrow raised. ''Looks like we'd better be careful,'' he said, with a teasing grin. ''One more little collision like that and I'll have to yell for the brakeman to stop the train.''

''Whatever are you talking about?''

His eyes, twinkling, held hers. ''If we touch again you'll jump right out that window—the engineer'll have to screech to a halt and pick you up off the siding.''

''I will not! I mean he won't have to . . .'' She stopped, flustered, feeling the heat rising in her cheeks. If only he wouldn't look at her that way: so . . . flirtatiously.

He leaned toward her, and without warning put his arm around her shoulders. She stiffened.

What in the world?

But he was only pulling down the shade at her window, keeping the too-bright sun from shining into her face. Even with it shut out, though, she was melting inside. Because King's eyes were still on hers.

And because for one brief moment his rugged face with its burnished copper skin had been so close she could've touched her cheek to his. Now that he was sitting up straight again she felt a strange loss that she had not done so. The thought struck her as nothing short of insane. What was happening to her?

"Agreed?" King asked. "No jumping out the window?"

She shook her head, first affirmatively, then negatively. "Yes," she said. "I mean, no."

"Do you?" His tone was deeper, more teasing than ever. It gave the words a double meaning and her a double identity. Some stranger inside her wanted to flirt with him in return.

He knew that, too. She could see it in his face. But her normal self prevailed. "I don't want to talk now," she said. "I need to think." She leaned back into the plush seat and closed her eyes.

King watched her from the corner of his eye. Incredibly stubborn woman, he thought. Although she certainly didn't look it. Only the set of her chin might give a man a clue.

He leaned back and stared out the window across the aisle, still seeing Celina's aristocratic profile instead of the rugged mountains that surrounded them. Yes, without a doubt she was the most stubborn woman he'd ever met.

And the most skittish. Both times he'd accidentally touched her knee, she'd jumped as if he'd struck her. And his arm around her shoulders had made her go stiff as a stick of firewood.

"Strictly business," she had said. And, obviously she had meant it.

Was she afraid of men because she had a blustering bully for a father?

"Celina?" he said, before he even knew he was

going to speak. "What do you think your father meant about bad blood between our families?"

Slowly she turned her head and looked at him. Her skin glowed like peach-colored porcelain against the deep red plush pillow on the back of the seat.

"I have no idea," she said. "It must be something that happened in the Cherokee Nation."

"I suppose Aunt Fee would know."

"*My* Aunt Fee? You call her that, too?"

"I always have even though she isn't really kin to me. She and my mother have been best friends since they were schoolgirls."

They smiled at each other like two silly children.

"Isn't that a strange notion?" Celina said. "It's almost like we're cousins or something instead of strangers."

"Kissing cousins, I'm sure," King said, without thinking. He could've kicked himself.

But she didn't turn away. She dropped her long lashes and blushed, but the surprised smile stayed on her lips.

"Mr. Chekote?"

King looked up to find the conductor standing over him. How long had the man been there? What in thunderation was the matter with him, anyway, not even knowing when somebody walked up behind him? He'd have to do better than that out on the line or he might not live to tell it.

"Yes?"

"We're not more than ten minutes from Bitter Springs, sir. I'll have yours and Miss Hawthorne's things brought from the baggage car."

"Thank you, George. We'll be ready."

When the train began to slow, Celina preceded King down the aisle, his hand on one of her elbows to steady her. To his surprise, she didn't jerk it away.

Only King's warm fingers kept her upright as she

tried to keep her balance in the lurching car. Celina let herself lean into them, luxuriating in the sense of his big body steady behind her, not swaying at all with the movements of the train.

He had the most contagious smile, she thought suddenly. And those clear, changeable eyes that let her see right into his thoughts drew her to him like bees to honey.

He stepped closer behind her as they passed onto the tiny outside vestibule of the passenger car. Another high, shrill blast of the whistle announced that they were stopping at last. The train gave one last, perilous lurch.

It completely robbed Celina of her footing. She turned half around, reaching out for the wall, for the railing, for any support.

King caught her in his arms. His big hand crushed her face into the starched front of his shirt; his smell of soap and spicy toilet water filled her nostrils. His skin heated her cheek, even through the cloth.

The rhythm of his fast-pounding heart invaded her blood and made it race to the same wild beat.

She clung to him; his embrace grew tighter, the muscles of his back moving under her hands like powerful ropes. He widened his stance for the final moment of the swaying stop; it threw the whole, hard length of his body against hers.

She stood transfixed. Never, ever, had she known that it would be such a marvel to be held in a man's arms.

The train stopped. King was aware of that, but he was afraid to move. Celina might vanish if he did— her body felt unbelievably delicate, so small-boned and fine that it could slip from his grasp like a puff of smoke. But yet her breasts were real, full and round against his chest. So soft against his own hard body that a fierce longing sprang up in his loins.

The lilac scent rose from her warm skin like a signature. His hands itched to move over her, to get underneath the stiff fabric of her dress and find that damp, smooth skin, to wipe that sweet, light smell onto his palms and keep it with him from now on.

"Please!"

He realized that she was struggling now, trying frantically to free herself. The conductor was pushing past them, carrying the portable steps. King dropped his arms to his sides.

Celina's veil brushed his chin as she turned away, a teasing, silky touch that made his fingers ache to take the hat off her hair and thrust into its richness. He almost reached out and caught her to him again, he wanted so much to do it, that instant, to cup her head in both his hands and turn her perfect face up to his so he could taste her mouth.

Treat *her* like a man? Small chance!

Then the conductor was on the platform, shouting "Bitter Springs!"; other passengers were crowding behind them, ready to leave the train; and another engine was hissing to a stop on a parallel section of track. Life in Bitter Springs, crossroads railroad town where the north-south tracks met the east-west ones, bustled out to meet them.

With a flourish, the conductor raised his hand and helped Celina down the steps. King took a deep breath and followed.

Again, Celina could feel him near her, as instinctively sure of his exact whereabouts as a swan would be of its mate's.

Her body still trembled with the wild mix of sensations she'd felt in his embrace. Why hadn't she tried to get out of it sooner? What must he think of her standing there clinging to him like that? She had certainly been helpless in his arms; it was incredible that her body could have such a mind of its own!

Then, as if to prove that point beyond the slightest doubt, her knees went weak beneath her. King's hand was around her arm; his lips were brushing her ear and every instinct in her was screaming for her to turn into the circle of his arms again.

"Promise to stay right here?" he asked in that low, velvety tone that made her feel he had run his hand over her skin. Even the deafening noise of the train did nothing to drown it out.

She looked up into his eyes—teasing eyes, sparkling eyes. His breath came hot against her cheek. "I'll go see about the stage."

His absence left her feeling empty, as if she'd been abandoned alone on a desert island, although there were people all around her. Good heavens! What was the matter with her, anyway? How could she let him have such an effect on her?

Exasperated, she whirled to look for her luggage. She watched the men take her pieces off the baggage car and stack them onto the handcart along with several other bags and bundles, then, without thinking, she followed them as they began to push it toward the depot. Almost inside, she remembered that King had told her to wait by the tracks.

She stopped. She wasn't following the luggage, she was looking for King.

Her body was doing it again! It was drawn to him by some force she hadn't even known existed until a few minutes ago. She had to get control of it this instant.

But she couldn't. Her heart lurched when she saw him striding around the corner of the building, his eyes searching the platform.

"King!"

He turned to beckon to her. "Have you seen the luggage?"

"Over there." She indicated the rolling baggage cart.

He gestured for its handlers to follow him and came to take Celina by the arm to hurry her along.

"Hank Austin's holding the stage for us," he said. "And he hates to be off schedule."

"Who's Hank Austin?"

"The legendary stagecoach driver—he's famous for racing over any terrain to make up lost time. They claim he's driven thirty miles an hour with two wheels hanging over a cliff."

"Good heavens, King! I hope we haven't made him very late. What did he say about it?"

"Nothing. He's also famous for not talking except to announce the stations. When he does say a few words, people hang on to every word like it's the gospel."

On the other side of the depot, down off the wooden platform in the dusty street, stood a battered stagecoach hitched to four restless horses. The driver held the lines and stared straight ahead as if he were as anxious as they were to go, and at any second might give them the command to be off. His assistant hurried to help the Southern Pacific employees load King's and Celina's baggage.

"Chekote and Hawthorne," King told them as they examined the tags. He strode forward and took hold of a canvas-wrapped bundle himself.

"Those are mine," Celina said. "The matching flowered ones."

King glanced at the other bags piled on the cart, then looked again. He turned to her. "Surely not all of them."

"Of course all of them," Celina said. "It'd be quite a coincidence if another traveler had bags just like mine—they were made especially for me." She moved toward the open door of the stagecoach.

"God in Heaven, woman!" King roared. "What're you trying to do? Haul around everything you own?"

Celina stopped in her tracks and glared.

His eyes blazed an even lighter brown as his face

flushed darker. "What the hell do you mean?" he shouted. "Any simpleminded schoolgirl would know not to try to bring all this claptrap on a camping trip!"

Celina looked at the offending objects: a round-topped steamer trunk, a boxlike wardrobe sized to hold full-skirted dresses without folding, and a large portmanteau. They were covered in matching lilac-and-pink flowered tapestry with black leather trim along the edges, made for her by one of "Mama's people," a Mexican craftsman who still lived on the remnants of her Spanish grandfather's old *rancho*.

How dare King be so unreasonable? He *was* just like Father. Simpleminded schoolgirl, indeed!

"But we're also going into court," she told him gently. "And you don't like the clothes I'm wearing. It's really fortunate that I brought some other choices, don't you think?"

She waited, her eyes locked on his, but he didn't reply. He seemed to have been struck dumb.

Finally, with a sharp movement of his head, he indicated that the men should get back to work; then he stalked around to the back of the vehicle and threw the bundle he held into the boot. It landed with an unsatisfying thump on top of the bags already there.

Celina turned her back, shook the dust off her skirts, and stepped into the coach. Well, that ought to take care of her problem, she thought. If she could remember what an arbitrary man King was, just like the one she was trying to escape, she shouldn't have any trouble keeping away from him.

After much sweating and swearing, all the luggage was finally stashed aboard: her trunk and wardrobe tied on top, the portmanteau dumped unceremoniously in at the door to land by her feet. King climbed in after it, and before he'd fastened the door closed, Hank Austin let the horses go.

They bounded down the main street of Bitter Springs, dust rising between them and the setting sun like a gathering storm. King sat on the seat opposite Celina and glared out the window.

He should have known better, he thought, seething with the effort not to start yelling again. If he had the sense God gave a wooden goose he'd never have hired the woman. Now they'd have to drag all that claptrap clear to hell and gone.

By Thunder, that ought to help him keep his hands off her. All he had to do was think about how much trouble she was to lug around. They never would get all that stuff into the little tent he'd brought for her.

Celina lifted her chin and looked out the opposite window, dropping the veil over her face against the dust. So, let him sit there and sulk. He couldn't dictate what she packed or what she wore. It'd do him good to realize that he couldn't control everything and everybody in the entire world.

And who cared if he wouldn't talk? It'd be best if they conversed only when necessary pertaining to business. Yes. That would be ideal, considering the fact that this was to be purely a professional relationship, camping out together in the wilderness or no.

They rode that way for five miles or so. Outside Celina's window, the terrain grew wilder, with scrubby trees and brush scattered over the gray-white hills. The summer dusk came gradually at first, then faster, until finally the world outside lay dark.

"Barton's Station!" Hank Austin shouted. "This here stop is Barton's Station."

He brought the stagecoach to a grinding, lurching halt in the night. One light showed: a lantern hanging in front of a small way station.

Four men, rough-looking and coarse-talking, came through the dim light and crowded up to the stage.

When the first man opened the door, King rose and, in one swift motion, swung over to sit beside Celina.

One of the men settled in on the other side of him, the other three stuffed themselves into the opposite seat.

Celina tried to keep from touching King, and he her, but even though he folded his arms across his chest and she shrank into the corner of the coach until the side panel pressed into her spine, they were wedged so tightly together that they might have been glued.

The whole length of his muscled thigh pressed against her leg.

Her elbow jammed into his side.

His bulging bicep nudged her shoulder with every breath he took.

The frothy veil on her hat blew upward and tickled his nose.

They stared straight ahead while the stage rushed on through the darkness.

But as the hours passed, Celina grew more and more exhausted. She let her eyelids close. She began to nod. Finally, just before she fell asleep, she gave a deep sigh and laid her head on King's shoulder.

With the utmost care he untied the ribbon and removed that obnoxious black bonnet. Then he lifted his arm and put it around her.

Chapter 4

"**C**-a-a-li-ente Crossing! This here stop is C-a-a-li-ente Crossing!"

The bellowed announcement woke Celina to the shivery cool of early morning. She lifted her head.

Where was she? Who was yelling?

Then she saw King on the seat opposite her and the entire day and night just past came back in a wild, rioting rush. It ended with an empty sensation of coldness around her shoulders.

Had she dreamed that King's arm belonged there? That it had been around her, keeping her warm all through the night? Surely that had not been real. No matter how tired she had been, she wouldn't have permitted such a liberty! Goose bumps popped up on her arms; she rubbed at them and sat up straighter.

The stage steadily picked up speed, running downhill, then the sound of the wheels changed as they hit the water. Big drops splashed through the open window into her face; Celina blinked and braced her feet on the floorboards to keep from slipping to the other side of the seat.

"We need our nighttime companions back again," King said, leaning forward to help steady her. "When they were here we didn't have room to slide around."

"Yes," said Celina, hanging on to his outstretched hand. "But you have to admit that we did almost suffocate. I hope Hank Austin dropped them off in front of a bathhouse." His hand warmed her through. While she held it she was safe.

"Nope," King said cheerfully. "We left them in the middle of nowhere, best I could tell. About an hour ago. Probably won't find enough water to drink for fifty miles, much less enough to bathe in."

"When they got out, did you . . ."

Move over there away from me? she wanted to ask. King, had you been holding me while I slept? But, of course, she could never say such a thing.

She reached up and touched her hair with her free hand—her gaze flew to the black bonnet on the seat beside her. She felt the heat rise in her cheeks. This was even worse! Had King taken her hat off for her?

The horses suddenly were pulling hard up a hill. They topped it and Hank cracked the whip. They picked up speed and then he brought them to a roaring, lurching stop. "Caliente Crossing!" he shouted again.

"I can't wait for you to see the place," King said, getting up before the coach had stopped swaying. "And to see how far the graders have come."

They climbed out, Celina feeling for the step with her foot while her eyes swept over the townsite she had come to save for King.

"Thanks for the ride, Hank," King called.

The laconic Austin only nodded.

Once Celina's feet were on the ground she stood in one spot and stared. Why, this place was nothing but a bunch of tents! Caliente Crossing was too big a name for it. There wasn't enough town here to even *have* a name.

"Well?" King said, barely giving her a glance he was so busy looking all around. "What d'you think?"

"Uh. It's . . . nice," she managed. "This really is a pretty place for a . . . town."

It was that. The white and tan tents, with an occasional blue one dotted here and there, were scattered over a gently rolling hillside, spilling downward to the bank of the river. There, several trees bent their branches out over the water. The rest of the vegetation in sight consisted of some scrubby bushes and a few gnarled Joshua trees.

Compared to the lush foliage and luxurious appointments she had grown up with, this would be a stark place to live, indeed. Even compared to Mrs. Moncrief's it would be extremely primitive, just as King had said.

But that would be all right. A few weeks of living here would give her her freedom for the rest of her life.

But only if she stopped clinging to King! She removed her hand from his, fast. Whatever had she been thinking? She had let him hold it ever since they'd crossed the river in the stage!

"Chekote!" someone called.

"So you're back, King," another man's voice said, closer by. "I need to talk to you."

They turned toward the voices. Two men were coming out of a spacious, open-sided tent with the terse sign SADIE'S EATS nailed to one of its poles. It was almost filled with men and a few women eating breakfast and talking. When they saw King, several of them got up and followed the first two men out to the stage.

"Somebody rode over here from Haileyville whilst you was gone," the larger one boomed, before he even reached Celina and King. "Said you don't have clear title to these lots you sold us. What's the story?"

The others all crowded up behind him.

"Yeah," a thin man in front chimed in. "You

cheatin' us, or what? If'n' we all pull up stakes and ride outta here you won't have much to haul on that railroad up yonder."

Celina stared at him. If they all pulled up stakes and rode out, King wouldn't have much of a title case based on his development of California, either.

"We want our money back!" said a tousle-haired woman with a small girl holding on to her hand. "Or else the legal papers saying you had a right to sell us the lots in this town!"

"You'll get them," King said.

He turned to Celina with a flourish. "I've brought the best lawyer in Los Angeles to get those papers for you. This is Miss Celina Hawthorne."

"Lawyer!" several voices echoed.

King introduced the large, loud man as O'Reilly, blacksmith and liveryman; the thin one as Bud Hanna, the keeper of the general store; and the woman who'd demanded the papers be legal as Isabelle Browning, dressmaker and milliner.

They, and all the others crowded behind them, stared at Celina as if she were Poker Alice Ivers or some other notorious character.

Her travel-weary legs began to tremble. None of these people looked terribly prosperous. They couldn't be or they wouldn't be living out here in the middle of nowhere trying to start businesses in canvas tents. They appeared to be honest and sincere.

Now they were depending on her, too. Not only her life and her dreams, and King's hopes and his business empire, but their fates, too, rested on her winning this case.

Oh, Dear Lord, could she do it?

Not if Judge Sullivan looked at her with that same skeptical look they had in their eyes.

"Don't you worry, folks," King said, as Austin's helper began to untie the luggage from the roof of the stage. "Your deeds will prove to be legal, right enough. That Haileyville bunch doesn't have a leg to stand on, and they know it—they're just trying to run you off."

He paused and looked around, meeting each person's eyes directly. "And we all know why, don't we? Because they know that inside a year we'll be the biggest and best town in Wheeler County!"

A few ragged cheers went up.

King waited another minute for effect and then finished, "But what's *really* galling them is . . . we'll be the county seat to boot!"

Everyone cheered this time, and the accusing glares changed to smiles. King talked some more, effectively whipping up their spirits and communicating his confident enthusiasm. Then he moved from person to person, shaking hands, introducing Celina, and inquiring after businesses and health. He seemed to know everything about everybody there.

Celina noticed, with a little pang that she assured herself could not be jealousy, that he flirted with all the girls. Every female in the group, from Isabelle Browning's small daughter to a wizened older woman in a wool shawl, had a special smile for him.

They ended up in the middle of the tent as most of the citizenry drifted back to their breakfasts. Outside, Hank Austin slapped his lines and drove away, leaving King and Celina's luggage piled in a heap on the ground.

Celina glanced at it longingly. What she would give for a bath and a change of clothing! She never wanted to see another black dress for the rest of her life.

"Boss! Welcome back!"

A short, stocky man got down from a stool at the rough wooden counter running across the kitchen end of the tent and came toward them. Behind him, at one of the two wood cookstoves, a red-haired woman looked up from her work to watch him go. Then she saw King and her eyes stayed on him.

"Glad you're here, sir," the man said. "I heard you was comin' in on this morning's stage, so I got the men started workin' and then come down here to wait for you."

"That's the way to do it," King said heartily, offering his hand in greeting. "Celina, this is Marshall Moseley, the leader of the gang of graders for the C and G. Best ramrod I ever had—I can always depend on him to keep the grade coming no matter what."

The man flushed, obviously pleased by the praise, and shook King's hand. "Thank you, Boss."

"This is Miss Celina Hawthorne, my attorney," King said.

The man touched his greasy hat brim and nodded to her. Then he turned back to King.

"There's a couple of things we need to talk over, Boss," Moseley said.

"Can't it wait ten minutes?" King asked. "We've had a long night's trip with Hank Austin."

"Uh, yeah. Yeah, it can."

"Good," King said. "We'll freshen up and meet you back here."

"Right," Moseley said. He turned away.

"Oh, Moseley, by the way," King said. "Would you mind bringing our bags to my tent?"

"Sure thing," the man said, and headed outside to the luggage. The red-haired woman passed in front of him carrying a tray full of steaming platters of pancakes; Moseley had to swerve to keep from bumping into her. She never even saw him. She was too busy looking at King and giving him a radiant smile.

Just like all the other women of Caliente Crossing, Celina thought.

"Come on, let's go wash up," King said, taking

Celina's arm. He walked her out into the sunlight, heading downhill toward the river.

"We can both use my tent."

When she threw him a shocked glance, his teasing amber eyes were waiting for it.

"In fact, I was thinking maybe we oughtn't go to the trouble of pitching your tent at all," he said solemnly. "That'd give the town something else to talk about besides clear titles and legal deeds."

He swung around to face her as they walked, letting his hand slide down her arm until his beguiling fingers rested on the sensitive skin on the inside of her wrist. They lingered there as if they had every right. They brought her blood to some primitive heat, stronger with every beat of her pulse.

"Celina!" he said, grinning. "That's the ticket! It'll stop this foolish chatter about pulling up stakes and moving out—why, this one idea could single-handedly save this town!"

He dropped back to walk beside her again, shooting a sideways, slanting look at her that made her whole body tingle. "Well? What do you say?"

She smiled, deciding to rise to the challenge. She might as well, she thought, since that was what she'd be doing from here on out.

"I don't know, King," she said, tilting her head as if she were seriously considering the suggestion. "That'd be fine for Mr. Moseley—he seemed to take my profession quite in stride. But from the way Mr. Hanna and some of the others looked at me when you said 'lawyer,' I don't think they could cope with any other shocking behavior on my part."

King threw back his head and laughed.

"You're absolutely right," he said, guiding her around a bend in the path to a battered tent set up beneath one of the riverbank's low-spreading trees. "We must protect Bud Hanna's delicate sensitivities at all costs. Even if it means the end of the town."

He raised his tent flap with a flourish. "Make yourself at home, Miss Celina. I'll be right back with some fresh water for you."

With a smile she watched him go, then closed the tent. But, just for a moment, she stood completely still, remembering that look, holding the inside of her wrist to her overheated cheek.

King was as good as his word, and Moseley arrived with the luggage a few moments later. Once it was unloaded and stacked, he left to take the hand-cart back to Sadie's, promising to wait for them there.

So, Celina thought, stepping out of the dust-encrusted black dress with a sigh of relief, the red-haired woman must be named Sadie. She, like all the other women of Caliente Crossing, certainly had eyes for King.

Through the closed flap, King gave Celina directions to the women's privy, inquired as to whether she needed any of the larger luggage opened, and said he was going to wash in the river.

"Be ready in ten minutes," he concluded. "We'll eat and then I'll show you the town quickly, before we ride up to the cut."

"All right."

She shook her head in amazement as she opened her carpetbag and took out a fresh blouse and a split skirt. Three days ago she would never have thought she could ride on a stage all night and still be eager to explore a new railroad town the next morning. King's energy and enthusiasm must be contagious.

They *were* contagious. She still couldn't believe how he'd turned that crowd of townspeople around.

Then, on the way back to Sadie's, she couldn't believe how he turned her head around. She couldn't keep her eyes off him. How could he be more attractive in worn, pale blue Levi Strauss denims and an open-necked work shirt than he had been in his tailor-made suit? But he was.

He wore battered cowboy boots, too, and a felt hat that obviously had seen better days. And he walked as if he truly were king of the Caliente.

The restaurant had cleared out a bit. Moseley was waiting at a table in the back of the tent. As soon as Celina and King sat down, Sadie appeared with a pot of coffee and platters of pancakes. She served them silently, her narrow face softening only when she glanced at King.

"But we haven't ordered!" Celina exclaimed. She accepted her plate gratefully, anyway, and began buttering the cakes.

"It's Saturday, so it's pancakes," Moseley said shortly, giving her a look that said any fool ought to know that. "Ain't no orderin' to it when you're eatin' at Sadie's."

"Now, Boss," he said, turning back to King. "I'm thinkin' the men'd be lots happier if they could eat here instead of in camp. That Chinese cook o' mine can't cook worth shucks."

King lifted one shoulder in a shrug and reached for the syrup pitcher. "Fine with me," he said. "But the cook'll go off salary, naturally."

"Right," Moseley said, blowing on his coffee to cool it. "Next, I'm thinkin' of offerin' prizes for record-setting number of miles graded in a day . . ."

Celina stopped listening and let their voices flow on while she ate the fragrant buckwheat cakes and drank the bracing hot coffee. She'd get right to work as soon as King had showed her around, she decided. The first thing she'd do would be to unpack her law books.

No, first, they had to set up her tent . . .

Suddenly she was aware that King and Moseley had stopped talking. They both sat frozen, looking toward the front of the tent.

She looked, too.

Two men were sitting at the counter that ran between the kitchen and dining areas. She had glanced that way when she and King sat down, but the counter had been empty then. Their backs were turned to the rest of the diners, but she could tell that they were both richly dressed, both tall and portly.

"Who is it?" she asked.

"Rudisill, the man I told you about from Haileyville," King said quietly. "It's a sure bet he's here to cause trouble."

"He don't know you're back, Boss," Moseley whispered. "He'd never have come in here so bold if he did."

Sadie moved back and forth between the counter and the stoves to serve the men, who were chatting and laughing. King watched them avidly.

"I'd give a hundred dollars to know what they're up to," he said.

"Call Sadie over here and ask her," Celina said.

Both men turned to stare at her.

"Sadie's not a talker," Moseley said, again in the tone that said he suspected he was talking to an idiot. "She's as closemouthed as Hank Austin. Everybody knows that."

"Moseley's right," King said. "Besides, that'd be asking her to eavesdrop."

"No, she's already eavesdropped," Celina said. "It'd just be asking her to repeat whatever she heard."

"She may not have even been listening to them," King said.

"Well, even if she was, she won't tell it," Moseley declared. "I never heard that woman say more than three words in a row all the time she's been here."

Celina shrugged. "It's worth a try," she said.

"Surely one of you two gentlemen can charm some information out of her."

Moseley narrowed his eyes and stared at Sadie. "I probably can," he said. "I've hornswoggled prettier women than her in my time."

King raised his hand and signaled for Sadie to come. Her thin face lit up. When she reached their table, coffeepot in hand, Moseley spoke right up.

"Sadie," he said, with elaborate casualness, as he held his cup for her to fill. "What's them two at the counter been talkin' about?"

She gave him a sharp glance. "You sayin' I'm in th' habit of eavesdroppin' on my customers?"

"No!" Moseley blurted, flushing with embarrassment at the vehemence of her reply. "I ain't saying—"

"I'm sure Mr. Moseley didn't mean to imply such a thing," King interjected smoothly, holding out his own coffee cup in turn. "It's just that, for the sake of the C and G, I need to know what business those men have here."

Sadie looked into his eyes and smiled back at him, letting the coffee almost run over the top of his mug. She tilted the pot back just in time.

"They're from Haileyville," King went on, lowering his voice to an even more confidential tone. "And you know as well as I do, Sadie, that they can't be up to any good in Caliente Crossing."

Sadie's thin lips parted. "Somethin' 'bout somebody Donathan," she replied promptly, never losing her besotted smile. "About talkin' him outta sellin' some land."

King sucked in his breath. "We could lose it all right here without ever seeing the inside of a courtroom," he said. His hand went to his shirt pocket and Celina heard the crinkling of paper. He pushed back his chair.

"Sadie, can you stall them?" he asked.

She hesitated, the coffeepot still poised in midair.

King said, "Maybe you could tempt them with some of your fine cherry pie. Have you baked any this early?"

"Jist taken one outta the oven."

"Well, then," Moseley said forcefully, as if determined to have *some* influence on the woman's role in solving the problem. "Wave it under their noses, then. It'll delay 'em some—they'll have to spit out the cherry pits."

King grinned, in spite of the worried look in his eyes. "Good idea," he said to Moseley, as if the crew chief had thought of the entire scheme. "Thanks. And thank *you*, Sadie."

He gave the cook the grateful look and one last smile, then turned to Celina. "The secret's out," he said. "We've got to get to Donathan first."

He stood up, trying to keep the tent pole between him and the front of the room. He nodded toward O'Reilly, who was sitting at another table, then looked at Moseley. "Tell him I took two mounts from the livery," he said.

At his signal Celina got up and followed him to the open side of the tent, keeping as far away from Rudisill and his friend as possible. Once outside, King took her hand and they ran for the horses.

The sunlight pulled them down the long hill and across the river at a fast lope. The rolling, grassy hills plucked them out of the flying drops of water and up onto the unbroken road.

"I'm glad you can ride," King shouted. "You *had* to come."

He meant because there might be last-minute changes in the contract which she'd have to legalize; he'd told her that on the way to the livery stable. He'd known from the beginning that the old man might waffle, although he hadn't mentioned it on the train. He hadn't wanted to think about the possibility.

But she wouldn't dwell on that now. She would pretend he meant that he couldn't have borne to be racing through this capricious day without her.

She had never felt so resplendently alive. The wind blew in her face and whipped her hair free; the air smelled like faraway snow and like flowers. Beside her, Kingfisher Chekote rode a shining sorrel horse. The land flowed beneath them like deep, gray-green water. She sensed, rather than saw, its going.

Partners. They were partners. And their joint fate rode on their skill in winning this chase.

Soon, too soon, they came to a narrow, hard-packed road. King turned the sorrel and took it at a fast trot. Celina followed.

"Just a mile or so more," he called back to her. "Pray that he's at home." He urged the horse forward again.

The old man met them at his gate, surrounded by three large dogs that had warned him someone was coming. King and Celina dismounted, King introduced Celina, and they walked with him leaning on his cane up the curving drive to his house. It was a sprawling red-tiled adobe that reminded Celina of her grandfather's old hacienda.

They sat on the patio, the dogs stretched out in the shade of the overhang. Mr. Donathan squinted at them, then at King and Celina.

"Where're you from, young lady?" he asked.

"Los Angeles."

"Los Angeles," he repeated thoughtfully. "I ain't been there for years. Come right through that town on m' way to the gold fields, back in '49."

He squinted at her. "Did you know," he said, "that not a one o' them gold-hungry fools found his fortune? It's the truth! No!" he said, shaking his head. "I still wonder that I had the sense enough to buy this here land."

Without waiting for a response to that, he pounded the tile floor with his cane. "Maria!" he shouted. "Lemonade! We've got company here, you know." He tilted the slatted back of his chair against the wall, tottering slightly, and peered at King.

King took the contract out of his pocket, unfolded it, and spread it on the low table between them.

"Eh, I dunno," Mr. Donathan said. "I been thinking about when you'd come with these papers. I might oughtta tear them up and keep my hand in."

Celina's heart sank. He couldn't, he just *couldn't* do this to them after that long, wild ride. He couldn't do this to them because it would destroy one whole argument for their case. But King had known that he might. Donathan had told him that he dreaded having nothing to fill his days if he gave up farming and ranching.

Maria came with a tray of lemonade and glasses. King barely contained his impatience until she'd set them on the table, served everyone, and gone.

"We had an agreement, Mr. Donathan," he said. "You gave me your word."

"Eyuh, that's right," the man said. "But no deal's done 'til the money changes hands."

King stood up and reached into the tight back pocket of his jeans. He took out his wallet.

"The money can change hands right now," he said. "I have a cashier's check with me."

"Hold on, now!" the old man said. "How come you're in sich a hurry? You know something I don't? Land value gone up again?"

King clenched his teeth; the muscle knotted along his jaw. He'd be yelling at the man next, Celina realized. Just as he'd yelled at her about her luggage.

She leaned forward, gripping her glass of lemonade in both trembling hands, but she kept her tone entirely casual. "Mr. Donathan," she said. "You did find a fortune here, even if it wasn't in the gold fields. When you cash that check you can go anywhere, do anything that strikes your fancy. Have you thought of doing some traveling now?"

The man's front chair legs hit the tile floor with a clink. He squinted at her, then spat out into the yard. "Well, I just might," he said thoughtfully. "I never gave that notion much thought. When I was young I used to love to see new country."

King flashed Celina a startled look, then fixed his eyes on the old man.

"That's right," he said, equally casually. "You could hop on my train and ride all the way to San Francisco."

Mr. Donathan smiled. "San Francisco," he said. "Now *that* was a town when I was young."

"I went to law school at California College," Celina said. "While I lived in San Francisco with some friends."

"Did ye, now?"

That prompted a dozen memories and comparisons, and, finally, when King turned the conversation back to the land contract, Mr. Donathan was much more receptive. He brought up some objections, about access to the river and the amount of land he was to keep, but King and Celina countered them or agreed to compromise.

After what seemed a veritable age, the man thumped his cane and called for a pen. Celina amended the papers while King rounded up Maria and her helper to serve as witnesses. Mr. Donathan signed his name.

King and Celina stood up, but Mr. Donathan sat still, staring at the check.

"Maybe I'll see ye someday in Los Angeles," he said. "And for sure I'm going to San Francisco.

Why, with this much *dinero* in my pockets, I might just sail around the world!" He watched them walk out into the yard and mount their horses.

"Close the gate when you go out," he said. Then he pounded his cane hard, even though Maria was hovering close by on the patio. "Maria!" he shouted. "Git in there and find my old trunk!"

King and Celina waved and rode away, laughing.

Just outside the gate they stopped. Horses were coming. The iron clang of the latch mixed with the dry whir of wheels turning on hard ground.

King grinned at her. "I wonder," he said, "who that could be."

She cocked her head. "Sounds to me like a man, no . . . two men who have just eaten their fill of cherry pie."

Laughing again, like two giddy children, they rode out to meet Mr. Rudisill's gig. When it rolled to a stop, King rode up beside it.

"Chekote!" the more red-faced of the two men exclaimed. "Why, is that you? We heard you were gone to Los Angeles!"

King gave a little salute and a nod that caught the sun in his tawny hair.

"Came back on the morning stage," he said pleasantly. "Couldn't waste such a beautiful day staying in town."

"Ah-h-h," the other man said, clearing his throat as if something were stuck in it. "The morning stage, you say?"

"That's right." King smiled at them. "You two are a long way from home. Enjoying your ride in *our* part of the country?"

Rudisill was struck speechless. The other one snapped, "Your part of the country! Well! What have you—?"

His companion's elbow jabbed him in the side and stopped his sentence in the middle.

King waited politely.

Both men's eyes shuttled in dismay from King to Celina and back again, as if they could read the answer to the unfinished question on their faces. But they already knew. Their bodies were wilting pitiably into the black horsehair bench where they sat.

"Well, gentlemen," King said, giving them the full benefit of his irrepressible grin. "My attorney and I must be going. A good day to you both."

He looked at Celina, swung his horse, and set off at a gallop down the road. She started to follow, but she surprised herself by turning back in a circle so she could bestow one of her own most charming smiles. Then she spun the gray and let him have his head. He followed the sorrel.

As soon as they were well away from the gig, King let out an earsplitting war whoop of victory. He reined in, wheeling his horse back to meet Celina's. Her gray danced to a stop beside him.

King, smiling and gorgeous, stood up in his inside stirrup and leaned across to catch her up in his arms. Laughing, he pulled her out of her saddle into a wild hug of celebration. He crushed her against his chest. "We did it, darlin', we did it!"

She threw her arms around him and hugged him back.

"I know! Can you *believe* it, King? We talked him into it just in time!"

Laughing deep in his throat, he drew her hard up against him until she stood in one stirrup, too, and she was entirely in his arms.

Only King kept her from falling. King and the strange, brand-new lightness of her heart. He smelled like sweat and horse and King, his own man-scent mixing into her nostrils with that trace of spicy toilet water underneath. He felt like a warm, firm rock to cling to, a safe place to run to, all happiness encased in one marvelous body.

His heart beat deep and sure against her cheek for one whirling moment. Her hands splayed flat against his back. His hand cupped her head and lifted it to nestle her face into the hollow of his throat. Her lips turned to kiss the raw closeness of his skin. Her tongue darted to taste its salty sweetness.

He quit moving, quit breathing. The tip of her thoughtless tongue stayed against his hot skin, burning itself into numbness.

King took a long, shuddering breath. "Celina?"

His voice sealed her palms to the muscles of his back through the thin cloth of his shirt.

He put his knuckles under her chin and tilted her head so that his eyes would meet hers.

They blazed topaz fire into her soul, bathed her whole body in a flaming light. The sun still shone, but it might as well have been throwing nothing but shadows from the sky.

"Celina?"

That one smoldering word asked a question she couldn't answer. What did he want of her?

Her body knew. It strained toward him so surely that her sleeping mind started to work once more.

What was she doing? This was worse, much worse, than the way she'd acted on the train.

She dropped back into her saddle and clutched at its horn as if only that could save her.

Chapter 5

The fear was so strong it wiped away the excitement in her eyes for one shaky minute. King watched her fight it down and then it was gone, leaving only a gloss of heightened color over her triumphant flush of victory.

She brushed back a strand of her hair. He tangled his fingers into his reins to keep from reaching across to help.

"You're the one who did it," he said, easing back down into his saddle. "How'd you know that Sadie would talk to me?"

"She's attracted to you. It's written all over her."

"I never saw it, and I spent three weeks here before I came to L.A."

"Then you weren't looking."

"I'm always looking for romance."

It was the wrong thing to say so soon after the hug and her own lack of restraint had scared her. She dropped her gaze and smoothed at her hair again, this time tucking the errant strand firmly into place.

He willed her to look at him again. "Shrewd work, Lawyer Hawthorne."

Her huge dark eyes blazed at him across the narrow space, this time filled with a question.

"I mean it," he said. "They'd have beat me to him if it hadn't been for you. You saw the shape he was in—they had a good possibility of talking him out of signing."

Her heart soared again, floating up and out of its heavy tangle of warring emotions. He really did mean it. There was genuine respect in his voice. So. She had won the battle. Maybe he would begin to believe she could win the war.

"You helped, too," she said modestly. "You're the one who mentioned San Francisco."

"We make a team, don't we?" he said, reaching for her horse's bridle to turn him around. "Rudisill and his bunch don't have a chance."

And neither did she, Celina thought, not unless she kept her guard up every minute. Words of praise from him could become as addictive as his smile.

They rode across the river at a slow trot, side by side. Coming up the bank on the far side, they reined in at the same moment.

"You have a new neighbor!" Celina exclaimed.

"Looks like the tent I brought for you." King urged his mount forward. "Somebody's pitching it for us."

Celina followed him.

The tent was up, but sagging on the sides, waiting for the support ropes to be tightened. A slender figure in faded blue pajamas was tugging at one of them, wrapping it around a stake while trying to keep the canvas smooth and stiff.

It straightened up and turned to face them—Celina saw that it was a Chinese girl with a long, black braid down her back and shy, dark eyes. She couldn't be a day over sixteen.

"Hello," she said carefully. "I Mei Lee. Mr. Moseley's cook."

Her accent was heavy, but her voice was light and musical as the wind. "He send me to help the lady."

"I thought his Chinese cook was a man," King muttered, swinging down from his horse.

The girl stared at the ground, holding her body perfectly still. Yet somehow she looked poised to run.

Celina dismounted and walked toward her, holding out her hand. "Hello, Mei Lee. I'm Celina," she said. "Have you done all this heavy work by yourself?"

The girl nodded, keeping her eyes cast down. When Celina reached her she sketched a small curtsy instead of taking her hand.

"Thank you for putting up my tent," Celina said. "Let me help you finish." She bent down and picked up the rope. Then she leaned back to throw her insignificant weight behind the effort and pulled mightily with both hands.

King watched her, grinning, shaking his head. She was the most unpredictable woman he'd ever met. The last thing he'd expected was for her to be trying to pitch her own tent.

She straightened the rope, though, and tied it around the stake with a knot that looked passably efficient.

"Not bad," he said, going to take the second rope from her. "But why don't you let me?"

"Mr. Moseley say I do it," Mei Lee objected. She was wringing her hands. "He be angry if I not."

King shrugged. "You can help Celina unpack," he said. He dropped the rope and reached into his pocket for his wallet. "And run up to Hanna's store," he said, giving the girl some money, "to get a wash pitcher and basin plus whatever else Celina tells you."

She did so while King finished pitching the tent and rigged another rope across its interior. Celina and Mei Lee unpacked clothes and hung them on the rope, set up the washbasin and pitcher on a packing crate King found, and took out the law books that had traveled in the bottom of the trunk.

Without being told, the girl sorted Celina's clothes by type of garment and arranged her paper, pens, and inkwells neatly with the books. Then she went to the river to fill the pitcher with water for washing.

Celina tried to draw her out, but she would say very little about herself. She made noncommittal remarks and exclaimed over pretty fabrics or colors or pieces of jewelry that she liked. She lingered especially over a varnished papier-mâché bracelet painted with bright red flowers, then closed the jewelry box and placed it carefully on the small, rickety table King brought over from in front of his tent.

"You two about done?" he asked. "Let's go eat lunch and then ride up to the cut. I thought I would've got up there by now."

"Mei Lee, come with us to Sadie's and eat," Celina said. "You must be hungry—you've worked really hard."

"No, no," the girl said, backing away. "I go to camp now."

"Let me pay you, then," Celina said, reaching for her bag. "And thank you so much for all your help."

Mei Lee threw up her hands. "No!" she repeated, in a perturbed tone. "Mr. Moseley said, 'Do not take any money.' "

"But Mr. Moseley isn't the one who has done all this work . . ."

Mei Lee hurried to the open tent flap, scuttled around King, and ducked outside.

Celina stared after her, then jerked open the jewelry box and grabbed the flowered bracelet. "Wait!" she called. "Wait, Mei Lee!"

Mei Lee was standing like a statue near the grazing horses, her head tucked down as if she were afraid to look and see what Celina wanted.

Celina ran to her. "Please take this," she said. "And my thanks. You've been a wonderful help."

Mei Lee took the bracelet and held it in both hands, staring down at it as if it were a treasure. Then she looked up and flashed Celina a look of pathetic gratitude.

"You're welcome," Celina said, but before the words were out of her mouth the girl turned and ran up the hill. She looked back just once before she slipped the bracelet onto her arm.

Celina speculated about Mei Lee all during lunch and after, as she and King mounted again and rode the horses uphill toward the track-building site. The delicate girl fascinated her. Where had she come from? Where had she learned to speak English? How had she met Moseley?

King had acted absentminded all through lunch; he hadn't seemed too interested in any of those questions. But he was bound to know the answers to some of them.

"King," Celina said, urging her horse into a faster trot to keep up with him, "why would Moseley send Mei Lee to help me, anyway?"

"I told him he'd made enough miles to spare someone to pitch your tent," he said, "not knowing that he had a female cook who could act as a lady's maid—that was his own idea. That's the way we work: as long as I encourage and compliment him he curries favor with me."

"Don't you get tired of such games? Why do you put up with him?"

"Because if I work him just right he'll get twelve or fourteen miles out of the men when they should've done only ten," he said. "And keep 'em laughing and joking while he does it. I'll put up with a little boot-licking any day to keep that track coming this way."

She digested that. "So that's why he told Mei Lee to take no pay. If she did, you wouldn't owe him."

"Right."

"But he wasn't the one doing the work. She was."

"Right. But he's her boss. He hired her, he tells her what to do."

"Sort of like lending you his slave, huh?"

King shot her a quick look. "Well, he was giving up whatever she could've been doing for him during that time."

He nudged his mount into a long, fast trot.

"I think she's too intelligent to be doing this kind of work," Celina declared, as they rode away from the northern edge of town. "Mei Lee should be in Mrs. Tolliver's school."

"What school?" King asked.

"A school in San Francisco for Chinese girls," Celina said. "Mrs. Tolliver and her Presbyterian Women's Mission members rescue the girls from horrible lives and educate them."

"Whether they want to be educated or not?" he teased.

"King!"

She reined in her horse and he rode on, then circled back impatiently to her. "What're you doing? Come on! I'm in a hurry to get up there—I've got to see how far they got while I was gone so I can figure when the tracklayers may reach the Caliente."

"I just had the most horrible thought. King! Mei Lee is Moseley's Chinese cook!"

He raised one eyebrow and squinted at her. "Yeees," he drawled quizzically. "And have you had any other momentous revelations lately?"

"No! Really, King, don't you see? *You* were paying Mei Lee's salary, but now you're not because the grading crew is going to eat at Sadie's. She's out of a job!"

He made an exasperated gesture and set his horse moving again.

"Celina, will you stop worrying about that girl? She's Moseley's responsibility. He found her in some dive somewhere and hired her to . . . cook. And now he'll find something else for her to do. He'll take care of her."

Celina shivered. "I'll just *bet* he will!"

She glared at King's broad back all the rest of the way to the top of the hill. How could he be so unconcerned? Couldn't he see that that girl didn't belong in a graders' camp? The child, and that's what she was, was helpless.

King reached the crest of the hill before she did and immediately reined in. He stared to the east for a minute and then raised his fist and let out a wild, exultant yell.

"Front of track!" he shouted back at her. "Come on!"

She followed at a lope, smiling in spite of her annoyance with him. He was so like a little boy, riding pell-mell to see the circus.

The clang of metal upon metal floated through the clear air. So that's what he'd meant by "front of track." The tracklayers were here.

When Celina reached the top she saw what King had seen first: the huge three-story rolling dormitory where the tracklayers lived, towering like a monolith far behind them while they worked. As she followed him she could see the legend, C & G RAILROAD, painted in huge block letters on its side.

In the shade of a scraggly pine tree, watching the men carry the rails and put them in place as fast as other men could drive in the spikes, sat Marshall Moseley talking to another man.

"Moseley, why didn't you tell me?" King shouted. "This is fantastic, man!"

The graders' boss gave an ingratiating grin. "Wanted to surprise you, sir!"

King swung off his horse and hurriedly helped Celina down from hers. He introduced Moseley's companion as Bill Sutton, boss of the tracklaying crew. Sutton doffed his hat to Celina, then all four of them went closer to watch the colossal work in progress.

A horse was galloping up to the front, drawing a flatcar loaded with rails. As soon as it stopped, five men ran to it and grabbed a rail, two at each end and one in the middle.

They came forward at a run, and when one man yelled the command, they dropped the rail into its place, right side up. A second later, another crew dropped the matching rail on the other side.

"They're so fast!" Celina gasped.

King nodded. "Less than thirty seconds to a rail for each gang. Four rails go down every minute."

Over the noise of the hammers hitting the spikes, he shouted, "Five men to the five-hundred-pound rail, twenty-eight or thirty spikes to the rail, three blows to the spike, two pairs of rails to the minute, four hundred rails to the mile!"

He was practically singing a litany of praise, she thought, smiling at the excitement in his eyes. Kingfisher Chekote was a man who had found his calling.

She continued to watch the fascinating expertise of the workmen, carrying rails and driving in the spikes with rhythmic speed and skill that were nothing short of miraculous. King and the other two men finally drifted a short distance away and squatted on their haunches to talk.

To the west, a long distance down the right-of-way, Celina could see their original destination: the crew of graders struggling to keep ahead of the tracklayers, running tipcarts and shoveling dirt with that same hurrying determination the tracklayers had. From here they resembled a colony of very large ants.

Finally King got up and shook hands with Sutton.

"Keep 'em coming," he said. "I'll be back in the morning. Right now I'm going to see how Moseley's crew's doing."

Celina rode toward the graders at a walk, with King and Moseley ambling beside her horse, King leading his sorrel. Moseley tipped his hat and looked up at her with an obsequious grin.

"My girl do you any good, Miss Hawthorne?" he asked.

"Yes, Mei Lee was a lot of help, thank you," she said. "She's a hard worker."

His girl, indeed.

"Thanks, Moseley," King said. "That was thoughtful of you to send her down."

"Any time," Moseley said, expansively. "You just holler if you need her—I've not got much for her to do all day."

Celina stared down at the top of his smug head. What did he have for Mei Lee to do all night? She couldn't think about it.

They passed the graders' camp on the way to the worksite. Celina gasped and looked away, then she looked back for Mei Lee. No one was in evidence, but the place obviously was inhabited.

By pigs. No, pigs would be neater than this.

Trash was everywhere—pieces of broken equipment, empty whiskey bottles, dirty blankets and pieces of clothing lay scattered at random around the ragged tents. A few cards from a tattered deck blew here and there in the wind.

What a depressing place! Caliente Crossing was Nob Hill compared to this.

Repulsive as the sight was, Celina turned in the saddle after they had passed by. Which tent belonged to Mei Lee? Did she have to share one with Moseley?

As they approached the end of the grade, King called, "They're coming up on you, boys! Think you can keep ahead of 'em?"

Several men looked up from their work and waved.

"Sure, Boss!" someone shouted back.

"Not you, Doan!" came the quick answer. "If you don't quit runnin' to the water bucket ever' five minutes, they'll catch you and lay track right acrost yore arm while you're reachin' for the dipper!"

General laughter greeted that remark, but nobody stopped working. Their horse-pulled dumpcarts went back and forth in a steady stream from the place where a dozen men were hacking at the hillside by hand. They were hauling earth and rock in thousands of tiny loads to dump into the defile. King watched them carefully for a minute or two, then examined the grading they had finished.

He looked at Moseley. "You've got it all in top shape, as usual," he said. "I always say there's not a crew chief in the West who can hold a candle to you, either picking men or working them."

Another little compliment of encouragement, Celina thought dryly, disliking the smirk on Moseley's face. She took another look at the men he had chosen. They were the wildest-looking, most motley men Celina had ever seen in her life.

She couldn't believe Mei Lee was living in the midst of them. They all looked like criminals—it was a wonder they hadn't lynched Mei Lee if they didn't like her cooking.

Finally King had finished inspecting the grade, planning the next day's goal, and looking over the survey with Moseley. Frowning over the number of miles they still had to go before the deadline, he swung up into the saddle and led the way back down off the cut.

"King," Celina called, matching her horse's gait to that of his sorrel. "We need to try to find Mei Lee a place to live in town. This graders' camp isn't fit for human habitation."

He turned in his saddle to glare at her. "Celina, for God's sake!" he exploded. "Will you forget about that girl? I've got too much on my mind to worry about somebody that's none of my business."

"But she's so young! She *is* our business—"

"She is not! You sound like some meddling, do-good fanatic."

The familiar phrase tore like hot knives through Celina's brain. She dug her heels into the gray and took off at a gallop.

Celina woke early the next morning, fighting a dream that had come again and again in the night. In it, King rode toward her across a field, scooped her up behind his saddle, and galloped to a grove of trees at the edge of a river.

He dismounted, then put his hot hands on each side of her waist and pulled her down to stand facing him. Slowly, slowly, he lifted her hand and pressed his lips to her palm, then to the thin, sensitive skin on the inside of her wrist.

A sweet trembling shot through her whole being. It made her want to kiss him on the mouth. But when she leaned toward him, he turned her loose and stepped away. In a suddenly formal way, he said, "Miss Hawthorne. You are an absolutely *shrewd* attorney. Good-bye."

She stared at him, speechless, until he turned and mounted the horse again.

"King?" she would call. "King?"

She woke then, every time, to the sound of his name hanging like a presence in the dark air of the tent. And every time, she drifted back into sleep so he could tell her again what a shrewd lawyer she was.

So he could kiss her again.

But now the pale walls of the tent showed new light coming through from outside—even when she closed her eyes she could see it. Sleep was gone for good.

King thought she was a good lawyer. King had said she was shrewd and had looked at her with true respect. She'd better get up and get busy so she could live up to that. She threw off the sheet, but she couldn't quite make herself move. She stretched out her legs and ran her hand along the smooth wood frame of the cot.

King had kissed her, too. She could still feel the imprint of his lips on her skin.

No, no, that was only in the dream. In real life, *she* had kissed *him*. Her face flushed hot at the memory. She sat up fast and swung her feet onto the dirt that was her floor.

She had never done such a forward thing in her life! And she wouldn't do so again. Not now. Not when King was, for the first time, thinking of her, not as a woman, but as a lawyer.

Not now? Celina was groping her way toward the washbasin and pitcher when the significance of that thought hit her. Not *ever!* What in the world had come over her?

Being in King's arms one time had destroyed every bit of control, and sense, that she had. But not for long. As soon as good daylight came she would get right to work. The joy of losing herself in her law books and research would banish that nagging dream with its disturbing memories for good and all.

She found the upturned packing box where Mei Lee had set out her toilet things, and fumbled around to find the towel. She would wash and dress now and be ready to work as soon as the light grew strong enough.

Her searching fingertips found the tin pitcher, its surface cool and damp with condensation from the night air. She located the bowl and poured some water into it, bending over to splash it onto her face.

The one long braid she'd made of her hair for sleeping swung forward. She tossed her head to throw it back over her shoulder. Then she bent to the water again. It hit her with a cool shock, and she washed in it repeatedly, reveling in the return to her senses. She lifted the towel.

She had a case to prepare, the most important one of her life, and only a short time in which to do it. Nothing would distract her; this was her chance.

The only one she would ever have.

King glanced toward Celina's tent as he left his own, heading for O'Reilly's and a horse to ride up to the railroad cut. The white canvas square reflected the pale first light, sitting sure and silent against the dark background of the hill.

She'd probably sleep until noon, he thought, with an indulgent smile. Yesterday had been quite a day for her. Besides all the traveling and the excitement over Donathan's contract, she'd worked herself into a fit over that little Chinese girl. Surely by today she'd have calmed down and realized that the world wasn't perfect.

He swung away toward the peeping sun, showing the slimmest sliver of pink at the edge of the hill, and strode fast around the edge of the sleeping town. The fresh smell of very early morning, the chittering of birds coming from the trees by the river, the teasing glimmers of the new sun filled his senses; he had to bite his lip to keep from whistling.

Yesterday had been quite a day for him, too, he

thought, visualizing Donathan's scrawling signature across the bottom of the page. Closing that deal had probably solved all his problems. No judge in his right mind would deny him title to Caliente Crossing when he showed that he owned both sides of the river and could lure hundreds of farmers— besides the ones he'd already signed to bring from Italy—to settle in this part of the state.

He threw back his head and began to whistle anyway, not caring if he woke the whole town. It was a beautiful day and everyone needed to be up to enjoy it.

Yes, if those graders would just keep it moving, his biggest problems would soon be a thing of the past. The C & G would be well on its way to the top of the heap. He and Celina *did* make quite a team.

Now all she had to do was prepare the title case just as he told her.

Chapter 6

But the next time he saw her, late that afternoon, King forgot the title case even existed.

He had spent the whole day on the route of the C & G, riding ahead of the graders for miles, doubling back to check the surveys and the terrain, planning with Moseley and Sutton, trying to foresee any problems or delays. While the bosses were gone, both crews set a record for the number of miles completed in a day. King, thrilled with such progress, praised them mightily and told the foremen to declare the workday done.

Then he had ridden the sorrel at a slow lope down the side of the sloping hill, trying not to push him since he'd already traveled so many hard miles in the sun, but wanting to, anyway. He needed to hurry back to town and tell this good news.

To Celina.

His few stray thoughts during the long hours of working had been of her. The feeling of her soft lips and her shyly wanton tongue on his skin had come back to him more than once, a sensual memory that had the same power to stir him as the reality had done.

Even if she *had* ridden away in a fury and left him yesterday.

The sorrel swerved to miss a small, scurrying lizard; King leaned into the stirrup on the other side.

He patted the horse on the neck, shaking his head at the memory of Celina, galloping ahead of them.

"She left us to eat her dust last night, didn't she, old chum?" he said. "Never know what that woman's gonna do next."

That must be the reason he'd kept thinking about her today—distraction was always a welcome thing in a railroad camp. He smiled and reined the horse to the left, to avoid the barrier of a rocky outcropping. He'd go straight downhill and follow the river to shorten his way home.

"Celina!"

One minute Celina was two hundred miles and ten years away, back in her childhood room in Los Angeles with Eli's scornful face leaning over her. The next she was in the present at Caliente Crossing with King.

Only King.

When she looked up, he flexed the long saddle muscles in his thighs and urged the big sorrel toward her across the open space that lay between their tents and the river, sitting the saddle like a smiling conquistador.

"Good news! Both crews set a record today for number of miles completed in a day!"

Her dream came rushing back, obliterating for one blessed moment the spiraling hurt that was cutting larger and larger circles inside her. One more time, she felt the sensual rush of his dream lips on her skin. When it had passed, she managed to say, "Wonderful! That's marvelous, King!"

He swung down from his mount, turned it loose to graze, and strode toward her with his sure, easy bearing that said the world was his, as, indeed, this corner of it was. If only he had the power to banish all unhappiness from it.

King could see Celina's face change, even from

several yards away. The bright surprise of welcome faded to that same devastated look that had come over it the day they met, when Eli charged into her office.

A bright yellow paper fluttered in her hand. The instant it caught King's eye, he knew. The old reprobate had just charged into *this* office, too, even though it was a rickety table and mismatched chairs set up in the shade of a tree two hundred miles away from the luxurious one in Los Angeles.

Celina forced her gaze not to drop to the telegram again; she had already read it a dozen times like some delirious fanatic bent on self-destruction. She watched King's lordly face instead and wished that her dream were real, that he would take her body between his big hands and make her forget this hurt.

He reached the table without taking his eyes from hers, grabbed the other chair and turned it around, straddling it before he sat down. He crossed his arms on its back and looked at her.

"Bad news?"

His voice was so kind the tears lurking behind her eyes multiplied in an instant. She dropped her gaze to the hateful words in her hand so he wouldn't see any more of her pain. How could she ever talk about it?

MY ONLY CHILD. WORK FOR ME. COME HOME NOW BEFORE MAKE COMPLETE FOOL OF YOURSELF. SURE TO HAPPEN.

YOUR FATHER,
ELI HAWTHORNE.

The black letters hadn't changed one bit since the first time she read them. They grew bigger and bigger before her eyes, then they blurred and she felt the sting of tears.

One of them fell onto the telegram. It landed just

beneath the word FOOL and raised an uneven spot on the paper like a blister.

"Sharing the sadness cuts it in half," King confided artlessly. "Didn't your mother tell you that, too?"

The unexpected aphorism pulled Celina's gaze up to his. He gave her a smile that was utterly reassuring.

"Better let me read that so I can take half those tears away," he cajoled, holding out his hand. "Remember the second rule of life: always do what your mother says."

To her own profound surprise, Celina let him take the malicious message and read it.

He made a quick sound of disgust. Or was it dismay? Was he regretting that he'd hired a lawyer who would make a "complete fool of herself"?

She snatched the page from his hand.

"Celina?"

Very carefully, forcing her hands not to tremble, she refolded the page and slid it back into the envelope.

"Can I help?"

"No," she said, standing up so abruptly that her chair fell over backward. "No. Thank you." Blindly she turned and walked away.

King waited a moment, then he got up and followed her.

Damn the old reprobate, anyway! Why'd she have to wire him her address?

Floating wraithlike along over the rough ground without ever looking down, she moved into the dim coolness of the trees that grew along the very edge of the river.

Wasn't anything fair in life? Celina was far too beautiful, too kind and too . . . game, too gallant, to deserve anything that would make her so unhappy.

She must deal with this once and for all and be done with it.

He trailed her, wondering for a minute whether she intended to walk right out into the river, until she stopped on a low, rocky verge of the bank that thrust into the water. Quietly he walked up behind her.

Celina shivered, then wrapped her arms around herself as it she were cold. Instinct urged him to go one stride closer and hold her. To warm her. And comfort her.

But she looked too remote to want that, too withdrawn into a shell of her own making. She wasn't a person who talked about her feelings, he had noticed that from the beginning. On the train, when he'd brought up the subject of Eli and his diatribe about bad blood between their families, she certainly hadn't mentioned Eli's treatment of her, his strange behavior, or how she felt about it.

Yes, she was accustomed to holding her deepest feelings close to her heart: her mysterious eyes had told him that the day they had met. But he wanted to know what they were—he *needed* to know, somehow. Surely he could persuade her to open up and talk; everybody he knew told him secrets.

She turned her head, staring out across the river with her face so still it seemed to be frozen in that expression of questioning sadness. He could have cried for her.

He vowed to himself in that moment that he would help Celina learn to unlock that prison of frigid silence in which she was shivering. And in the process he would come to know her.

But he couldn't question her now. No, the way to destroy this problem was to sneak up on its blind side.

"An *Uk'ten'* will get you if you don't watch out," he said. "They live in rocky places near water."

She whirled to face him, her eyes hugely dark and shiny with tears. But his childish warning had made her sensual mouth lift at the corners. Good.

"What's an *Uk'ten'*?"

"A huge snake with shiny scales and a blazing, brilliant crystal implanted in his forehead."

"Is he good or bad?"

"Both. If he breathes on you or smells you or sees you with his inescapable eyes, you die. But if you kill him—by shooting him in his seventh scale—you can look into the crystal to see the future and use the scales for protection and healing."

She smiled. A ravishing, innocent smile.

"I love it! Is that a Cherokee legend?"

He nodded. She was so beautiful standing there framed by the wide, glittering water. His throat ached. His hands hurt to touch her.

"Then let's find one!" she cried. "I need a magic crystal and all the shiny scales I can get."

He laughed and held out his empty hands. "How are we going to shoot him? We don't have a bow or any arrows."

"A blowgun!" she said. "Cut one of those reeds and make us a blowgun!"

"Celina!" he said, laughing harder at the fierce expression on her face. "You're a real Cherokee. Where did you ever hear about blowguns?"

Her smile faded. "From Father. That's one of the few stories he ever told me about life in the Cherokee Nation—his father helped him make a blowgun and he actually killed a rabbit with it."

She walked toward King, then past him, to the shade of one of the low-hanging Joshua trees on the bank. Taking hold of a branch, she leaned her forehead against her arm.

Then she straightened and turned around. "He acted as if that were something so brave and wonderful that it took a great hunter to do it—probably the only one he ever did—so that's why he talked about it. Otherwise he pretended the Nation didn't exist, no matter how many questions I asked.''

He went to her. The shade fell across her hair, leaving her creamy face in the light, a light that made her look like an elegant lady in a painting. It was all he could do not to cup her cheek in his hand. To trace her full lips with his thumb. To hold her mouth still so he could bend down and . . .

He caught himself. Was he crazy? He wanted to cheer her up, not scare her away. ''You can ask me all the questions you want about the Nation,'' he said. ''I promise to answer them without telling you a single brave-hunter deed I've ever done.''

She laughed and he had to hook his thumbs into the pockets of his jeans to keep from reaching out for her.

''All right.''

He turned away, walked to the base of the tree, and dropped down to sit on the ground beneath it. Celina hesitated. Then, slowly, tentatively, she came closer to him and did the same.

He fought the urge, pounding in his blood now, to somehow pull her closer to him. He ached to ask more about Eli, press to get that sadness out of her eyes and into words and tears, tears that might wash it away forever.

But he couldn't bring himself to do it. She had laughed—she'd forgotten the hurt for now. Her coming to sit by him like this was a gesture of trust and he wasn't going to betray it.

He would urge her to talk, though, another day. That was a promise. He would bring her here to this quiet spot beside the river until she opened up her heart to him.

''Let's see,'' she said. ''What was the most exciting thing that ever happened when you were a child?''

"The coming of the railroad," he said promptly, and stretched out on his back to get comfortable for the telling. "The M K and T. I was eight years old."

"And it came through your town?"

"We lived on a big farm, a plantation—the nearest town's ten miles away. No, it came several miles away from us, but my dad used to load up the whole family and drive us over to watch the trains come thundering through."

"Who was in your whole family?"

"Then it was just me and my brother William, who's three years younger. But now there's also my sister Jessee, who's fifteen, and brother Colin, who's ten, and baby sister Laura, who's seven."

"Oh," Celina breathed. "You're so lucky. I always wanted brothers and sisters, but I never had any."

He grinned. "They're great. I sure miss them sometimes."

King shifted closer to her, crossing his arms behind his head for a pillow. Instinctively Celina moved nearer, too. She wanted to take his head into her lap, cradle it there. Her fingers itched to loosen the thong that bound his hair back and made him look like pictures of . . . an Apache brave. She would smooth it away from his face . . . trace his cheekbones . . .

The strength of the wanting astounded her. She picked up a smooth stone that lay beside her and stroked it, instead.

"The engine was just a little four-four-oh," King said, staring off into the distance, remembering. "But it was the most exciting thing I'd ever seen. It'd roar through those crossings snorting louder than the most powerful animal on earth, blue smoke rolling, flying down those shiny rails pulling those beautiful, bright-painted cars."

She smiled. "So you decided right then you wanted to have one of your own."

"One or more," he agreed with a grin that made her see the little boy he must have been then. "Preferably more."

"Your father must have liked them, too, if he took you boys to see them."

The grin disappeared. His face went as hard as the dry ground. "He did, then. Now he can't stand to hear the word 'railroad.' "

"Why not?"

King heaved a great sigh. "From the minute I was born he planned for me to follow in his footsteps, to build a dynasty of River's Bend Plantation."

"And you didn't want to."

He shrugged. "I didn't *not* want to. And I didn't *not* want to serve on the National Council nor be an official of the Canadian District, nor give advice and counsel and hospitality to everybody all over the country and be a legendary pillar of the Cherokee Nation. I just wanted railroads more."

"What did he do that made him a legend?"

He turned his head and threw her a quick, sharp glance. "Oh, during the War Between the States he kept the Confederate Cherokees from raising their flag at Tahlequah. And he escaped from their prison and ran all the way home, exhausted and half-starving."

He made a sweeping gesture with one hand. "There's nothing he hasn't done. He negotiated for the tribe in Washington City during the war—he helped build schools and newspapers and churches when it was over."

King looked at her again, his tawny eyes blazing with feelings she couldn't quite read. He respected and loved his father, that came through in the pride in his voice. But there was a bitter frustration in it, too.

"And it hasn't ended yet. His horses always win the horse races. At fifty-two he can still outwrestle, outrun, outshoot, and outtalk a man half his age. He can settle disputes that've been going on for years. He can grow more corn, more sorghum, more cotton. You get the picture . . ." King threw up his hands, then dropped them. "He's bigger than life."

So are you, Celina thought, watching the flames in his eyes getting hotter by the second. So are you, King, but you don't know it. And until you do, until you prove that you're every bit the man your father is, you're going to have this fire burning in your belly.

The intimacy of the insight sent a thrill through her—one stronger, even, than that created by their physical closeness. She ached to touch him, to tell him that he could do it.

But the words wouldn't come. This maze of emotions about his future and his father was one he'd have to find his own way out of, just as she would have to do with her own. Still, it galvanized her to know that they were so alike in this.

"It seems strange to know that I'm not the only person in the world whose father wants to run her life," she blurted, to her own astonishment. What was it about King that brought her feelings right out of her heart and out of her mouth?

He turned his head and gave her a long look. "That's why I hired you," he said. "When you told me that it was your only chance to prove him wrong."

They were quiet for a moment. Finally Celina dropped her eyes. She could only share so much at one time, and King was looking right into her soul.

So she said, "Do you think you'll ever live in the Nation again?"

"I can't imagine not spending most of my life there. That's why I partnered with Travis Gardner even though we never work together. He's building his own line in Oregon right now and he won't leave the West, but I had to have a white man's name on the permit requests. I'm applying to build the feeder lines all over the Indian Nations.''

''In the Nations! Then why do you need a white man's name on the applications?''

''Because all Indians are shut out of the railroad business back there. They're allowed no control of lines coming across their lands.''

Celina dropped the stone she'd been holding. ''I can't believe that! It's so unfair! You need someone to go back with you and fight that through the legal system.''

He gave a bitter chuckle. ''For thirty years *everyone's* been fighting it through the legal system. Hasn't done a damn bit of good.''

''What have they tried?''

''Promotion and cooperation. Buying stock and selling land in exchange for seats as directors on the railroad board. Memorials to Congress. Appeals to the president. Denying rights of way. Taxing railroad property. Finally, tearing up track.''

''And none of that worked?''

''None of it. And then, five years ago, Congress ruled that eminent domain applies to Indians as well as to whites. There's no way to stop the railroads now—you've heard of Manifest Destiny.''

''But surely not every Cherokee will sit back and accept that,'' she said slowly. ''Not after fighting for so long.'' She thought about it for a minute. ''King, if you get your permits won't you be in a difficult position?''

His gaze flew to hers. ''That's my lawyer,'' he said, with a wry grin. ''Going straight to the heart of every problem like an arrow to its mark.''

She gave a mock bow of appreciation, sketchy because she was sitting, and grinned back at him.

Then he said what they both were thinking. "My *father* will put me in a difficult position," he said quietly. "Never mind anybody else."

"Is he still that determined for you to run the farm?"

He nodded. "Ridge Chekote does not give up easily. I keep telling him that Jessee could run the plantation and the whole Nation on top of it—he ought to pin his dreams on her."

"What about William?"

"He's frail, from rheumatic fever. He's not strong enough to spend all day in the saddle." He shrugged. "We'll just have to wait," he said. "If I ever get the permits, then we'll see what happens."

The resigned tone of his voice told her this was a statement he'd made to himself a thousand times. Yet there was a sad apprehension in it, too, a foreboding that moved her and gave her the courage to put out her hand. Not enough to stroke back his hair as she'd been longing to do, but enough to touch his arm.

He turned and gave her a look as strong, as disturbing, as a caress. But he didn't touch her in return, even though she could see the desire to do so in his eyes. She let her hands fall loose at her sides.

"Tell me about the rest of your family and your childhood," she said. "I want to pretend that I grew up there, too."

"My mother's name is Lacey," he began. "She has as much energy as Jessee and is as much fun, besides. She runs the house and the gardens and sees after everybody who needs her . . ."

Celina sat and listened to King talk about home, and to the soft-running river, until long after darkness had fallen.

Three days later, in the middle of the afternoon, King found himself at the open doorway of Celina's tent instead of on the hill at the right-of-way, where he'd planned to be. He'd ridden all the way back from Haileyville at a long, hard trot so he could oversee the construction of a new trestle; then, to his own consternation, had spent only a bare hour up there on the railroad.

That was because he and Celina needed to work on the title case, he'd told himself. Now that Donathan's deed was registered in his name it was safe to plan the case around that land acquisition.

But all thoughts of business flew out of his head when her soft voice floated out to him from inside the tent. Who was in there with her?

"Celina?" he called.

An instant later she appeared in the door, her arms full of clothes. Behind her, similarly laden, stood the Chinese girl.

"King!" Celina said, with a teasing grin. "You've come just in time to help with the laundry! Mei Lee and I have gathered it up."

Mei Lee gasped and put her hand over her mouth, apparently shocked by such a suggestion; she stepped around Celina to take the garments she held. "I do laundry," she murmured. "I go to river, now."

"No, Mei Lee, I'll help . . ." Celina began, but the girl scooped all the clothing into her own arms and scurried away.

Celina looked after her, shaking her head in dismay. "She does everything for me," she said, glancing up at King with a flustered look that made him ache to touch her. "She carries my water, washes my clothes, straightens up my things—all before or after she goes to her job. Did you know Sadie hired her to help in the kitchen?"

King looked down into Celina's eyes, darkly intense with concern for the girl. He couldn't help himself: he reached out and tucked back a strand of her hair that had slipped from the pins as she worked in the warm tent. He shook his head. "No," he said, "I didn't know."

"Well, she's working very hard at the café." Celina turned away and frowned after the girl. "I hope she isn't doing all this for me as pay for that silly bracelet I gave her. She wears it all the time."

"She's probably doing chores for you because she likes you."

"I feel I need to do something else for her," Celina mused.

"You can," he said. "Later. But right now, how about doing something for me?"

She turned to look at him. "What kind of something?"

"A walk-by-the-river kind of something. It's too hot to work."

She put her hands on her hips and smiled up at him, then she began to laugh. "I cannot believe that those words came out of your mouth," she said. "Is this the same Kingfisher Chekote who's been on that railroad from dawn to dark every day? Too hot to work?"

She schooled her beautiful face into a stern expression. "Well, Mr. Chekote, *I* am not too chickenhearted to work in the heat," she said with dramatic mock scorn. "I have no time for a walk by the river."

She left him abruptly and began stalking toward her table beneath the trees which was piled high with papers and open books. King stayed right behind her, matching her step for step, watching the tantalizing motion of her small hips as her skirt swayed from side to side.

"But you don't understand, Miss Hawthorne," he murmured, coming closer. "We *will* be working. I intend for us to discuss our title case as we walk."

"Oh, well," she said, another mercurial change

coming over her face. "Under those conditions, I'll
be most happy to go."

She rushed around the table, thrusting pencils and
scraps of paper into the books to mark her places
and gleefully slamming them closed. He burst out
laughing.

So did she. "We might as well laugh as cry," she
said. "I've scoured these books for three days now
and haven't accomplished a thing. I don't know why
I even bothered to mark my places."

She snatched up her straw hat by the ribbons and
came to him; he took her arm, looking down at her
with that utterly irrepressible smile of his.

"Don't worry about it," he said. "I registered the
Donathan deed this morning. Emphasize to Judge
Sullivan that the C and G's all set to single-handedly
develop California, that we have already contracted
to ship a hundred Italian immigrants and their farm
equipment and winepresses. Tell him we're all set
to irrigate and bring this valley to life!"

Celina shook her head. King's smile and his contagious enthusiasm made it sound so easy. But he
was wrong—some deep instinct told her that.

She wouldn't argue with him now, though. Not
with his fingers warm and strong around her arm
and the breeze brushing the leaves together over
their heads. She needed to give her mind a rest;
then, maybe, the solution would come to her.

They strolled south, toward the spot where they'd
sat and talked through that recent long, dusky evening, King rambling on about how this valley would
look a year, two years from now. When they reached
"their" tree, King, still talking, dropped to the
ground to sit beneath it and held up his hand to pull
Celina down beside him.

But she stood without moving, looking at him. He
sounded so content; he would be devastated if Judge

Sullivan decided against them. She banished the thought.

"I've decided you were right after all," she said. "It's too hot to even talk about work. Let's make a blowgun, instead."

King only stared up at her.

"I mean it!" she said, laughing. "Right over there's the cane you said we could use!"

He shook his head, laughing back at her. "That's what I like about you, Celina," he said. "I never know what you'll think of next."

She felt herself blush a bit at the personal remark. "Really, King," she said. "I want something of the Nation to be real for me, something I can hold in my hand."

"You can hold me," he said, his expression changing from smiling to solemnly sensual in an instant.

"King!" Celina could feel the warmth rising higher in her cheeks. "Please?"

But she couldn't remember what she was begging for. She stood transfixed by the heat his words created in her veins. On the train, when she had fallen back into his arms . . . on the horses, when he had reached out to hold her . . .

"Please?" he echoed, stretching his arm out to reach her.

She had to distract him. And herself. "King," she said helplessly, "will you?"

"Anytime," he drawled, and opened his arms.

She almost walked into them. It took every shred of strength that she possessed to stay where she was. "Kingfisher Chekote! Your conversation is shocking," she chided, but she couldn't keep from smiling down at him.

He shook his head slowly, his amber gaze teasing her, challenging her. "Your interpretation's what's shocking," he said, one eyebrow lifted, his wide mouth curved in a lazy, voluptuous smile. "Admit it."

"Oh!" she exclaimed, and stamped her foot in frustration. "I don't know what I'll ever do with you!"

"Let me show you," he growled, getting to his feet and lunging at her in one swift motion, lithe as a panther.

With a silly squeal like a little girl's, she turned and ran into the patch of cane that grew along the river, King at her heels. They rushed through it, dodging each other, in a wild game of tag that soon had Celina breathless.

She stopped in her tracks, gasping for air, but King didn't run up behind her. He didn't catch her in his arms. She turned to look; he had disappeared.

"All right, you win," he called, a minute later. "I've found the perfect piece of cane for your gun."

She felt elated, and at the same time curiously disappointed. Why? Wasn't this what she'd wanted him to do? Hadn't she run from him? Her heart beating against her rib cage like a striking clock, she turned and made her way to him through the stiff, clacking stalks of cane.

He had already cut a piece almost as long as she was tall; he held it up to her to measure. His hand on her shoulder sent a brooding warmth all through her.

"Are they supposed to be a certain length in proportion to a person's height?" she asked.

"No," he said, turning to lead her out of the canebrake. "They're supposed to be a comfortable length to hold. I'll show you in a minute."

Celina followed him, her eyes fastening on his broad back at the shoulders, then drifting to the center of it and following the indentation of his spine down to his narrow waist. It was so clearly defined by his damp clinging shirt that the need to trace it with her fingertip became a primitive heat. Why hadn't she gone to him when he'd asked her?

Then they reached the shade of the tree and he turned. Without warning, he reached out and pulled her to him, turning her around in the process. His arms went around her.

"Try it," he said, fitting her body to his. He placed the end of the cane at her mouth and both her hands on it. "Can you hold it up comfortably?"

His chest pressed against her back; she could feel his heart beating against her shoulder. His arms held her in a charmed circle. Her nostrils flared to draw in his scent; his chin brushed the top of her head.

"Needs to be about a foot shorter," he said, and stepped away from her, taking the piece of cane, and her breath, with him. He shot her a quick look.

"I don't know if this'll work," he said, taking his knife from his pocket, unfolding it, and cutting off the piece of cane. "Normally we'd burn out the inside of the cane. This one's nice and hollow, though, so maybe it won't need it."

Celina nodded. She couldn't take her eyes from his supple, brown fingers. They cradled the blowgun and raised it to his lips; then she couldn't take her eyes from his mouth.

He puffed air through the hollow shaft. "It'll actually work!" he chortled. "As soon as I make a dart, I'll kill you a deer."

"A deer! No! This is my blowgun, remember? I'll use it only if we're attacked by an *Uk'ten'*." She reached out to take it from him as if he were about to kill a helpless deer before her very eyes.

He let her take hold of it, but he didn't turn it loose; he slid his hands along its slender length until they rested on hers.

"If you won't let me kill you a deer, then how can we get married?" he teased, in that deep tone that made her legs go weak. His smile was slow and sensual.

"Married?" she gasped. "What does a deer have to do with marriage?"

The words hung in the soft river air between them. Celina bit her lip. What was she saying? She should've challenged the very subject instead of asking for cultural enlightenment.

"In a traditional Cherokee ceremony," he said, "I would give you a haunch of venison and you would give me an ear of corn."

His hands were sending a hot thrill into her veins that raced up her arms and spread into her body. If he hadn't been holding the stick of cane, too, she would have dropped it between them.

"Celina," he said, before he even knew he would speak. "Did you mean what you said that first day about not having any suitors?"

The minute the words left his mouth he wanted to call them back for fear they'd make her withdraw, that they would destroy the new feeling of closeness that had been pulsing between them this afternoon. But he didn't. He was more afraid, for some reason he couldn't quite name, that she'd tell him there was a man whom she loved.

"I meant it," she said softly, her wide eyes open and honest on his. "There's not one suitor in my life."

She lowered her lashes then, shyly, as if the very personal exchange had embarrassed her. But his heart sang in victory. Eventually she would talk to him, trust him. And he would know her heart.

"Come," he said happily, switching back to their playful tone. "Now we need thistles and a little stick to make a dart."

They ran up the hillside together to pick several of the purple flowers, and on the way back to their place beneath the tree, King picked up a slender twig.

"This is way too crooked to be accurate," he said, sighting along it, "but with no ax and no bois d'arc what can we do?"

"What would we do with the ax and the bois d'arc if we were in the Nation?" Celina asked. After a heartbeat she added, "What's a bois d'arc?"

They laughed together.

"For a second there you sounded as if you knew," he said. "It's a tree with really hard wood. The Osages always used it to make bows—that's what the name means in French."

"I know," she said impatiently, holding out her hand for the twig. "What would we do with it?"

She held up the tiny stick and imitated King's sighting along it.

He chuckled. "I've never had a student in such a swivet to learn. Are you interested in Cherokee culture or do you want your weapon because you're thirsty for the blood of an *Uk'ten'*?"

Celina gave him a fierce glance which she finally ruined by returning his grin. "Both," she said firmly. "Now tell me."

"Chop down a tree, cut a piece, and then split it to get a straight shaft out of the core."

"And the thistles?" she asked, as they reached their favorite spot and sat down cross-legged on the grass. In her lap, she cradled the flowers they'd picked.

"Watch," he said, taking back the twig and then reaching for one of the purple blooms. His hand brushed her thigh; even through her skirt and petticoat she could feel his heat. It lingered for a moment, then it was gone. But it left a question that burned into her brain all the while she watched him break off the blossom, turn it upside down, and pull the airy puff of thistle from inside and circle the cot-

tony softness around the end of the makeshift shaft.
How would his lithe brown fingers feel on her skin
right there?

He tied the dart together with a thread he took
from the tail of his shirt and inserted it into the
blowgun.

"Do it this way," he said, and blew. Sure enough,
the dart came out the other end to fly several yards
before it fell to the ground. He got up and retrieved
it; when he returned, he sat down even closer to
her.

And his arm came around her again. Then his
other arm. She leaned back against him.

He replaced the dart, his muscles working against
her upper arms. They felt powerful enough to . . .
kill an *Uk'ten'* barehanded.

"Shoot," he said, low in her ear.

She sat up very straight to take in enough air; her
cheek brushed his, then rested firmly against it. His
skin clung to hers. His cheekbone fit just above her
jawbone as if they were pieces of a puzzle. A wild
surge of new sweetness washed through her; she
would never move again. She couldn't.

"Now," he whispered. "See if you can hit that
clump of grass." He lifted his arm to show her the
target, but his cheek never left hers.

She drew in a long, trembling breath and blew.
The dart wobbled out of the gun and dropped to the
ground at their feet.

They burst into delighted laughter. King leaned
forward to pick it up; his arms tightened around
Celina. She had a sudden, overwhelming desire to
turn her head so her lips could find his.

"You'll have to blow harder than that," he said.
"I know you can do it—lawyers are full of hot air,
aren't they?"

"What an insult!" she squealed, pretending to try

to struggle free. "You're the one full of hot air—you blew it the farthest!"

He held her fast. "No escaping," he said. "You have to shoot until you hit that grass."

Laughing, so dizzy with King's scent and his closeness that she could hardly hold the blowgun, she tried twice more, sending the dart a few inches farther each time.

"You're getting the hang of it," he said. "This time you'll hit it—it's your fourth try."

"Why on the fourth?" she asked, lifting the cane to her lips.

"Four is a sacred number to the Cherokee," he said. "And so is seven. The incantations have stanzas of four or seven lines . . . the medicine man takes only the fourth of each healing plant he finds . . ." His voice trailed away. He swallowed hard.

Celina pulled away to look into his eyes. They were tantalizing, calling to her.

"Then I may not hit it until my *seventh* try," she said in a wary voice, shaken by what she had just seen.

"That's true, I guess."

Their breaths mingled softly, their lips separated only by inches.

"Celina, kiss me."

But she didn't quite dare. Her eyes drifted to the hollow of his throat, to the sweet spot her lips had found that other time he'd put his arms around her.

"King, I can't," she whispered. "I mustn't lose control again." Then, quickly, as if she'd surprised herself as much as she had him, she turned away and lifted the blowgun to her lips.

He watched her in silence, not protesting because a surge of joy was rising now through the ache of his frustration. Celina had actually spoken the feelings he had read in her eyes!

Chapter 7

After that their days fell into a pattern. At daybreak King rode to the right-of-way, where he spent most of the day; Celina spent hers working in her makeshift office. But every evening they spent together by the river.

Every day Celina told herself that they must break that habit, but each time King appeared, smiling and confident, she couldn't bring herself to refuse him. She loved being with him. She loved it too much.

He was fast becoming the best and only friend she had. He was giving her the part of her heritage that she'd always wondered about, for not only did he describe life in the Nation, he recounted every traditional tale and legend he knew and taught her some words in Cherokee besides. Underneath those satisfactions, though, he was creating in her a terrible hunger for more, hunger for his hands on her skin, his mouth on hers, his body fitted to hers.

Every day she vowed not to think about it, but whenever she wasn't working, it was all she could think about. So she tried to work every waking hour that she wasn't with him.

She spent hours upon untold hours searching her law books for cases that had any connection to theirs. She read the current statutes concerning transfer of ownership of real property, as well as the contracts King had signed until the words blurred before her eyes.

Three days before the trial, panic hit her again. With a half-suppressed cry, she pushed the tedious books away and got up to pace the bank of the river.

She and King wouldn't be coming here very many more days. They wouldn't be together anywhere— not as friends, not as employer and employee.

His business would be in shambles and so would her dreams of having her own practice.

She stared out across the river to the shallow water on the other side where she could see the rocky bottom. She wished an *Uk'ten'* did live there; she was strong enough in her fury and frustration to wrestle him barehanded for his magic jewel.

In that instant it came to her. She saw the pages she had read that morning as clearly as if she held an *Uk'ten'*'s crystal in her hand and looked through it to the future.

Peterson vs. *Guiterrez*. One of the old Spanish land grant cases.

She stood as still as if a bolt of lightning had struck her numb. This was the way, the only way, to win.

She couldn't wait to tell King.

He might as well have laughed at her.

No, it would've been better if he'd laughed at her. At least then she'd have known he gave some credence to her theory.

Celina sat across from King at their usual table in Sadie's and watched him talk to Marshall Moseley. Something about a bridge. The degree of the downgrade from the hill to the river. The supplies and the labor and the earliest day they possibly could arrive.

She could only hear a word or two here and there through the roaring in her ears. How dare he?

When she'd finished telling him about her great discovery, King had nodded, barely grunted in reply, and promptly turned to hail Moseley, who was just coming in with the men for supper. A pesky *fly* buzzing around his head would've drawn more response from him.

She picked up her cup of tea. Her hand trembled so badly the liquid sloshed out onto the table. "Would you please excuse us?" The words rushed out, her voice much louder than she had intended. "Mr. Chekote and I were discussing something important," she said to Moseley. "Perhaps you could talk with him later."

Both men stared at her. Their eyes mirrored the surprise she felt beating like a trapped bird in her throat. Was this really herself, Celina Hawthorne? She had never been so bold in her life. But her very life hung in the balance this time. And so did King's, if he only knew it.

"I'm sorry," she said, her manner only a bit more controlled. "But what I have to say is rather urgent."

Moseley looked at King for corroboration.

King dismissed him with a short nod. "Come to my tent after supper," he said. "We'll thrash it out then."

Moseley moved on, with one last backward glance at Celina. It was a mixture of resentment and wonder and the age-old curiosity to which she had become accustomed.

Well, what else could you expect from a woman lawyer? He might as well have spoken the words aloud.

She looked back at King. His face was set, his eyes shooting amber fire.

"Don't you ever do that again," he said, biting off every word, but keeping his voice low so Isabelle Browning and her little girl, dining at the next table, couldn't hear.

"Don't *you* ever do that again," she said, giving

him a look as good as the one she got, although the old Celina at the back of her mind was screaming caution. "We were discussing an important topic when the 'fastest ramrod in the West' walked in."

He picked up the heavy case knife beside his plate and slammed it down. It rattled on the bare wood of the table. "We were not discussing anything," he said. "On the train, on the way up here, I told you how to argue this case. I've been telling you the same thing ever since. All you need do is—"

"Emphasize the development angle," she finished sarcastically. She took a deep breath and sat up very straight in her chair, gripping the splintery edge of the table with both hands.

"On the train, on the way up here, I told you that I would decide how to argue this case. Well, I've decided. The old Spanish land grant case of *Peterson* versus *Guiterrez* is a perfect precedent."

"It's a perfect trap. Any judge, especially an old traditionalist like Sullivan, who hears the phrase 'Spanish land grant' will remember that ninety-five percent of those cases went the other way."

"I doubt the percentage is that high. I'll go over to Haileyville tomorrow and go through the deeds and other land records—"

"You'll do no such thing!" he roared.

Isabelle Browning turned to stare at them. So did half the other people in the tent. King glared back at them. He didn't have the grace to look embarrassed, but he did lower his voice.

"You can't go over there," he said. "No telling what'd happen to you. Why, when I went to record my deed to the Donathan property the other day, everybody I ran into had something rough to say— one yahoo even spit at me on the street."

"I'm going," she said. "We have *two* days, King. Only two. I have to use every minute."

King glared into her dark, determined eyes while

he digested her curt announcement. She was learning to say what she felt, all right. He clamped his lips together to keep from yelling at her, to keep from calling her stubborn and stupid. He had to get control of himself and the situation, had to remember that persuasion worked better than force.

"Now, Celina," he said smoothly, although the words came out between his clenched teeth. He forced his jaw to relax. "You're not in a position to make that decision because you don't have all the facts. Lawyers like to have all the facts, don't they?"

She answered with an even harder glare.

He shifted in his chair, leaned back casually, and gave her a smile. "You're used to a different world to the one you'll find in Haileyville," he said in his most persuasive tones. "You must listen to me—"

"Don't try to charm me into your way of thinking the way you do everybody else," Celina interrupted. "It won't work, King."

He crashed his chair to the floor on all four legs and thrust his face close to hers. "You have to use a little sense!" he snapped. "I can't go with you, I don't have time—there's too much to do about this bridge, even if the trestle *is* low."

"I don't *want* you to go with me! I can take care of myself."

"That statement proves you don't know what you're talking about. Or what you're doing. In Haileyville, you'd be a lamb among wolves."

"I do know what I'm doing! I'm saving my practice, my future. And yours!"

"Drop it. Right now."

Each word was clipped clear as a black silhouette against a white-hot sky. Celina looked at him. She wished that her stare could be a weapon, that her eyes could throw the fire in her heart against his smooth, red-brown skin and burn that cool, dispas-

sionate assurance right off his handsome, arrogant
face.

How could she ever have felt close to him? She
hated him.

She leapt to her feet. "You are exactly like my
father," she said. "You are every bit as unreasonable and overbearing as that 'malicious old reprobate,' Eli Hawthorne!"

Then she turned and ran for the shelter of her
tent.

The next morning Mei Lee woke Celina at daybreak as Celina had asked her to do.

"Mister O'Reilly, he say horse and gig be waiting
at Sadie's, not at blacksmith shop like he tell you
last night," she said, once Celina was on her feet
and at the washbowl. "He say, 'You sure you can
drive all right?' "

Mei Lee's tone showed that she shared O'Reilly's
doubts.

"Don't worry, Mei Lee," Celina said, dropping
the towel from her face to give the girl a reassuring
smile. "My grandfather taught me to ride and to
drive. There aren't very many horses I can't handle."

"Grandfather have *rancho*?" Mei Lee was always
intensely curious about any details of Celina's life.

"He managed to keep the house and a few acres
until I was thirteen," Celina said, accepting the blue
divided skirt and matching short jacket that Mei Lee
took from her hanging row of clothes. "And then
he lost those, too. My grandfather was a hopeless
gambler."

And I may be, too, she thought, going to her
wardrobe for a fresh white shirtwaist. I'm gambling
everything I and King and everybody in Caliente
Crossing owns on one shaky idea.

"I go now," Mei Lee said, edging toward the tent's flap. "Miss Sadie waiting."

" 'Bye, Mei Lee, and thank you."

Her heart thumping like a wild thing, Celina dressed and grabbed the reticule filled with blank paper, ink, and pens she'd packed the night before. King should be heading for the tracksite by now. If everything went well, she would be to Haileyville and back before he even knew she had gone.

The morning was cool, with a mist rising off the river. Celina hurried through it, coming out into the clear air a few yards in front of Sadie's. O'Reilly's gig wasn't there.

Well, maybe he'd left it around on the side where Hank Austin always parked the stage. Hank wouldn't be due quite yet. The bag bumping against her knees, she hurried around the corner.

And stopped dead in her tracks.

The gig was there, all right, hitched to the gray horse as she had requested. But King sat in the driver's seat.

She took one shocked minute to assimilate that fact, then she straightened her shoulders and strode up to him. "There must be some mistake," she said briskly, throwing her bag in and climbing up after it. "I've rented this gig. You can get out now."

She sat down and reached to take the lines, which were lying limp over the front of the floorboard. His broad, bronzed hand swept them out of her grasp.

For the first time that morning she looked him straight in the face. "Give me those lines," she said, amazed that she could actually issue a command under the unwavering arrogance of his gaze.

For answer, he lifted the leather straps and dropped them lightly onto the horse's back. "Hyah," he said, his eyes cutting away from hers to look ahead. "Giddup."

The gig began to roll.

"Stop!" she cried, and reached for the lines as the poles of Sadie's tent began to slip past. "You get out of this gig, King. You aren't going with me."

"I *am* going with you," he snapped. "Although God knows I shouldn't take the time for such a wild-goose chase. Remember that the next time you announce that all men are unreasonable and over-bearing."

"Oh?" she said, her voice slipping into an embarrassingly high register. "So I'm supposed to feel grateful, am I? And guilty for taking you from your work?

"Well, I won't! And I won't give you any credit for being thoughtful and cooperative, either. If this, this . . . highway robbery of the gig *I* rented isn't overbearing, I don't know what is!"

"Stop screeching," he ordered. "And you *will* give me credit. I realize this is something you have to do for your own satisfaction, and I'm going to help you do it, even though it's a criminal waste of time for us both. I won't let you use a word of it in court."

Struck speechless, she stared at him. "What do you mean?" Her lips felt so stiff and numb she could barely form the words.

"I mean you'll have to do as I tell you when it comes right down to the wire," he said. "We're doing this for your peace of mind—so you can feel you've explored every possible avenue."

"So I can prove myself wrong?" she murmured, her tongue thick with fury.

"Right." He drove around a jutting rock and turned back to the west, guiding the gray onto the dusty Haileyville road.

She couldn't take her eyes off his classically beautiful, imperiously lordly profile. What would it be like to be so naturally self-assured? This man simply assumed that he was right and the rest of the world was wrong, and that was the end of it. How could she possibly fight that? She stared out into the early morning.

With evidence.

She'd go into those land records with a will stronger than his. She'd find so much evidence to back up her theory that he'd have to admit he was wrong. For the first time in his life, no doubt.

The wheels hummed along over the soft, sandy road. A few early-rising birds called back and forth down by the river which the gig was fast leaving behind. Up in the hills, just ahead, rumbled a noise like thunder.

King shot her a quick, quizzical glance. He expected her to keep on arguing. He was waiting for her next defense so he could tear it down.

She gave him a dazzling smile.

He looked at her, squinted at the road ahead, and looked at her again.

Celina kept smiling.

"Sounds like we might get wet," she said pleasantly. "Did you, by any chance, bring an umbrella?"

He stared for a minute, then rolled his eyes skyward as if asking for divine help.

"That's not thunder. Moseley's bunch is blasting today."

"Oh," she said, disappointed. "I thought maybe it was an omen."

"Of what?" He sounded disgusted by his own curiosity. But it was genuine. He was waiting for her answer.

"Oh," she said airily. "That Thunder would help us today."

King cocked an eyebrow at the word 'us' as if he would like to protest that they had no common goal on this trip.

Celina brushed the dust from her shoulders and

settled more comfortably into her seat. "You never did tell me how we Cherokee came to be Friends of Thunder," she said. "Except you mentioned it had something to do with the *Uk'ten'*."

He slanted a long, suspicious look at her. What the hell was the little minx up to now? Her smile didn't waver, it only grew more charming.

The tension went out of his mouth and he felt its corners begin to lift. He shrugged. Oh, well. It was a beautiful morning and he was out alone with a gorgeous woman. Even if she was a champion at exasperating a man.

Fortunately, for some unknown reason, she wasn't wearing a hat today. Her hair shone in the sun like a blackbird's wing. She had dressed it differently, parted it in the middle and rolled it back on each side, then again across the nape of her neck. Unbound, how heavy and lush would it feel in his hands?

And her eyes, those enormous, dark eyes, combined with that smile like sunlight dissolving a cloud of mist fair shook his bones.

There was nothing to worry about. Moseley and Sutton could handle anything that might come up today. He deserved a day off, and so did she—she'd been poring over those books for days. They might as well enjoy the drive over and back.

"Thunder and the *Uk'ten'*," he said thoughtfully, looking ahead down the winding road while he stretched the horse into a long, steady trot. He took a deep breath and began with the classic opening for a Cherokee tale: "This is what the old men told when I was a boy."

Celina scooted around and leaned into the corner of the seat so she could watch his face.

"In olden times two boys went hunting. Down in a valley they saw Thunder and *Uk'ten'* who had hold of each other in a fierce fight. The *Uk'ten'* was long and strong—he was on top of Thunder.

"The boys looked at them fighting. Thunder was rumbling, very low. When he saw the boys, he cried, 'Nephews, help me! He'll look at you and kill you!'

"The *Uk'ten'* said the same things. 'Nephews, help me! When he thunders he will kill you.'

"Because Thunder was being beaten, the boys felt sorry for him. They decided to shoot the *Uk'ten'*. The first arrow that hit him weakened him. So did the second. Thunder began to rumble louder. He made the thunders louder and louder, and on the fourth thunder, the fiercest ever heard, the boys killed the *Uk'ten'*.

"That is why Thunder is our friend today. Some human beings helped him.

"If the boys had helped the *Uk'ten'* and he had won, I wonder what it would have been like. *Uk'ten'* would be lurking everywhere. Thunder would have killed us whenever it thundered and an *Uk'ten'* can kill you just by smelling you."

The story was over. King smiled and drove on. "So what do you think is the moral of the tale?" he said, finally.

"Oh . . . I don't know," Celina mused. "Oh! Yes I do! People and Nature must be friends. Neither can exist unless they respect each other."

"Hmmm," King said. "Maybe."

"Well, what do *you* think it is?"

"The boys killed the *Uk'ten'* because they felt sorry for Thunder, who was the underdog."

"So we should always help the underdog?"

"No," he said, and gave her a measuring look. "The truth in the legend is that we should always follow our feelings."

King's voice was low and rich. Celina felt as though he was throwing it out like a velvet ribbon to draw her in, a smooth, soft band for her to follow, hand over hand, when she was ready to let her feelings pull her to him.

The idea hit her like a bolt from Thunder himself.

Haileyville was much more of a town than Caliente Crossing. As King had said, several of the buildings were brick or sandstone; almost all of them and the wood frame ones on the main street had two or three stories. There were wooden sidewalks in front of some, paved brick ones in front of others. A large brick building in the middle of a landscaped square had an ornate sign which read WHEELER COUNTY COURTHOUSE.

Celina stared at it. So. That was the place where her fate would be decided; hers and King's and that of a dozen others.

"It's early enough that there aren't too many people out," King said. "That's good. Be as close-mouthed as you can about who you are and what you're doing and maybe we can get out of here without an incident."

He left the buggy in the shade on one side of the square; they entered the courthouse through a side door.

The clerk in the land records office became mildly hostile when King and Celina identified themselves, but there was no way around it—as long as they tried to remain anonymous she maintained that they had no business searching the records at all. When Celina insisted that they be admitted, citing their legal rights, she became even more antagonistic. "The records room's not open," she said flatly. "It's closed for the day."

Then King smiled at her. He glanced at the carved nameplate in front of her, leaned toward the woman, and said, "If all our public officials were as conscientious as you are, Miss Burton, we'd have no worries at all about the government. Now, if you'll just tell us the procedure to follow in looking at this material, I give you my personal assurance that we'll follow the rules to the letter."

The woman's small gray eyes stared into his intense amber ones as if she were mesmerized. Finally she smiled back at him. Then she pushed back her chair, got up, and led them past her desk, through an open door, and into a room lined with shelves of dusty boxes. More shelves stood in rows down the middle.

"You can't take nothing out with you," she said. "Use that table under the window if you want to write."

King drew two chairs up to it, but then he remained standing, leaning against the window frame, moodily staring down from the second story into the street. Celina dropped her bag onto the table and went to work.

She spent more than two hours searching the boxes' labels, withdrawing and glancing over stacks of old records, and copying information. She became more and more elated, for four challenged titles, all cases extremely similar to *Peterson* vs. *Guiterrez*, had been decided in favor of the defendant. Her idea would work. It definitely should be used as the foundation of their case.

But she wouldn't tell King yet. There was no time to start that argument again—he'd been constantly urging her to hurry. "Just this one more," she murmured at last. "Then we can go."

He answered with a curt nod, his gaze still fixed on the street below.

She bent her head and began to write. When she was almost finished, she felt King stiffen beside her.

Celina stopped writing, her pen poised over the page. "What is it?"

He didn't answer. His eyes were hard, fixed on

the outer office. Celina turned around and leaned past a row of shelves to see.

The portly man from the gig outside Donovan's gate, Mr. Rudisill, loomed in the open doorway.

"Well, Chekote," he said, and began to advance down the narrow aisle. "Somebody rode clear out to the mine to tell me you were here."

He waited until he had almost reached them to repeat the taunt King had thrown at him and his friend. "Welcome to *our* part of the country."

"Thank you," King said. "But you needn't have ridden all the way into town just to greet us. We're leaving soon."

"That's just what I was going to suggest," Rudisill said, smoothly.

He was so close now Celina could see individual drops of sweat standing on his temples.

He turned to her and swept off his black bowler hat. "I rode in to encourage the two of you to head out of Haileyville," he said, "for your sake, Little Lady. A mining town can be a dangerous place."

"Is that a threat, Rudisill?" King growled.

"No, no!" the man said. "Not at all. But you know this country as well as I do, Chekote. There's drunken miners and rattlesnakes and rock slides and nobody knows what other dangers around here."

"I'll be fine, thank you," Celina said coolly.

"Living in a tent, traveling these winding roads . . ." Rudisill stared at her with flat gray eyes that had no depth at all. "Watch yourself, Honey," he said. Every trace of false heartiness had fled from his voice.

He turned to King. "You've got a hell of a nerve comin' in here like this, you arrogant Greaser bastard," he said, in a low, cold tone that made the hair stand up on the back of Celina's neck. "You no-good Indians're all alike, I don't care how many railroads you own."

King stared him down.

Rudisill's empty eyes slid back to Celina. He reached down and scooped the stack of records she had used—the cases similar to *Peterson* vs. *Guiterrez*—from the desk.

"My attorney'll want to look at these," he said. "One glance and we'll know your strategy. All that scribbling you just done is wasted ink."

"No!" Celina cried, snatching at the pile of folders. "Give those back to me!"

Rudisill turned as she leapt to her feet. His long legs carried him away before she could untangle her skirt from her chair.

"King, do something!" she cried. "Stop him!"

"You two have made me mad, now," Rudisill called from the doorway. "Watch your backs from now on." He tucked the folders underneath his arm and marched into the outer office. He muttered something to the clerk, but Celina couldn't catch the words.

She whirled to King, her breath catching in her throat. "Now they'll know our whole case!" she cried. "King, I can't believe you didn't make him leave those files here!"

King leaned over and picked up her reticule.

"Those records are the property of the county. You heard the clerk say you couldn't take them out of this room!" she raged. "How could you let Rudisill do that?"

"I'm not the sheriff."

She jerked the bag away from him and began stuffing her notes into it as fast as her hands could move, then she slammed the latch shut.

"You let him take them on purpose because you didn't want me to use my strategy! You deliberately sabotaged me right in front of my face just because you're so sure that your way is right!"

He took her by the elbow and began pushing her

toward the door, even though she tried with all her might to break away.

"We'd never have gotten out of this town alive if we'd interfered with Rudisill," he said. "How many men do you think I can fight and protect you at the same time?"

"You don't have to protect me!" she muttered, as he propelled her through the outer office where the sour-faced clerk sat watching.

"Somebody does," he said. "Think of me as an instrument of God. They say he protects fools and children."

She gave an incoherent cry and tried harder to free herself, but he crossed the hallway and started down the long staircase at such a fast pace that her feet hardly touched the ground.

Downstairs, they rushed through the vestibule and out the door—and right into a small crowd of angry citizens who were blocking the path to their buggy. Celina would have stopped in her tracks, but King's long legs kept up their momentum. He switched hands on her arm and put his other arm around her, pushing their way through what now seemed to be a horde of horrible people.

"Greaser!" somebody shouted behind them.

"All Injuns is yellow-bellied," the huge man said. "And you, you greasy redskin, you're the yellowest of 'em all." One man, as tall as King, but heavier by a hundred pounds, stepped directly in front of them.

"Get out of my way," King said.

The man patted the butt of the pistol he wore on his hip.

"This here's what says who passes and who stays."

King laughed. He actually laughed.

Celina looked into his face—he seemed to be genuinely amused.

"A big man like you ought to be able to do his own talking," he said. "Now get out of the way."

The man stared at him, frowning as if he were trying to understand what King had just said.

"Move, or drop it and put up your hands," King ordered. He no longer sounded as if he were amused. "I'm not armed."

"Fight!" somebody in the group yelled. "Take off the gun and fight him, Buster!"

"Yeah!" someone else called. "I'm bettin' on th' Injun!"

King stiffened his arm, pushed the man back a step, and squeezed Celina through the opening, leading her toward their rig at a quick walk.

"Don't look back," he said.

She could hear the crowd milling behind them; they sounded as if they were coming closer. After what seemed a lifetime, he was handing her up into the buggy.

He climbed in after her, his movements deliberately unhurried, and picked up the lines. They drove down the street at a brisk walk.

"Hurry," she said. "Can't you make him trot?"

King gave her a look, one eyebrow raised, and she met his eyes. They were afire with exhilaration. He was actually enjoying himself!

"You don't want Buster to think we're afraid of him, do you?" Then his anger reemerged. "You're damn lucky, Celina," he said. "Buster could've shot me and you could've been . . . hurt. Bad. If that crowd had got organized, they'd've been ugly."

"I'm lucky? What about you? You practically begged that monster to shoot you!" She trembled, just remembering how brave King had been. He had walked right over that enormous man. Who had had a gun!

His natural self-assurance was one thing, but that had been sheer courage. And his arm around her had been sheer comfort. Whatever would she have done without him? What if she *had* come to Haileyville alone, as she had intended?

In the next second she wished she had.

"I'd never have seen 'that monster' if you hadn't come chasing over here after nothing." King said. "You've stirred up a hornet's nest."

"I have not! I've won our case!" she cried, then she wilted against the back of the seat, clutching the reticule to her breast. "At least I would have if you'd have saved those files from Rudisill!"

They rounded a corner and he clucked to the horse, lifting the lines. Once the gelding was trotting, King looked at her and said flatly, "Believe what you want." He glanced over his shoulder. "The trial's not our biggest problem right now. Rudisill's thugs are."

Celina looked behind them, too. No one was following as King guided the gig through the few wagons and horses of the morning's traffic.

"Rudisill's a big windbag. He wouldn't dare do anything violent with the trial so close—it'd be too obvious."

King's jaw tightened. "We can't take a chance. You'll have to come up to the cut with me tomorrow and stay all day," he said. "I can't think of anybody I can trust who has time to watch you."

"I can watch myself! Don't be ridiculous! There's no way I can spend a whole day on the railroad. I have one day—*one*, King—to prepare our case!"

"You can't use those notes now. You said so yourself."

"I did not. I have to use them, even if Rudisill will be prepared for this strategy."

"Celina, you are the most muleheaded woman I have ever met."

"And you are the most stubborn man."

They sat silent, seething, on opposite ends of the

seat. King squeezed the thin leather lines between his fingers.

Celina crushed the soft reticule with both hands. Well, this certainly promised to be a miserable ride home! And after the ride out had turned out to be so companionable. Follow her feelings? Follow her feelings! How in Heaven could she when she couldn't sort admiration from anger, or frustration from gratitude, in that rising thunderstorm of emotions exploding inside her?

It took them the whole interminable afternoon to get back to Caliente Crossing because the horse picked up a pebble that made his foot sore. Part of the time King walked and led him, part of the time he sat beside Celina, but the whole time they went no faster than a walk.

King had had Sadie pack a lunch, and they let the horse rest for a few minutes while they ate. They stopped another time or two to drink from a spring, but aside from that, the journey seemed endless. Occasionally they argued again, but they made no progress toward an agreement and finally gave it up. The traveling was wearying enough.

They reached Caliente Crossing just at nightfall, as the enormous yellow moon showed the first sliver of its fullness at the top of the hill. King's presence on the seat beside her had gradually become Celina's world; her mind had whirled itself into exhaustion during the tedious trip—by the time they pulled up in front of her tent she was so stripped of all thought that she could function only through her senses.

And they drew her to King as if he were a lighted candle in the dark. She couldn't get out of the buggy. She couldn't leave him, though he seemed to expect her to.

He got down off the seat and came around to help her out. "I'll sleep outside tonight," he said, in that same protective tone he'd used when he'd talked about her safety earlier. "Where I usually do. So you don't worry—just get some rest."

"All right."

She let him lift her and set her feet on the ground. His nearness, his big, warm hands on each side of her waist, reminded her of her dream. A sweet yearning flowed through her—if only he would take her hand and press it to his lips as she had dreamed. Instead, he handed her her bag.

"I'll get this poor horse to O'Reilly and see to that foot," he said. "Then I'm riding up to the cut. Want me to stop at Sadie's and have her send Mei Lee with your supper?"

"No, thank you," she murmured, forcing herself to turn from him toward the flap of her tent. "I don't want to eat."

He walked away, leading the horse, the buggy creaking along on its high wheels behind them.

Celina opened the entrance to her tent and went inside. A scrabbling noise came from deep in the back of it. She held her breath.

The noise came again.

Whatever . . . or whoever . . . was making it definitely was located inside her tent. Fear raced along her nerve endings, alerting every inch of her tired body. Her mind leapt back to life.

Rudisill? Had he sent someone riding fast to lie in wait for her? He had mentioned that she lived in a tent—he no doubt knew which one was hers.

Her lungs begged to breathe, but she couldn't make her muscles move. She tried to reach for the flap again, to open it and dart outside into the poor haven of the moonlight. But her arm couldn't accept the message from her brain, nor could her legs.

The noise stopped. Whoever, whatever, was there listened silently now; she could barely hear the whisper of its breath.

She forced her lungs to take in air to push out words. "Who's there?"

The answer came on a soft wail of misery. "Mei Lee."

Blood flowed again in Celina's veins. "Mei Lee! Well, where are you? Why didn't you light the lantern?" Celina moved toward the box where she kept the light.

"No lamp!"

Celina heard a scrambling noise; then she saw Mei Lee's dim silhouette separate itself from that of the luggage at the back of the tent.

"Why shouldn't I light the lamp?"

"Nobody can see Mei Lee. Hide."

"You're hiding! From what?"

Celina made her way past the box holding the pitcher and bowl; Mei Lee shrank back into the shadows.

"Miss Sadie. She say Mei Lee must run away."

"Why in the world would she tell you that?"

Celina dropped to her knees near the girl; her eyes adjusted to the dimness enough to see that Mei Lee was sitting huddled against the long wardrobe.

"I not sleep in her kitchen. Not leave Moseley."

"What does Moseley have to do with it?"

The girl gave a trembling sob and covered her face with her hands. The pitiful whimpering started up again.

"I too scared," she said, in between sniffles. "Get lost in hills. Wild animals, they come eat me. Bears. Graders they see bears and big cats, too."

"You can't go into the hills alone!"

Mei Lee's sobs began to subside. "No," she said. "Moseley follow." She dropped her hands and looked straight at Celina. "Moseley never let go nothing belong him," she said, in a voice so thin and calm that goose bumps stood up on Celina's arms. "I run away, he beat me 'til I die."

"He beats you?"

"No place to run to," the small, eerie voice went on. "Old master gone. He beat me, too."

Celina's hand froze in the motion of reaching out to Mei Lee. She'd known it. Somewhere, deep inside, she'd known all along that Mei Lee was a slave girl.

She forced her voice to sound calm. "Mei Lee," she said gently. "Why would Sadie tell you to run away?"

But even as she asked the question, her mind was whirling, giving her the answer.

"Miss Sadie want Moseley for herself. Only her. But he don't want her."

"I see." So, Celina thought wryly. Sadie must've given up on King and set her sights on Moseley.

"He want Mei Lee. He own me. He won me in card game."

"Mei Lee . . ."

The girl sobbed again, one deep gasp of pain. Celina leaned forward and took both Mei Lee's hands. It was too dark for her to see the girl's eyes, but the lines of her head and shoulders bespoke pure despair.

"What to do?" the Chinese girl whispered. "Miss Sadie fire me if I not run away. Moseley beat me if I not give salary from her to him."

"I will help you, Mei Lee," Celina said. Why, *why* hadn't she done something sooner?

"How?" Mei Lee asked. "What can you do?"

"Send you to San Francisco," Celina said, "to my friend, Mrs. Tolliver."

Mei Lee sat limp.

"She started a home for girls just like you!" Celina squeezed Mei Lee's hands, willing her to hope. "She and her friends march into Chinatown and face down armed guards to rescue Chinese slave girls. Mrs. Tolliver will give you a place to live and send you to school, Mei Lee!"

"I go on train?"

Celina heard a germ of eagerness in Mei Lee's voice. "Yes!" she said firmly. "You'll go on the train. We'll have King arrange it all and get your ticket."

"Not on telegraph. Jensen could tell. Moseley must not know. Miss Sadie must not know."

"Don't worry. We'll be very careful. Now, listen to me. Tell Sadie that you'll go in a day or two, that you have to get ready. Try to keep Moseley from suspecting anything."

Mei Lee stayed with Celina for a long time, exulting in their whispered plans. She would tell Moseley Miss Sadie had her working late, she said. He would believe that.

She insisted on bringing Celina fresh water and helping her get undressed and into bed. She plumped up her pillows and turned back her sheets, took her clothes outside to shake off the dust, brought them back in, and put them away. Finally she bowed and bowed again, thanking Celina profusely each time, and slipped away to go back to the graders' camp.

Celina lay in her bed and watched the tent grow lighter and lighter as the moon rose. It seemed to be expanding as it climbed the sky, taking over the world and promising that the night would last forever.

She closed her eyes. She wanted the moon to set and morning to come so she could tell King about Mei Lee!

She flounced over onto her stomach, buried her face in the pillow, and willed sleep to come. Instead, a mélange of images and feelings from the day assaulted her: the hardness in King's voice when he called her stubborn, the protectiveness in it when he told her he would sleep outside. The bravery in his eyes when he had pushed past Buster, the camaraderie in them when he'd told her the Thunder story.

She flipped over onto her back again. The moonlight flooded into her face as if the flimsy cloth roof were not even there. King.

Did she dare go find him now?

She shouldn't; Mei Lee's problem could wait until morning.

No, it couldn't. They needed to have messages ready to send out on the early stage. She sat up on the side of the bed and reached for her wrapper.

Chapter 8

The minute Celina stepped outside, the night filled her senses to bursting. Every pebble, every clump of dirt thrust at the soles of her feet through her thin slippers. A night bird called, high and sweet, so close it seemed she ought to answer. The breeze swirled down out of the mountains, smelling of dust and pines and, from some summit far away, of snow.

The moonlight bloomed everywhere, overpowering the dark mountains, filling up the valley, illuminating even the shaded places, showing all their secrets.

For a moment she was blinded to the spot where King had said he would sleep, then she turned her face away from the moon and she could see his long form, rolled up in a blanket beneath one of the river's low-hanging trees. Was he still awake?

She moved over the rough ground stretching between them, feeling her way, keeping her eyes fixed on him.

"King?" She dropped to her knees by his bed.

The whispering wind swirled her hair into her face; she brushed it back. Then it stirred the low branches of the tree, bathing King in moonlight and suddenly she was motionless on her knees.

His face would beguile the Furies of Hell. It caught the moonglow red-golden on the strong bones of his

138

brows, his cheeks, the arch of his nose. That made him a warrior, a hard god of these mountains.

But his mouth!

His lips curved in a half smile sweet as spring water. *That* made him an angel, defenseless, unguarded.

His one bare shoulder gleamed, alluring as satin. She could almost feel his skin on the tips of her fingers and the palm of her hand.

The quilt rode high against one side of his neck, then cut a diagonal across the slow-breathing breadth of his chest. Her breasts tingled, remembering how it felt to be pressed against him there.

Her whole body thrilled. It felt as if she had nothing on, no protection, nothing between her skin and the air. Every pore was open, every nerve ending awake.

"King?" she whispered. She reached out to touch him. His naked flesh was softly sleek, over muscles that were startlingly hard.

"Mmm?" he murmured. He opened his eyes.

He smiled at her—no hesitation, no surprise—then he raised up on one elbow and slipped his strong, sure hand beneath her hair to clasp the nape of her neck.

"Celina."

The word was a fleeting whisper against her lips, then his mouth was devouring hers.

She opened to him purely by instinct, immediately, the sweet shock of it wiping away her inexperience, her reservations, and her fears in one instant. A shiver ran through her like the wind through the trees, then her tongue was entwining with his.

The melting wonder of his lips took the strength from her body. But not from her mouth. She stayed still on her knees, begging him, impelling him with long, throbbing caresses of her tongue and tiny whimpers in her throat to kiss her forever, never to stop.

King complied, drawing the life, the very soul out of her and then pouring it back again. His hand held her to him, but it didn't move. The marvel of the kiss made him powerless to even want more, much less to take it.

Surely there had never been another woman like this, certainly not in his experience. Not in his lifetime. Never had such a fire been banked and hidden so well.

The silk curtain of her hair swayed against the back of his hand, her mouth burned against his. Desire flared like a sudden conflagration in his blood.

He sat up straighter so he could have both hands free for her, plunging the one deeper into her hair to press her mouth even closer, reaching to caress her body with the other. It found her waist, slid up to her rib cage, absorbing the heat of her flesh through the thin silk.

Her tongue pushed deeper into his mouth, teasing his, entwining, then drawing away. He groaned and moved his hand higher to cup the roundness of one perfect breast.

Her mouth went still on his.

His thumb found her nipple. He caressed the hard bud through the smooth fabric of the wrapper. Once. Twice.

She gasped. After a moment she melded her softness closer in the cradle of his hand, thrusting the nipple against his thumb in a silent demand for more.

He gave it, resuming the kiss at the same instant, taking her lips and her tongue with an all-absorbing passion. She leaned even closer for one heart-stopping instant; then she took her mouth away from his. Her head came up and her hair brushed his face. Fragrant, fine, soft as a feather's touch.

His mouth found her small, determined chin and sucked it once, fast, then fastened itself to her throat, high at first and then lower and lower in a wild succession of kisses, begging, pleading, importunate kisses as she tore herself away from him.

He placed both hands on her hips to keep her against him, but she was moving desperately fast and he was too late.

"No," she whimpered. "Stop. We must . . . stop."

"Celina, what . . ."

"No, King. No. I didn't mean to . . . I mean . . ."

His nostrils flared to catch the lure of lilacs. And to take in air to give vent to the anger beginning to swell in his veins.

She was backing away from his bedroll. He caught her by one wrist and held her.

"You mean to drive me crazy, that's what! Where do you think you're going?"

"I . . . King, I didn't come out here for this."

He stared into the huge pools of her eyes, even more darkly mysterious in the revealing moonlight. The one emotion he could read in them was fear.

Of him? After she'd just kissed him like that? "Just what the hell *did* you come for, then?"

"I came . . ." She made a sound that fell somewhere between a hiccup and a sob. "I came to ask you . . ."

He sat up straight. Ramrod straight. "Ask me *what*?"

She jerked back as if he'd slapped her; she was still on her knees, sitting back on her heels so stiffly she looked as if she were carved out of ice. But she wasn't. He sure as hell knew better.

"To . . ." She made that noise again. It sounded so pitiful he ought to feel sorry for her, but his body was pounding with frustrated desire.

"To help me rescue Mei Lee," she said in a rush.

"King, she's a slave. I suspected it all along, deep inside, but I just wouldn't face it. Moseley owns her, and Sadie wants her to run away, and she is so scared that he'll beat her again . . ."

Were those tears? Tears glistening in those magnificent eyes over some pathetic tale of woe? With no thought of what she'd just this minute done to him? Damn! Had she already forgotten the exultant passion they'd both been feeling? How the hell could she turn it off like that?

She had come to him in the moonlight to ask him something about a slave girl? Not to say, "King, will you hold me?" or "King, I want a kiss?" She hadn't come to him because she'd been dreaming of him the way he had been of her?

"Make sense, woman!" he roared. "Say whatever the hell it is that you've come here to say."

"You have to get her a train ticket, King. I don't have enough money left out of the advance fifty you gave me. And you'll have to make the arrangements to get her to Bitter Springs without Moseley's knowledge."

"Catch the train at Bitter Springs. And just where is it that we're secretly sending this girl who belongs to Marshall Moseley, the best foreman I ever had?"

"To my friend, Mrs. Tolliver, in San Francisco. She has a mission for Chinese slave girls, remember? She'll take Mei Lee in."

He dropped his fingers from around her waist. She didn't seem to notice. She lifted both hands, brushed back her hair, and tucked it behind her ears. It was all he could do not to drive his fingers into it and drag her mouth back to his.

Goddammit . . .

He clenched his fists. She sat looking at him with those wonderful, glistening eyes, marvelously dark compared to the moon.

"When do you think she can go, King? I want to tell her in the morning."

"Celina," he said slowly. "Miss Hawthorne."

She froze in place. Now his face was completely that of the mountain god. And an implacable, merciless god he was! He was furious with her. He thought she had led him on. It was all ruined now—he would never kiss her again.

But that was good. She couldn't let him, anyway. Kissing King was the most dangerous thing she'd ever done.

Never, ever, had she felt such intoxicating sensations, such seductive desires. Never had she known that passion could go so deep as to stir her very soul—no, *King* could stir her very soul. King could set free all the wild emotions she had held in check for so long. He could set them, and her, on fire. And she, and the whole world with her, would be destroyed in the conflagration.

"Listen to me," he was saying. "That girl belongs to Marshall Moseley."

She opened her mouth, but he stopped her words with an uplifted hand.

"Right or wrong, taken by hook or crook, she's his. Now, I want you to know that I feel sorry for her. It's too bad for any human being to be in such a position. However, by no stretch of the imagination can I see that she is any of our business, yours or mine."

She gasped. "I can't believe you said that! Any human being in misery is naturally our business!"

He continued as if she had not spoken one word. "And I have no intention of delaying the construction of the C and G Railroad by alienating Mr. Moseley. Remember, we owe the success of the Donathan deal partly to him—we're in his debt."

"I'm not!"

King ignored that. "Buying his girl a ticket to San

Francisco and putting her on the train is almost certain to antagonize him," he said emphatically. "He could, and probably would, stop those graders from doing another lick of work."

"King! Surely saving someone's life is more important than your infernal railroad!"

"I hardly think her life is in danger. She's lived with the man this long."

"But things are different now!"

"Nothing's different. If this track's not laid by the deadline we lose half our capital in fines."

"You're putting your railroad, your steel-and-wood railroad, above flesh-and-blood people?"

"This is business, Celina," he said coldly. "Remember? You want to be part of the business world, don't you? Well, here you are."

She got to her feet, fast, as if he'd shot at her with a pistol.

"Yes," she said. "Here I am. And up there in that horrid graders' camp is Mei Lee, depending on me to get her out of it."

"It's not your place to get her out of it. Your only responsibility here is to secure a clear title for the C and G."

"The C and G! The C and G! All right, if that infernal railroad is more important than people's lives, then let's make that true across the board!"

Celina clenched her fists until her fingernails cut into the palms of her hands. "If my only responsibility is winning in court, then it's not my place to keep coddling your feelings, either. Therefore, I am putting you on notice at this very moment that *I* am the one in charge of arguing this case."

She stopped to draw a deep breath, to hold in the cry tearing at her throat.

"I *am* a qualified attorney," she said, forcing herself to speak more calmly, "even if *you* see me simply as a woman, someone to be kissed without

warning and ordered around without courtesy. I will
not be told how to do my job. I will prepare this case
the way I see fit, I will argue it the way I see fit, and
I will win it. Don't ever try to tell me how to approach it again!''

Then she turned her back to him, and, on legs that
wanted to run, she walked, slowly, through the
mocking moonlight all the way back to her tent.

Celina took her notes and a law book with her
when she went up to Sadie's for breakfast. The stubborn moon still hung above the western horizon
even though the whole sky already glowed with light
from the sun. She turned her eyes resolutely to the
ground.

Today was here; tomorrow would be the trial. Last
night was gone and nothing like it would ever happen again. She would make sure of that.

The outside table farthest from the kitchen sat
empty. Celina took it and spread out her papers,
ignoring the looks she got from the bunch of sleepy-
looking graders at the next table. Sadie would forgive her this once for monopolizing space before
rush hour was over; twenty-four hours wouldn't be
enough time if she worked every minute.

''Coffee, Miss Celina?''

Mei Lee had appeared at her elbow, a tray of
empty mugs balanced on her hip, a tin coffeepot in
her other hand.

Celina took two mugs from the tray and set one
on a stack of her notes. She held out the other to be
filled. ''Yes, please.'' More softly, she said, ''Don't
worry, Mei Lee. I'm working on a plan.''

The girl nodded, shot her a grateful glance, and
glided away to refill the mugs of the graders.

Celina sat down and took a sip of the scalding
brew. She had no idea what the plan would be yet,
she thought, but as soon as the trial was over, she'd

think of one. She'd get that pathetic child out of
Caliente Crossing if she had to forfeit her job to do
it.

She took another, deeper, drink of coffee and began to sort her crumpled notes. Within a minute,
they had absorbed her completely.

"Celina?"

King's voice jerked her back to reality in an instant. And beyond that to memory.

"Celina," he had said. And then his lips had
taken hers, and herself, into sweet oblivion.

He towered over her, staring down at her, his
weight thrown onto one hip, loose and relaxed. In
his tight-fitting blue denim clothes. His battered
leather work gloves were folded in one hand.
Rhythmically, arrogantly, he tapped them into his
other palm.

"Yes?"

Yes. That's all he had wanted to hear last night.
Why hadn't he ripped down her thin canvas walls
and finished what that one kiss had started?

"I need to talk to you for a minute."

She touched the top button on her shirtwaist,
tucked a tendril of hair into her tight chignon. He
fought the urge to reach down and pull it out again,
to drag every pin from her silky, midnight hair and
let it loose so he could crush it in both his hands and
hold its fragrance to his face.

"Sit down," she said.

He stepped around the corner of the table and
pulled out the chair across from her. When he laid
his gloves on her papers he had all he could do not
to brush her hand with his fingertips.

He folded his arms on the table and leaned across
it toward her. Too close. Her lilac scent caused his
heart to pound; it brought back every sensation he'd
felt last night. But his body refused to move away
from her.

"I've been thinking about it all night," he said.

For one wild heartbeat she thought he meant the kiss: he could see it in her eyes. And so he did. Although he hadn't said the words with that in mind.

He tried to force his thoughts back to business. "I've decided that you're right," he said. "I hired you to be the lawyer; I have to let you call the final shot."

Her eyes flew to his. They looked like deep, deep brown velvet, except that they held so much life. She was surprised, they said. And a bit disbelieving, as well.

"I mean it," he said. "Although it ties my guts in a knot to say it. It's hard for me to give up control, Celina. Of anything."

"I know," she said. "I understand."

She made a quick movement, and for an instant he thought she would reach for his hand. But she picked up her pencil instead. Celina smiled at him, and the plaguing desire stirred stronger in his loins.

"I appreciate your decision, King," she said. "I want you to know that I'll do my very best."

A sudden mental tension made his jaw tighten; he felt a muscle jump along the bone. "I'm putting my railroad, my life's work, in your hands, Celina."

"You won't be sorry, King," she said. "I know I'm right."

Her soft-spoken confidence lessened the tautness in him. Without thinking he started to touch her.

But she let go of her pencil and picked up his gloves instead, holding them in one hand and tapping them in her other palm, as he had done, so she could avoid the physical contact.

Well, she'd never get away with it, he vowed, watching her hands mold themselves around the worn leather that had to be still warm from him.

When this trial was over he would kiss Miss Celina again, and this time he wouldn't let her leave him.

She laid the gloves aside and pulled the papers and the book around where he could see.

"Let me show you what I have," she said, "and I think you'll feel better about your decision."

They reviewed *Peterson* vs. *Guiterrez* and all of Celina's notes for an hour or more, agreeing at the end that they had an excellent chance of winning, even if the opposition did know their basic strategy. Celina promised to use King's development-of-California argument as a backup and in her opening and closing statements.

Then King pushed back his chair and stood up.

"I have to get up to the track now," he said. "Are you ready?"

"Me? What . . ." Then she remembered Rudisill's threats and King's declaration that she shouldn't be alone until the trial. "I'll be fine, King," she said. "Look—there's a town full of people."

He glanced around, at Isabelle and Sadie and the burly O'Reilly, who was bent over, concentrating on his hearty breakfast. Then he stared down at her, frowning.

"Will you stay in it? Work here in the café and not down by the river?"

"Yes," she said.

"Promise?"

"I promise."

"Don't go anywhere alone, please." He picked up the gloves and slapped them onto the table for emphasis, still looking at her with that unwavering stare.

She wished she could read it the way she usually read his face. He was still worried about her safety. Was it because he cared about her personally or because he didn't want to lose his lawyer?

It had better be the latter because his lawyer was

all she could ever be. Anything else was far too
dangerous.

The next morning, after a day that held no unto-
ward happenings, King escorted Celina to the Haileyville stage. They boarded and sat silent while
Hank Austin and his helper loaded mail, express,
and half the population of Caliente Crossing.

Everyone going to the trial talked to King, and he
had to make small talk back; they expected him to
hand out reassurances of victory as if he were a pol-
itician running for office on the basis of promises.
On the surface, he managed to be the epitome of
confidence.

Inside, though, he was wishing Celina would
come out of her shell and reassure *him*. He couldn't
stop going over every detail she had told him the
day before and praying that each would have the
effect she planned.

She was shrewd, he thought, trying to comfort
himself. And she had common sense. Maybe it
would work the way she said. Pray God that it
would work.

"Can you even hear yourself think?" he asked
her as the stagecoach lurched into motion, carrying
chattering citizens sitting on each other's laps, clinging to the roof, standing on the back, and sitting
doubled up in the boot.

"Just don't let them talk to me," she whispered,
shrinking as far as she could into her corner. "I'm
trying to concentrate."

But that proved to be impossible. Although King
shielded her as much as he could, Isabelle and a few
others insisted on getting Celina's estimates of their
chances to win straight from her own mouth.

The sight of Haileyville's main street disturbed
her, too. There was so much hatred boiling just beneath the surface of this town; would it erupt in the

courtroom this morning? Or after the decision came down? Would King be in danger if they won? Or even if they lost?

Danger or no, if they lost he would be ruined. And so would she.

Her hands shook and she gripped her reticule in a stranglehold to stop the trembling. However, once she and King had been swept out of the stagecoach and into the courthouse in the center of the group of raucous Caliente Crossingites, everything changed.

Celina walked down the wide hallway, echoing now to the sounds of dozens of voices and twice that many feet on its bare wooden floor, becoming calmer by the minute. Here it was, that moment of reckoning that would make all the difference in her life. She was ready for it. She had done all that she could do.

Her steps were brisk and sure as she went down the center aisle, through the swinging gate in the divider, and across the space beneath the judge's bench to the long, polished table set to his right. She opened her document case and laid out her books and papers before she sat down.

She looked back for King: someone had caught him in the back of the room and several others gathered near, waiting to talk with him. Celina heaved a thankful sigh. None of them resembled Buster or the other Haileyville residents who'd reviled him three days before.

She slipped into her place, took one glance at her notes, and shut out the rest of the world, her concentration complete. She immersed herself in the case again until King came to take the chair beside her. He leaned close to speak with her.

"Ever hear of Everett Martin?" he asked.

She nodded, throwing a quick look at the opposition's table. "He's a well-known, well-respected attorney from San Francisco," she said. "Don't tell me that's who Rudisill has hired."

"That's what I just heard."

"Could be," she said, her eyes on the tall, bald-headed man who sat with the obnoxious Mr. Rudisill and the other man whom she and King had raced to the Donathan house that day that now seemed a lifetime ago. "I've never seen him."

A tiny kernel of fear burst to life in her stomach. Everett Martin would be tough, very tough, to beat.

The bailiff called for order and for all to stand while Judge Sullivan entered the room. When the attorneys introduced themselves, that seedling of fear became a strangling vine climbing up the inside of her throat.

"Everett Martin," her opponent had said, in a mellifluous voice that carried all the confidence in the world. Celina forced herself to turn away from him and look at Judge Sullivan.

He was older than she had expected, with a wise expression in his sharp blue eyes. She hoped he wouldn't be prejudiced by the sex of an attorney. Or the prestigious reputation of the other attorney.

The audience was an unruly one, exchanging cat-calls and colorful insults while the bailiff tried to restore order. At last the room was quiet and, at a signal from Judge Sullivan, Mr. Martin got up to present his opening argument.

Celina's heart sank. He was good. His reputation obviously was well-deserved and his confidence appeared to be boundless, like King's. What could she do?

Nothing except what she had prepared to do, in a manner that said she was every bit as competent and talented as Mr. Everett Martin.

As Martin finished and acknowledged the applause he had generated with a ceremonious bow, the light caught on the gleaming dome of his head.

It flashed and shone as brightly as if it had been carefully polished.

King leaned over to Celina and whispered, ''See that? All you have to do is shoot him in the seventh spot.''

She stopped in the act of rising from her chair as Martin walked back to his and flashed King an incredulous look.

He was grinning a totally relaxed, completely confident, sincerely amused, questioning grin. Isn't it fun that Mr. Martin is an *Uk'ten'*? it asked. And that we are the underdog who is going to win?

It took a minute for the message to soak in. King had as much confidence in her, now that he'd decided to trust her judgment, as he had in himself.

Celina stood up very straight. She would prove to him and to Mr. Martin and to Judge Sullivan and to all these people and to herself, and to Father, that King was right.

She flashed him a grateful smile and walked around from behind the table on legs that shook only a little.

''Your Honor,'' she said, ''I would like to base my defense on the basis of several precedents, the first of which is the 1879 case of *Peterson* versus *Guiterrez*, decided in Tulare County, California.''

Celina hardly had to look at her notes; the long hours spent poring over them the day before paid off. A few minutes into the argument and she was so passionately involved in the intricacies of her work that she had forgotten everything else, even the feeling of King's supportive gaze at her back.

She kept her eyes on Judge Sullivan and spoke directly to him. He listened intently, but she couldn't tell whether she was convincing him or not.

At last she sat down, to enthusiastic applause and cheers from the spectators from Caliente Crossing—even Mr. Hanna, who usually sneered at her, was waving his hat in the air. The other two thirds of the audience, from Haileyville, responded with boos and jeers.

The bailiff pounded and called for order; the judge warned that the courtroom would be cleared if such a rude display of emotions were repeated.

Everett Martin got up to refute. His first sentence made Celina clench the arms of her chair. The man *was* good—his reputation was well-deserved. But then she thought of his bald head and Thunder and the *Uk'ten'* and her fear dissolved.

When it was time for her to take the floor again for her closing argument, she leaned nearer to King and muttered, "I almost feel sorry for *him.* He needs a whole army of little boys with bows and arrows."

She walked to the front of the judge's bench with a smile on her face and confidence surging in her blood. She had to use every shred of her skill, but she had a feeling, even before she began her summation, that she had won.

The feeling stayed with her through the fifteen minutes of chaos while Judge Sullivan deliberated in his chambers. She and King didn't talk; they simply sat at the table together, bound by a feeling of closeness stronger, even, than that she had felt that first evening they had talked by the river.

At last Judge Sullivan returned and banged his gavel, his blue eyes darting to every corner of the room in a warning for decorum.

He cleared his throat and announced, "The precedents so carefully researched by Miss Hawthorne have convinced me that the C and G Development Company should be issued clear title to the purchased townsite of Caliente Crossing and its environs."

He banged the gavel again. "Effective immediately."

Celina stared at him, fighting to absorb the meaning of the words.

She had won!

The Caliente Crossing people went absolutely wild—despite the bailiff's shouts and the judge's continued gaveling. They began screaming, cheering, and stomping their feet. They threw hats, handkerchiefs, and small children into the air.

But Celina couldn't watch them. King had eyes only for her. And they were fired with admiration. Now he saw her as an attorney, as well as a woman. And Papa would, too, as soon as he heard the news.

Then, before she could form another thought, King pulled her out of her chair and into his arms. He whirled her around, hugging her so tight that she could barely breathe, singing in her ear like a victorious little boy, "The *Uk'ten'* is dead, the *Uk'ten'* is dead!"

He stopped and held her away from him. "Didn't I always say that *Peterson* versus *Guiterrez* was the argument to use?" he teased. "Aren't you glad you took my advice?"

Celina gasped. "*Your* advice?" She took a playful swat at him.

"Miss Hawthorne," someone said in her ear, "you done a mighty fine job."

She turned to accept a hug from Isabelle and one from her little girl, then a blurred succession of congratulations from all of "their" settlers who had accompanied her and King to the trial. Finally, when the celebration had boiled out into the hallway, where some Haileyville residents were threatening to cool it down with fisticuffs, King drew Celina aside.

"This could go on all night," he said. "But if it doesn't, even Hank Austin'll wait for us now. Let's go send some telegrams."

"To my parents," she said, working her way through the crowd with him toward the front door.

"I want them to know that I won. Papa will have to send me congratulations when he hears this!"

"Holleman will have to give us our money, too," King said. "And I want Travis to know. The C and G is rolling now!"

"What about your parents?" she asked. "Are you going to send them word?"

"Not yet," he said, frowning a little as they started down the graveled walk. "It'll put Dad in a mood just to hear the word 'railroad.' I think I'll wait until the track's all laid."

Hank Austin did wait for them. And the celebration did keep going, fistfights, shouted insults, Irish songs, and all. Finally, more than an hour after the trial was over, Jed O'Reilly and three other men carried King and Celina to the stage on their shoulders, everyone piled in behind them, and they started for home.

Celina sat in the middle of the coach in a state of bliss. She had proved to everyone that she knew her business. She couldn't ask for anything more. Except maybe an approving telegram from Papa, and that would be sure to come tomorrow.

The minute they set foot in Caliente Crossing, though, she forgot all about Papa. Her happiness transformed itself into an exuberant joy she had never felt before when the good citizens carried her into Sadie's chanting her name.

It was a few minutes after dark, but the café was blazing with what seemed to be every lantern in the entire camp. The delicious, spicy aromas of barbecue and dried apple stack cakes Sadie had stayed home to make added to the sense of welcome, which was magnified a thousand times when King shouted that he was treating the town. That brought on even more shouts that he and Celina were heroes, and the revelers set them on their feet in the middle of the restaurant as a place of honor.

As Celina looked from one happy face to another and then another, she felt a swift sensation of gratified delight so sharp it took away her breath. She felt like singing; she felt like dancing.

To her own astonishment, she took a few rhythmical steps, picked up King's hand, and twirled herself under his arm. A roaring cheer went up.

"Ned! Ned Sloane! Run home and get your fiddle!" someone yelled. "We're a-gonna be dancin' tonight!"

Several of the town's larger boys began to clear out a good spot for the square dancing just outside the tent, still in the circle of light, and others besides Ned went to get their instruments.

"Here, now, don't let this grub get cold! Better eat before you dance!" another voice called, and someone thrust an overflowing plate into Celina's hand. Before she'd taken two bites, Dan Jarman jumped up onto a table and started an endless speech about what a great town and new county seat Caliente Crossing would be.

When he finally finished, the crowd roared for Celina. King lifted her onto the table in Dan's place. She spoke to their laughing, friendly faces, but she had no idea of what she was saying—her excitement was so intense she was dizzy with it.

Then they called for King. When he swung himself up to stand beside her, he announced the purchase of the Donathan land and, therefore, the full water rights. The cheers of the citizenry became so boisterous that they filled the valley and echoed back and forth out of the hills. Celina thought her heart would burst.

After that, Moseley's crew of graders came in, Ned Sloane and Jed O'Reilly began to fiddle, and everybody chose up partners. King held out his hand to her.

They formed one side of a square and danced the

Texas Star and the Virginia Reel and Sally Good'in. Celina's hair began to slip from its careful moorings and she let it go—in the middle of "Old Joe Clark" she shocked herself by deliberately shaking the rest of it loose to fly behind her as she danced.

Then the fiddles struck up a waltz that flowed into her veins like a surging, tantalizing dream and she turned with fevered haste for King to take her into his arms.

Moving with him, in the circle of his embrace, she danced the slow dance with the same utter abandon as she had the fast ones. The strong beat of his heart against her cheek lured her into craving the hot honeyed taste of his mouth, the haunting magic of his hands on her breast.

She ran her hand up onto his neck and caressed his skin with her fingertips. His arms tightened around her. Celina melded herself to him and closed her eyes.

The sweet sounds of the music grew fainter. The wind in her hair grew stronger. So did the pressure of King's strong body against hers.

He danced more and more slowly. They turned again, once, and then drifted to a stop, out in the open somewhere, standing still and so close together she could feel the urgent pressure of his manhood. It set every nerve in her body on fire.

King buried his lips in her hair. When she lifted her face, he pressed them to her forehead.

"Celina," he murmured, as he had done that day by the river, "kiss me."

This time she raised up on her tiptoes, put her arms around his neck, and lifted her lips almost to his. Her hands stopped on his shoulders, though, intrigued by the muscled slope of them, lured over and over again by their power, refusing to have this fascination obscured by the stronger sensations of a kiss.

The tips of her breasts brushed the hardness of his chest. A thrill shot through her, so fine that it was a torture of pleasure. She did it again.

That same torment, that teasing touch through the thin cloth of his shirt, made King truly desperate. He scooped her up and crushed her mouth to his needy one.

They came together in a ravenous hunger—lips caressing too hard and fast to taste; tongues stroking, moving on to explore before the first touch was familiar. King slowed them down.

He cradled her small, round hips in one calloused hand and slid the other one up the back of her neck to cup her head and hold it exactly where he wanted it. He held her still against him and measured the strokes of his tongue on hers until she, too, fell into the languid rhythm of true delectation.

His hand on her neck relaxed, and moaning in protest, she tilted her head to trail her tongue into the corner of his lips. He groaned.

She brought her tongue back to taste the tip of his, and they kissed until they were breathless, bruised, completely sated. At last Celina drew her mouth away and pressed it, trembling, into the hollow at the base of his throat.

King kept her there for a minute, then pushed his fingers into the wild tangle of her hair and cupped her cheeks. He held her away from him so he could see her face.

Her enormous eyes gleamed at him in the moonlight, darker than ever with the driving excitement that flushed her cheeks. Her just-kissed lips gave him a pouting smile.

"Oh, God, Celina," he groaned, and slid his hands up to caress her breasts.

She closed her eyes and moved closer to him. Moaning with pleasure, she put her hands at his waist and then moved them down to cup his hips as he had done hers.

With an incoherent cry, he bent to find her mouth again and she gave it with a fiery desperation that made colors explode in his head. But her beautiful body began trembling in his hands—shaking in the warm breeze as if she were cold. As if she had a fever.

Which she did. The thought jolted his mind back to life. She'd been in a fever of overpowering excitement ever since their victory, especially since they had returned to Caliente Crossing.

Celina arched away enough to put her hands on his chest and began to unbutton his shirt.

A bewildering hurt flashed through him: she wouldn't stay with him when she woke him in the moonlight, when there had been nothing and no one in the world but her and him. But now, when she was in one of the wild emotional swings of this exceptional day, excited by her first trial and her winning, and the adulation of the people, she would.

He didn't want it to be that way. When he'd vowed to keep her with him all night the next time they kissed, he had meant that she would stay because she wanted him too much to go. Because she would be entranced by the magic between them, not in a fit of abandon created by new feelings outside of the passion they aroused in each other.

Besides, what if she were too carried away by this excitement to really know what she was doing? What if she would wake tomorrow and be sorry?

He broke the kiss and caught both her hands in his. She was unspeakably gorgeous in the bewitching moonlight. He fought to keep from wrapping her again in his arms.

"We'd better stop now," he said, hardly recognizing his own voice, it was so hoarse. "This isn't the right time for us, Celina."

She looked up at him with glistening, soul-shattered eyes.

"Another night," he murmured, and cupped her chin in his hand. "This one has been too full already."

"King, I . . ." she murmured.

"No need to say a word," he teased, placing his finger lightly across her lips. "I'm just trying not to distract you—you need to stay sharp so you'll have lots more victories like you won today."

Chapter 9

The morning stage brought a spate of mail. Celina got hers when she went up to Sadie's—Bud Hanna had dumped the bulging sack onto a table and sorted it instead of taking it over to the store—and half the town was there, reading letters and opening packages.

Celina took her letter from her mother to a table on the outside edge, in the half of the tent now washed in yellow sunlight. She read it quickly, and then more slowly, letting Dolores's words of support and encouragement warm her through. Then she laid it aside. She couldn't wait to hear from both Dolores and Eli once they'd received her message about the trial.

She glanced up to see King striding through the scattered tables, his horseman's long thigh muscles moving like magic beneath his tight pants. He came straight to the spot where she sat.

After a long minute she trusted herself to look up at him. "Good morning," she said.

He threw a sheaf of letters onto the table and pulled out a chair. "Sadie!" he called. "Coffee over here."

Mei Lee was there instantly with the pot and two mugs. He nodded his thanks to her as she poured. When she had gone, he took a drink of the coffee and looked at Celina.

161

She wrapped her shaky hands around her warm mug. "Have you recovered from yesterday?" she asked.

"Are you all right this morning?" he asked.

"Yes," they both said together, and smiled. But his smile was strangely subdued.

After a minute she said, "I see you got a lot of mail."

He took another sip of coffee.

She waited.

"A letter from my dad," he said. "The A T and SF has completed their line across the Unassigned Lands and he's sure the whites will overrun the Nation any minute now."

"But didn't you tell me that's to the west of the Nation?" She loved calling it "the Nation" instead of "the Cherokee Nation." It made her feel like a real member of the tribe.

"It is. But he sees even one railroad as a spreading plague."

"Maybe all fathers are narrow-minded about one thing or another," she said.

He gestured at her letter, folded in front of her. "That from Eli?"

"No, from my mother. Of course, they hadn't heard that we won the trial when this was written."

He nodded and sipped at his coffee. "Want some breakfast?"

"Yes, thanks." But she didn't, really.

He lifted his hand to signal Mei Lee, his shirt sleeve rolled up across the bulging muscle of his forearm, faded palest blue against the coppery tan of his skin. Celina had a sudden urge to trace that dividing line with her fingertip, a desire so strong it made her go weak.

He turned back to her. "The permits came," he said.

It took her a minute to comprehend, to concentrate on his words instead of his presence. "To build the feeder lines?" she cried. "In the Nation? Oh, King! That's wonderful news! Congratulations!"

"Well, I don't know," he said. "The permits are for me to start within the month, and, really, Celina, I'm not so sure I can get away."

She stared at him. "But, King! The crisis is over here. We won, remember?"

"Yes," he said, dropping his eyes to the tabletop. "But they haven't finished laying the track and you never know—"

"You told me this was your dream," she interrupted. "You formed this company, took a white man for a partner, came out here and did all this backbreaking work, took all those hair-raising risks so that you could be the one to build the feeder railroads in the Cherokee Nation. So you could be the one Indian who had some control in the railroads at last!"

Mei Lee refilled their coffee mugs.

"All that's true enough," he said, when the girl had gone. "But this is too soon—it's not enough notice. I'd need to meet with the Council and get them prepared. My father says they've just met and passed a resolution . . ."

He raised his eyes to hers and, as always, she saw the truth in them. All the pieces of the puzzle fell together in her head. King kept on talking, explaining, but she wasn't listening. For the first time since she'd known him he was lying to her. And to himself.

No, only to himself. And only with words. His eyes, his handsome face, his calloused hand lying open on the table conveyed another message, a plea for her to put into words what the other half of him was yearning to say.

Celina had never felt so close to King as in that

moment. He was deliberately asking her to help him with the fiercest, oldest battle in his heart.

She reached across the table and tapped his palm gently with her fingers. "King," she said softly. "King."

His words trailed off into silence.

"I know what you're doing because I've done it a thousand times myself," she said. "You're putting off the confrontation with your father one more time."

His hand went still as stone beneath hers.

She leaned toward him. "You've avoided it for years and years," she said. "That's why you came so far away from home in the first place. That's why you've stayed all these years in California."

His face—his wonderfully handsome, tremendously open face told her that she was right.

"You'll be so much happier when it's done," she said. "I am. I'm so thrilled every time I think about facing up to Father. It was worth all the pain a hundred times over: here I am, a free woman, starting my own law practice, with a victory he said I never could win."

King's amber eyes were already accepting what she was saying. He turned his hand palm up under hers.

"King, if I can do it, you can too," she said.

He squeezed her hand. "You're right. I have to do it," he said. "I knew it the minute you started to talk. It's time for me to grow up and face this."

Mei Lee brought their food, but neither of them looked at it or at her. They couldn't stop looking at each other.

"It feels splendid," Celina said. "You'll find out. It makes you free to go on with the rest of your life, to live it the way you want."

He nodded. "I'll go," he said, his voice so quiet she could barely hear it.

The warm feeling of togetherness that filled her drained away in that instant. He would go. He was going far away. More than a thousand miles away.

The same shock hit him. She saw it in his eyes. Was this the end? Were they parting?

"Go with me," he said, and his hand tightened on hers. "You hired on for a year, remember?"

But she hadn't hired on for those kisses, or for that desire that had racked her soul and body all night long last night.

"I don't think so, King," she said, dropping her eyes from his to avoid their powers of persuasion. "I've just started my career here, in California, and the Nation is so far away . . ." She swallowed and took a sip of her coffee.

"You're always wanting to know about the Nation," he said, leaning across the table, so close that their heads almost touched. "You wanted the blowgun so you could have something of it to hold in your hand. Well, this is your chance! You can *live* in the Cherokee Nation and become a real Cherokee!"

Celina picked up her knife and began spreading the butter melting on her toast, watching the yellow swirls disappear into the rough surface of the thick brown bread. Watching it instead of King's face.

He reached across and lifted her chin. She looked up into blazing topaz eyes.

"Besides," he said, with that grin the devil himself couldn't resist. "Remember this: you're the only lawyer I have and this is the only job you have."

She couldn't help but smile back, although her heart was beating in an awful, pounding rhythm like that of a tracklayer's hammer. "Let me think," she said. "Eat your eggs."

Celina took a bite of her own eggs and then the toast, although all she could taste was the desire to go with him. Did she dare?

Yes. She could meet Aunt Fee and others of her

relatives, see what it was like to live in a real community, maybe even become part of it. She could use her legal skills to fight for its very existence.

Now King read her face as she had read his. He spoke her thought aloud. "You could even help in the legal battles to keep the Nation from being assimilated."

She nodded and took a sip of coffee, deliberately keeping her eyes away from King's.

No! What was she thinking? Of course she couldn't go with him! If she couldn't look at him right now for fear he'd influence her decision, she certainly couldn't hope to keep her hard-won independence in any kind of long-term association with him. She'd lose everything she'd gained, everything she'd dreamed of all her life if she went with him.

"Miss Celina? Telegram."

Isabelle's little girl stood beside Celina with a yellow envelope in her hand. "Mr. Jensen give me a penny to bring this to you."

"Thank you, Mary."

King gave the child another coin and she ran off. Celina tore open the message.

"Maybe it's from Papa and Mama," she said, "answering my wire about the trial!"

She unfolded the pages and began to read.

DAUGHTER CELINA:
WHAT VICTORY TO BEGIN CAREER? DECISION WAS LUCK, FLUKE, OR BRIBE BY CROOK CHEKOTE. MAYBE NOVELTY OF WOMAN LAWYER. NOT CLEARCUT, ANYWAY. NEVER HAPPEN AGAIN. CHEKOTE RUINED YOUR REPUTATION, WILL DUMP YOU. NO ONE WILL HAVE YOU BUT ME. COME BACK TO WORK NOW WHILE I WILL TAKE YOU.

At first, shock numbed her. Then every successive sentence hurt so much that she tried to hold her eyes still, to keep them from moving on. But they wouldn't obey her brain; they slid from each wounding word to the next, taking every one of them in and sending them straight to her heart.

Why, why had she ever hoped that Father would be proud of her, praise her? Why hadn't she known that he would react this way?

The vitriolic tirade went on for three full pages and she stubbornly read every one of them. She should have stopped, though. She should have quit and ripped the crisp little pages in half before she got to the end. Because it was the worst: Eli's parting shot shattered even the already broken pieces of her heart.

IF I HAD A DOZEN CHILDREN I WOULDN'T CARE WHERE YOU GO OR WHAT YOU DO. BUT I HAVE ONLY ONE. YOU ARE MY CHILD AND YOUR PLACE IS WITH ME.
ELI HAWTHORNE

Eli Hawthorne? He signed it with his full name as he would to a stranger? He couldn't even call himself "Father" to her, much less "Papa"? Furious pain raced through her. But the formal signature wasn't its source. She had to acknowledge that; the mortal hurt was in those words just above his name.

He wouldn't care? If he had a dozen children, then he wouldn't care what she did? She wasn't a real person to him—she wasn't an individual; he didn't know her, Celina, any more than he knew "Crook Chekote." He didn't love her for herself and he never had; she was just "his child."

And after all her hard, painstaking work! What would it take ever to please him?

Her heart hurt so much she couldn't breathe; her insides churned with the hopeless, dying dreams of her childhood. Then, boiling up out of the hurt, bubbling from its thickening residue like water boil-

ing in a pot, surged the hottest anger she had ever
felt. Its tears filled her eyes as she raised them to
meet King's. She folded the hateful pages and
stuffed them into the pocket of her skirt.

"Celina, are you all right? Do you want to tell
me?"

His tone spoke volumes: that he knew she was
hurting and he hated it; that he was hurting with
her; that he would like to bash whoever had done
this to her. That he guessed it was Eli.

"I can't," she said.

"Why not?" he challenged. "I've gotten the dis-
tinct impression that we're friends."

"I'm too angry to talk," she said, biting off each
word.

"Good," he said, the corners of his mouth lifting
although his eyes kept their concerned look. "It's
about time you got mad at somebody besides me."

"I don't get mad at you! What are you talking
about?"

"Don't you remember how mad you got when I
criticized the amount of your luggage?"

She gasped. "You have the memory of an ele-
phant! Besides, *you're* the one who had a temper
tantrum over my luggage."

He shook his head. "Not true," he said.

"It *is* true."

"There's only one way to settle this," he told her.
"We must take another trip together and see who's
the first to fall into a fit of temper."

"King! You are the most treacherous opponent
I've ever faced in an argument!"

"Aren't you glad I'm not a competing attorney?"

She actually laughed, in spite of the angry hurt
spreading through her. She wanted to cry because
King was trying so hard to talk her into going with
him. The idea made her heart lift with excitement.

But it wouldn't be good for her in the long run: it would put them in too close a proximity for too long. And then he would be controlling her with his charm, as he'd proved a dozen times that he could do so well.

She was not going to live under someone else's control! Celina silently repeated her familiar promise.

He stopped laughing and fixed her with his piercing, sparkling stare. "Come to the Nation," he said, daring her. "Leave your troubles behind."

She looked back at him, but instead of his face she saw the hateful, black letters again: IF I HAD A DOZEN CHILDREN . . .

"You'd love it there, Celina," he said, with his most persuasive smile. "The blowguns and darts grow on trees."

She laughed. He had actually made her laugh again. "I'll go," she said, and her voice didn't break in the slightest.

His voice got as solemn as his face. "When?"

"Any time. Tomorrow. Now. This minute. When do *you* want to leave, King?"

"How about tomorrow morning's stage? Since our minds are made up, we might as well do it."

She pushed back her chair and stood up. "Perfect," she said. "Now I need to go and send a wire."

He got up, too. "I'll go with you. Travis will have to find me a boss to finish off this line."

King took Celina's arm and guided her through the maze of tables and out into the purging sunlight. They walked side by side in its healing heat, in silence, all the way up the hill to the telegraph shack.

Celina refused to go first; while King talked to Jensen and sent several wires, she stood at the rough counter and printed on a tablet of coarse, lined paper the one message that she would send:

FATHER ELI:
WHAT CHILD TO COME HOME AND WORK FOR YOU?
YOU SHOULD ADOPT A DOZEN OTHERS. I AM GOING
WITH KINGFISHER CHEKOTE TO THE CHEROKEE NATION.
                              CELINA HAWTHORNE

Jensen pecked out the letters one by one, and the
telegram was sent. There was no calling it back, but
she had no desire to do so.

"Should be delivered by noon," the telegrapher
said genially. "We're gonna miss you two around
here."

"Thanks," King said, steering Celina to the door.
"But we'll be back. Wouldn't miss dedicating the
courthouse for anything."

"Right!" Jensen, laughing, called after them.
"Shouldn't be more than a year or so 'til we build one."

King and Celina hurried down the hill, past Isabelle's home and shop and Hanna's store. King
stopped when they were opposite the livery stable
and rope corral.

"I need to get a horse and ride out to the end of
track," King said. "Will you be all right if I leave
you?"

"I'll be perfectly fine," she said, calmly.

He watched her face for a moment. "I won't be
long," he said. "I'll hurry back to help pack up all
those clothes of yours."

When she didn't even smile in response, he said,
frowning, "Think I ought to bring Moseley's crew
to help? The stage'll be in by daylight. That would
only give us . . . uh . . ."

He took out his watch with a flourish and made a
dramatic production of opening and consulting it.

". . . approximately twenty-two hours to fold
shirtwaists and petticoats, riding habits and ball-
gowns, hats, bonnets, and mourning costumes and
stuff them into the various pieces of your luggage."

She chuckled, although a minute earlier she would've said that she'd never smile again.

"Bring the tracklayers, too," she said. "We'll need all the help we can get."

He snapped his fingers. "That's how you can help Mei Lee," he said. "And me, too. I just thought of it. Give her a lot of your clothes and I won't have to haul them to the train."

"What a weakling!" she said. "Afraid of a few little pieces of luggage."

He laughed. "More like a wagon load," he said. "Admit it." He touched her cheek once, then strode toward the stable.

Celina ran down the hill. Mei Lee. That was the one piece of unfinished business left in Caliente Crossing.

The Chinese girl was just outside the kitchen area of Sadie's tent, scrubbing the huge tin pitchers from which they'd poured the eggs into the skillets. Sadie stood a few feet away, just inside, cleaning them.

Celina stopped beside Mei Lee, but she called out to Sadie, "May I borrow an ice pick, please? The lock on my trunk is stuck and I have to pack. I'm leaving tomorrow."

Sadie didn't look up. "In there," she said, tilting her head toward the boxes of cooking and eating utensils on a table behind her.

Celina hesitated. Obviously there'd be no getting rid of Sadie by sending her on errands. "Thanks," she called back.

She glanced down and met Mei Lee's worried look, but before she could speak, Sadie called out, "Leaving tomorrow, you say?"

Mei Lee glanced away and dipped her dishcloth into the pan of soapy water.

"Yes. I need to do my packing right away."

Without looking at Mei Lee again, Celina muttered, "Come to my tent very early tomorrow. Long before time to go to Sadie's."

"Well, you want that ice pick or not?" Sadie sounded even grouchier than usual.

"Yes," Celina said, hurrying toward the boxes of utensils. She rummaged around in the largest one, pushed aside spatulas and long forks, and took an ice pick.

For the second night in a row, Celina hardly slept. Even the exhausting task of driving the ice pick through the three layers of the wardrobe—tough tapestry fabric, wood frame, and quilted cotton lining—a minimum of thirty times had not tired her enough to sleep.

Now, lying on her cot in the darkness, she worried about whether there'd be enough air in the wardrobe. Should she have made at least fifty holes? How much air would Mei Lee need?

Would she be too frightened to stay locked in the wardrobe all those long, jouncing miles to Bitter Springs? Probably not; she was more frightened of Moseley and Sadie.

And would King and Austin's helper notice anything wrong? The wardrobe would be heavier than it had been when she arrived and so would the trunk and the portmanteau; they were loaded with extra clothes from the wardrobe, even though she'd given several things to Isabelle and Mary.

Celina flipped over onto her stomach and covered up her head. What would King do when she let Mei Lee out at Bitter Springs? God knew that he thought more about that railroad of his than he did of people. Would he fire Celina and send her packing? Rush back to pacify Moseley so the railroad could keep going? Horror of horrors, would he try to return Mei Lee to Moseley?

She tried to visualize such a scene: Mei Lee in

tears; King, wearing his implacable mountain god's face . . .

She threw off the quilt that covered her. No thinking about King. That had been her rule all night and one of the reasons she'd clung so to her worries. No thinking about King and the consequences of traveling across the country alone with him. No thinking about his kisses . . .

Another vision of him flashed before her eyes: the sensuous face of a vulnerable angel.

She sat up and brushed back the hair from her face. Oh, Dear Lord, what had she done?

"Missy Celina?"

Mei Lee's voice was no more than a breath at the open flap of the tent.

Celina was on her feet in a flash. "Mei Lee!" she whispered, hurrying to draw her inside. "Thank goodness you're here in time! Come here and see what I've planned."

She led the girl to the wardrobe, showed her the air holes, and helped her climb in and lie down. The two of them experimented with stuffing various pieces of clothing around her for padding and using a rolled-up shawl for a pillow. Finally Mei Lee proclaimed herself comfortable and Celina closed the lid.

"Celina, are you about ready?"

She froze with her hand on the lock of the wardrobe. The voice at the flap was King's. And somebody else's.

". . . help you get loaded and see if there's any more orders . . ."

Marshall Moseley! Good heavens, what was *he* doing here at this time of day?

Politicking, of course. Cozying up to King. Being his usual overhelpful, charmingly deferential self. Mei Lee would be terrified when she heard his voice!

"Just a minute, please," Celina called, without opening the flap. "I'm almost ready."

She unfastened the lock and opened the wardrobe. Mei Lee lay in the bottom of it, cushioned around the sides by rolled-up pieces of clothing. Her face was calm, but her eyes were full of fear.

"Moseley is here to help with the luggage," Celina whispered. "But don't be scared. I won't let him find you." She hoped.

Quickly she closed the lid and double-checked the lock. Then she opened the flap and went out. "I'm ready," she said. "I'm sure you can't believe it, King, but I managed to pack all my clothes with only half the town helping me!"

Moseley had brought a mule and sled normally used on the grading site; the two men made quick work of adding her luggage to King's. Hank Austin's first cry of "C-a-li-en-te Crossing!" came floating across the river just as they started up the hill to meet him.

Celina was thankful that both Moseley and King were obsessed with work; all the way to Sadie's they talked about the boss that Travis would send and finishing this line to Bakersfield and where the next branch line would run. Hank brought the stage rolling in just moments after they reached the café.

It seemed to Celina that they stood around there forever, talking—except for Hank, of course, who kept his seat and stared off at the mountains while his helper offloaded the mail. King tried to hand Celina in to her seat, but she pleaded the long ride ahead and stayed outside to watch them load her things.

"Maybe do the wardrobe first?" she suggested. "It was tied on top on the way down here."

"Right," King said, but he stowed the portmanteau full of books in the boot and Moseley lashed her trunk to the side before they turned to the wardrobe.

They picked it up; Moseley grunted and took a better grip on it. When they had it balanced on their shoulders, King turned to Celina.

"How'd you do it?" he asked.

She gave a start. Did he know, somehow? "Do what?"

"How'd you buy clothes in Caliente Crossing? I swear this thing is heavier now than it was when we came."

"I filled it with rocks from the river," she teased. "For souvenirs."

"You ain't just whistling Dixie," Marshall Moseley said, taking a deep breath and a second try to heave the long box to the top where Hank's helper caught it.

"Gotta be rocks in here," he grunted. "You oughtta make her leave it, Boss."

Celina smiled.

Moseley climbed up on top to help tie the wardrobe down, and Celina watched every motion he made with the utmost pleasure. She only wished she could see his face when he found out he'd helped send his own slave girl away.

"B-it-ter Springs!"

Celina's heart gave a mighty thump. All the way she'd been longing for the trip to be over, but now she wasn't ready. What would King do? More importantly, how was Mei Lee doing? Had she survived the trip?

They pulled up to the back side of the train platform; the minute the swaying stage stopped, Celina got up. King followed her out the door, grumbling that she should wait for him to go first and hand her down. But she knew she couldn't have. She couldn't look him in the face.

The minute Hank's helper was on the ground, Celina said to him, "Please unload my wardrobe first."

She felt King's startled look. The boy said, "Have to, ma'am. It's what went on last. Last on, first off."

Celina paced the platform while they untied and lowered the long box. "Careful," she cautioned, and again she felt King's eyes on her.

The minute the wardrobe was on the ground she was on her knees beside it; working at the lock. Several travelers had stopped in their tracks to watch.

Finally the latch came loose. She raised the lid.

Mei Lee had slid all the way to one end, where she was lying completely still. Her eyes were open, huge, and very much alive. They held such a look of triumph that it made Celina want to shout with joy.

"Thank God!" Celina cried, reaching in to help her up. "Mei Lee, are you all right?"

The girl sat up, then stood up, holding on to Celina's hand for balance, and stepped out onto the wooden planks of the platform. A lacy petticoat caught on her foot and came with her, draping itself over the side.

"Well, I'll be damned!" muttered the man with the bowler hat who'd ridden with them from Haileyville.

"Mr. Woodson, can you beat that?" squealed a woman traveler to her husband.

But it was King's words that were going to matter. He would share the exultation of the moment, though. How could anyone look at Mei Lee's face and not be moved by it? She put her arm around Mei Lee, threw back her head, and smiled up at him.

He towered over them, his eyes blazing with anger, his lips compressed into a hard, thin line that barely moved when he spoke.

"Celina, what the *hell* is this?"

Chapter 10

Celina's spine stiffened. How could he take that attitude? Well, what was done was done. No matter what the consequences—if she had to go into a restaurant and get a job scrubbing pots like Mei Lee—she was glad she had done this.

"Answer me!" King roared.

Mei Lee cringed. Celina pulled the girl closer.

"She was in danger," she said, angrily. "I told you, King, Moseley beats her."

Mei Lee's eyes darted furtively from side to side. "Moseley? Where?" she said, her voice cracking.

Celina said, "We left him back in Caliente Crossing. Don't worry about him; we'll never see Marshall Moseley again."

"We'll never see a branch railroad completed on time, either," King said, spitting each word at her. "I told you, Celina, alienate Moseley and you'll shut down the line. Dammit! You've done it now! Why can't you *listen* to me?" He was so angry his voice was shaking.

Mei Lee's thin shoulders trembled beneath Celina's protective arm. "Branch railroad!" she cried. "Branch railroad! I am so sick of hearing those words. Look at this poor, scared girl and then tell me about your precious branch railroad!"

King glared at her, then turned and looked behind

him at the stagecoach. "I ought to take her back to
Caliente Crossing this minute," he said.

Hank Austin, startled out of his fabled reticence
by a Chinese girl's stepping out of a wardrobe that
had ridden right behind him for the last forty miles,
called down from his perch. "Not in my coach," he
said regally. "I've got a schedule to keep."

"Besides, we'd miss our train," Celina said.

King turned back to her. "Of course we'd miss
our train!" he shouted.

"You mustn't do that," chirped Mrs. Woodson.
"This is a terrible station to wait in. Why, the last
time we had a layover here . . ."

King glared her into silence.

"King," Celina said quietly. "King, don't worry.
I have it all planned. I'll telegraph Mrs. Tolliver to
meet Mei Lee in San Francisco—we'll put her on the
northbound train before we go."

He stared at her. "You've already checked the
train schedules?"

"Yes. Jensen let me use his."

He kept looking at her, shaking his head. "You
never give up, do you, Celina?"

"No," she said. "I never do."

And she gave him a smile. Not a triumphant,
gloating smile, but a friendly smile that said, "King,
I trust you to do the right thing."

He couldn't think *what* to do. Nor what else to
say. She was, without a doubt, the most exasperating woman on the face of the earth.

"I'm going to take Mei Lee into the washroom
now," Celina said, bending down to stuff the petticoat back into the wardrobe. "I'll help her change
into some of my clothes. While we're gone, would
you buy her ticket, please, King?"

She closed the wardrobe, had Austin's helper
bring her trunk and open it, and asked Mei Lee to

pick the clothing she wanted, then shepherded her to the ladies' washroom.

Dumbstruck, King watched her graceful progress.

Celina! That little minx! She had the nerve! She really did. The thought made his anger lessen. A person couldn't help but admire her—she had risked a lot for someone she hardly knew.

Really, when he thought about it, in a way it was funny. That obnoxious manipulator Moseley deserved to have the girl stolen out from under his nose. Especially if he'd been beating her, which, no doubt, he had.

King turned and paced back in the other direction. Would the man stop the graders' working, though? What a mess-up if he did! They could end up still losing the business, thanks to Celina's misplaced charity.

King looked toward the station, but she was still in the washroom. What would he do, anyway, when he saw her? He ought to shake her until her perfect teeth rattled.

But, deep down, when he remembered her beautiful face turned up to his out there by the stagecoach, all he really wanted to do was kiss her again—kiss her until they were both senseless with the pleasure.

After an age, the two women came out onto the platform. Mei Lee was wearing a pink dress instead of her customary faded blue pajamas, and Celina had outfitted her usually sandaled feet in high-topped shoes. She carried a small bag which, he suspected, held more of Celina's clothes. The girl looked very nice and much more relaxed. Celina was clucking over her like a mother hen, giving glowing accounts of Mrs. Tolliver and her school.

King bought their tickets, arranged for their luggage to be put aboard, and then went back to wait

with Celina and Mei Lee for the northbound. After
another age, it came.

He smiled to himself as Celina hovered around
the departing Mei Lee as if she were her child,
straightening the collar of her dress and making sure
that she had her ticket ready for the conductor. They
both cried when it was time for Mei Lee to board;
they hugged, then cried again.

At last the girl was settled in a window seat where
she could wave to them, tears and joy mingled in
her face, as they were on Celina's. The big engine
began to build up steam; its chuffing noise filled the
station. The engineer gave two long pulls on the
whistle, the train started to roll, and suddenly, Mei
Lee was gone.

And he was alone with Celina.

She looked up at him with her wide, intriguing
eyes. "King, I do so hope you understand. I could
never have lived with myself if I'd gone off and left
Mei Lee."

It came again, that powerful urge to shake her.
No, to kiss her. "I understand," he said. And suddenly he knew that it was true.

"But, King, I *am* really sorry if Moseley blames
you and stops the graders."

He shrugged. "All we can do now is wait and
see," he said. "And deal with whatever happens
when it happens."

He looked down at her and grinned. His heart
turned over.

"Moseley may not blame me at all," he said. "If
Hank Austin's talking streak holds out, he'll testify
that I was as surprised as anybody else when Mei
Lee popped up like a jack-in-the-box."

She laughed. The low, musical sound sent molten
heat through his veins.

The rails began to hum, and then to vibrate. From
the west sounded one long, galvanizing whistle, the

signal that a train was approaching the station. A minute later it came roaring in.

They stood up in the swirling dust of its wake. King took Celina's reticule in the same hand as his portmanteau, and her arm in the other. He led her along the cindery side of the track to a car ornately painted in purple, blue, and silver. A sign on its side read THE WESTERN ZEPHYR. As they approached, the conductor opened its door and set out some portable steps.

Celina stepped up onto the bottom one, King's hand under her elbow to help her board.

"Mr. Chekote!" someone called. "Message for you!"

They turned to see a man wearing a green eye-shade running from the station, a telegram waving in his hand.

The sight of the yellow paper made Celina go cold. Would she never see another one without being reminded of the all-time most-hateful message from Father? She slipped her hand into her pocket to find it still there. Why couldn't she bring herself to throw it away?

Because it was a token, a reminder that this decision to go with King was the right one. Any time she doubted that, all she had to do was to touch these crackling little pieces of paper.

King gave the man a tip, stuffed his message into his pocket, and he and Celina finished climbing the steps. They entered the vestibule.

The porter, an immaculately groomed black man in a starched uniform, bowed and indicated that they should pass through the door he was holding open.

"This way, ma'am. Sir."

Celina stepped into the Western Zephyr and into another world: a beautifully appointed, utterly lush, new world.

It was like falling into a feather bed: the sheer se-

duction of so much comfort lured her into immediate relaxation. The deep armchairs and couches
arranged in conversational groupings looked plush
enough for sleeping after her Spartan cot in the tent.
A few scattered passengers occupied them, reading
or chatting or looking out at Bitter Springs through
the wide picture windows that let in sparkling sunlight from both sides of the car; it reflected and multiplied in the gilt-framed mirrors that lined the ends.
It caught in the rich lavenders, purples, and blues
used in all the appointments, too, and somehow
gave the impression that the room was full of flowers.

"I would've hired a private car for us," King murmured in her ear. "But for such a long trip I had to
think of your reputation."

She smiled at him over her shoulder. "I thought
all railroad magnates *owned* their own private cars
just like this one."

"Give me time," he muttered, making a face at
her. "Give me time."

The porter ushered them across the deep,
diamond-patterned carpeting to a small table and
two chairs upholstered in blue plush and swinging
silver tassels. The same fringe trimmed the heavy
damask drapes that framed the windows.

"Just let me stow away that hand luggage, there,
sir, ma'am, and I'll bring you some drinks," he said.

Celina gave him her reticule and then dropped
into the soothing restfulness of her seat.

"Oh, King," she sighed. "I'd forgotten such luxury existed."

She tilted her head against the back of the seat
and gasped, delighted.

"Look!" she said. "King, look up!"

The high, broadly arched ceiling was as beautiful
and interesting as any gallery wall. Divided into sec-
tions, it was decorated with hand-painted land-

scapes, each one a majestic scene from somewhere in the West, each one "framed" by intricate filigrees of gilt paint.

"Ahh," she sighed, "wonderful. I love this."

King grinned at her. "How can you be so impressed, accustomed as you are to the luxury of Caliente Crossing?"

Celina sat up and laughed at him. "You have a point there. Caliente Crossing is the very reason all this feels so good. Three weeks of living in a tent and bathing in a river will make plush seats and painted ceilings seem like heaven."

"Be kind," he teased, reaching into his pocket for his telegram. "You know you'll miss having breakfast at Sadie's. Now when it's Saturday you won't have any idea what the menu is."

He unfolded the message and read it. A broad, satisfied smile spread over his face. "We got it," he said, looking up to beam at her. "Holleman says he's proud to give the loan to the C and G."

"Thank goodness," she said. "Things won't be quite so tight now if Moseley does shut down."

"Don't talk about it," he said. "We'll just hope that he won't."

Celina let her head rest against the back of her seat again while she watched him. He really *had* been wonderful about Mei Lee, she thought. He was a good man.

The noise of the engine, far away at the head of the train, grew louder. The cars jerked once, then again.

"It's your doing, you know," King said. "Holleman wouldn't've let us have the money if you hadn't won the title case."

He folded the crisp yellow page of the telegram once, then again, and idly drew it through his fingers. Celina kept staring at them.

The train jerked again; it began to move forward. Bitter Springs started slipping past, faster and fas-

ter. Then it was gone. All the old world was gone.
It had faded away and left her alone with King,
safely enclosed in this luxurious car, falling into the
depths of his empathetic eyes.

She dropped her hands into her lap and leaned
toward him. "I'm happy for you, but the only telegram I can really think about is Father's," she
blurted, as the engine sounded two long whistles.
"I had my mind on Mei Lee all yesterday and last
night, but now, every awful word of Papa's message
is beating at my brain."

"Was it that bad?"

"It was terrible. The worst. But King, the *worst*
thing is within me. Somehow, in spite of all the pain
he's caused me, deep, deep down I still want him
to love and admire me."

She sighed and stared out the window at the wild
landscape sliding past. "I guess you were right when
you said I never give up."

King leaned forward, too, amazed. Was she actually going to trust him enough to talk about her
relationship with Eli? "That's only natural, Celina,"
he said.

"That's only hopeless, I'm afraid," she retorted.
Then she looked at him again. Was she really telling
him all this? Only to King could she speak of these
deepest feelings that drove her. "Is it? Is it really
natural to feel that way?"

"Of course it is. He's your father in spite of all.
You want to love him and win his approval."

Celina dropped back against the chair, letting her
body sink deep into it. "I've always admired my
father intellectually," she began. "Papa is the one
who encouraged me to go to college and to read for
the law," she said. "He always seemed truly proud
of me and my desire to learn."

"He should be proud of you," King murmured,
afraid to move. If he did, he might break the spell.

She didn't seem to hear. Her face was turned half away from him; she was staring out the window, obviously without seeing anything. "Now it hurts so much to know that he only wanted me to be a lawyer so I could be his 'right arm' for the rest of his life."

"Are you sure that's true?"

She lifted her eyes to his. The hot pain in them seared him. "I'm sure. I should've known it all along. He totally dominated my life as a child and he never had any intention of letting up just because I had become a woman. The only thing that changed as I grew up was that he stopped sneaking up behind me to see what book I was reading."

"He did *what?*"

"Yes!" she said, leaning toward him again across the small table. "I loved to read—especially novels—ever since I learned how. My mother had Emilio drive me to the library twice a week and she also bought me lots of books. Any time my father found me reading one of them he would tiptoe up close and read over my shoulder to see whether he approved or not."

"Did he ever take any away from you?"

Her eyes blazed. "Oh, yes! For years I've been searching for a copy of *Maggie's Choice* so I could see how it ended." Suddenly she looked like a hopeful little girl. "Have you read it, by any chance? I'd love to know whether she chose to go live with her uncle in his castle or to come to America with her big brother."

King looked into her huge, dark eyes. "That son of a . . . gun," was all he could say. But he made a mental note of the title. He would find that book for her if there was a copy left on the face of the earth.

"Exactly," she said bitterly. "It used to make me so *furious.* I felt so powerless!"

King's fist clenched. "Of course you did."

"And it wasn't just books, King! He chose my friends, what few I was allowed to have—he even arbitrarily chose the number of chocolate candies I could have in a week." She sighed. "Chocolate is one of my favorite things in the whole world."

"How many did he let you have?"

"Three! Isn't that stingy? That isn't even one every other day!"

"What did he do, lock them up?"

"Yes, and in a glass cabinet where I could see them, too. He said it would help build my character."

"I'd like to help build his," King said tightly. "It isn't too late for that—even at his advanced age."

"Yes, it is," she said, ripping the telegram from her pocket and thrusting it at him. "Read this and you'll see."

King took the crumpled pages, smoothed them out against his thigh, and began to read. By the time he had gotten to the last words, IF I HAD A DOZEN CHILDREN I WOULDN'T CARE, he was cold all over.

He crushed the papers in his fist as if they were Eli himself, and dropped them into the cut glass ashtray in the middle of their table. He arched up to get his hand into the front pocket of his pants, took out a match, and struck it, thrusting the flame to the paper.

How must *she* feel? If those terrible words had struck *him* so deeply, how could the poor darling bear it?

"Do you think he ever could change, King?" she asked. "After reading that, do you think he can ever let me be free and still love me?"

There was hope in her voice, in spite of her just having told him that it was too late for Eli. Her beautiful eyes were swimming in tears.

Free or not, he doesn't love you now and he never has, King wanted to say. Give it up, sweetheart. Eli can't love anyone. But his throat was so tight he couldn't say anything, even if he'd been so insensitive as to actually blurt out those words. He was sick to his stomach, too, and, for the first time in years, he wanted to cry.

Damn the bastard! Damn him!

He stared blindly out the window for an instant so she wouldn't see the depth of his rage. It was so strong, though, that it pulled him to his feet. He had to move, or else he'd explode. "I'll go see about those drinks," he muttered, and strode down the aisle to look for the porter.

Somebody like Eli didn't deserve to have a child. He'd strangle him. No, he'd forget him. And he'd make Celina forget him, too. But first he had to answer her question: could Eli let her be free and still love her?

He signaled the porter who was at the other end of the car and went back to Celina, trying to get a grip on his anger. "It's hard to tell," he said, dropping into his seat. "I know from experience with my father that sometimes it's nearly impossible for parents to give up on their own plans for their children."

She nodded, obviously too overwrought to speak.

The porter appeared with a tray. When he'd served their iced lemon drinks, King handed him the ashtray to empty. Then he reached for Celina's hand. "I guess the answer to this question about Eli is the same as the one to the question about what Moseley will do. Only time will tell."

She nodded. "You're right. And there's no point in even discussing it any more at the moment."

"There is if it'll make you feel better," he said.

She squeezed his fingers. "I already feel better," she said. "You're the only person to whom I ever felt I could really talk. Thank you, King."

"Any time you want to talk—about anything—I want to listen," he said. "Will you remember that?"

Celina smiled through her tears. "Yes."

The train puffed into a station for a stop. "Great!" he said, and jumped to his feet. "I'll be right back. You sit right here and wait for me."

Local peddlers came through the train selling everything from newspapers and fruit to homemade bread; two new passengers boarded and settled into their seats, and, finally, the conductor began calling, "All aboard."

Celina got up and crossed the car to look up and down the platform for King, but there was no sign of him. The engine began building up steam. Was he going to miss the train? What would she do if he did? Should she go look for him?

Then she saw him, bursting out of the door of one of the shops built in a row beside the station, running across the platform like a little boy afraid of being left behind, the tail of his fine tan coat streaming out behind him.

He bounded up the steps and appeared the next instant in the doorway of the car. Under his arm was an enormous box, wrapped in shiny red paper, tied in both directions with a thin, gold cord.

"This is for you," he said. "Come open it."

As soon as she was seated, he placed it in her lap. The luscious aroma of sweet, bitter, thick, creamy, delicious chocolate filled her nostrils.

"It's all yours," he said, smiling. "Ten pounds. You may have as many pieces as you want, now or later, without asking permission from anyone."

"King!" she cried. "Ten pounds!"

"Of course," he continued, grinning, "you may feel an inclination to share it. That is a great deal of chocolate for one small woman to eat all by herself."

Celina began to laugh, pure delight bubbling out of her like a song.

He reached out and touched her cheek. "Open

it," he growled in mock impatience. "See if it's the kind you like."

"There's never been a chocolate I didn't like," she said, wanting to touch him back, the way he had touched her, but not quite being able to dare. But a new burst of warmth at his kindness gave her courage; she reached out and returned that one sweet, caressing touch.

His eyes blazed. "Open it anyway," he said.

She untied the cord, unwrapped the stiff paper with fingers that trembled only a little, and opened the lid.

"Which one looks the best?" he asked.

"This one."

She chose a heavy, dark square and picked it up, lifting it to King's mouth. Eyebrows raised in surprise, he bit into it with his strong, white teeth, caressing her fingertips with his lips as he did so. She held them still just a moment longer than necessary, then brought them to her own mouth with the taste of King still on them. They savored the burning, bitter sweetness together.

Celina leaned back in the hot soapy water and rested her head against the curving top of the bathtub. She let her eyes drift closed.

But they opened again, immediately, to her reflection in the polished walnut panels of the ceiling. Her whole face was suffused with the strange, languorous excitement that King had created in her this afternoon. She could still taste his lips, sweeter than the chocolate by far, on her fingertips.

King.

And now they were going to dress up and go to dinner alone. She had never been to dinner with a man alone—Papa wouldn't permit it and Professor Tolliver had acted in his stead. Even in a group on college outings she'd never been linked with one particular young man.

But King was as different from any of those college men, from any other man she'd ever met, as . . . a lion was from a rabbit. King had a power she couldn't begin to understand. Who else could have gotten her to spill out her deepest feelings the way he had done today? Who else could have understood them so well?

Her glance went to the half-wrapped box of chocolates sitting on her marble washstand.

Who else could have soothed her wounds so surely?

She shivered and wrapped her arms around herself, although the water had not cooled. Her body still burned for King, for what he had denied her after they had danced in the night.

Now it seemed he might get that same terrible hold on her heart.

Chapter 11

King's knock at her door froze Celina in place, her arms lifted to put the last jeweled pins into her hair. Remember, she cautioned her reflection. Be calm and act as if you do this every day.

She took one last glance in the mirror. She loved the rich, rose-colored fabric, but was this dress cut too low? Did it leave too much of her neck and shoulders bare? No, it would make her appear more worldly, more accustomed to romantic dinners for two.

King knocked again. Celina took a deep breath, picked up her bag, crossed the bedroom and then the sitting room to open the door.

King filled the passageway. His broad shoulders touched the walls, his head threatened to brush the lowered sides of the ceiling. He wore a black suit, cut even closer to his form than the tan one, and a stiff shirt, so white that it gleamed.

He was incredible. Handsome beyond belief. And that look in his eyes! Had she really put it there?

"Hello." She barely breathed the word.

"Celina."

She bent her head to take the key from her small, beaded bag. King held out his hand for it and, when she had stepped out into the passageway, locked the door for her. She replaced the key and wrapped the woven cord of the bag around her wrist.

The train lurched, rocking her gently against him, then away. He put one hand on her waist to support her, but his touch made her even more unsteady.

"I'd offer my arm," he said. "But there's not much room here."

He guided her ahead of him along the aisle of their sleeping-and-drawing-room car, the Palmyra, brushing past two of their neighbors, King steadying Celina carefully with each movement of the train. They crossed into the observation car. Outside, dusk was just beginning to fall—a half dozen or so passengers were watching the sky, streaking rapidly with bright vermillion.

The reddening sky showed through the windows of the dining car, too. It and the raw, pale earth beneath it looked like a deliberate backdrop for the scene inside the elegant diner—another elaborate luxury provided by the Atchison, Topeka & Santa Fe for its passengers' pleasure.

Celina said as much to King as the waiter escorted them between rows of snowy linen-draped tables with dark cherrywood chairs. He stopped at a table for two, complete with wine in a silver bucket of ice, near the end of the car where the organist played.

"It *is* a service of the company," King teased, as he held Celina's chair for her. "Now, when the moon comes out, be sure and let me know if it isn't to your liking and I'll call the management. Do you want it to be a full one?"

"How did you know?" she asked, smiling at him over her shoulder. "Can you read my mind?"

He leaned toward her and murmured, "If you could read *my* mind, you'd be blushing bright red right now."

"King!"

That look she'd seen in the corridor was still in his eyes. She felt herself blushing, anyway.

He raised his wineglass and held it up to touch hers. "To us," he said. "And to this night."

Her heart took a great leap inside her chest. What, exactly, did he mean? She lifted her glass; her arm felt as languorous as if she'd already drunk half the bottle of wine. It must be that look; she was drunk on the look in his eyes.

"To us," she whispered.

He clinked his glass against hers.

The scent of the wine gave her a heady feeling; its fiery taste heated her blood.

King leaned back in his chair, his eyes intent on hers. "You know," he said, "that rose color you're wearing is my favorite."

"Oh?" She sipped at her wine again so she would have a reason to drop her gaze from his. "I remember reading somewhere that most men overwhelmingly prefer blue."

"I used to prefer blue," he drawled thoughtfully, "but the minute I saw you standing there tonight I knew that rose was definitely my new favorite."

"And black and white is mine," she blurted, surprising herself with such boldness. "You look extremely handsome tonight." She dared to meet his gaze again. It was hot enough to burn. Her hand shook a little as she lifted her glass.

He grinned. "Thank you, ma'am."

She met his gaze briefly, then glanced out the window at the coming night. The music swelled, sweet as the scent of the flowers in the center of their table, to fill the room. The organist began to sing a love song: "Aura Lee." Celina could feel King's eyes on her face as she listened to the slow, tender melody.

He sipped his wine. "That first line about the Blackbird singing reminds me of Cherokee love songs. They always start with calling on a spirit, often a bird."

A week ago that remark would've precipitated a storm of questions about those love songs. Tonight she didn't care to know any more. She only wanted King to keep looking at her in that intense and dreamy way.

The waiter came with the menu and lingered to light the candles on their table while they made a choice from oxtail, blue points, or green turtle. Celina said "Blue points" without even knowing what she was ordering.

King's eyes gleamed in the candlelight. His skin glowed like copper and the flame caught his cheekbones and brow. Her fingers ached to touch them. She smiled at him over the top of the hand-painted menu.

He moved the silver bowl of flowers to one side, nearer the wall. "Those flowers are in our way," he said.

She laughed. "So are the candles and the wine and the water glasses and the silverware," she said, "if we order all twelve courses on this menu. Why, there are forty-five or fifty dishes here, at least!"

"What's wrong with your appetite?" he teased. "You must've eaten too much chocolate after I left you in your room."

"Never!" She dropped her eyes demurely. "I can't have eaten more than seven or eight pieces during my bath!"

She looked up at him, then, and they laughed; Celina felt happier than she ever had since she'd known King. They joked their way playfully through the soup and the fish, the beef and roast quail, the orange fritters, the chicory and lobster salad, and the half dozen vegetables until time for dessert. But she talked only about the present moment, and so did he, as if they had an unspoken agreement to banish the past and the future.

Outside, true dark had fallen. The waiter came to

close the curtain, but King wouldn't let him; the night was so thick and black around the narrow body of the rushing train that it truly cut them off from the world and everyone else in it.

"I like the feeling it gives, too," Celina said, when the man had gone.

King finished his coconut pudding as Celina ate her Charlotte Russe, and they fell silent. While the waiter came to pour them coffee and after that, time and time again, King couldn't keep his eyes from straying back to Celina's, which were always waiting.

Her hair was piled high, very high onto the crown of her head in curls, with soft tendrils escaping at her temples, on her forehead, and down the sides of her neck. It shot black fire in the candles' glow, it called to his hands like a siren's song; if he could take out the pins and let it fall into his palms, fill his fingers with its richness, he could die a happy man.

When the waiter had removed the cake and New York ice cream, when they had nibbled at the Edam cheese and Bent's crackers, when they had tasted the grapes and nuts, King picked up the fruit knife and a perfectly formed, shining apple.

Celina couldn't take her eyes from his long brown fingers, holding the fruit absolutely still with no effort at all. Then he wielded the knife—so surely that, one movement, then another stroke, and the fruit fell apart, divided into perfect pieces. He picked up one and bit into it; the juice shone bright on his lips.

King took the piece of apple from his mouth and held it to hers. With her eyes locked to his, she took tiny bites until his fingertips met her lips. He leaned across the table, and she did the same, still caught in the snare of his gaze.

She let her eyelids drift closed, willing at last to fall headlong into a world composed only of the coffee and apple smells of his breath and the hot, sweet, firmness of his lips.

The kiss ended. Their lips came apart, but only by inches.

"I think we got this backwards," she murmured. "Wasn't it *Eve* who offered *Adam* the apple?"

King took her by the hand and drew her to her feet.

"I think so," he said. "But we can do it any way we want to."

The words brought her dark gaze straight to his, a sudden realization flaring in her eyes. It made his heart catch, and then beat faster in a hard, quick rhythm.

They threaded their way back through the cars without saying another word. With their fingers entwined.

At the door of her compartment she gave him her key; he fitted it into the lock and twisted it. He hesitated, then withdrew it and laid it in her waiting palm.

She took an interminable time putting it into her bag.

He propped his hands against the frame on either side of the door to keep them away from her, to keep them from taking possession of her glimmering alabaster shoulders, perfectly boned, perfectly curved.

She turned her head and looked at him over her shoulder. She wanted him. He couldn't be mistaken about that look in her eyes.

His hands dropped, he cupped her shoulders in both hands and turned her around. She came straight into his arms, fast, with an importunate cry. He hooked his finger beneath her chin and lifted it, but she was the one who melted against him, standing on tiptoe to offer him her mouth.

King groaned and let himself take what he'd

wanted since the moment he first saw her. He slanted his lips across hers and kissed her ravenously, letting the hunger rise in him, naked and strong.

She pulled away, but not far; only far enough to whisper, "Don't leave me, King. Not tonight." Her eyes were huge, limpid in the dim light of the aisle lamps.

He placed his hands, very carefully, at her waist. To his surprise, they were trembling.

She slipped her arms up and around his neck and then *she* kissed *him*. Slowly, slowly, she traced his lips with her tongue.

Primitive heat rose in the center of him. He stood the delicious torture as long as he could. He savored the taste, the sweet softness of her mouth—above all, the thrill of her invitation—then he gave in to the impelling urge to kiss her in return.

He tried to keep it slow at first, to let it build, but his pulsebeat quickened, throbbing throughout his body, until the hot blood pounded in his ears. Irresistible desire drew them back against the door, then through it; King nudged it closed without breaking the kiss.

Celina took her mouth away and looked up at him. His glittering topaz eyes held her still as stone. Only his hands moved. They went to the tiny buttons down the front of her dress.

He slipped the top one through its loop.

Then the second one.

A little shiver of shock raced through her. How bold of him! And of her! She ought to pull away. But his heavy-lidded gaze burned through her, set every nerve in her body on fire, destroyed her ability to move—until she thought of lifting both hands to the front of his shirt. She pulled at the soft silk of his tie and slowly untied the bow.

When it hung loose and rakish around his neck,

she took hold of the button beneath his collar. Her fingers touched the warm pulse-point, rising and falling at the base of his throat. They trembled, but she turned the button and slipped it through the buttonhole. Then the next one. Was she really doing this? Was she Celina, or had she turned into some stranger? She unfastened the next button.

So did he.

Celina let him. She helped him. She arched her body toward him and let him unfasten her dress all the way down to her hips while she unbuttoned his shirt and pulled it loose from the tight waistband of his pants. This was herself, her real self, setting free all the wild feelings she'd restrained for too long. She threw back her head and looked King boldly in the face.

His eyes blazed down into hers from beneath lids heavy with wanting. "Celina?"

The low, ringing tone of his voice stroked her skin as surely as if he had run his fingers along the side of her neck. In response, she edged up on her toes to slide his coat off his shoulders. It dropped to the floor.

She would have sent his shirt to follow it, but when she took hold of it, her thumbs brushed the quivering muscles of his chest. She hesitated, then slid both her hands beneath the starched white linen to place her open palms against his brawny power.

He groaned. "Celina . . ." He could she? How could she contain that passion he knew was there beneath that cool exterior?

He thrust his hands into her hair and pulled her mouth to his for a quick, voracious kiss. Then he held her away for one more look: the deep hue of the rose-colored dress contrasted against her creamy skin. Behind her, lit by the glow of the lamp, the turned-down bed beckoned: pale satin sheets against polished dark wood.

His hands dropped onto her shoulders and swept the dress off and away as if it had never been there. The burning urge to possess her pounded in his blood like a drumbeat, like a primal command, but he took the time to push away the rest of her lacy clothing.

Then, without pausing to remove his own, he picked her up and strode across the sitting room and into the bedroom, her bare skin rubbing in precious torment against his own where the shirt lay open on his chest.

Celina pushed it off his shoulders the instant her arms were free, and reached for the fastening of his pants.

This was right. She was more alive at that moment than she had ever been in all her life because she was with King. King, who truly cared for her.

And wouldn't hateful Papa be horrified? What better revenge on him than to make love with this man he despised . . . this wonderful, sexy man who had been tempting her for weeks?

That was her last conscious thought. King threw the top sheet and the blanket all the way back and knelt on the bed. He bent over her in all his golden glory and she held her mouth up to his.

That kiss took them rushing headlong into the night faster than the train they rode.

Celina undid his trouser buttons, her fingers brushing against the hot hardness straining there. When he tore his lips away to take off his boots, and then the pants, she raised up and pressed her breasts to his back, slipping her arms around his waist so she could keep touching his skin.

At last all his clothes were gone, too, and he was laying her down again. His mouth and his hands were everywhere on her body, melting her flesh and her bones until she had no strength left to breathe.

He slipped one of his long thighs between her own

and kissed her chin, her throat, her breast. Her breast.

She cradled his head in both her hands and held it there until his tongue had called up every dancing flame inside her and whipped it into a blaze. Until he had brought her back to life again and built her pleasure to a glistening peak.

Then his mouth was gone from her breast and hovering near hers again, his breath like warm wine against her lips.

"I have to do this," he murmured urgently, leaning on his elbows over her so the hard peaks of her breasts brushed his harder chest.

The sweet agony made her cry, "King . . ."

"Not yet," he whispered. "I have wanted to do this since the first moment I saw you."

He took the first pin from her hair, then the next, slowly, deliberately, all the while gazing into her eyes with that heavy-lidded look. She held her breath.

The train rolled on, rocking her up into, then back down from the heated enchantment of his body. His hands weren't touching her anyplace but her hair. How could he do this with her breasts crying out for them? His marvelous hands.

Her thighs, her belly . . . they needed his hands. "King," she murmured. "King."

He smiled.

Later, an endless age later, he spread her hair out around her head and lay looking down at her.

A cloud, it was, a cloud of glossy black against the white satin. It framed the most perfect face he had ever seen, the most wonderingly passionate face.

He hesitated, his hand gone still between them. "Celina," he said. "Do you know what you're doing? I mean . . ."

She raised her head and nipped his lower lip, then traced its shape with the tip of her tongue, blotting out the last traces of his ability to think. His mouth fell onto hers and devoured it.

Her hand took his and put it back where it had been; he traced his own golden fire along the crevice there.

''King,'' she demanded.

He came into her as unerringly as the train roared through the night, melding them into one spirit for swift passage, each to the heart of the other.

Celina clung to him and buried her face in his neck, learning how to move with him away from the rails, from the earth itself. She melded her body to his, within and without, each rocking thrust setting off a stronger sensation inside her, each one causing an even brighter flare of colors to chase across the black sky of her eyelids. She wrapped herself tighter around him, digging her nails into the powerful muscles of his back.

They sent, not pain, but a fiery delight through King's veins, an invitation to take her higher, and faster, into the mysterious night. He answered with growing fierceness, setting his primitive hunger loose to drive him more deeply into her. A strangled cry tore from his throat as the almost unbearable sensual joy, and the need for still more, shot through his veins.

He opened his eyes so he could see her pleasured face, arched back against the pillow, and then, slowly, deliberately, he brought them both to the brink of flight, to the willingness, no, to the plea, to be taken, whirling and helpless, far out into the hot oblivion of the exploding stars.

Then, mouth to mouth and skin to skin, they threw themselves into the brilliant bursting of shattering sensation and went spinning like a comet into the night, away from the gleaming, glorious world that was the Western Zephyr and out into the sparkling darkness.

Afterwards they lay, her head on his shoulder, floating, letting the train rock them to sleep. King's hand moved slowly on her hair, stroking it over and over again.

The train began to slow, its smooth speed gradually reducing itself to a rhythmic jerking. Finally it stopped.

"Where are we?" Celina murmured.

"Together."

Her breath caught in her throat. She raised up and dropped a kiss into the hollow in the middle of his chest. Then she whorled the tip of her finger there before she tilted her head to smile up at him.

She closed her eyes and snuggled close once more. King buried his face in her hair.

Soon the train was in motion again.

A few moments later a knock sounded at the door. King sat up and started to call out, but Celina put her finger to his lips.

"It's my compartment," she said. "I'll answer." She got up and went to the closet for her wrapper.

"Conductor," a voice called through the door, "with a message for Miss Celina Hawthorne."

Her heart leaped, even through all the new, wild feelings that filled it. Could it possibly be another telegram from Father? One saying that he was sorry, that she really did do a great job in court?

She ripped the robe off its hanger and slipped into it, tying the belt around her as she hurried into the sitting room, pausing to half-close the bedroom door. Swiftly, she turned the handle of the lock and opened the door to the hallway.

"I'm Miss Hawthorne—"

The door swung violently inward, clanged back against the wall. A man came in with it.

In the fleeting second it took her to realize that this was not, after all, the conductor delivering a telegram, Celina could see nothing but the knife.

Even the dimness of the aisle lamps' glow caught the blade the man brandished in one hand and made it glitter. Another second and he was thrusting his face into hers.

Marshall Moseley!

"Where is she?" he growled. "Let me have her now!"

Celina's numbed limbs wouldn't move.

Moseley grabbed her and spun her around, one beefy arm pressing hard against her neck and chest. The other hand held the knife to her throat.

"You took my Chink slave girl," he said. "Give her back or I'll kill you."

She couldn't scream. Fear took her voice, but it set her mind frantically to work. Moseley didn't know that King was there. King could overpower him, but she'd have to get away from him first. If he were surprised now he'd cut her throat for sure.

King. He had to save her.

Celina twisted around to put Moseley's back to the bedroom door. She caught a glimpse of King in the space where the door was ajar; she prayed that Moseley hadn't seen him.

"I can't . . . talk," she gasped.

Moseley loosened his grip.

"Now you can," he said. "Where's Mei Lee?"

"How would I know? I don't know what you're talking about."

"You'd know because you took her away from me. You're the one helped her get away."

"What do you mean, get away? Were you holding her prisoner? I thought she just worked for you."

For one second, King remained frozen where he stood. Then, holding every muscle taut to contain the urgency that threatened to send him rushing out into the other room, he moved back and reached for his pants. He stepped into them as stealthily as if he were stalking a deer. He looked through the crack at Celina again.

God! How could he stand it? Moseley ought to have his hairy arms ripped off his body for putting them around her, much less for threatening her with that knife.

But he couldn't interfere. Not while the edge of the blade lay against her throat. He clenched his fists and tried to slow his breathing. Thank God Celina had maneuvered the bastard so that he couldn't see the bedroom door: at least there'd be a chance of surprising him.

"Mr. Moseley," Celina was saying, "I don't understand why you've forced your way in here like this. Turn me loose or I'll have you arrested."

"I'll turn you loose when you tell me where that girl has gone."

"All right."

King could see Moseley's start of surprise at Celina's sudden capitulation.

"Put that awful weapon away and I'll tell you."

Slowly, taking an age to do it, Moseley lowered the knife.

"And turn me loose, Mr. Moseley, if you want Mei Lee."

He dropped his other arm. Celina stepped away.

King swung the bedroom door all the way open and barreled through it. Moseley turned; he had the knife half raised when King crashed into him.

The force of their grappling bodies pushed Celina down, hard, into one of the club chairs of the sitting room. She watched, silent, horrified, while the two men struggled, Moseley to raise the knife, King to keep it lowered.

Finally they stood in the middle of the room, panting, King behind Moseley, towering over him, pinning his arms tightly to his sides. King's right hand squeezed Moseley's wrist until the knife dropped soundlessly onto the Brussels carpet at his feet.

"Lemme go!" Moseley demanded. "Lemme go and lead me to that Chinee girl, Chekote, or the front of the track on your C and G'll damn sure be the end of the track, too."

King's worried eyes found Celina's and for a second she thought he was concerned about Moseley's threat. But he said, "Celina, are you all right?"

"Yes," she managed. "Yes." She got to her feet.

With an abrupt nod of relief, King dragged Moseley backward toward the door.

"You gonna lead me to her?" the shorter man said. "Lemme go!"

"Conductor!" King shouted out into the aisle of the car. "Conductor! We need the marshal here!"

Moseley struggled mightily, but King held him with little effort.

A door slammed open somewhere and muffled footsteps sounded. Then voices.

"What's the trouble?"

"What's going on?"

"I heard somebody thumping around and then some shouting," came a prissy voice that Celina recognized instantly as Mrs. Woodson's. "I thought the train was being robbed is why I've come out in public in my nightie."

A babble of other voices replied.

The conductor appeared in the doorway, fully dressed in his uniform. Only his slightly askew tie indicated that this was the middle of the night. Mrs. Woodson's round face hovered just behind his shoulder.

"I want to turn this man in to the federal marshal," King said.

"Think again," said Moseley. "The damn C and G Railroad will never make that deadline now."

Mrs. Woodson gasped and put her hands over her

mouth. Her eyes found Celina, then traveled back to King's bare torso.

The conductor yelled, "George! You, there! Go for the marshal, right now."

Mrs. Woodson stepped aside and the porter scurried away toward the end of the car.

"You'll regret this, Chekote," Moseley said. "You're the one been worrying about losing your money. Better let me go."

"What's going on here? Mr. Chekote, do you know this man?" The dignified conductor looked stern as a judge. In fact, he reminded Celina of Judge Sullivan.

"This man forced his way into Miss Hawthorne's compartment," King said.

Mrs. Woodson gasped.

King glanced down at himself, casually, as if he were accustomed to running around barechested and barefooted.

"I was asleep, but I heard the commotion," he went on, "and rushed out to see about it."

Moseley made a strangled sound as if he would contradict the story, but King tightened both his arms around the man and he subsided, except to say, "Forget the marshal. You want that crew workin', don'tcha?"

"Who is this man, Mr. Chekote?" asked the conductor.

"He's a disgruntled former employee of mine," King said. "He must've been trying for my compartment and broke into Miss Hawthorne's by mistake."

"Here comes the marshal!" squealed Mrs. Woodson.

"Step aside, folks, step aside," the conductor called. "Let the marshal through."

The marshal had a far sterner look than either the conductor or Judge Sullivan, Celina thought. She would hate to be in Moseley's shoes.

Without a word, he took the handcuffs from his belt and put them on Moseley, who was yelling at King.

"Think about this, Chekote. You owe me. Is this the gratitude I get for all I've done for you?" He was still raving when the marshal led him away.

King went straight to Celina, feeling all those pairs of eyes on them.

"I'm fine," she assured him, holding her trembling arms firmly at her sides to keep from throwing them around him. "He didn't hurt me at all."

She repeated that for the conductor, recounted a brief story to back up what King had said, and then, blessedly, everyone was leaving. Another minute of this and she'd be running into King's arms, crying with shock and relief.

With a last, long look into her eyes, King said, "Be sure and lock your door now, Miss Hawthorne; don't open it unless you know who's there."

He gave her a smile that made her want to kiss him. "I'll be right next door. You call if you need me."

He stepped to his own door and tried the knob, then turned to the conductor.

"Would you please open this for me? It must've accidentally locked behind me when I ran out."

Once inside, with the door closed behind him, he collapsed against it and buried his face in his hands. The skin of his palms still held Celina's scent.

He was shaking.

My God! That crazy bastard could've killed her right there in front of his eyes! But hadn't she been the cool one, though?

A new knowledge flooded through his consciousness, a realization that he'd had in that helpless eternity he'd stood waiting behind her bedroom door. This—this bone-deep, skin-tingling, blood-pounding desire that gripped him combined with the tenderness he felt, the respect, the admiration and fascination she created in him—could only be love.

For the first time in his life, his teasing and flirting and kissing had pulled him in a lot deeper than he had expected to go.

He had fallen in love with Celina Hawthorne.

Chapter 12

He loved Celina! The awareness made his blood sing.

King raised both fists in a wild salute, then dropped them to his sides and did a few whirling steps of a war dance.

Celina had been right the first time—people *were* more important than railroads. Or anything. She was more important to him than life itself.

Of course! That's why watching her suffer over that wicked telegram had hurt him so. He had shared her pain because he loved her.

She was his! He wouldn't stop for a minute until she was by his side night and day, until he'd never have to leave her again. Then he wouldn't have to worry whether she was safe. He would personally protect her, and enjoy her, every second of their lives together.

He rushed to the wall that separated them and pounded on it. "Celina!" he shouted. "Open the door. I'm coming over!"

He threw open the door again and stepped out into the aisle, heedless now of who might be watching. He reached her door just as she clicked open the lock.

Rushing inside as abruptly as Moseley had done, he kicked the door closed behind him and swept her into his arms.

"I love you, Celina, I love you!"

He wrapped her tightly against him and began spinning around, lifting her feet off the floor.

"We'll get married as soon as we reach the Nation!" he cried. "Then I won't have to explain to anyone why I'm in your rooms wearing nothing but my pants!"

Humming the opening bar of "Aura Lee," he waltzed them into her bedroom. "Just think!" he chortled. "Three days from now you'll be my wife!"

Celina froze to her core. His arms were a vise, squeezing the life out of her. His words were a trap, waiting to spring on her. The killing cold fear spread out to her skin with a bullet's speed. It made her lips so stiff she couldn't speak.

"Everyone'll be so surprised," King was saying. "My parents . . ."

Celina forced her mouth to move. "Will they really? Somehow, I have a feeling that *I'm* the only one to be surprised." She pushed at his arms, struggling to get free of him. Her efforts were too feeble, but he did stop the spinning dance and hold her away so he could look into her face.

"Yes," she said, and the hostility in her tone made him loosen his arms, "*I'm* the one to be surprised . . . by my *own* wedding."

He locked his hands behind her waist and stared down at her, completely amazed. "Celina! What are you talking about?"

The innocence in his tone changed the ice in her stomach to fire. She hit at his forearms, trying to break out of their confining circle.

"I'm talking about the fact that you've tricked me!" she cried. "You've planned this all along—you're just as overbearing as Father!"

Struck dumb, he dropped his arms to his sides and let her go. "What in hell does your father have to do with this?"

"You're treating me the same way he's always done." She paced away from him, back into the sitting room, tightening the belt of her wrapper as she went. "Imagine! Rushing in here to tell me I'll be your wife in three days!"

She spun on her heel to glare at him. The look fastened his feet to the floor in the doorway.

"How long have you been planning to get me alone and tell me that I belong to you, King?"

"For about three minutes! How long could it be? Stop and think, Celina! You're the one who urged me to make this trip."

"Well, you're the one who suggested that I come, too! You teased me and charmed me into it!"

She turned away from him, trembling all over. He narrowed his eyes and watched her.

"You don't love me," she said, and now her voice trembled, too. "You're only trying to protect my reputation and, I might add, that of your beloved C and G Railroad by marrying me."

She whirled and marched back to him on her bare feet. Her eyes blazed black as the midnight sky rushing by outside the train. "You have thought of me only as a woman, not as an attorney—even though I did win the title case—from the minute we met!" she proclaimed. "I left home to avoid a marriage that Father had arranged and now here you are arranging another one!"

Her voice was still shaking; a sheen of sweat glistened on her forehead. She pushed her hair away from her face with both hands and gathered it at her neck, holding it there as if she needed something to fasten it.

She was afraid. Afraid of letting her hair flow loose and beautiful into his hands. Afraid of being held in his arms and hearing that she would stay there forever. Afraid of those sparkling passions they had shared this night.

He shook his head. Damn! Why hadn't he been smart enough to think before he'd spoken? From the very beginning he'd known she was scared, had sensed in her that instinctive terror of getting close to a man.

"I'll admit that," he said gently.

Her head snapped up; those magnificent eyes accused him. Of lying. Of trickery.

"At first I did have trouble seeing you as an attorney and my intellectual equal," he said, forcing his hands to remain loose at his sides. "But, Celina, you changed that."

She frowned and folded her arms across her chest as if to say he'd have to prove it. The rocking motion of the train made her hair swing loose like a black silk curtain. He would have killed for the privilege of pushing it back from her face.

"Your seeing into Sadie's character, not to mention the way you understood the old man, saved the Donathan deal," he said, raising one hand to grasp the door frame. "You already had me convinced that you could do anything—long before you won our case."

He lifted his other hand and took hold of the other side of the slick woodwork. It'd never do to touch her now. "But I do see you primarily as a woman, Celina," he finished softly. "And that's because I'm so in love with you."

She came a step closer, like a wild deer tempted by a bunch of ripe berries.

Shaking her head she said, "No. You just think you are. If you loved me you could see me as an individual."

"I do . . ."

She held up one hand in a graceful gesture for silence. More calmly now, she said, "You went back on your first promise to hire me when you knew I was a woman."

"No man could not know you were a woman, Celina."

"Hush," she said, "and listen to me. You said on that first train ride that it'd be hard to treat me like a man. For ages you ordered me to argue the title case the way you thought best. And when I asked you to help Mei Lee you rejected the whole idea, in no uncertain terms, without really considering it for so much as one red-hot minute!"

She shook her head, her huge eyes filled with sadness. "All those examples prove it, King. You'd be just as tyrannical a husband as Eli." She swallowed hard. "Oh, you'd be charming instead of hateful as Father would, you'd dance me around in your arms while you informed me of my fate, but you'd decide it for me, all right."

King straightened, hurt to the quick. Her words didn't really surprise him, though. Nor was he discouraged. Hadn't Ridge always said that King didn't know the meaning of the word 'quit'?

He gripped the door frame until his fingertips hurt. "I've listened to what you've told me all along and I've tried to change my behavior," he said soothingly. "Think about it, Celina. I did hire you and keep you on, didn't I? I did defer to your judgment in the title case. And tonight, if you'll remember, I did refuse to betray Mei Lee to Moseley, even though I'm risking my railroad."

Holding his breath, he reached out to touch her, just once, on the cheek. "I sensed your feelings the night of the victory celebration, too, you know. I wanted you that night, Celina, like I've never wanted anything in all my life. But I wouldn't go ahead because you were in such a state: I wanted to wait until you were sure about what you were doing."

He dropped his hand and clenched it by his side to keep from touching her again. Her eyes were huge, dark pools of mysterious light and he was falling, falling, into them.

"And I won't stay now if you don't want me here," he said. "All you have to do is tell me and I'll go."

She didn't speak. She didn't move.

"However, as an attorney *and* as a woman you can see how I could've misunderstood you," he went on. "After what we shared earlier tonight surely you can forgive me for assuming that you might love me, too, and not be insulted by the mention of marriage."

Great tears sprang, full-blown, into her eyes. Her heart filled with a tumult of new feelings just as huge as the tears. She had no idea what names to put to them. Or how to quell them.

King stood in front of her, close enough to touch. Waiting. With his archangel's face and his honest, amber eyes assuring her that he'd told her the truth. She tried to speak. But she couldn't.

So she held out her arms and King walked into them.

King woke to the sounds of the clanging bell and the hissing steam that meant they were pulling into a station; and to the feel of Celina's soft skin against his.

Miraculously, the jerking, halting motions of the train hadn't disturbed her. He shifted slightly to cradle her head more deeply in the hollow of his shoulder. He'd hold her like this for the rest of his life if she'd stay.

He lay, barely breathing, listening to the noises outside and the faint sounds of voices inside the train. The wine-colored brocade drapes drawn across the windows were growing rosier as he watched; the morning sun was well up. They must be somewhere in Arizona.

When they were in the Cherokee Nation, would they still lie together like this? A terrible longing, a need so strong it almost choked him, mounted in his chest. He tightened his arms around Celina.

She would say yes to him eventually. Wouldn't she?

Of course she would. She loved him, too, although she hadn't admitted as much in words. It had been written on her face, though, when she'd opened her arms to him. And it had been implicit in every kiss, every touch, every look she had given him as they made love again and again while the train rocked on through the night. Celina loved him.

He pulled back a little so that he could look down into her sleeping face. The crescents of her long, black lashes lay against her flushed cheeks without moving, her breath came slow and even, so softly that he could barely hear. How could she be right here and still be so far removed from him?

The sudden, desperate need to know that in her mind she hadn't left him, that she did love him, that she would be his forever, surged to a fever pitch. He brushed her tousled hair back from her face and kissed her.

She smiled. But she didn't open her eyes.

He tickled her nose. She murmured a protest and turned her face away, untangling their arms and legs for a long, languorous stretch.

He caught her to him again, tucking her back into place against the front of him, burying his face in the fragrance of lilac in her hair. He kissed her on the ear and then kept his lips against it.

"Celina," he whispered, "let's wake up this way every day. Marry me. Say you'll marry me."

She went stiff in his arms. Panic spiked along his nerves. Then she turned her warm cheek against his to give him a kiss and twisted around in his arms.

She stroked his face. "Let's not talk about that, King, please. I'm not ready to think so far ahead."

He folded his lips into a thin, straight line. "What's there to think about?" he asked, forcing his tone to be light.

"Why, everything! Getting married would—"

"Would what?" He tried, but he couldn't keep all the anger out of his voice.

She put her fingers across his lips. "Can't we just take one day at a time?" she asked, and the pleading in her beautiful dark eyes made him begin to melt inside. "This train is a world apart, darling, one all our own. We can treasure this time to the very utmost and not even think about life after we leave it."

He looked at her. Unsmiling.

"Please, King. Can't we just pretend that this trip will never end? That we'll never get off the Western Zephyr?"

She gave him that marvelous smile. The one that had made him hire her in the first place. The one that had made him buy Mei Lee a ticket to San Francisco. The one that took his heart right out of his body.

Darling. She had called him darling.

Finally he smiled back and dropped a kiss of agreement into her tousled hair.

For the next three days the train called the Western Zephyr did become their world. They lived only for each moment as it came and never spoke of the present or the past, for they had no need to. The present consumed them.

Making love consumed them. By the fourth day, Celina had been newly created as a sensual being; her worries, even her work, everything and everyone else she had ever known had been left a thousand miles behind in California. Only King existed now.

As they climbed out of bed late that morning, though, she did have one lucid thought: soon they would be arriving in the Nation. Soon they'd step off the train into a different world, one filled with people, and she'd have to share King with them. She needed to start getting used to that, even though the very idea made her go cold all over.

"Maybe we should have breakfast in the dining car this morning instead of having it brought in," she suggested.

King's amber gaze flew to her face. "Why?"

She touched his cheek, then sat up and reached for her wrapper. "Oh, just for the sake of variety." There was no way she could bear to say aloud that this idyll was about to end.

"Whatever you say, Miss Celina," he drawled. "Your every wish is my command."

She gave him a playful swat with her belt and went to her own room to get dressed. Yes, she would use today to begin curbing this awful new addiction of hers, this compulsion to be physically in touch with King every second. She smiled to herself. Lord! This was worse than her craving for chocolate!

During breakfast she did fairly well, only brushing his hand as she passed him the marmalade and touching his arm when she pointed out a rabbit running alongside the train. But afterward, when they went into the observation car, she couldn't resist sitting shamelessly close beside him on the sofa seat. She kept his warm shoulder firmly against her arm while they watched the white-and-yellow buffalo grass glide by.

George, the porter, brought them fresh coffee as the train slid, huffing and puffing, into a stop at a station. He spoke to King, "Might want to get off the train and stretch your legs, suh," he suggested. "Be a while here, gotta check somethin' 'bout the brakes."

"No, thank you, George," King answered, "it won't be necessary—we still have a good supply of chocolates."

He and Celina laughed, smiling into each other's eyes, and George, with a puzzled look on his face, moved on. Then King raised his coffee cup in a toast. He said, "To problems with the brakes: may they last forever."

Celina touched the rim of her fine china cup to his, but her hand shook a bit and a tiny tendril of dread twined itself around her heart. So. King had thought of it, too; the end of this dream.

She suppressed the thought as she never used to know how to do: she buried it beneath the physical pleasure of simply being with King. She leaned her head back against the smooth, polished paneling and feasted her eyes on him. He was dressed in pale blue denim again, but a newer shirt and jeans than he had worn in Caliente Crossing, and his skin glowed like bronze fire against the cloth. She lifted her fingertip and traced that line where the pale and dark colors met along his collar at his throat.

His eyes went dark. "You'd better not do that in public," he warned, with that sensual, sideways glance of his. "I won't be responsible for my reaction."

She glanced around. There were other people in the car. And that was what she had wanted, wasn't it? Protection against herself?

Resolutely, she stood up. "Let's play checkers," she said, setting her cup into her saucer with a definite clink. "I'll get them."

"Checkers?" he protested. "It's too early in the morning for checkers! What's this world coming to? I just thought of something better to do."

Celina laughed and walked to the large lamp table halfway down the car. She took the wooden box that held the game out of its drawer. "What can I say?" she teased, returning to King. "I'm just a wild, unconventional woman. I can't help myself."

He drawled, "Don't ever try to help yourself, sweetheart. You're perfect just the way you are."

Those words and the melodious bass of his voice sent a blissful thrill along her skin. When she sat down again their hands met on top of the table as if they were permanently magnetized.

They unfolded the board, set up the game, and tried to play, but neither could concentrate enough to keep track. The third time King crowned one of her men out of turn just so he could trail his fingers across hers, she looked into his warm, tantalizing eyes and gave up.

"You were right a few minutes ago," she murmured hoarsely. "We'd better not do this in public."

Without another word they got up and made their way back to the Palmyra.

"My skin has been hungry for yours all my life," Celina said, late on that last afternoon which neither of them was calling the last.

King scooted closer and slid his hand over her belly.

I can satisfy you for the rest of your life. Tell me now that you'll let me. But he couldn't say it. Push any wild thing in the taming and lose it.

So he said, instead, "Which have you been hungrier for, me or chocolate?"

"Chocolate, of course!"

He jerked his hand away.

She put it back. "I can't believe you're so sensitive," she teased, holding her lips up to his pouting ones. "You knew how strong your competition was when you asked that."

He moved his hand lower. "But when you answered, you didn't know all the weapons I have in my arsenal."

"Oh?" she said archly, barely brushing her lips against his. "I don't care. I still love chocolate the best."

He caught her chin in his fingers to hold her mouth still for his. "Lady," he growled, bending over her. "I'm gonna make you eat them words."

Her full lips took over his mouth and his mind. And then his soul. The kiss went straight into the center of him, sharpened the aching shaft of wanting there, and plunged it deep into his very core. His lips parted to take her in, all of her, when her tongue flew to seek his. Her heat melted his body as fast as the speeding train. Celina. This was Celina and he loved her. He would love her forever.

They kissed until there was no breath left, and finally she tried to wrench her mouth away. But he couldn't let her go. He finished the kiss with a bruising caress, changing at the last instant to the feathery touch of the tip of his tongue. It traced the shape of her lips, then trailed onto her cheek. Even as she tried to resist, she turned her face to follow it.

Yet she didn't bring her lips back to his.

"Celina? What's wrong, sweetheart?"

The high whistle of the Western Zephyr gave two long, lonesome blasts.

A little shiver of fear ran through King. She couldn't stop. There was no way on earth she could close him out of her thoughts now, and no way she could leave his bed. Not when it would be their last night like this.

"The curtain," she whispered. "Close it, King. We must be coming into a town."

So he reached across her, his arm brushing her

silken thigh, and drew the drapes across the dusk-filled window. When they were shut into their own dreamy world again, together, she came back into his arms.

"Web-bers Falls!" the conductor shouted, working his way through the narrow aisle of the day coach on the M K & T. "Gather up your bags and your children, folks, we're pulling in to Webbers Falls!"

The train began slowing. King glanced out the window. "There they are," he said. "The whole family's come to meet us."

"Because they're dying to see you after two whole years." She managed to keep her tone light, but her stomach tied itself in a knot. Why should she be so nervous?

King stood up and reached for his portmanteau and Celina's reticule. "Celina?"

She looked up. He was grasping the luggage rack with both hands, staring down at her so intently that it shook her.

"Yes?" But even as she said it, she knew what it was he was asking. The question had hovered between them ever since they'd wakened this morning. King was too smart to put it into words again so soon, though, too smart to give her an excuse to bolt.

At last he said, very quietly, "How would you like me to introduce you?"

As your one true love. Forever and ever. Amen. But she couldn't say it. She couldn't even let herself think it. Because then she would be exchanging Eli's steel cage for King's gilded one.

"As your attorney," she said, just as quietly, and looked away.

The car clanged against the linkage that held it to

the one ahead once, then again. They lurched to a stop.

Celina sat where she was, the backs of her knees clinging to the front of her seat. It was over. Their magic, loving time had vanished down the long, silver track this morning when the Western Zephyr had left them standing on the platform in Muskogee. And now they had to live in the real world and share it with other people.

King held out his hand to her and she rose. They followed an elderly woman and her sister to the door and down the steps.

"King!" a high, child's voice called. "There they are!"

The minute their feet touched the ground they were surrounded, caught in a web of hugging arms and welcoming words. Celina lost hold of King's hand.

He was moving everyone farther back on the platform, out of the way of passengers trying to board the train, when, for the first time, Celina became aware of his father.

That man had to be Ridge Chekote.

He was an older, darker-skinned version of King, right down to the long hair pulled back and tied. His hair was black instead of amber-brown, though, and shot through with a few streaks of silver.

There was tremendous force in his very presence, just as there was in King's. No wonder King had gone to California to avoid doing his bidding; this man would be infinitely hard to defy.

His dark eyes were resting on her.

King gently put down the little girl who'd thrown herself at his neck and began to introduce Celina. He began with his mother, who looked so young Celina hadn't actually picked her out at first from the group of siblings.

She should have known, though—King had told

her that Jessee was darkly beautiful and looked very Indian. His mother was a petite, blue-eyed blonde who gave Celina not one but two genuinely welcoming hugs.

"We're so glad you could come with King," she said, smiling. "Please feel at home with us and please call me Lacey."

Jessee's flashing brown eyes took Celina in in one swift, judgmental glance. Evidently she passed the test—Jessee's smile was truly friendly, too.

Baby Laura, who was seven, and the brothers; William, who was twenty-two, and Colin, who was ten, both of whom looked more like their mother than like King and Ridge, seemed to accept Celina without question.

Not so his father, who came forward to take his turn at last. Although his courteous smile was like King's charming one, Celina could feel his reserve.

"You all don't act a bit surprised to meet Celina," King said. "I didn't tell you I was bringing her with me."

Everyone laughed. "Aunt Fee told us," Jessee said. "Celina's father sent her a telegram."

Just the mention of her father shriveled Celina's insides, but King's frustrated expression and the shrieks of delight it inspired made her laugh, too.

"Leave it to Fee to ruin your surprise," Lacey said. "She's been telling everyone's secrets for as long as I can remember."

They all chatted while King and Ridge made arrangements for the luggage to be loaded on the farm wagon they'd brought, then Celina found herself being swept away toward two carriages waiting at the side of the station. Being in the middle of this group was something like being caught up in a whirlwind, she decided; they, like King, were too strong a force to resist.

* * *

That night, long after the big house at River's Bend lay quiet, Ridge stood in the window staring out into the moonlight. Lacey turned over for the dozenth time and peeked at him from under her arm.

Poor darling. He had seen it, too, almost as soon as she had.

She sat up, then gathered all the pillows in the bed and propped them in two stacks against the carved walnut headboard. "Why don't you come on over here so we can talk about it?" she said softly.

He turned where he was and looked at her. "Can you *believe* it?" he asked, crossing to the bed in three long strides and dropping down to sit facing her. "Eli Hawthorne's daughter! Of all the young women on the face of the earth!"

"She's King's attorney, Ridge. In the parlor, after supper, she was telling me that she's always wanted to have a career and that she never intends to marry."

"Well, King intends to, I can tell you that right now. And she's the one he wants."

"Maybe it's just another of his many infatuations. You know how many times he's been in love."

"Hmph," Ridge snorted. "In that case he wouldn't have brought her fifteen hundred miles with him. No, Lacey, that boy's finally come home to settle down and run this plantation. He's ready to get married now, and for some reason that only God knows, the woman he's picked is Eli's daughter."

"Now, Ridge," Lacey soothed, stroking the top of his bare shoulder. "I believed Celina when she told me she's interested only in her career."

"You needn't try to fool me, Miss Lacey," he drawled. "You didn't believe that for a minute."

She laughed, that trilling bell-like sound that he loved. "Are you telling me that here I am, an old woman in my forties, and I'm still as transparent as ever?"

He grinned at her, his face in the moonlight as handsome as the day they met—more handsome, even.

"You are," he said. "Just like your son. Neither one of you could hide your feelings for five minutes if your life depended on it."

Lacey's heart turned over. "I admit it," she said, with a catch in her breath. She reached up to run one finger along the line of his jaw. "And at this moment my life depends on your knowing exactly what my feelings are." She leaned forward so he could see her face in the moonlight. "Can you read them?"

He put his hand on her naked neck and slipped it up to cradle her beautiful head. "I sure as hell can," he growled, bending to kiss her. "And they're calling to mine."

Later, much later, they lay twined into the tangled sheets together, her head nestled on his chest.

Long after he thought she was asleep, she roused.

"Ridge?" she murmured. "If what King and Celina feel is half as deep as our love, it would be wrong to try and interfere."

"I know," he said slowly.

"You won't, will you, sweetheart? Promise me."

An eon later, he said it.

"I promise."

In the wee hours of the morning, Celina woke with a start.

"King?"

The sound of her own voice surprised her, brought her fully back to consciousness in the strange room. Her eyes flew open and moved from one unfamiliar object to another until she realized where she was.

At River's Bend. King's home.

Where she'd spent the evening telling his mother, and herself, that she was only a casual visitor. King's attorney. A dedicated career woman. Who never, ever would marry.

And here she was, a few hours later, crying out for King in the night. Waking because she was alone and lonely in the bed. She flopped over onto her stomach, hid her face in one pillow and pulled another one over her head.

Oh, Dear God, what had she done? Now that she had let him be with her, it would take all the strength she could muster to do without him.

Chapter 13

By late the next afternoon, when Jessee came to Celina's room to dress, Celina had decided to let herself pretend. Just for tonight, just for the big party, she would pretend that she really was a part of this family and of River's Bend. Because, except for the time spent with King on the train, she had had the best day of her life there.

She and King and Jessee and William had gone out very early, on horseback, riding down the long slope of the hill where the house sat and along the wide Canadian River. It had flowed far below them, at the foot of a steep bank, furrowed into curves along the top as if carved with a giant's knife.

When she had said as much, the three Chekotes had regaled her with ancient tales of giants and Uk'ten's and the recounting of hilarious river adventures when they were children. Somehow, even though Celina had no such stories to tell, they had made her feel entirely a part of them.

When they'd returned home for an enormous country breakfast that rivaled the fancy food on the train, the whole family had sat around the table until almost noon, talking about the farm and the neighbors. Then, and during the rest of the day as they'd all rushed around preparing for the evening's social in King and Celina's honor, Celina had felt that same

spirit of welcome from Lacey and Ridge, especially
Lacey.

One reason was because they had asked and followed her opinions on questions as diverse as
whether to hang lanterns on trees all the way down
the driveway to the road or just around the house,
whether to prepare one outdoor dance floor or two,
and whether or not most people like ice cream with
rhubarb pie. It gave her a heady feeling of power to
decree that lanterns hung all the way down the
driveway would be wonderful, two dance floors
would be quite necessary if Jessee's report that half
the people in the Canadian District would be coming
was true, and that heavy cow's cream was much to
be preferred than ice cream over rhubarb pie.

Never before had she made a single decision that
affected an entire family: certainly not *her* family.

And now, here was charming, quicksilver Jessee,
at Celina's door with her dress, petticoats, and hair
ribbons filling her arms and her mane of black hair
flowing everywhere.

"I thought we could get dressed for the party together," she said, flitting into the room and dump-
ing everything on Celina's bed. "Celina, will you do
my hair in French braids the way yours was this
morning? I never can do them right, and Mama's
too busy."

"I'd love to, Jessee."

"Oh, good! Then when we're all dressed, let's go
down to the honeysuckle bower and weave some of
the flowers into our hair. We'll look like sisters!"

We will. And I'll pretend we are, just for tonight.

King was the only problem in her make-believe
world. He had no patience with anything pretend;
he wanted it all to be real.

He ran into them coming back from the honeysuckle bower and sent Jessee chasing after her new
puppies. "Silas said to put them in a stall in the

barn," he called after her. "They're all over the place while Joe and Talley set up the tables for the party and someone's bound to step on them."

"You could've done it for me, King," Jessee called back over her shoulder. "*I* want to introduce everyone to Celina."

"And *I* want to keep Celina all to myself," he murmured, grabbing Celina's hand and pulling her into the private nook formed by the brick fireplace and the crepe myrtle bushes.

"King!" she remonstrated. "We're practically out in public here."

"No, no," he said. "There's not a soul on this place paying us one bit of attention."

He held her just an arm's length away from him, his hands engulfing hers in a warm embrace, his eyes so brightly approving that they caused little thrills to spark along her skin.

"I can't stop looking at you long enough to kiss you," he murmured. "Which was what I intended to do in the first place." He lifted her hands and pulled her closer. "That soft yellow dress makes your skin look like cream," he said, kissing her fingertips between words, "and the white-and-yellow honeysuckle against the black of your hair . . ."

Celina had to touch him. Gently, she untangled one of her hands and laid it against his cheek. One touch, no more. In a pretend world, all things are possible.

"You look pretty handsome yourself," she said.

"Pretty or handsome?" he teased. "Make up your mind."

She laughed and let him reclaim her hand for more kisses.

He was dressed in a white shirt and tan pants, which made his skin look rich as copper. His shirt was big-sleeved and flowing, the fine cotton fabric catching in every little gust of wind; his pants were tight as a second skin. He had pulled back his shining hair and tied it with a dark leather thong.

Sunlight slanted through the bushes and fell across his face. His eyes sparkled with mischief and desire. And love for her.

She couldn't help herself. She moved even closer to him. "King," she murmured. "King."

Just outside their charmed circle made of bricks and red flowers the wheels of a carriage rattled on the gravel of the drive. When they stopped, Lacey's voice rose in greeting.

"King and Celina," called Lacey, her voice floating around the corner of the house. "The Swimmers and the Campbells are here."

"I'll find them, Mama," piped Laura. "I saw them. I know where they went."

"Damn!" King muttered, letting their still-clasped hands drop to swing loosely between them. "Why's she growing up to be such a little gossip?"

Celina sighed, a sharp surge of mixed emotions, half disappointment, half relief, washing through her.

Laura and Lacey appeared with the Swimmers and the Campbells in tow; soon it seemed to Celina that half the district was indeed there, as Jessee had predicted. Guests arrived in a steady stream, and although a few settled on the veranda of the house to talk and the children scattered to the stables and the riverbank, most of them gathered around King and Celina, who had strolled with the early arrivals to sit in the pecan grove at the lower edge of the yard.

Ridge soon ambled across the wide lawn to join them, signaling Joe and Talley to bring more chairs and Pearly, the cook's helper, to serve pitcher after pitcher of fresh lemonade and tea. He settled into a plank chair with wide arms; Lacey perched on one of them, her hand on his shoulder, when the pleasant chatter began.

They looked at each other as if they were newlyweds. Celina had trouble keeping her eyes off them. She was trying not to look at King—partly to prevent gossip and partly because it made her want to touch him—and his parents kept catching her gaze. Perhaps that was because when they weren't looking at each other they were looking at King with such love and pride in their faces. It was plain to see that they were joyously happy to have him home.

Were some families really like this?

Everybody talked, but King's stories of life in the West were in special demand. There were questions about Celina's work, too, and how he had found her. The general implication, which gave her a deep thrill, seemed to be that she was a lost Cherokee who had only needed a guide to show her the way to the place where she belonged.

She learned to be deeply grateful for her Aunt Fee's colorful personality and propensity for gossipy nosiness because most people talked to her about Fee instead of about Eli when the inevitable discussion of her heritage began. Or maybe their discretion was due simply to a natural sensitivity and tact that she began to think was a general Cherokee character trait.

In any event, they did seem to be deliberately avoiding the subject of her father. Had he been hateful and obnoxious as a young man, too? Or did nobody much remember him because he'd been in California so long? Why had he left the Nation?

She put those questions out of her mind. This was a perfect day and she wasn't going to let thoughts of Father spoil it.

And it was a perfect day. The sun slanted into the pecan grove and filled it with light that rose from the ground like a mist in the morning. A fresh breeze played in the leaves overhead; once in a while it sent a pecan plummeting to the ground. Ice clinked in their glasses and the fragrances of lemons and tea and sugar mixed with the watermelon smell of freshly cut grass.

Up the slope, halfway to the house, several children ran, screaming, after the puppies. Here, all around Celina, softer voices laughed and chatted, in English and in Cherokee, pulling her into a family of friendship so strong she felt she could touch it.

Their peaceful talk—of people, of crops and the river and the weather, of cattle and horses—fit perfectly into her cherished fantasy. And she was included in it, by smiles and nods and quick meetings of the eye, although she knew nothing of the topics of conversation.

Then an ancient man, inexplicably introduced as Young George Sixkiller, turned to Ridge and said in his quavery voice, "Glad to have your boy back home again, are you, Ridge?"

Ridge turned to look at King, who paused in his conversation with his friend, Nicatoy Swimmer, to look back at him.

In the truth-telling late afternoon sunlight the two men looked like mirror images, both dressed in flowing white shirts. The lines of their profiles were strikingly the same: the hooked Indian nose; the hard, strong jaw; the chin that bespoke pure determination. Both had the club of long hair tied back, both held ponderous shoulders easily straight.

"Uncle, I couldn't tell you how glad I am," Ridge replied, looking King straight in the eye. "I've waited a lot of days for this one to come home." He smiled at King, then, a smile that sent him all the love in the world.

Tears sprang into Celina's eyes. If Eli ever looked at her that way, she could die happy.

Lacey rose from her seat on the arm of Ridge's chair and moved around behind it, her skirts dragging lightly on the grass, to lay one hand on each of their shoulders, Ridge and King.

She hadn't been able to keep from touching them, Celina thought. That same urge had been in her, the need to create a physical expression of that tacit bond between father and son.

"So?" Young George Sixkiller piped. "You finally realized you're a farmer instead of a railroader, huh, Kingfisher?"

Celina's heart stopped.

"No, Uncle," King said. "I haven't come home to farm. I'm here to build—"

Then, to Celina's infinite relief, he bit off the next words and looked around him. He didn't want to ruin the day, she saw, as one emotion after another flitted across his open face. He, too, treasured this moment of peace and welcome.

"Farming's too much hard work," he teased, visibly willing his body to relax. "You remember I grew up working for this slave driver, here." He gave Ridge an affectionate smile.

Everybody laughed.

"That slave driver can turn out the cotton and corn and the wheat," Young George Sixkiller said flatly. "Not to mention the fine horseflesh."

So the conversation turned to horses, and Celina let herself be drawn back into the warm camaraderie of the teasing talk. Soon Pearly came to tell Lacey that dinner was ready, and the children, bearing the same news, went to call everyone else on the place.

Walking back up the hill to the long, cloth-covered tables set up on the lawn near the house, Celina thought that she would burst from the simple happiness that filled her. King had one of his hands on her arm and the other on Nicatoy's; the setting sun and the fragrant breeze wrapped them all in an airy cocoon.

Joe and Talley came around the house carrying a

side of beef they'd just taken from the pit where it
had been cooking since before Celina and King had
arrived at the train station. Other servants brought
bowls of fried corn and fresh string beans, platters
of fried chicken and baskets of hot yeast breads and
beaten biscuits to the already groaning tables.

As the food was passed around, the spirits of the
group grew even livelier. Laura and Colin teased
Celina mightily when she asked what was in the
bowl of *connuche* that Pearly served her; first they
told her ground-up peanut shells, then turnips, then
butterbeans. Finally, when she had tasted it and
pronounced it too delicious for any of those ingre-
dients, they admitted it was made of pounded hick-
ory nuts rolled into balls and cooked in sugar and
boiling water. They, and Jessee, and especially King,
continued to tease Celina and to make sure that she
sampled everything; by the time the meal was finished she felt even more a member of the family.

Finally the servants cleared the tables and filled
them again with Lane cakes, tea cakes by the dozen,
rhubarb pie and heavy cow's cream, blackberry cob-
bler, three kinds of homemade ice cream, and Lacey's famous brownie cupcakes made from a recipe
her mother had brought from Virginia.

"Please try all the desserts," Lacey said. "And
Pearly will bring us some coffee."

But Celina couldn't eat another bite. And the mu-
sicians were getting up and drifting over to the front
veranda where they began to tune their instruments. The children ran to catch the lightning bugs
flashing in the falling dusk, and some of the men
left the table to smoke. The fiddles slipped into a
heartfelt rendition of "Lorena."

She turned and looked up at King; he was already
looking at her. Without a word, they stood up to
dance.

The minute they stepped onto the dance floor,

they turned to each other; he took her into his embrace with a mighty sigh.

"It's been a lifetime since I've held you," he said, beginning to move in time with the music. "Last night went on forever."

"I thought it would never end," she said, the words bursting straight from her heart.

He held her so close, then, that she thought surely people must be staring. But she didn't care if they were. She was in King's arms.

King tightened his arms around Celina and pulled her even closer, breathing in the sweet smell of the honeysuckle in her hair. This night was so perfect, just as this day had been—except for the moment after Young George Sixkiller's question when he should have announced the reason he had come home. He just hadn't had the heart to ruin the party. But tomorrow he'd have to tell Ridge and then there'd be hell to pay. The thought tied his gut into a painful knot.

"Celina?" he said, turning to dance her away from another couple who were coming too close. When she lifted her face, though, and he looked into her wide brown eyes, he couldn't speak. Whatever he had wanted to ask couldn't be put into words.

She smiled at him, anyway.

Night fell, coming fast after the long, slow summer dusk. King floated through it, willing all thought to leave him, losing himself in the tangible dream of sparkling lanterns, bright dresses, and beautiful Celina in his arms. He had to give her up to dance two dances with Nicatoy and one with Ridge, while he danced with his mother and an importunate Jessee, plus a girl named Sally, whom he used to think he loved. Then his world came right again when he reclaimed her for his partner in the reels and party games.

Soon everyone gathered around the long tables

again for refreshments. King found a private spot in the shadow of a spreading silver maple tree and left Celina sitting there while he went to get tea cakes and lemonade.

Celina watched him go, already yearning for him to come back. After what seemed an age, he did so, and, legs crossed, sat down beside her on the grass. He held a crystal plate of tea cakes in his right hand and one matching goblet in his left.

"We'll have to share a glass," he said. "I only have two hands."

"What an excuse!" she said, smiling, only pretending to complain. Eagerly, she took a drink when he held it out to her: the lemonade was twice as sweet with the taste of King's lips on the goblet's rim.

She broke one of the sugary cookies and shared a fragment with him; he leaned toward her, his hair catching the glint of the moonlight, and took a bite with a quick kiss on her fingertips like the ones he'd given her that afternoon.

The midnight moon rose high.

Without warning, one fiddle began a winding, minor melody. Then an old man's voice, hauntingly high and sweet, joined it, singing in Cherokee. The lovely sounds, like water slipping over smooth stones, made her heart leap up and the wet glass go warm beneath her fingertips.

"*Gha!*" the old man sang. "*Tsisa'tinige'suna.*"

King put his arm around Celina, leaned forward and whispered into her ear, translating each line after it floated out onto the night in Cherokee.

"Now! No one is ever lonely when with you.
Your eyes draw love from my heart like the night
  unsheathes the stars.
Ha! I am the White Kingbird!
Very quickly when you and I conjure

My soul wings down upon your body
Like the fire panther pierces the night.''

Celina's body melted into the sinuous curve of King's shoulder. The song transported them into their own idyllic world again, this time a world made of haunting music and heartrending words, honeysuckle and moonlight.

When the music had ended the earth lay quiet for a long, long moment beneath the climbing moon. Then King drew her away without speaking a word, around the maple tree and along the moonlit path to the honeysuckle bower. The instant they were inside it, they were in each other's arms.

The moonlight slanted through the twining vines and fell across his face. Her eyes caressed it, consumed the precious sight, until he took her head in both his hands and brought his lips closer to hers, slowly, slowly, his eyes blazing with untamable desire. Then she had to close her eyes so nothing, nothing would distract her from the taste of his mouth.

His breathing grew ragged and deep, and then they were kissing as if they would devour each other, giving each other air and life and then taking it away, only to give it back once more; giving each other the souls out of their bodies.

Finally King tore his mouth free and folded her against him, tight, so tightly that he could feel her heart beating wild against his.

He had to know that she was his; he needed that surety at this moment more than he'd ever needed anything in all his life. Tomorrow his father and most of the neighbors and friends here tonight would be against him. Soon he would hurt his whole family, slash at their hearts without wanting to do so.

Tomorrow he would be starting the confrontation

with Ridge that he had been avoiding all his life.
Celina had to be his rock to cling to.

"Celina," he said roughly, his voice ragged with
wanting. And with need. "Marry me. Tell me this
minute you will."

She froze in his arms. He wasn't supposed to ask
that, not tonight! Not while she was pretending all
things were possible and everything was perfect.

The shock of his words made her shiver, even
though all evening she'd been thinking that her answer might be yes. Hadn't she told him she couldn't
talk about this yet? He was pushing her, giving her
no time to find the sure direction buried deep in her
heart.

His arms tightened around her and became a vise
once more.

"Celina?" he demanded. "Answer me."

She turned her face away and stared out at the
night through the tangle of sweet-smelling flowers.

"I don't know if I'll ever marry," she murmured,
through lips stiff with pain. "I'll always need my
work, King."

Chapter 14

Her soft words reverberated from one side of his brain to the other, back and forth like a spider making a web, filling his head with cotton batting that, for an instant, rendered him blind and deaf. Her *work*!

What the hell kind of an answer was that?

He put her away from him. No wonder he felt as if he weren't half the man his father was—Dear God, he couldn't even get the woman he wanted. And after he'd worked so hard to win her!

A terrible fear raced through him, chilling his blood. Maybe he couldn't *earn* her love! If not, how would he get it?

No! Damn that kind of thinking. Kingfisher Chekote got what he wanted; when he worked for something, by Thunder, he deserved it and he got it. And what he got he kept.

His fingers tightened around her arms. "There's plenty of work to do on my railroad for you, too," he growled, and drew her close again for a kiss.

She held her head stiff and straight.

King slid his hand across the bare skin of her shoulder and caressed its curves, ending with his thumb circling in the hollow of her throat. A little gasp of pleasure escaped her. However, she stayed stubbornly as she was.

He trailed one finger up the side of her neck. She

quivered. He let it trace the line of her brow, the sublime shape of her cheek. Then her mouth—her luscious, perfect, breathless mouth. She turned her face to his.

He cupped her chin in his hand and slowly, inexorably, prepared to kiss her. "You're my woman, Celina," he muttered against her lips. "And after I make love to you tonight you'll damn well know it." After he made love to her tonight, she'd never have the strength or the will to say no to him again.

He kissed her. His hand found the ruffled edge of her gown and followed it, over the tops of her breasts, then around them. He took one into the hollow of his hand; his thumb went immediately home to its swollen tip.

She wanted him so much she could die.

He moved his hand to her other breast. She reached for his other hand. Just this once. This one last time.

His mouth left hers to kiss her throat, but with a little moan, she made him bring it back again. Just this last kiss, and then no more.

However, he dropped his hands to cup her hips against him and deepened the kiss until it took her, spinning, into sweet oblivion. The next thing she knew they were tangled together, lying in the sweet-smelling grass, surrounded by the even sweeter fragrance of the flowers. Celina took a long, shaky breath.

King's hot whisper, "Celina?" trembled against her lips, his enthralling mouth so close that one small movement would suffice to make them touch and melt into each other again.

He took her face between his hands and looked up at her in the dancing moonlight.

"You're mine, Celina, do you hear me?" His voice was low and richly soft, his face handsome and hard.

His warrior's face that she had first seen by the light of the moon.

She reached down to touch it.

He groaned and drew her mouth down onto his, scooping her onto his chest to hold her even closer. Her arms twined themselves around his neck, her hands cradled his head between them and the ground.

And she kissed him back. She poured all her heart and soul into the kiss. Into King. So that somehow he would always be part of her and she of him.

The muscles of his arms curled strong as rope ribbons around her back. His big body protected hers from the hard ground. She would pretend that she was safe with him forever.

King gave a tortured groan and rolled over, settling her into the curving cage of his embrace, pressing her desperately between him and their grassy bed so she could never escape.

But they couldn't stay there. The ancient passion was rising in him with such wild need that it had become pain. He tore himself away from her and pulled her to her feet.

They left the honeysuckle bower running blindly into the night. King felt it close around them like an indulgent accomplice; no one called out to them as they left the lanterns and the music and the people behind.

The path, too, was his confederate; it took their feet without touching them and sped them toward the dark sanctuary of the woods.

Night birds called back and forth; the long, high sounds they made were sweet as shadows on skin. Overhead the summer leaves rustled. But it was King's breathing and the sounds of his light footsteps that held Celina spellbound. King.

As soon as they hit deep shadow, he stopped and pulled her into his arms, kissing her again until all breath was gone. Then, holding her to his side, clinging so close that his leg moved against hers, he took her through a last blessed curtain of trees and into a moon-drenched clearing.

"This is my place," he whispered, turning to look down into her face. "It was my refuge when I was a boy." And now you are my refuge. Aren't you, Celina?

But she had forbidden the words. Tonight it was their bodies that had to ask and answer the questions.

He dropped his lips to hers and her mouth, without speaking, said yes.

They undressed each other without separating. King wouldn't, *couldn't*, move away from her—only far enough to let her dew-dampened skirts slide down between them and then his pants. The tousled clothing lay in a deep pile around them, making an inviting bed.

But he fell into it by instinct, drawing her down with him, not willing to break apart from her to try to see. The blind passion that had brought them running to this place was growing, robbing him of every sensation that came from anything but her.

The dark night, with its moving white pathway of moonlight, the fragrance of pines and the river, the bird and wind sounds of the moonstruck meadow faded away, as did the earth beneath. Only Celina in his arms kept him from disappearing, too.

Nothing was left but the hot honey of their starving tongues and eager lips, the heavy perfume of the honeysuckle that fell from her hair, the feathered touch of their breaths mingling, then brushing light against each other's skin. And the unspoken question that burned between them.

Will you? He asked it with the tantalizing caress of his tongue, and the smooth, sweet stroking of his hands.

At first his tongue was on hers, twining with it, sending shards of fire into her body through her moaning, willing mouth. She gave it up to him, gloried in the feel of his sensual lips moving against hers, caught at them with tiny, tantalizing bites that brought them down harder on hers. She gave herself up to the kiss, body and soul, so that it would never end.

Yet when it did she didn't protest, for his lips were leaving hers to follow his hands. They trailed a tingling path down the curve of her throat and into the valley between her breasts. Her breath caught in her throat, her blood stopped in her veins as first his calloused fingers, and then his sweet, rough tongue, moved up over the curve of one breast to its swollen, needy tip. He took it fully into his mouth and encircled it with his tongue. He did it again.

Her bones melted into the waiting earth. Her breath stopped completely. As long as she had this, this unspeakable delight, she had no need for air. Only when his mouth moved on, going lower, did she draw in a long, ragged breath of the sweet-scented night.

You will. He answered the question with the captivating embrace of his powerful hands on her legs. With the wet warmth of his mouth on her thighs, circling, then circling again to come back higher.

I will. She answered with the open invitation of her thighs. Her hands moved in the silky weight of his hair, soft and sleek as satin; her fingers found the sensitive spots around his ears, as he pressed one hard kiss onto the triangle between her legs.

Celina whimpered deep in her throat and reached with both her desperate hands to bring his mouth back to hers. He gave it, and the fiery thrust of his irresistible manhood, as well; she arched her back and gave herself up to the caress of his powerful arms.

They moved, then, into the ancient, primal rhythm, melding, creating a heated perfection as pure as if the night itself had put them together to search out its mysteries. Celina let herself fall into the dark abyss of its magic, clinging to the rock of King's broad shoulders, melding her lips to his as if she would speak volumes to him without words.

The night's most precious magic found them, at last, and King threw back his head and cried out into the darkness.

The sound pierced Celina through the heart.

He could not stop calling her name.

Later, much later, the love song came.

The low, insistent beat of the drum floated out to them through the quiet; Celina raised her head from King's shoulder to listen. But he pulled it back into its place and cradled her to him while the high, haunting notes of the music filled the air.

The next morning when Celina went downstairs for breakfast the song was still floating in her head. She hummed it, trailing her hand along the smooth banister of the stairs, letting the homey atmosphere of the big, old house enfold her. Being at River's Bend was so different from being at her parents' house in Los Angeles: for one thing, their house was new, built as a monument to Eli's success. But that wasn't the only reason it had no soul. The laughing voices that echoed from the dining room were not quiet and polite like those of Mama and the servants—they were full of life, and love.

Like King. She touched her lips with the tip of her tongue; the taste of his honeyed mouth still lingered there.

She began to dream again, seriously this time, as she stepped down into the huge hallway and followed it toward the inviting voices. What if she did marry King? What if this hospitable home filled with loving people became hers, too? What would Christ-mas be like at River's Bend, and the Fourth of July?

What if she and King could belong to each other forever and could always make sweet love as they had done last night? A deep yearning to know that that could be true had been pulling at her heart since the moment she left him.

At the dining room door, Celina paused. There were two tables full of people this morning, for the party had lasted almost all night and nearly every one of the guests had stayed over. Jessee looked up from the smaller, round table and beckoned for Celina to join her and the other children.

But Lacey saw her, too. "Please come and sit with us, Celina," she said, smiling her welcome. "Let's hear what you thought of our party."

With an apologetic smile at Jessee, Celina slipped into a chair at the long table. King wasn't here yet, she'd noticed that the moment she looked into the room, but there was an empty chair beside her. Maybe he'd come down soon.

"Since there're so many of us we're eating in shifts today," Lacey said, from her place at Ridge's right. "And that's going to cause Ridge and me to get fat because we feel obligated, as the hosts, to have breakfast with everyone." She laughed her tin-kling, silver laugh.

Ridge gave her a smile that was so full of affection it twisted Celina's heart. "Speak for yourself," he rumbled. "I haven't eaten half as much as you."

"Now, now, Dad," King boomed from the door-way. "Pearly told me you ate every biscuit in the house, fast as she could cut 'em out and throw 'em in the pan!"

Everybody turned to look at him, chuckling at his scowling imitation of Pearly's face. The chuckles changed to roars of laughter when Pearly appeared behind him, a plate of fresh biscuits in one hand, a platter of sausage and eggs in the other.

King turned and saw her, then, and, pretending to be terrified of her displeasure, hurried to the table and pulled out the empty chair beside Celina. "Please don't thump me on the head, Pearly," he begged. "I was mocking Dad's mean face, not yours."

When the laughter had subsided and King had endured pretend thumps from both Pearly and Ridge, he turned to Celina and squeezed her hand under the linen tablecloth. Then he took a deep breath and reached for the bowl of sausage gravy directly in front of him.

"Well," he said, with elaborate casualness, "the party's over. Today we'll have to get to work."

Ridge nodded. "Right. The north pasture's ready for another cutting of hay and there's the cotton to see to. You've come home just at the right time, Son."

"Kingfisher, I think you was right about him being a slave driver," Young George Sixkiller called cheerily in his quavery voice from halfway down the table.

King threw him a tight smile, then his eyes went back to his father's. "I haven't come home to farm, Dad," he said. "I can't stay that long. I've got to get to Tahlequah and start ordering supplies: I'm here to build the Nation's railroad feeder lines."

His words fell with merciless clarity into the comfortable hum of conversation. It stopped dead.

Ridge didn't move. His gaze never dropped from King's face. But his expression changed in that swift instant of silence from the soft one of love and pride to a shocked, hardened enmity.

"What do you mean?" he blurted. "You didn't say anything to me about coming home to build railroads."

"You didn't ask," King replied.

"Well, I assumed . . ." Ridge clamped his lips shut, his face darkening like a thundercloud.

"You always assume," King said, in that same tone of bland innocence. "That's a dangerous thing to do."

"Building railroads in the Nation's a dangerous thing, too!" Ridge roared. "Don't you know there's people who'll kill to stop them?"

"Please!" Lacey cried, her voice high and trembling. "Couldn't we discuss this later?"

But neither man even heard her.

Ridge leaned forward to glare into King's face. King gave back a look so coldly hostile that it drove all the warmth of both food and fellowship from the table.

"Nobody can stop them," King said. "The last thirty years of trying should've taught you that. Assimilation with the whites is inevitable. You ought to know that."

Ridge jerked his head up and straightened his spine into steel. "Well, *I* can stop you," he shouted. "No son of mine'll be the one to let the railroads and the trash that comes with them into this Nation. Not as long as there's breath in my body!"

King didn't flinch. "If I'm the one who builds the feeder lines—and if you'd take off your blinders you'd know that somebody's going to do it, and soon—at least I can have some control over what kind of people comes in with them."

"Like hell you can! The boomers and the other land grabbers and the thieves and the prostitutes and drunks'll be pouring into the Nation by the trainload!"

"Not necessarily! That wasn't true in Caliente Crossing, was it, Celina?"

Startled, she stared at him as all eyes at the table turned to her. "Well, not thieves and prostitutes," she said thoughtfully, "but the graders *did* drink a great deal, at least to judge from the empty bottles strewn around their camp with the rest of their trash. I've never seen such disgusting habitation for human beings."

King glared at her, his expressive face filled with shocked anger and hurt that accused her of betraying him to the enemy. She glared back.

All she had done was tell the truth. What was he doing, anyway, dragging her into this?

His gaze swung back to Ridge; he gritted his teeth and ground out, "I'll be in a position—"

Ridge leapt to his feet. "The position you'll be in is that of traitor!" he stormed. "You'll be the next Elias Cornelius Boudinot!"

The words hung in the air like hawks hovering.

King replied in a deadly quiet voice. "I've worked my whole life to see this railroad succeed. You've made your living *your* own way, and I, by God, have that same right to choose how I'll make mine. You can't stop me with insults nor any other way. I'm my own man—I'll live my own life."

Ridge's mouth flattened into a straight line. He and King glared daggers at each other, then he threw his napkin at his plate, turned, and stalked out of the room.

Never, ever had Celina seen such pain expressed in the lines of a person's body, in the very way he moved.

Lacey got up and started to go after Ridge, then she made a motion toward King. Her eyes were enormous and dark with hurt, her face as white as the tablecloth. Finally she dropped back into her chair and helplessly covered her face with her hands.

The conversation began to hum again, but the sweet harmony in the sound was gone. The word "railroad" cropped up again and again, sometimes in derision, sometimes in approval. King had driven it like a spike into the peaceful fellowship. Only Nicatoy talked directly to him.

Celina's throat closed tight. How could he do that to Ridge? And to Lacey? How could he deliberately hurt his mother and father so?

He had sounded absolutely ruthless when he'd told Ridge he couldn't stop him. How embarrassing in front of a table full of guests! Couldn't he have waited, at least until tomorrow, to announce that he'd come home to build railroads? Maybe by then most of the visitors would have been gone. And the awful way he had looked at her! As if she were a loathsome turncoat!

Was the C & G still taking precedence over people in his heart?

Suddenly the room fell completely silent again. Ridge had reappeared. He stood in the doorway for the space of two heartbeats, then he walked back to his place at the table.

Poor Ridge. Somehow, even the awful anger on his face wasn't deep enough to hide a bewildered look of pain. Celina could have cried for him, and for King, too.

And for Lacey. When she lifted her face to Ridge and then turned it to King, it was the living embodiment of the word "hurt."

Ridge stopped behind his chair and grasped the top of it with both hands.

"I happened to think," he said, speaking to King in a voice so strained Celina could hardly believe it was his, "it's nearly time for Council Holiday. Why not wait and go to Tahlequah when we all go?"

"Because I've got a business to start, holiday or no holiday," King snapped. "And waiting around here won't make me change my mind."

To Celina's surprise, Ridge didn't snap back. Instead, he pulled out his chair and sat down.

"This place has outgrown one manager," he said

tightly. He placed both arms on the edge of the table and leaned toward King. "Your duty is here, Kingfisher, keeping all the work we've done and investments we've made from going to nothing."

King stared at him coldly. "I have full confidence that you can handle it by yourself," he said. "You've always done the work of two men."

Was this, after all, the real King?

The quiet in the room was so complete that it hurt her ears.

After a moment, from the other end of the table, Nicatoy said quietly, "It *might* be a good idea to wait, King. Won't be much business going on 'til after holiday's over."

King lifted his arm and laid it along the back of Celina's chair to lean toward Nicatoy. It felt wonderfully familiar, yet strangely alien, too, for there was no affection in the touch; the muscles of his forearm felt like iron ropes.

She didn't even hear what he said to his friend. Then, in the next breath, he was speaking her name as he spoke to Ridge again.

"Celina agrees that I need to get started as soon as possible," he said. "She urged me to come to the Nation as soon as I got the permits."

Ridge's hard, angry eyes, and Lacey's soft, hurt ones, immediately went to Celina's face.

"Isn't that right, Celina?" King asked, his arm dropping away from her.

She hesitated, shocked by the question. He was challenging her, giving her one last chance, his glittering topaz eyes told her, to back him up. To choose to be on his side. How unreasonable!

Did she really know this man at all?

He understood that her urging him to come fulfill his dream in the Nation didn't mean that she was averse to his spending a few days visiting his family first. After all, they had been dying to see him and he'd only been here two days.

And it had obviously cost Ridge a great deal of pride to come back into the room and try to reason with him like this in front of everyone. He hadn't done that solely to try and stop the railroad. Part of his motive was simply to keep his long-absent son where he could see him for a few days more. That hunger was there, beneath the angry frustration in his face.

And it was filling Lacey's face, overpowering the shock and hurt. Didn't King know how blessed he was to have parents like these?

"I have no idea how long it will take to get the supplies," Celina said tightly, "but surely ordering them two or three days later wouldn't make a critical difference."

Lacey made a hopeful little sound of agreement. More softly, Celina said, "After all, King, it's been two years since you've visited your family."

King frowned and gave her that terrible look again. It said she might as well have stabbed him in the back.

She tore her eyes away. King was sitting beside her, he had been talking to her, but something had changed between them. Her fear was returning.

"We'll leave right after breakfast," King said sharply, and she could tell by the sound that he was speaking to the side of her face, trying to make her turn and look at him. She looked straight ahead, at the lace curtain, lifting and falling in the late-morning breeze.

"Oh, no, not *that* soon!" Lacey blurted. She had just picked up the teapot; she set it down so hard its lid rattled. "Whatever for?"

"I need to get contracts for timber for the railroad ties and for gravel. I also have to hire freighters to haul them," King said, his tone a bit kinder. "It'll take a little time to get the bids."

Laura jumped up from the children's table in tears and ran to King, grabbing his arm. "Can Celina stay here?" she begged. Then she said bossily, "Now, King, you come right back before dark."

"I need Celina to draw up the contracts for me," he said. His face softened as he scooted his chair away from the table and turned to take his little sister onto his lap. "She's my lawyer, you know. But I'll bring her back one day soon."

"Before dark?" Laura asked, drying her eyes on his napkin.

"Not tonight," he said gently, and pulled out his handkerchief to help wipe her face.

"The two of you should have a chaperone," Lacey said, clearly leaping at a change of subject, one over which she might have some control. She poured Ridge some more tea without asking whether he wanted it. "To travel that far."

King gave a bitter laugh as he settled Laura more firmly on his lap. "Mother, we just traveled fifteen hundred miles alone together."

"I know," she said. "But your father and I didn't know any of the other people aboard that train and if they gossiped, we didn't have to hear it."

"Besides," King said, as if he hadn't heard her, "Celina is my attorney, remember? Ours is a business relationship. Why would anyone think differently?"

He shot Celina a piercing look as he said it. He was only pretending to talk to his mother, she thought. Really that sarcasm was meant for her. Answering anger flared in the pit of her stomach. Why, indeed?

"Never mind that," Lacey said, signaling with her eyes that he should be aware of Laura's sharp ears.

"You two make a very attractive couple; Jess must go with you."

Jessee gave a shriek of delight, Laura set up another wail, and everyone in the room started talking at once. Celina listened to the pleasant cacophony. Tahlequah would be very lonely with only Jessee and King, furious as he was with her.

But by the time they were packed, loaded into the buggy, and started on the road northeast from River's Bend, King was his old charming self again. Too much so.

Celina eyed him warily as he chatted and laughed in response to Jessee's high spirits. He had refused to let Celina tell him how she felt about his dragging her into the confrontation with Ridge, saying that he was too busy packing and getting the papers together for the railroad. And that feeble attempt of hers to talk with him was the only moment he'd spent alone with her all morning. Yet he was constantly turning to her with supposedly solicitous remarks.

"I'll bet you're excited about meeting Aunt Fee and her boys at last," he said, now. Then he looked at Jessee and said in a confidential tone, as if he were letting her in on a great secret, "Celina has been saying that she can't wait to meet some Cherokees of her own blood; then she'll really feel that she's one of us."

What was he doing? Trying to charm her, somehow, into parroting his opinions the next time he got into an argument? Trying to pretend that he'd never looked at her in that monstrously accusing way or talked to his parents so unfeelingly?

Was he this happy just because he was about to begin work on his blasted railroad?

The longer they traveled, the angrier his attitude made her. He had been thoroughly vexed with her only a few hours ago: were feelings between them so shallow that they could be wiped away with a snap of his finger? If so, then what about the feelings they'd shared last night?

A little before dark they drove across a bridge where King said there used to be a ferry and up into the yard of the weathered inn where they would spend the night.

"Look at the sign, Celina," he said.

It was a graying shingle swaying between two short poles near the porch.

"Hawthorne's Inn," she read.

A little chill raced through her. She really *did* have roots in the Nation!

"This is the place Mama was telling you about—where your father and Aunt Fee grew up," he said.

"King! You never told me we would stay here!"

"We wanted to surprise you!" Jessee burbled. "All the furniture and the rooms are still the same."

"I'm sorry your grandparents aren't alive for you to meet them," King said, helping her step down onto the hard earthen yard. "But maybe you can know them a little bit this way."

His tone was low and rich, the voice she'd heard in California telling her all about her people whom she'd never known; it wasn't the hard, implacable one that had talked to his father this morning. Which was the voice of the real King?

After supper they took a tour of the inn and its grounds, King holding her grandfather's old lantern high between her and Jessee. When that was over and they had gone to their rooms, Celina lay awake for hours beside Jessee, forcing her mind to review, minute by minute, the events of this cruel, capricious day.

But she wouldn't let her memory even touch on last night—the thought of King's passionate love-making brought a terrible sadness that drained the

very life out of her body. For he probably hadn't
truly meant it from his heart. Most likely, he'd only
been trying to get her on his side for the confrontation he had been planning to start the next morning
and take some pleasure for himself into the bargain.

Tears welled in her eyes. In fact, now that she
thought about it, didn't he always want something
when he was at his most charming? One example
after another flashed through her brain: King charming Sadie into telling him what she'd overheard,
King flattering Moseley (and even admitting as
much) so he'd get more work out of the men, King
joking with the townspeople so they wouldn't pick
up and move away, King talking the records clerk
in Haileyville into letting them in.

Her throat tightened. King trying to manipulate
her, Celina, at the breakfast table this morning. King
cajoling her into telling him what was in that first,
awful telegram from Father. King remarking, that
night after the dance, that they mustn't make love
and distract Celina from her work: "You've got to
stay sharp," he'd said, or words to that effect. "So
you can win some more victories like today's."

Victories for the railroad. Always, eternally, forever for the railroad. Every one of these instances of
his using his charm had one purpose and only one:
the good of the C & G Railroad.

Why, this thoughtful, sentimental interlude here
in her grandparents' old inn had been planned for
that very same purpose, no doubt. King was manipulating her yet again, encouraging her to accept her
Cherokee roots so she would want to stay in the
Nation and help him fight for that blasted railroad.
He had seen how upset she'd been after that scene
this morning; he must've thought she would want
to leave and go home.

How dare he be so ruthlessly calculating! Why, a
child could see where his priorities lay!

Suddenly the disappointment and the pain were simply too much to bear. She had to do something. She had to move.

She got up and strode to the window.

That was no help. The shimmering night outside looked too much like the one they'd spent in the meadow, making love.

Finally, in desperation, she turned back into the room and crossed to the old, high-backed rocker in the corner. Whipping it around face to the wall, she plopped down in it and closed her eyes, determined to think about something else.

Had this chair been one of her grandmother's favorites? Had she come here to rock and think—maybe about her only boy, Eli?

Surely, then he had been different, had been close to his family and friends. It must have been his excessive ambition that had crushed that out of him as a man.

Surely, someday, he could learn it again.

In the next room King tossed in his bed, wishing that the wall between him and Celina wasn't there. Wishing Jessee was back at River's Bend.

But would it really make any difference? There'd been no walls between them in the night when they'd listened to the love song. He had poured his very heart and soul into loving her then, and still she hadn't come running into his arms to stay.

She hadn't even told him that she loved him, although they'd lain for hours, sated, in each other's arms. Maybe if *he'd* told *her* again . . .

But, no. A man had his pride. He had told her on the train with words and again in the meadow with every fiber of his being.

If she didn't break down after that lovemaking, what would it take?

After that lovemaking! What had it meant? Nothing. Instead of telling him she loved him, that she would marry him, she had betrayed him!

At last, alone in his bed, he let himself actually feel the pain of that. He still couldn't believe that Celina hadn't had the loyalty to support him in the argument with Ridge. How could she desert him when she'd encouraged him to come here and begin this confrontation, to try to resolve the old, festering conflicts? Didn't she even care enough about him to take his side?

He groaned and turned over to stare at the wall standing blankly between them. Celina. Celina, didn't you mean a single thing you told me with your sweet body last night?

Evidently she hadn't, and the hurt of that realization was growing by the minute, cutting into his very core. He hadn't let her see that today, though, and he never would. After all, a man had his pride.

But King's pride was no comfort when the sweet agony of the previous night flooded through him again, setting his nerves on fire. He kicked the sheet away from his feet and got up to prowl naked around the room, listening, wishing to hear the soft sound of her voice through the wall.

Chapter 15

The next day's trip into Tahlequah went quickly, thanks to Jessee's hilarious characterizations of Aunt Fee's many children (nine in all and all of them boys) and of her hot-tempered, redheaded husband, Uncle Isham Battles. By the time they drove into the pretty town and down its hilly, tree-shaded main street, King thought Celina would be able to recognize any of her relatives on sight.

He also thought he would lose his mind if he didn't get away from her pretty soon: she had sat beside him all morning, keeping her eyes straight ahead and directing most of her conversation to Jessee. Whenever she spoke to him it was in the most businesslike tones possible. It irritated him beyond belief.

What was her complaint, anyway? *He* was the one who'd been wronged. He stopped trying to hide his hurt and began treating her with as much cool indifference as she was treating him.

He pulled the team of bays to a stop in front of Aunt Fee's immaculately kept two-story house. A sign on the picket fence announced in ornate script:

Battles Boarding House
Clean Rooms, Good Food
By the Day, Week, or Month

The door opened, and slim, dark-haired Fee, as lithe as a girl, came flying down the path to the gate.

"Hi, Aunt Fee!" Jessee trilled.

"It's about time you all came to see me!" Aunt Fee cried. "Get down out of that buggy this minute and give me a hug!"

Within seconds, it seemed, she had wrapped all of them at once in her wiry arms.

Then she stepped back and held Celina away so she could look at her. "I'm so glad you're here, honey," she said. "Eli never would bring you to see me, even though I wrote and wrote how much I needed a little girl to help me with these nine wild boys."

They all laughed, and then Fee turned to gaze up at King with her small, sharp eyes.

"So you're the one brought me my beautiful niece," she said. "Don't you think she's beautiful, Kingfisher?" Her voice held that I've-got-a-secret tone that everyone in the Nation knew so well.

King returned Fee's mischievous grin, but he didn't let his eyes quite meet hers. "I do," he said, smoothly. "Why, everybody knows the Hawthorne women are the most beautiful in the Nation!"

"Oh, Kingfisher," Aunt Fee said, giving him a playful swat. "You old charmer! I'm talking about Celina, now!" Taking both girls by the hand, she continued to chatter about how fortunate it was that he and Celina had met.

Fee has had this planned all along, King thought, picking up Celina's valise and carrying it along behind the three women as they swirled, talking and laughing, up the stone-paved path to the door. That skinny little busybody had been hoping he'd meet and fall in love with Celina when she sent Eli's address two years ago. *She* was the cause of all his misery.

Once the luggage was unloaded and the team

taken care of, King left the boardinghouse without bothering to speak to anyone, his blood pounding in his ears like a woodpecker's working song. He stretched his legs in long strides that ate up the ground, heading for town, or the hills on the other side of it, heading for anyplace away from Celina.

No. He wouldn't let her affect him like this. Deliberately he pushed her out of his thoughts and fastened them onto the railroad. He had a business to run, by Thunder, and he intended to get on with it. By the time he walked into Duncan's Lumberyard he had the estimates already figured in his head of how much gravel he would need and where he wanted it dumped.

Gourd Duncan was sitting outside beneath a tree, watching his employees offload logs from a wagon. He greeted King with a wave toward the chair beside his, and a slap on the arm.

" 'Bout time," he said, without removing the pipe between his teeth. "Haven't seen you in a coon's age, son."

"California's a long way off," King replied, reluctantly taking the offered seat. He always liked to talk with Nicatoy's uncle, they had been good friends, but today he wasn't in the mood for a visit. He had too much to do.

There was no getting around it, though. He had to remember that this was the only way to do business in the Nation.

"Haven't seen that Nicatoy, neither," Duncan said, totally disinterested in California or any other place outside his range of experience. "Looks like he would come to see me sometimes. Lots of days I think about when you two would stay at our place a week at a time and fish out that creek 'til there wasn't no catfish left."

King laughed. Just thinking about those memories loosened the knot in his nerves. "You took quite a few yourself," he said, "I don't remember very many days you weren't right there on the bank with us instead of here in the lumberyard or in your fields."

Gourd nodded. "Can't work *all* the time," he proclaimed, using his favorite saying.

The reminisced, King fighting the urge to bring up the subject of gravel too soon. Finally he ventured, "Uncle Gourd, I want you to make a bid on a contract I'm planning to sign pretty soon. I'll need a hundred and fifty tons of gravel to start with— delivered to a spot out by Park Hill."

Gourd Duncan clamped his teeth down harder on his pipe, puffed, and eyed King through the smoke that curled upward. "And what might ye be needin' that much gravel for?" he demanded. "You buildin' a road or what?"

"A *railroad*," King said. "I'm going to build feeder lines all over the Nation. Farmers can ship their crops and livestock . . ."

The words died in his throat as Gourd began shaking his head. He took his pipe from his mouth and knocked it out against the sole of his boot.

"Nope," he said sharply. "Don't need the trade that bad. Ain't havin' nothin' to do with no railroad." He got up and stood looking down at King. "White man's plot," he said. "That's all it is. They're using you, Kingfisher, and you oughtta be smarter than that. Be the ruination of the Nation."

He stared at King for another long minute, as if waiting for him to renounce the railroad, then abruptly turned and walked away without another word.

King sat looking after him, anger and hurt disappointment surging in his gut. Was this the way it was going to be?

The way it was going to be was a finished railroad. The thought jerked him to his feet and onto the road to Blackbear's Quarry, his heels hitting the ground like the beat of a drum.

During the next week King looked back on that first day in Tahlequah as a pattern for the ones to come. Blackbear didn't blink at the idea of a railroad; he and two others promised to submit bids. Immediately, without thinking about Uncle Gourd anymore, King moved on to requesting bids for the timber for ties. Davis Smith wanted nothing to do with railroads, but the idea didn't bother anybody else he approached.

One night, though, riding back into town from the C and G's route, Gourd Duncan's words and the look on his face came back to King. Gourd had been an important part of his childhood: would they ever be friends again? Would Nicatoy still be his best friend when this railroad was finished and done?

He clamped his jaw together and squeezed the sorrel he was riding into a faster trot. This railroad would be finished and done if it killed him, and maybe by that time these sickening feelings would be gone. In the meantime, they'd be submerged beneath the work.

The sorrel pinned his ears and tried to slow; King stuck his heels to him and demanded a lope. He'd learned from the best how to hide his emotions under his work, he thought, his dry lips stretching into a bitter half smile. He'd learned that from Attorney Celina Hawthorne.

The lilac scent came back to him with the thought of her name, so strong it filled up his nostrils. What was it she had said that time by the river, with the blowgun, when he had asked her to kiss him?

I don't want to lose control again, King.

And that night in the moonlight when she *had* kissed him, kissed him like a wild wanton, she had been able to take her mouth away from his and get her mind right back on Mei Lee and the upcoming trial. And ever since she'd refused to back him up at the breakfast table that day—the day after a night of magic lovemaking in a moonlit meadow—she'd been all business, that little lady.

Well, if she could do that, he could keep his mind on business and not on Uncle Gourd, or his father, or . . . on her. This railroad might be separating him from them, but if that was so then it was all he had. That made it all the more urgent for it to be a success.

When he rode the sorrel into Aunt Fee's barn a half hour later, King was glad he had straightened out his thoughts and gotten rid of his emotions. For Ridge was there, supposedly rubbing down the horses he'd driven up from River's Bend, but obviously waiting for King to come in.

He came to help as King unsaddled. "Looks like you've ridden a few miles today," he said, taking the saddle and pad.

"You all just get in?" King asked.

"About an hour ago. The children and your mother are excited about the holiday."

Does Mama still have that hurt look in her eyes? But King couldn't ask. He'd see for himself soon enough. Instead he asked, "Have a good trip?"

"Not bad." Ridge set the saddle onto a rack and turned the pad sweaty side up across it. His hands dropped to his sides, then, and he swung around to look at King in the light from the lantern.

"There's a whole element of the people that are calling you a traitor, Kingfisher, just as I predicted. You might want to think about that."

"I might *not*."

"Well, if that doesn't bother you, maybe this will." Ridge's tone turned hard as the stall post beside him. "Young George Sixkiller's giving up his plantation—just moving off and leaving it at the age of seventy-six—the place he's poured his sweat and blood into for fifty years, his home, and is moving way up into the flint hills.''

King froze with the bridle in his hand, his fingers clamped around the leather straps, staring at him, knowing in his gut what was coming.

''Because your railroad is going to cross his good bottomland farm! He's going to a falling-down cabin on land that won't grow a thing but berries and rocks to get away from the riffraff and the no-goods you're bringing into this Nation!'' By the time he had finished, Ridge was shouting.

The sorrel snorted and kicked the stall.

King forced his emotions, surging forward now, to the back of his mind. The railroad was all he had. So he had to build it.

''That's Young George's decision,'' he said tightly. ''I didn't make it for him.''

''Well, I sure as Thunder wish I could make a decision for you!'' Ridge roared. ''God knows you haven't got sense enough to make one for yourself!''

King stared back at him without answering, without moving, until, at last, Ridge stormed away toward the house. When he had gone, King finished wiping down the horse with hands that trembled in spite of his fierce will to stop it. Then, his heart pounding against the sides of his chest like a warning, he climbed up into the loft and collapsed on a pile of loose hay.

He could not go into the house, not yet; he couldn't face everyone and make conversation. But the longer he lay there, staring at the rough roof of the barn, feeling the sadness wash through him, the more he knew that it wasn't ''everyone'' he was afraid to see.

It was Celina. Whether she loved him or not, even if she would never marry him, if he saw her this night he would walk right up to her and take her into his arms. This night he needed the comfort of her body next to his.

Fortunately, by the next morning, King had his feelings back under control. He sat with Celina in the room next to the dining room which Aunt Fee and Uncle Ish used for a combination study and office, and kept his hands on his papers with no effort at all.

Well, hardly any. Her hair glistened like satin in the morning light from the window and for one fleeting second he saw it loose and wild, spread on the creamy pillowcase in their bed on the Palmyra. He locked the vision away.

"I need you to examine this survey," he said, picking up a thick envelope and holding it out to her.

She took it from him, carefully grasping it from the other side so that their fingers wouldn't touch.

"Compare it with the land descriptions on the permits, please."

"Do you have the permits?" she asked.

Her voice was so crisp and businesslike he hardly recognized it. When they had first said hello he had thought it held a whisper of warmth, but he must have been mistaken.

"The permits are there with it."

"I know you've been working day and night since we got to Tahlequah," she said coolly. "But there hasn't been time to have a survey done, has there?"

"No. This was made when I applied for the permits, months ago."

She looked directly at him; her eyes were as cool as her voice.

Months ago. The words hung in the still room between them. One month ago. One month ago they hadn't known each other very long, had never kissed . . .

For an instant King felt that she had shared the

thought. Some stray emotion, some flicker of feeling flashed through her eyes—but then it was gone. If only he could've looked into those deep black pools last night when he was hurting so much and found them warm and caring!

"Will that be all?" she asked.

"For now," he said. She turned and left.

Once she was outside in the hallway, Celina closed the door quietly and leaned against it. She took two deep breaths, then straightened her spine and headed for the stairs to go up to her room.

She would get this work done as quickly as possible and then go shopping with Lacey and Fee and Jessee, exploring the town as she loved to do. It made her feel free and independent and it helped keep her from thinking about King and whether he had ever really loved her.

He must not have. He was certainly immersed in his railroad now, which was where his heart really had always been.

As Celina passed the front door on the way to the foot of the stairs, voices and a bit of commotion floated in to her from the porch. She stopped and glanced out. A tall, gaunt man stood at the door, his hand raised, ready to knock.

She stared at him. Her heart slowed. It couldn't be true. Could it?

He stood there, that hand in the air, unmoving, like a scarecrow without any wind. Then a breeze from nowhere sprang up and chilled Celina's skin. She squeezed the envelope in her hands until it crackled.

"Eli?" Fee questioned, her hurried footsteps sounding from somewhere in the hall behind Celina. "Eli?" she repeated, as if she were seeing a ghost. "Is that you?"

"It is," he declared, stepping through the doorway into the entry hall. "Is this all the welcome I get?"

Felicity squealed and ran past Celina to hug him.

Celina stood frozen where she was. Had Father come to say that he was sorry? That *he* wanted to bring her to her place in the Nation? She glimpsed her mother behind Eli on the porch.

"Mama!" she cried, and Dolores, too, came into the house. She took Celina into her arms. In the confusion of cousins running to see who had come, Celina tried to avoid speaking directly to Eli.

But he would have none of that. He removed his hat, hung it carefully on the oak coatrack, turned to her, and growled, "So. You think you can run loose all over the country with that worthless bum, do you? Didn't I tell you you'd become nothing but a wanton?"

The words shriveled her inside; the old, sick hopelessness washed through her.

Dolores slipped between Celina and Eli. "Please, not now, Eli," she said. "We've just arrived."

Celina stared at her. When had she ever heard her mother criticize her father?

"I've just come fifteen hundred miles," Eli retorted, "and—"

Felicity took his arm. "Don't you want to go freshen up?" she asked. "Then we'll have tea."

"Serve the tea now," Eli ordered. "My throat's dry as dust."

Felicity shot Celina a startled look, raising her eyebrows in puzzlement. "Very well," she said quietly. "The dining room is right this way; the last of the boarders have just finished breakfast."

She sent one of the children to tell Nanny, her housemaid, to bring tea and coffee, then she led Celina, Dolores, and Eli into the dining room.

"I can't believe you two are really here," she said, squeezing Dolores's hand. "And that I'm meeting my only sister at last."

Dolores's eyes held sudden tears. "And I, too, am happy to meet my sister."

The three women made small talk for a moment while Nanny brought in a tray and set it on the table.

The minute she left the room, Eli said, "Well, I didn't come here for this." He fixed his beady eyes on Celina. "I've come to see to it that the low-life Chekotes don't take my only child away from me the way Ridge took Lacey."

Astonished silence, like a glass bell dropping down from the ceiling, covered them. They could still see each other, but no one could speak. Finally Celina's lips moved. "What are you saying?"

"I'm saying you will come home with me and your mother when we go. Until then, you will not associate with that scum, Kingfisher Chekote, or any other Chekote, for another minute. You will never speak to him again."

Pure, hot anger stirred deep within her. It warmed her enough so that she could talk. "I work for the man," she said. "Of course I will speak to him."

Eli ignored her. "What you don't know, child, is that Ridge Chekote has no character and no conscience, therefore his son has none either. You'll stay away from him."

His blazing eyes held Celina's, but she could sense Felicity's shocked stillness beside her, then her leaning forward to try to get Eli's attention.

"That's not true!" Fee said. "And you know it."

'Then why do you say it, Father?" asked Celina.

Eli flicked his eyes back and forth from her to Fee behind his round glasses. Then he swept them away disdainfully, stalked to the table, and with his long, thin fingers picked up a cup and poured himself some tea.

"Lacey Longbaugh should have been my wife," he said, whirling to stare at them confidentially, the cup resting in the fingers of both his hands as if it were sitting in a basket made of sticks. "She belonged to me. She loved me boundlessly. But Ridge

Chekote snatched her from my arms by telling her vicious lies. He destroyed a sacred bond.''

Felicity gasped.

Eli gave a short, quick nod. "May he burn in hell.''

Felicity said sharply, "Eli, get ahold of yourself. That's a bunch of hogwash and you know it.''

He shook his head. "No. It's the truth and *you* know it.'' His small eyes stared out from behind the gleaming glass, fixing on Felicity for a moment, then moving slowing to Celina and last, to Dolores. Celina couldn't bear to turn her head and look at her mother.

Eli had wanted Lacey?

Eli still wanted Lacey. A lustful possessiveness was evident in the very timbre of his voice when he spoke her name. Poor Mama! After she had given him all these years of unquestioning devotion!

"Now,'' Eli said, "you know the truth, Celina Esperanza. Are you ready to drop this foolish, misbegotten connection with the Chekotes, come home with me and work for me?''

Celina wanted to cry so badly that her lips were stiff. Oh why, why couldn't he understand her? Why couldn't he see that they'd never have any kind of bond between them so long as he tried to own her?

"No,'' she said, not letting her burning eyes waver from his. "Never.''

His sallow coloring lightened, flushed, then faded out to paleness again. "Think, Daughter,'' he commanded. "Have you considered what you're saying?''

"Yes,'' she said, letting all her cold fear and fury wipe out the plea she still, somehow, would like to make. If she showed any weakness at all she'd be lost. "Don't ever tell me what to do, Father, not ever again.''

"You disrespectful little jade!'' he cried. "I told you you'd be selling yourself on the streets if you left me, and that's what you've done!''

"Eli!'' Felicity and Dolores said, at the same time.

"That isn't fair, Father," Celina said. "I've worked hard—I always have, at school and on my cases—so you would be proud of me." Her voice broke. "Why can't you be proud of me, Papa?" She continued to stare at him, although his face was so full of hatefulness it hurt her eyes.

"Because you are nothing but a faker, a deceiver. Pretending to be a virtuous woman. Pretending to be a competent lawyer. You'll never be a fit attorney!"

Eli turned his face suddenly away from Celina as if she no longer existed. He swayed and clutched at the air, letting the teacup and saucer crash to the floor. He didn't appear to notice.

"Felicity," he said. "I need to lie down. My heart condition seems to be bothering me again."

Aunt Fee, her face tight with bewilderment, took his arm. She led him from the room. To Celina's intense surprise, Dolores did not follow them.

For a long minute both women stared at the empty doorway. Finally they looked at each other.

Celina's hurt and hopelessness were mirrored in Dolores's face—her huge dark eyes had filled with tears. But this time Celina had no desire to run into her mother's arms.

King. She wanted King. Nobody else could make this pain go away. With a whispered, "Mama, I'm sorry," she turned, ran out into the hallway, and down it to the study door.

In her moment of weakness she was so intent on finding him that she didn't even think to knock; she opened the door and rushed in. The only important question was whether King was still there where she had left him.

He was. Thank God, he was.

"King!" she said, closing the door behind her without taking her glittering eyes from his. "I . . . need to talk to you for a minute."

His heart quit beating.

At last! Thank God! These horrible days of holding her at arm's length had hurt her as much as they had him. The cold businesslike meeting they had just finished had made her, too, yearn for the old closeness they'd once shared.

King stood up, his mind whirling with questions, trying to answer them as fast as they came. Had she realized that she loved him? Had she come to say that she hated this distance between them? That she would marry him? It must be. Why else would she have rushed back in here like this?

He took a step toward her, lifting his arms to take her in. "Celina!"

She burst into tears and ran into his embrace.

He pressed his lips into her silken hair. "Cry it out," he murmured, wishing as he said it that he could do the same. The relief rushing into him was making him weak. Thank God. She had come to him at last.

"Oh, Celina . . ." He hugged her tighter, rocking back and forth, drawing her heady fragrance of lilac into his nostrils, into his bloodstream.

He could not live without her. He never could. Now he knew that beyond a doubt. And she knew it, too. He loved her and she loved him. He couldn't wait to hear her say the words.

"Tell me, sweetheart," he said. "Talk to me."

"My father is here, King," she said, lifting her tearful face to his as if she wanted a kiss. King almost obliged her; he wanted it, too. So badly. But her words finally traveled from his ears to his brain.

"He dragged my mother all the way back here to the Nation so they could take me home."

King's arms went limp, as if a sudden paralysis had taken them. They dropped away from Celina to hang useless at his sides. "Is that what this is all about?"

"He called me a wanton and a jade for running all

over the country with you," she said, hiccuping one last sob. "He said I'm selling myself on the streets."

"And that's what you wanted to talk to me about?"

"Yes," she said.

Her magnificent eyes had never been more honest, more earnest.

He had wished a hundred times that she could be more open about her feelings. Well, this was one time she was being exactly that. She was being openly cruel.

How could she? Her running to him for comfort was a charade, a travesty, a mockery of the closeness they had shared in the past. Now, thanks to her, they had only business between them. Couldn't she remember how she'd spoken to him not ten minutes ago?

"Oh, King!" she cried, tightening her arms around him, "I feel as bad as I did when we got on the train. He just keeps on hurting me over and over again. I don't think he'll ever love me."

King tore her arms away from his body and thrust them away. "He won't," he said, through lips so tight he thought they'd surely crack. "He can't. Your father is mad, Celina. Can't you see that?"

He stood staring down at her beautiful face, a million other words swarming to his tongue. But he couldn't catch one of them long enough to spit it out. He stepped around her and left without looking back.

Chapter 16

Celina stood in the middle of the room, her face in her hands, and cried. She wasn't aware that her mother had come in until Dolores put her hand on her arm.

"Sit, sit," she murmured, moving closer to guide Celina into the big chair that King had sat in. "Try to build a little wall around your heart," she said. "So he can't hurt you so."

For a minute Celina stayed stiff. She couldn't talk about King, not even with her mother. She simply could not.

"Eli knows he speaks lies," Dolores said.

Celina let herself collapse into the soft leather seat.

"I don't know why he does it," Dolores went on. Her voice broke on the last word.

Celina glanced up: her mother's eyes were still swimming in tears. Poor Mama.

"He hurts you, too, Mama."

"Yes. Because I can hardly bear to see him cause you such pain."

"He hurts you, too. I'm sorry about what he said about . . ."

Dolores picked up a cup of tea she'd left on the table by the door and brought it to Celina. "About Lacey?" she said. "That's all right. I have known always."

With a gasp, Celina said, "Did he tell you?"

"You have reason to think he might be so cruel, I know," Dolores said, pulling another chair close to sit beside her. "But, to his credit, he did not mean to say it. He came home drunk, not long after we married, and it was in his whiskey ravings that he spoke of this Lacey."

"I'm sorry, Mama."

"Don't be," Dolores said resolutely. "What your father doesn't know is that the situation is . . . mutual. He was never my first choice."

A little thrill of mixed gratitude and curiosity tempered Celina's hurt. Never, ever, had her mother talked with her so intimately. "Who was your first choice, Mama?"

"A magnificent bullfighter called Manuelo," she said, staring into the middle distance with a dreamy smile. Then the smile vanished. "He was gored to death three days before our wedding would have taken place. Six months later I married Eli."

"Why?" Celina whispered.

Dolores shrugged. "My father urged it. A trade, it was: my family's old California connections to advance Eli's career and me in exchange for enough money to pay my father's gambling debts."

"Oh, Mama!"

Again the resigned little lifting of her shoulders. "I could have cared less," she said. "At the time all I wanted was to die too."

Felicity appeared in the door.

"Eli's lying down," she said. She came in and pulled another chair close to theirs. "Is he always so . . . unbalanced and upset?"

"More or less," Dolores told her. "The doctors say he has no heart condition."

"He has no heart," Celina said bitterly. "Saying all those things about me when he knows they're untrue. And about the Chekotes, too! How in the world did he ever make up such a story?"

"Lacey did nearly marry him," Fee said quietly.

Celina set her cup into her saucer.

"I can't believe it! She and Ridge are still so much in love even an insensitive clod like Father couldn't help but see it. Haven't they always been that way?"

"Yes. Lacey was in love with Ridge from the minute she met him," Felicity said. "But he disappeared during the war and she found herself orphaned with her home burned to the ground."

"And Father . . ."

"He'd always been crazy about her and she was hoping that that would be enough to make a good home for her baby. She . . . was going to have Ridge's baby."

King! Celina thought. And then in the next breath: So? That has nothing to do with me. "And she assumed Ridge was dead."

"Yes."

"Where was he?"

"Being held prisoner by a band of Confederate Cherokees who had a grudge against him. They captured him up in the hills where he and Lacey had been stranded alone together for weeks."

"Then what happened?"

"He came back right in the middle of her wedding to Eli—he'd broken out of prison when he heard about it. Eli was mortified when Lacey ran to Ridge and married *him* right then and there, when she'd been hesitating about saying her vows to him."

"I can just imagine the state Father was in," Celina said. "So that's what he meant by 'bad blood' between the Hawthornes and the Chekotes."

She told her mother and Aunt Felicity the story of hers and King's first meeting and Eli's furious rantings when he heard King's name.

Felicity nodded. "Evidently he's kept the old wound festering all these years," she said. "Instead of forgetting about it and letting it heal. I'm afraid it's nearly driven him crazy.''

"Because his pride was crushed when Ridge displaced him as the bridegroom at his own wedding,'' Celina mused. "I hope he doesn't bother Lacey and Ridge now that they're all here together again.''

"Ridge can handle Eli,'' Felicity said firmly. "And so can Lacey. But I hope they don't have to—they have enough troubles without that.''

Everybody has enough troubles, Celina thought, and the next few days seemed to prove that true. She, herself, had to accept the fact that King had never been the man she had thought he was; more and more it seemed that the railroad was his only love and that he would do anything for its benefit.

She decided that she had never really known him. The protective, understanding King she'd known on the Western Zephyr and the loving King who'd drawn her into the magic moonlit meadow only a few nights before had not been the real King. They had been actors, manipulating her so she would use her legal skills and her loyalty for the good of the C & G.

That would be typical of a bossy, controlling man, no matter how much he professed to love her.

Had he ever really loved her?

Yet she hadn't wanted him to love her, had she? Because she didn't want to love him in return. That would mean losing her independence, something she could never do.

She knew King had his troubles, too, although she saw him rarely: much of the time he was gone eighteen hours a day on the business of the railroad, either riding out to the site where the track would be built or in Tahlequah making arrangements for supplies and equipment. Yet when he was at the boardinghouse, he and Ridge were at loggerheads.

Eli attacked King, too, every time he saw him, but

most of the time he was either out on his own mysterious errands or shut in his room with his "heart trouble." When Lacey and Ridge first came back from town, he'd flirted clumsily with her and bristled at Ridge, but Lacey's cool smiles and Ridge's indifference had soon discouraged him.

Troubles and tensions seemed to Celina to be everywhere, infecting the very air she breathed, and, except for those created by Eli, King's obsession with the C & G seemed to be the cause of them all. She was thankful that she had seen his obsession in time to bring their association back to a purely business footing, before she had let herself fall in love with him.

But when he stalked into the parlor the next evening, his shirt caked with dust and sweat from riding and the familiar, battered portmanteau full of papers in his hand, the blood raced hot in her veins.

She hadn't been in the same room with him for nearly a week. They hadn't spoken directly to each other, except for the most perfunctory of necessary greetings, in that same length of time.

Five and one-half days. And three hours.

"Celina," he said. "I need you to come with me."

And I need you, her traitorous heart cried back to him. King, I need you. No, she thought, deliberately drowning the desperate voice inside her. No. I do not need him.

Aunt Fee and Dolores looked up from their game of checkers.

"Here," Fee said, "you two use this table." She started to stand up.

King made an abrupt gesture that stopped her. "We'll use the dining room table, Aunt Fee," he said. "Don't move."

Celina walked past him to the doorway and down the hall into the big dining room.

He set the portmanteau down in a chair at the end

of the table and moved two of the upside-down plates, turned over the silverware, ready for breakfast, into the middle.

"I have acceptable bids for all the supplies," he said. "I'm ready for you to start writing the contracts. Sit down and I'll bring you up to date."

He moved down the table to get the lamp, then brought it back to set it in front of her, his long, brown fingers cradling the bowl of it as they had once cradled her breast. If only he could do that again, just once . . .

Celina smashed the thought as it was born. No. Her perfidious body would not destroy her resolve. She wouldn't let it. She attached her gaze to the blank, white peace of the tablecloth directly in front of her. But almost immediately her eyes drifted up and back to King.

He shifted his stance, throwing one hip forward to run two fingers into his front pants pocket for a match. Celina's heart slowed to a yearning, thrumming beat; she gripped both arms of the chair where she sat.

He lifted the globe and held it with his left hand while he struck the match with his right. When he held it to the wick, the light caught and flared. His craggy face was hard as the wood beneath her hands.

"I've been talking timber for the ties, gravel for the grades, and freighters to haul both," he said, and the tone of his voice was one he might use with a stranger. It was businesslike and impersonal, right to the point. Exactly what she had wanted when he had first hired her.

A lifetime ago in a place as far away as the stars.

He pulled out the chair around the corner from hers at the end of the table and sat down. She caught a whiff of his scent that brought back those long evening talks by the Caliente River . . . sweat, and dust, and horse, and . . . King.

"You'll need to write up the contracts for the bids I've accepted."

He set the bag on the table between them and began taking papers from it. Celina's hand lifted, completely of its own volition, and stroked the soft, worn leather. Then she jerked it away as if the bag were hot.

"King," she said. "Perhaps you shouldn't go ahead with these contracts right now. Besides the fact that this railroad is tearing your family apart, it's hurting a lot of other people as well: I heard that Young George Sixkiller is leaving his home and moving off into the hills to get away from it! He's an old man, King."

He ignored her and spread out the papers with quick, sure movements, keeping his eyes fixed on their headings so he could put them in the order he wanted. Anger flared hot in the back of her brain. "Did you hear me?"

"Young George is old enough to make his own decisions," he said shortly. "He isn't my responsibility."

"I can't believe you'd take that attitude!" she cried. "Just think about him at our welcome party at River's Bend: how he was so glad for you and Ridge both that you're home, how he loved talking about the farming! Now he won't have a good farm anymore!"

"All right," he said thoughtfully, his eyes on the papers under his hands. "Here you have the bids for the timber, with the lowest one on top. I need you to write a letter to each one—"

She gasped. "Are you so wrapped up in your eternal railroad that you don't care what it does to people you've known all your life?"

"No," he said brusquely. "Now, look here at these bids and listen to what I tell you."

His tone chilled her through and through. He really didn't care. She was much better off without him.

When King had finished outlining Celina's duties for her he went into the darkened kitchen and jerked open the breadbox. By the dim light that filtered in from the hallway, he found bread, cold roast beef, and a knife. He hacked the bread into thick pieces that fell away from the loaf like a deceitful lady's white fan, then he stuffed the sandwiches into the flour sack, jammed his hat down onto his head, and left the house through the back door.

He chose a different horse from the one he'd ridden all day and saddled him in record time, hung the sack of food on the horn, then stared at it as he felt for the stirrup to mount. Why had he even bothered? The thought of eating made his throat contract, even though he'd been starving when he'd ridden into town a short while ago.

No, it was listening to Celina that had destroyed his appetite, he admitted, as he swung into the saddle and headed out to hit the road to the south. He'd sleep on the ground tonight at the tracksite to get away from that lilac scent and those deep, dark eyes. Those beautiful, perfidious eyes.

And that sweet, melodious voice! *King, perhaps you shouldn't go ahead with those contracts right now.*

Thunder! Not only would she not take his side, now she'd given up her neutrality as well. She was working against him! She might be doing the legal work of getting the railroad built, but her heart was clearly in the same camp as Ridge and Gourd Duncan and Young George Sixkiller.

His stomach tied itself into a knot so tight he

feared it would never come undone. That had happened every time he'd thought about Young George Sixkiller since Ridge had told him the news. The old man was good clear through and it was a crying shame that he was giving up his home.

But he didn't have to do it. The C & G across his property wouldn't be that bad. What was really bad was Celina.

King took a deep seat and forced his mount into a fast lope through the night.

How the hell could she be such a traitor?

Celina finished the contracts and the letters the next day. She took them to Aunt Fee when she was done and asked her to leave them in King's room, because, somehow, she couldn't bear to look into his face and know that she would never touch it, never kiss him, again. Not yet.

But she wouldn't succumb. She'd known from the beginning that she shouldn't, and her instincts had been right. Someday she'd find comfort in knowing that. And someday she'd be able to walk into his empty room and put some papers on his desk without feeling compelled to throw her body across his bed and sob until there was not another tear left in her.

But not today.

Her anguish must have been written all over her face, for Fee didn't ask a single question about why Celina wasn't giving the papers to King directly.

And when she came back downstairs she gave her a hug. "Let's go down to the square," she said. "Tahlequah's so exciting when everybody's coming in for Council!"

Jessee happened through the hallway just at that minute. "Can I go with you?" she squealed. "No telling who we'll see!"

And so she went with them—it was the beginning

of a tradition. Every afternoon for the next few days the three of them drifted down the street in the cool circles of the parasols they carried to shade them from the late-summer sun, stopping to visit with everyone Fee knew (which was everyone), and ending up at the square, where colorful booths selling everything from blowguns to fry bread surrounded the Council House.

It became Celina's favorite time of day. Mornings were awful because Eli had taken to getting up early and sitting at the dining room table through the entire two hours Nan and Aunt Fee served breakfast, alternately charming and harassing each resident of the house, from the regular boarders to the traveling drummers to Celina.

She stopped going in there at first, but he always found her, even if he had to lurk outside her room. So she deliberately faced him down every day and felt her strength grow as she did so. He was losing his power to hurt her.

But King hadn't lost his.

The nights were worst of all, because then she dreamed about him. Or lay awake thinking about him, remembering, until her body burned for his touch.

What would she ever do? She'd have to get another job if she couldn't forget their personal history and make their association an entirely professional one.

If she tried to do that here in the Nation, could Father poison her every attempt, the way he had done in California? He seemed to have Cherokee friends left—although she never saw them and he never took Mama with him, he was away many afternoons visiting them.

Should she begin now to study Cherokee law? But if King stayed in the Nation, she couldn't. Not if she continued to think so constantly about him.

Oh, why, why had she ever permitted him to teach her how to let her feelings out of that neat, locked box where she used to keep them? Now it was impossible to gather them up and force them back in even though they threatened to pull her apart: so she lived for the distractions of the afternoons.

On one of them, two days before the official Council meeting was due to begin, Lacey and Dolores went with her and Fee and Jess as far as Sloan's Mercantile, where they lingered to look at the new shipment of fabrics and lace. Celina had no interest in clothes anymore (to Dolores's shocked surprise), and Jessee was more eager than ever to get to the square, so the usual three of them moved on downhill along the shady street.

"I know why you're in such a hurry," Fee teased, twirling her parasol in a gesture that made her look as young as Jessee. "You're wanting to shop for a fan. Let's see, now, would that be a turkey-feather fan?"

Jessee gasped. She turned around and began walking backward so she could see her aunt but still not lose any time getting to the square.

"Aunt Fee! How did you know?" she said. "You won't tell, will you?"

"Tell what?" Celina demanded.

"That Blue Hawk Deer-in-the-water has caught Miss Jessee's eye," Fee said.

"No, he has caught my heart," Jessee said baldly. "I love him."

She caught her heel on a rough spot, but she recovered and kept on walking without ever taking her flashing eyes from Fee's.

"My parents know that," she said. "They just don't know I'm coming to see him today. Really, Aunt Fee!"

They passed Maud Vann's Millinery and were approaching the busy cross street that ran beside the square.

"Auntie Fee, are you going to tell?"

"Not if you behave yourself," Fee said. "Remember always to be a lady."

"Oh, I will," Jessee squealed. "Thanks, Auntie Fee!"

She broke away from Celina, hugged Fee, turned, and ran into the dusty cloud filled with creaking carriages and high-stepping horses. Celina and Fee stopped dead and watched Jessee's sure progress in front of a dangerously fast-trotting team, around a freight wagon and behind it, then up onto the grass of the square.

Celina wondered why *she* couldn't be like that. Jessee was hardly more than a child, but she knew her own heart and she had the courage to follow it. But Celina couldn't follow hers. That would mean her own destruction.

"Aunt Fee?" she said, when Jessee had disappeared into the deep shade of the elm trees. "Why doesn't she want Ridge and Lacey to know that she's seeing this boy?"

Fee shrugged and took Celina's arm, waiting at the edge of the street until the traffic cleared. "It's the old story," she said. "The Deer-in-the-waters are penniless full-bloods, dirt farmers and hunters from way back up in the hills. A far cry from the Chekotes of River's Bend."

"But if they're good people . . ."

"Oh, they are," Fee said. "But they're proud. Proud as peacocks. Blue Hawk tries to ignore Jessee. He's no more than nineteen or twenty, but he knows right now that he'll never be able to give that girl a life like she's used to."

"And Ridge and Lacey . . ."

"Have told her not to make a fool of herself. You know how proud Ridge is."

She did, indeed. And how proud his oldest son was.

He'd proved over and over again during these last awful days that his pride in his railroad was more important than anything else in his life. If she'd kept that in the front of her mind all along she'd have seen that all he wanted from her was help in attaining his goals.

They crossed the street and came out onto the edge of the square. Booths and tables crowded with pots and baskets, bright shawls and beadwork stood in lines around its edge. Other proprietors sat cross-legged in the grass surrounded by their wares, sharing the shade of the tall elm and hackberry trees.

Jessee stood in front of a ramshackle booth half a block away, talking to a handsome boy. He leaned against the corner of the shelter, working with what looked like a bunch of feathers in his hands, but every few minutes he looked up to smile at her.

"He doesn't appear to be trying to ignore her," Celina said.

"That's not Blue Hawk. It's his brother Moses. Hawk's a year or two older and twice as good-looking."

"Moses is very handsome. . . . Hawk must be beautiful."

"He is. And hotheaded and wild as they come," Fee said. "Moses is quieter, but they're close as twins. They're good boys—they've worked from can-see to can't-see on that flint-hill farm of their Mama's."

Celina and Fee wandered through the square, keeping half an eye on Jessee. Aunt Fee bought some new brooms from Andrew Swimmer, who promised to deliver them later, and an appliquéd shawl as a gift for Dolores. They had just sat down to rest on a bench beneath one of the spreading trees when someone shouted.

"No! Hyah! You boys stop that!"

The sound rang through the square like a clarion call.
Fee and Celina turned toward it in time to get a glimpse
of two boys hitting and shoving each other, then curious
onlookers got in their way. There must have been a
dozen of them crowding around the Deer-in-the-water
stall, the place where they'd last seen Jessee.

"Jessee!" Fee gasped, jumping to her feet. "Dear
Lord, Lacey and Ridge will kill me if that child gets
hurt. I nearly forgot she was here." She and Celina
ran toward the commotion, dodging people coming
from all sides of the square.

When they got closer, Fee shouted, "Move,
please! Let us through! Jessee!"

The spectators stepped apart. Jessee stood, un-
harmed, directly in front of Celina and Fee. However, she was on the other side of the two struggling
boys, her horrified face pale as sand. She stood with
her arms outstretched and her lips parted as if she'd
been petrified in the act of trying to prevent the fray.

"Why, it's Moses and Blue Hawk!" Fee said.
"They surely aren't fighting each other!"

But they were. One of them broke free for a moment and threw up his arm to defend his face; blood
streamed from a cut on his brow.

The other stood with his fist drawn. "Moses, say
you'll quit," he ordered. "Say you'll go right back to
him and quit. There'll be no Deer-in-the-water on the
crews building railroads in the Cherokee Nation."

Moses dropped his arm and straightened his back.
Sweat was pouring off him.

"It's good money!" he cried. "We sure can use
it, Hawk."

"Traitor's money," Hawk spit back. "Money
stained with the blood of the Nation."

"You say!"

"I say we'll tear up the track as fast as the white
men can build it!"

The brothers stared at each other, their handsome faces strained to the point of breaking beneath the sweat and blood. Moses's face was pale and splotchy as the turkey feathers fanned out on the wall behind him. Hawk's was dark with rage.

"Well?" Hawk demanded, shaking his fist at his brother. "Are you gonna quit or not?"

"No."

Hawk dropped his head and charged at Moses, driving him backward into the flimsy wooden arbor. With a cracking sound like bones breaking, it tore into pieces and began to fall.

The boys fought like wildcats right through the growing destruction, oblivious to roof branches and upright poles hitting their backs as the pieces came crashing down. First one was on top, then the other.

The two brothers rolled deeper into the shambles of the booth, hitting each other with blows that sounded like hammers striking meat. Moses slipped out of Hawk's grip and staggered to his feet; blood was pouring even faster, now, from the gash in his forehead.

Hawk came up, too, dangerously quick, grabbing for a broken pole as he rose.

"That's right, hit the little coward!" a tall man yelled. "Teach him not to work for traitors, Hawk!"

"Shut up!" the stout man yelled back. "You oughtta know better than to tell him that, Drum-thrower!"

Moses staggered; Hawk lifted the pole with both hands, ready to bring it down.

"Hit him, Hawk," some people yelled.

Others shouted, "Don't fight, boys!"

"They don't know what they're doing," Felicity moaned. "Those boys have never fought each other in their lives! What if he kills him?"

At that instant Jessee moved. Like an unexpected gust of wind, she ran, skirts swirling, into the messy debris, screaming, "Stop it! Stop it, now!" over the noise of the crowd. She jumped over a piece of the roof and threw her body between Moses and the threatening pole. "Hawk, you put that down!" she shouted. "You can't hit him for working on King's railroad!"

Hawk glared at her, an expression of mingled shock and frustration mixing with the blind anger on his face. "Get away from here!" he roared. "Jessee, you get away!"

"No! Don't you hit Moses!"

They stood frozen for an endless moment, then Hawk brought the pole crashing down, missing Jessee and Moses by a foot or more, but at the same time he threw his body at his brother and toppled them both into the ruins. Jessee managed to keep standing for one precarious instant, then she sat down, hard, in the middle of the wreckage. The boys lay still.

Jessee's cry tore the sudden silence. "Hawk!" She was up and scrambling headlong toward him before anyone else could move.

"Oh, no," Fee moaned. "Lacey will have my hide!"

She and Celina tried to go to Jess, but several men pushed ahead of them, hurrying to pull the brothers out of the ruins.

They dragged Hawk out, shoulders first. Jessee came with them, holding his head, touching his shoulder where his shirt had been torn away before they'd even laid him down. She knelt beside him on the grass, crying. He opened his eyes and spoke to her.

Then she was up again and darting back into the shambles of the booth where some men were lifting Moses out. He was limp and pale as the sunlight.

"Moses?" Jessee called. "Moses? Are you alive?"

His hand, dangling like a leaf on a broken limb, fluttered slightly.

"It's Jessee," she cried, hurrying to keep up so she

could look into his face. One of the men carrying him tried to brush her away, but she held her ground.

"Hawk is so worried," she said. "He didn't mean to kill you, Mose."

They put Moses on a blanket that somebody spread on the ground several yards away from Hawk. Jessee stood over him for an instant, wringing her hands, then she ran back to Blue Hawk.

"Jessee," Fee called, moving past the men who had carried him and around a rotund woman in a fancy shawl to get closer to her. "Sweetheart, you need to calm down."

But Jessee was wild. She bent over Hawk, crying, wiping the sweaty streaks of blood and dirt from his face with the tail of her skirt.

She glanced up at Celina. "Celina, will you go and stay with Mose?" she pleaded. "Watch for him to open his eyes and keep telling him Hawk didn't want to hurt him."

She waited for Celina to nod her promise, then she turned back to Hawk, the frantic movement loosening her hair from its pins. It fell onto her shoulders and swung down across the boy's chest.

Felicity grabbed Celina's arm. "She'll never listen to reason, now," she said. "I'll go find Lacey."

"No, Fee, you stay with Jessee. I'll go," said a calm voice behind them.

They turned to find a slight older woman whom Celina didn't know. But, of course, Felicity did. "Oh, thank you, Trudy," she said. "She was at Sloan's a little while ago."

"I'll have her here in a minute," Trudy said in her soft, slow way. "You-all help Jessee look after these boys. They'll be my new neighbors, you know."

Even in the turmoil of the moment the strange remark struck Celina. And it piqued Fee's curiosity, of course; she took time to demand an explanation. If the town were burning down around them, Fee would stop carrying water to get the latest news, Celina thought.

"You're moving? Back up in the hills? But what about your good river plantation?" she demanded.

"The railroad's coming across it," Trudy said, her voice brittle with a hurt so grievous it made Celina's throat go tight.

Oh, Dear Lord, not another one! she thought. Poor old Young George Sixkiller was bad enough.

Trudy turned away and started for the street, hurrying along as if she could run from the truth of the statement she'd just made. Her thin form in the pale blue dress cut a winding path through the growing crowd of people; little knots of them were forming everywhere, even in the street, and the buzz of voices was getting louder every minute.

"The railroad," someone shouted. "Fighting over working on King Chekote's railroad."

"Better him, a thousand times, than the M K and T!" another voice called.

Several incoherent yells rose in answer.

But King wouldn't listen to them or to her. His pride was at stake, now, and his need to prove himself to Ridge; his blind self-confidence and determination were driving him to save it. Even the sight of these bloody boys lying on the ground wouldn't deter him one whit. Lacey's obvious desolation hadn't done so.

Her fists clenched in helpless frustration, Celina turned away and pushed through the milling people to Moses. She dropped to her knees beside him.

The boy's desperate gaze clung to hers and he made a guttural sound deep in his throat. He tried to move his lips, but they were so badly bruised and swelling so rapidly that he couldn't speak. The bloody cut through his brow was gaping. It definitely would leave a scar.

Celina reached out slowly and touched his forehead. She brushed back his hair. "Your brother sent you a message," she said. "He didn't want to hurt you—he was so angry he didn't think what he was doing."

Suddenly, on the other side of Moses, two women appeared, bringing water and cloths to wash and bandage him.

Celina closed her eyes. She could still see the boys' faces, so alike and so beautiful, in that one long moment in the sunlight when they had faced each other. Now Moses would always be scarred. And, in a different way, Hawk would be, too.

"Son," one of the women muttered, "this is going to hurt. But not as much as the sight of you and your brother fighting hurt me."

Celina opened her eyes. The woman's wizened face was ancient, impassive. Her eyes shone bright with unshed tears. She dabbed at the deep wound in Moses's forehead. His body arched with pain, but he didn't make a sound.

"He signed up to work on the railroad," said somebody standing nearby.

The old woman dropped her cloth back into the basin of water and shot to her feet. She raised both arms in the air and held them still until many people were looking at her.

"Take this word to Kingfisher Chekote," she cried. "He is the cause of my suffering and that of my grandchildren. He is a traitor to his people."

She paused. Then she called out again in a voice so high it was eerie. "For many, many years, since before the time of Doublehead," she said, "the Cherokees punish traitors by death."

Silence fell.

A louder buzzing of voices rose then, all over the crowd. "Death," someone repeated, and then all the sounds blurred together in Celina's ears except for King's name over and over and the world "railroad." Always the word "railroad."

Her blood stopped running in her veins. Would someone really try to kill King?

She sat back on her heels and held her breath until the grandmother dropped her arms to her sides and squatted on her haunches beside Moses once more. He opened his eyes and muttered something to her.

Another woman materialized behind her with a large drawstring bag that smelled of herbs and medicine. They would take care of Moses. She should get up and go see about Jessee. She should go see whether Trudy had found Lacey. She should find Aunt Fee.

She couldn't move.

Then a different noise ran over the crowd, a rippling wave of motion and sound that pulled each person's head up to attention. As if a giant had passed his hand over his hair or his hat. People began turning away from the scene of the fight, began leaving the two wounded boys behind to move out to the farthest edges of the square.

Some ominous premonition brought Celina to her feet. She followed three men until she reached a clear spot where she could see into the street. A procession of some sort was coming up it from the south. She arrived on the sidewalk just as the first trotting horse came into her direct line of vision.

"It's the Lighthorse!" someone cried, and she saw that, indeed, the four outriders were in the uniforms of the Cherokee police. They formed a circle. In the center of it, on a spirited sorrel horse, rode a man with his reins looped around the saddle horn and his hands tied behind his back.

Celina stared at him for an endless age before her mind would accept what her eyes tried to tell her.

The man in custody was King.

Chapter 17

Her heart lifted out of her body to go to him.

That was just as well—she would have no more need of it. Her blood would move through her veins without a heart to pump it, because all the laws of nature had been rescinded. Gravity had disappeared and left her hanging, cut loose from the earth, the air had turned to solid matter that refused to enter her lungs, and the smells of food and crushed grasses and dust on the square had turned acrid.

They were cheering! Some of the people were actually cheering to see King like this.

Her stomach lurched. She could hear Mrs. Deer-in-the-water's chilling proclamation still ringing in the air over their heads.

The Cherokee punish traitors by death.

Was this some awful plot to try King as a traitor? Could his life actually be at stake?

King sat his horse like a conquering chief riding into a town to accept its surrender. He looked straight ahead, staring out across the rolling landscape as if he owned every inch of it as far as his eye could see. His muscular shoulders and arms moved in rhythm with the horse. They ought to be powerful enough to rip his bonds to shreds. Yet the rope held him helpless, although every line of his proud body said it wasn't so.

He was brave enough to face anything. She knew that. He had proved it in California. But bravery wouldn't save him if most of the Nation decided he had betrayed them. Oh, Dear Lord, this had to be some horrible bad dream.

The leading Lighthorseman turned at the corner and rode along the north side of the square. Celina's eyes stayed on King's set face, keeping him in sight as his horse turned the corner.

She leaned toward him. He was too far from her already—farther away than she could bear. Yet she couldn't go to him. A tremendous stirring deep in her heart held her in place; a profound knowing, locked in the box of her secret feelings for a long, long time.

The four Lighthorsemen reined in at the long hitching post and began to dismount. King sat his horse, looking down on them.

They tied their horses, they spoke to the people coming up to them, they spoke to each other. They looked at each other. And then at King.

He made them wait.

Then he stood in one stirrup, as perfectly balanced as if he had the use of his hands, and swung his leg over the cantle. He stepped to the ground.

All Celina could see was his bright head and his broad shoulders, but it was enough. Enough to smash that box inside her heart to bits and let the sweet truth fly free forever.

She loved him.

She loved King with every shred of the passion born in her. And she always would, as long as she lived.

Celina took one step, then began to run in his direction. What was the charge? She didn't care. No matter. She would refute it, get it dismissed.

She ran past the shambles left by the fight and Jessee, still kneeling beside Blue Hawk, with hardly a glance. Aunt Fee called her name, but she didn't slow down.

By the time she had crossed the square all the Lighthorsemen had gathered around King and were moving up the graveled path toward the Council House door. She could catch glimpses of him—the white of his shirt, the amber fire of his hair—but now it was impossible to see his face.

Once inside the wide hallway she was able to push through the growing crowd.

"Cut this rope," King snapped to the Lighthorseman who had been leading the procession. "And go get the judge."

Celina reached him. "I love you, King," were the first words to rise in her throat, but they didn't pass her lips. This wasn't the time. "What happened, King?"

He dropped the chieftain's mask. "They say I stole some timber!" he said, furious. "After I've spent two weeks looking at samples and taking bids and having you write up contracts to pay for it." He turned back to the Lighthorseman. "Cut this rope, I told you, and do it now. I've got to get out of here."

"What's the procedure?" Celina asked. "Whom should I see for your release?"

"Nobody," he snapped. "I don't need a lawyer. All I want is to talk to the judge—this is some asinine mistake."

The captain of the Lighthorse nodded at one of his men, who drew a hunting knife from a sheath on his belt. With maddening slowness he turned King around and sawed at the rope that tied his hands.

When it was severed, King flung it aside and rubbed at his wrists. "There was no need to tie me in the first place, and you know it!" he bellowed.

"Get somebody in authority in here and let's get to the bottom of this."

Without replying, the Lighthorse captain escorted King down the hall and into a large room, probably the Council meeting room, Celina decided. Or maybe a courtroom. It had long wooden benches, placed in rows, and, in the front, an enormous oak table surrounded by chairs.

They were still standing beside it, with the Lighthorsemen pulling out chairs, when a contingent of men, obviously officials, trooped in behind them. The sight chilled Celina.

This *was* some kind of a plot. These people had been waiting to be called in—King hadn't been in the building five minutes.

King turned and looked at them; he made a noise of disgust under his breath. "McKisick," he muttered.

"Chekote!" the first man replied. He was short, with a round face distinguished by the most extremely smug expression that Celina could ever remember seeing. He pulled out a chair at the head of the table. "Sit down. I'm afraid, however, that your friend will have to go."

King ignored the invitation and stood rooted to the floor. "Miss Celina Hawthorne," he said. "My attorney."

"Well, in that case, welcome, Miss Hawthorne," the oily McKisick said.

He glanced at the secretary sitting down and arranging papers and pens beside him. The third man, wearing a badge which proclaimed him to be sheriff of the Goingsnake District, walked around the end of the table and sat down on the other side.

McKisick didn't ask King to sit again. He, Celina, and the Lighthorsemen remained standing.

"As Solicitor of the Goingsnake District," Mc-

Kisick intoned formally, "I charge you, Kingfisher Chekote, with theft from the Cherokee Nation—"

"You surely are not serious." King was the regal chief once more.

But McKisick was the relentless prosecutor. "With taking timber from forests owned in common by the Cherokee People for use as ties on the privately owned C and G railroad."

"That is not true."

Again, McKisick ignored King. He simply looked at the Lighthorsemen, and each of them, in turn, testified that logs marked to identify them as coming from the common land had been found on the grade of the C and G's short-line railroad.

"Why were the logs marked, anyway?" King barked.

For the first time, McKisick hesitated. His beady gray eyes flicked to King, then to Celina. "We recently began cutting them for use in building bridges," he said firmly. "Marking them is standard procedure before hauling them to the sites."

"Why?" King demanded.

"That's not the question," McKisick shot back. "Were marked logs found at your railroad or not?"

"Yes," King admitted stonily. "But they were not there by my hand. I contracted for logs with Old Man Kell Rabbit and with Jack Gowan to haul them. That's all I know."

"Solicitor McKisick," said Celina, "as Mr. Chekote's attorney may I say a word?"

One sharp glance from those pale eyes and then a nod of the man's head gave his permission.

"If the logs in question came from land held in common by the Cherokee Nation," she said, "then it seems to follow that they would not be in Mr. Chekote's possession illegally in any case. Mr. Kingfisher Chekote is a citizen of the Cherokee Nation in good standing, a member of a prominent family long engaged in service to its government."

The solicitor, the sheriff, and the secretary all stared at her for a long moment.

"How can Mr. Chekote be accused of stealing these logs?" she asked. "He is a Cherokee: the logs belong to him, too."

"Not to be used to build a railroad that will destroy the Nation," McKisick snapped. "Not to be used to make himself and the white men rich. This is nothing but theft from all the people for use in creating their own destruction."

A murmur of agreement rose from the other officials and the Lighthorsemen.

"You will be held in the National Jail," McKisick said, "until such time as Judge Adair returns. He is expected back in Tahlequah tomorrow."

King stared at him, obviously stunned that this mistake could have grown so huge, so fast.

"Your Honor," Celina said quietly, although she wanted to scream at the vain, closed expression on the solicitor's face. "Mr. Chekote is being accused of theft from the Nation. He contends that he is innocent. I propose that he be left free to aid in his own defense."

"That would be impossible. The sheriff and I have agreed."

The sheriff ducked his head, refusing to look at either King of Celina.

"When convicted murderers run loose on the strength of their word that they'll come back for hanging?" King burst out. "When the entire Nation knows that my word is good, when my father is a distinguished member of the National Council? I refuse to stay in jail."

"That choice is not yours, Mr. Chekote," the solicitor said. "It is our considered opinion that you should be jailed as an example."

"Of what?" King shot back in a tone of withering sarcasm. "Of an innocent man, wrongly accused?"

"As an example of a traitor to the Nation," the man replied, in a slow, cold way that made Celina's skin crawl. "To discourage others who might be tempted to put personal gain before patriotism."

King's fiery eyes went dull, and he suddenly looked sick, as if the strength had been sucked out of his face, leaving only a mask of hurt fury behind. Never, ever, had Celina wanted so to go to him. To hold him.

"I am not a traitor," he said hoarsely. "Anybody with half a mind knows that. I am not a traitor."

"The trial will tell," the solicitor said. He gazed at King, and then Celina, with a tight, conceited smile. "I feel sure that the judge will decide that there should be a trial."

King stared at him. The man's eyes didn't waver, and the longer they glared at each other, the more the old spirit came back into King's.

He said, "You're a yellow-bellied snake in the grass, Dothan McKisick, and you always have been. I'll have your job for this."

He turned on his heel and strode toward the door. The startled Lighthorsemen scrambled to move with him, but none tried to stop him.

"Make sure you note this gesture of disrespect," McKisick ordered the clerk, tapping his notebook with one finger. "And the threat of political reprisal." He looked up to find the Lighthorse captain and called after him, "Lock him up!"

"Not yet," Celina said. "I have the right to confer with my client."

She followed King and the Lighthorsemen into the hallway, where he drew her to one side, out of earshot of the men.

"The freighters I hired had to have hauled those marked logs in mixed with the ones I bought," he said tightly. "Somebody at the freight yards has to know something. That'll be the place to start."

Celina nodded. "I'll go straight there."

She looked at him, her heart thudding against her ribs. If only he would say something personal, just one thing that would acknowlege their old closeness and the fact that they were both suffering inside, sharing this bewilderment and fear, something that would admit they cared about more than just legalities here!

"You'll have to watch McKisick," he said. "He's a slimy one; he could do anything."

Did he love her? She loved him. He ought to know that. Did she dare tell him so? "King," she said.

"Go, Celina," he said, in a voice drawn so tight she thought it might crack. "Maybe you can clear me right away. I'm going to hate jail more than any place I've ever been."

She whirled and rushed down the dim hallway toward the rectangle of light that was the open door, disappointed and yet relieved that she hadn't spoken. Right now she was King's attorney, not his lover, and she had work to do.

The tiny voice of honesty that had come to life in her that day whispered, "Coward. Celina is a coward," but she ignored it. Later would be time enough to deal with her feelings.

Because what if King had changed his mind? Or, as she had been trying to convince herself, had never loved her?

When Celina dashed, breathless, into the hot, lifeless expanse of the freight yards she could still hear King's stricken voice saying, "I'm going to hate jail more than any place I've ever been."

He was so accustomed to wide spaces and living

outdoors—he had even slept outside his tent most of the nights in California, just to be out in the open.

She had to get him out. He must feel like that lion in the cage they'd seen the day they met. A lifetime, no, two lifetimes ago.

Now, in this dusty street she wished he were with her.

The long lines of wooden docks and dozens of wagons stood weirdly quiet in the heat of the lowering sun, except for the swish of tails and stamp of feet as the mules fought the flies. There wasn't a man in sight.

Sudden goose bumps broke out on Celina's arms. Had they known she was coming? Were all the freighters hiding so as not to talk to her? Was this another twist in the plot that had entrapped King? What was going on? Who was behind it?

She forced herself to keep walking. Several hundred feet ahead loomed the faded sign OFFICE, its letters almost as tall as the small, weathered building on whose side they'd been painted.

Celina had nearly reached it when a rough voice spoke, almost at her elbow.

"He'p you, pretty lady?"

She jumped and whirled to face the sound.

A short, bandy-legged man of about sixty or so stood on the ground, at the end of one of the wagons. Celina blinked. Behind him, up on the side of the hill in the shade, ten or more men lay sprawled, resting. She had come close to walking right past without seeing them. Sudden cold touched her and she shivered. Somebody walking over your grave, her old nurse had called it.

The little man stood still, staring at her through slitted eyes.

"Yes," Celina said, forcing her voice to sound firm. "I need to talk with the men who hauled logs to the C and G Railroad yesterday."

"What about?"

"The load they took. May I see them, please?"

He appeared to consider the question for an interminable time. "You're lookin' at one of 'em," he said.

"I'm Celina Hawthorne," she said. "Attorney for Mr. Kingfisher Chekote of the C and G."

He answered with a slow nod.

Finally she said, "What is your name?"

After another long wait he replied, "Jack Gowan."

"Well, Mr. Gowan, it seems that there were some stolen logs mixed in with the ones Mr. Chekote had bought that you took out to the railroad site. Did you oversee the loading yourself?"

Again the slow nod. "No stolen logs. I haul only what Chekote order."

He was lying. Some thin thread of deception ran through the words. Celina's heart leaped. If she could beg or force or trick this little man into telling the truth, she could set King free.

But ten full minutes of questioning got her no other answer than that. Reluctantly Jack pointed out two other men who had been his helpers on that load and they came slowly down off the hillside.

As she expected, the replies were the same. Jack translated the questions and replies, since he insisted that they spoke no English, so Celina didn't spend much time with them. Jack Gowan could tell her anything, and Jack Gowan was lying.

Celina trudged through the late-slanting sunlight back to Aunt Fee's. She must go to King and get more information so she could take another tack. But she couldn't bear to face him yet—not when she had nothing to report but running into a brick wall.

At least she did have the names of the freight yard employees. Aunt Fee could send a trustworthy interpreter to talk with them away from the job.

She heard the commotion inside the boarding-house before she even got up on the porch.

"Deliberate lies, I tell you!" Fee was shouting. "No one is going to believe it!"

Lacey answered, but Celina couldn't make out the words. She sounded as if she were crying.

They and Dolores were in the front parlor. Lacey *was* crying; Dolores, her face pale, was trying to comfort her, and Aunt Fee was pacing the floor, absolutely furious.

"Celina!" she said, pouncing on her niece in the doorway. "I want you to file a lawsuit against Donald McIntosh and Renny Fourkiller and the rest of the lying nitwits that are spreading these awful rumors. Sue them—every one of them!"

Celina took off her hat and brushed at the dust she knew must be clinging to her face.

"What rumors, Aunt Fee?"

"It's already all over town and half the Nation that Ridge is the one who framed King. That he swore to stop the railroad and that now he's done it."

"But how could anyone believe that Ridge would want to see his own son in jail?"

"They say Ridge Chekote would rather his son be branded a thief than a traitor."

Celina threw her hat onto the round arm of the sofa. "But that doesn't even make sense! He's being branded both right now!"

"None of it makes sense!" Fee snapped, suddenly crossing the room to put her arms around Lacey. "If I could just get my hands on those monsters!"

Lacey wiped her eyes and looked at Celina over Fee's shoulder. "You'll prove that they're innocent, won't you, dear? Both King and Ridge? Oh, Celina, you have to be able to do it!"

* * *

King heard the rumors, too. He lay on his bunk with his arms crossed behind his head and listened to the guards and the other prisoners speaking in the soft syllables of the Cherokee language, peaceful sounds like that of water bubbling over stones in a stream, telling hard, troubling things.

His father plotted this to stop the railroad, they said. That railroad would be the destruction of the Nation, they said. Think of the white men who would come pouring in. Ridge Chekote was a proud man, they said. And his son had defied him in front of his friends. Ridge had many friends.

King thought about that. Ridge did have many friends. Mixed-blood friends, full-blood friends. Friends who would die for him. Friends who had already been hurt by the railroad, or thought that they had.

King shifted his hips on the hard cot, uncrossed his feet and crossed them again the other way. He closed his eyes and clenched his teeth until his jaws hurt.

Everyone, Celina included, thought he was heartless, he knew. They had watched him push on, in the face of Lacey's trembling, worried frown and Ridge's angry hurt and the arguments that had torn the family apart, and they had thought him made of iron and steel like the engines and the rails.

But it wasn't true. He was flesh and blood and he was heartsore. Every one of those sad happenings caused by the railroad had been a bruising blow to his spirit. He had hurt over them, hurt deep.

The worst of those hurts had come from Celina. Why couldn't she have understood and stuck by him? After all, she had encouraged him to come.

And now! Now what would he give for some personal sign of worry from her, some indication that she was trying to get him freed because she cared about him? But, even knowing that he was on his way to jail, she hadn't said one comforting word, hadn't signaled her concern with the tiniest touch on the hand or the arm.

She had rushed away, already caught up in building the legal case, on his side again, but not because she loved him. No. Because this could be a boon to her law practice, another victory feather in her professional cap. She would enjoy it, would love digging into Cherokee law just as she had the intricacies of the old Spanish land grants.

In spite of the fact that she didn't love him back, though, he hated to drag her into this mess, for a truly nasty mess was what it promised to be.

The thought stung his muscles into action. He sprang up and began pacing the sides of his cell, first one way and then the other. Was there anything he could've done to foresee or prevent this arrest? Nothing short of stopping work on the railroad, or delaying it as Celina had asked.

But Ridge had given him no choice. There had been literally nothing else he could've done but forge on.

No matter. Ridge wouldn't have done this to him. He wouldn't have conspired against his oldest son, nor let any of his diehard friends do it.

Would he?

Chapter 18

Moonlight limned the rough-cut stones of the National Jail and threw the shadows of its high board fence long across the yard. The double gate swung shut behind Celina with a creak. The guard who had let her in led the way toward the stark building.

So far, so good.

"I wasn't sure that the . . . prisoners could have visitors this late," she said. "But I really need to see Mr. Chekote."

The man shrugged, as if to say that it mattered little to him. She followed him up the steps, into a small vestibule, then off it into a bare waiting room. He left her there and, in a matter of minutes, he came back with King.

"Leave us, man," King said. The guard went out and closed the door. King's eyes had never left Celina's. "Did you talk to Gowan? What'd you find?"

"He's lying," she said, stepping suddenly to the rickety table and chair in the middle of the room. She had to sit down. Her legs wouldn't hold her.

If King would touch her, would even smile at her, this horrible burden would be easier to bear.

But he was driven.

"How d'you know he's lying?"

She told him every word of the interview with

306

Jack Gowan and assured him that Ridge was going to personally talk to the two employees in Cherokee.

He frowned. "Rumor has it that this plot is his."

That brought her to her feet. "You can't believe that, King! Your father is absolutely beside himself."

He turned away and strode to the black rectangle of the window.

"You don't really think Ridge would do such a thing, do you?"

His shoulders slumped. "No. I don't. But he did swear to stop the railroad and I can't think of anybody else who would go to such lengths."

"Why, half the Nation, at least!"

He whirled to face her. "No, this is different."

If only he would say her name. Just that. Just "Celina."

" 'Half the Nation' will tear up the track and intimidate my crew," he said. "They'll start rumors of white invasion and run off game and kill cattle and blame it all on the railroad. But I can't think who would do *this*."

She sighed. "So much destruction."

He looked disgusted. "That's the price for refusing to see that assimilation is inevitable."

"But it's still a few years into the future," she said quickly. "King, listen to this."

His face hardened, as if he already knew and resented what she would say, but he tilted his head to one side and waited.

"The Bushyheads decided to give up their good farm and move to the flint hills to get away from the railroad," she said. "The Deer-in-the-water brothers almost killed each other today over Moses's working for you, and several other fights broke out on the square when people started taking sides." Just remembering that horrible time made her legs tremble. She dropped back down into the cane-bottomed chair.

For a fleeting moment, raw hurt showed in King's eyes. He waited.

"And Jessee made such a spectacle of her concern for Blue Hawk that if your arrest hadn't distracted your parents, she'd be on her way back to River's Bend right now in disgrace. She'd be locked in her room until she reached twenty."

"So?" he demanded. "Do you have any other good news to bring me?"

"What I'm trying to say, King, is that maybe you should think about holding the permits for a while and postpone the actual building of the lines. That would still keep the other companies out and it would give the people time to get used to the idea."

His jaw went slack. Then he snapped it shut and the muscle knotted along the bone. He stalked toward her.

"Let me get this straight," he drawled, his voice so low it was dangerous. "You *are* the same Celina Hawthorne who urged me to fulfill my lifelong dream of building railroads in the Cherokee Nation, are you not? You *are* my attorney who begged me for a chance to start your career as my personal lawyer? Have you changed your mind? Whose side are you on?"

"Yours! As your attorney I'm thinking that if you announce tomorrow that you're postponing your plans for the C and G, whoever's behind this plot will let the whole thing drop."

She got up and went to meet him. They stood in the middle of the barren room, in the circle of light from its one small lamp, and stared into each other's eyes.

"You'll go free, we'll have time to find out what this is all about, and your family and the Cherokee Nation, which I have grown to love, will have time to work out a way to stay in one piece and still accept your railroad.''

He took her by the shoulders, but his touch was not gentle. ''What are you talking about! I'd be giving up—letting them win!''

''No! You wouldn't be quitting. You'd just be postponing—''

His fingers dug into her flesh. ''I won't postpone one mile of that track! I'll drive the C and G through right on schedule no matter who moves to the hills or bashes his brother's brains in! None of that is any of my business. The railroad is!''

Celina ground out the words between her teeth. ''How can you be so utterly selfish?''

He let go of her so fast she almost tumbled backward.

''Ha!'' he yelled. ''That's the crow calling the raven black!''

She staggered back into the table; she reached behind her to hold on to it with both hands.

''You are more selfish than I am, Celina. You're suggesting this so you can be looked up to by the whole Nation as a famous peacemaker, a crafty diplomat.''

''No! I am not!''

''You've come up with this cockeyed notion because you don't have the slightest idea how to get to the bottom of this plot and get me out of here,'' he said. ''And you can't bear to be seen as a failure.''

''Not true! I feel sorry for—''

He ranted on as if she'd never spoken. ''And the reason you can't bear to fail,'' he chanted, ''is that you want only one thing in this world, Miss Celina, and the rest of us be damned. You want Eli Hawthorne's praise.''

Celina never could remember how she got out of the jail that night and back to Aunt Fee's. But she

didn't forget for one instant what King had said.
The hateful words were engraved in the stone that
used to be her heart.

King didn't love her! It was truly amazing how
much more that hurt now that she knew she loved
him.

During the next few days she questioned so many
people that it seemed she had talked to everyone in
the Nation. Her voice grew raspy and hoarse, her
head—and her heart—constantly ached.

Judge Adair returned to Tahlequah and she went
to see him, but, in spite of every argument she made
that this had to be a conspiracy, his decision was
that the evidence warranted a trial for King. He set
the date for October 7, a week away.

King grew more agitated every time she saw him,
and so did she. The long nights and days in jail filled
him with a bitter frenzy to be free. His restless pacing never let up, and every time she visited him in
the tiny room he looked out the window so desperately that she thought he would surely hurl himself
through it.

Some instinct told her to grab him, to hold him
still and shout that she loved him until he went quiet
in her arms. And that urge filled her with a confusion of pain as racking as the agony torturing him.

She borrowed a gig from Aunt Fee and asked William to drive it so she wouldn't have that to distract
her. They drove so many miles that they changed
horses twice each day. But they accomplished nothing.

The freighters were lying. Pure instinct and Jack
Gowan's small, sly voice had told her that the first
time they'd met. But on two subsequent visits all
their answers had been the same as on the first.

And they had been identical when they talked to
Ridge in Cherokee.

Each time she questioned them, Celina had then

followed the trail of the logs back from the freight wagon to the place where they were cut. Here, at least, on the twenty acres of hardwood timber that was part of Old Man Kell Rabbit's farm, she received longer, more detailed answers to every question each time she asked it. There must be progress in that.

"We talk many things, me and Kingfisher Chekote," Kell Rabbit said, on her second visit. "He say I have good timber, like all such timber on the Bald Knob Mountain. He say cut one wagon load every day for a week, he send freighters to haul it."

"Did you hire someone to cut the timber, Mr. Rabbit?"

"Yes," he said, as he had on her first trip to see him.

But this time he grinned and added slyly, "You think Old Rabbit still strong and do it himself?"

Celina grinned back at him. "I think you probably could," she flattered him. Then she asked, as she had done on her first visit, "Whom did you hire, Mr. Rabbit?"

That first time the question had met with a stubborn silence. William had drawn her aside and explained that Rabbit might see giving the names as some sort of betrayal of the men he had hired.

Celina had then gone back to the old man and explained that the men wouldn't get into any trouble with the law if they had done an honest job. But still he refused to answer.

This time, though, he shocked her by giving the immediate answer, "James Oostenacah and Ned Crawler."

Elated with the seeming breakthrough, she and William had traced the two men to their isolated cabins farther up in the hills of the Goingsnake District.

But the interviews were completely disappointing. Oostenacah and Crawler knew nothing of any shady dealings, they said. They had cut Rabbit's timber as he had hired them to do and had left it piled for the freighters. That was all.

Later in the day Celina went back to surprise them, but their bland, closed faces and their stories never changed.

The next day she took another tack. She'd lain awake half the night going over and over again in her memory the scene in the courthouse following King's arrest. King kept insisting that Dothan McKisick had to be involved.

The man certainly had acted shifty enough, but the whole family said that was his normal behavior. They all thought King was right, though, because McKisick was known to be dishonest and the office of District Solicitor offered innumerable opportunities for him to satisfy his greed.

Ridge was surprised to hear that the Nation was marking logs for the bridge work, but it certainly wasn't a matter important enough to have been mentioned in a Council meeting. Neither was the actual building of the bridges—there was a committee, which included two of McKisick's cousins, to make the decisions on such matters.

Aunt Fee and Ridge sent out feelers all over town and Celina and William questioned hangers-on around the courthouse and the freight yards, but there was no visible connection, anywhere, between the solicitor and the marked logs.

By late in the week Celina hated walking through the gate of the high palisade fence that surrounded the jail every evening and telling King that she had found nothing to use in his defense more than she had ever hated anything in her life.

Finally, two days before the trial, she decided that she couldn't face him again unless she had some scrap of comfort to offer. "You can come to supper at Aunt Fee's tomorrow night," she told him as soon

as the guard had brought him into the visitors' room.
"I went to see the sheriff and the judge today."

King stopped in his tracks, halfway from the door
to the rough table where she stood. "To supper?"

"Yes! Aren't you glad? The sheriff said that to
keep McKisick off his back he'll have to send a couple of guards with you, but you can stay all evening."

He finished crossing the room in three long strides
and leaned both hands on the table to face her.
"How kind of him! Did you and sheriff also plan
the menu for my last meal? I thought it was the cus-
tom to let the condemned himself do that."

"Your last meal? King, don't be ridiculous. The
death penalty wouldn't be invoked if you were convicted, but you won't be—as soon as the trial's over,
you'll be a free man!"

"How so, Celina?"

His face was still and set. His voice was so quiet
it made her skin crawl.

"King!" Impulsively she reached for his hand.

He wouldn't give it.

The air in the room was so hot and close there
wasn't a deep breath left in it.

"Have you found proof that anybody involved in
this whole miserable mess is lying? Do you know
who marked those logs and put them in that load?
Do you have even a theory as to why that mysterious person did such a thing?"

She could not meet the misery in his eyes. Her
gaze dropped to the tabletop. His fingertips had
gone bone-white clutching at it.

"Well?"

"No," she said.

"Then get me a paper and pencil and let me write
out what I want to eat," he said. "You and Fee and
Mama had better start cooking."

Her eyes whipped up to meet his. "So you're

sending me back to the kitchen, are you?" she said. "Where a woman ought to be? Well, you'd better know, King, that I'm doing everything humanly possible to clear your name. Nobody—I'm telling you, nobody—could do more than I've done."

"Then it really is hopeless, isn't it?"

"Don't say that!" she screamed, slapping her hand flat on the table. Dust flew up into their faces. "We're going to win! I'll . . . I'll break somebody down in court."

"Of course you will, Celina. Of course you will."

His sarcasm created a hard knot of pain in her throat. When she swallowed it tasted bitter as gall.

She turned and walked out of the room.

The next evening, as Fee and Lacey fluttered all up and down the shaded side porch, putting the finishing touches on the long tables loaded with food and making sure that there were plenty of places to sit down and eat, Ridge paced the length, and then the width, of the yard like a restless cat. Like his jailed son.

Celina stood in the corner and looked out through the climbing clematis vines, watching for King. Surely he would come, no matter how horrible it would be to stay only a few hours and then go back to the jail for one last night.

It would be one last night, wouldn't it? Please, God?

By tomorrow morning the time would be up. She had only a few hours left to find the key to this whole crazy puzzle. She took a long, deep breath and leaned her forehead against the painted post.

"Tired, Daughter?"

Celina whirled to see Eli dragging one of the ladderback chairs over to the wall. His glasses caught the low sunlight and winked at her.

"A little bit," she said cautiously.

He sat down and leaned the chair back onto two legs, propping it, very carefully, against the house.

"You're working too hard," he said.

Celina didn't answer. She was still listening to his words in her head, trying to gauge the meaning of his tone.

"It'll be a good lesson for you," he went on thoughtfully, as if he were talking to himself.

"What will, Father?"

"Attempting to analyze information. Questioning witnesses. Trying to prepare a case without anyone to guide you."

"You might recall that I've done so before," she snapped. "I've even won a very difficult case with no one to guide me."

"Beginner's luck," he said. "Chekote chicanery. This time you'll see."

"See what?"

"How the world really is."

Celina stared at him for a long time, but he folded his lips closed over the cryptic remark and made no effort to meet her eyes again. For a second she could hardly breathe. The air here on this open porch seemed as thin and close as that in the jail last night. Far away, behind the hills to the west, thunder rumbled.

Dolores came to stand beside her. "It is so hot, tonight, darling," she said, fanning both of them with a folding silk fan. "Why don't you come out from hiding in this corner?"

Because I'm afraid for King to come, Mama. I can't look him in the face. Because I'm failing him. And he's failing me. He doesn't believe in me, after all, and he doesn't love me. Worst of all, Mama, he doesn't love me.

They went to sit in the rocking chairs beside Jessee. But the girl's eyes, like Celina's, kept straying to the street in spite of Dolores's attempts to start a conversation. Finally the three of them sat silent, rocking faster to catch the breeze.

It had begun to rise almost cool out of the still, slow heat of the day, Celina realized suddenly. From the west. Again it brought the sound of the grumbling thunder.

Maybe it was a good omen. Maybe Thunder would help her save King.

"I hope it'll rain and break this heat," Lacey said, walking to the top of the steps to look down the hill toward the jail. "I wish it would."

Ridge, pacing the opposite direction, grunted agreement.

"I wish it'd storm like it's never stormed before," Jessee said. "Then maybe everything would change."

Just then the children set up a cry of "King! Here comes King!" and they ran down the steps to meet him. Two Lighthorse walked behind, but they stayed in the yard when King came up on the porch.

Laura was clinging to one leg and Aunt Fee's youngest, Jeremy, to the other; Jessee and Lacey went to hug him. He held out his arms and bent his head over them; he didn't even look at Celina.

She got up and walked to the porch rail, looking out to the purple-gray clouds beginning to boil in the western sky. They were the same colors as the hills, held the same tumult as her riotous heart.

Aunt Fee and Ridge and the others greeted King. They all chattered at him at once, at first sympathetic, then falsely encouraging. King's voice sounded tight, barely under control.

Finally, after what seemed an age, he appeared at her elbow.

"I want you to know that I don't blame you for anything, Celina," he said. "Don't beat yourself— an outsider can't be expected to get to the bottom of something like this. If Ridge is telling the truth, *he* can't penetrate the scheme, even with his connections.''

She gave him one quick glance, then lifted her face back to the breeze, fresh now with the smell of rain. But she couldn't keep her feelings silent as she would have done three months ago. As it had from their beginning, the honesty in him unlocked the truth in her.

"I can't believe you're giving up," she said. "I hate it when you don't trust me. That's all." But why should he trust her? He was going back to jail tonight, wasn't he?

She had no idea why she'd said such a thing. Except that King's native self-assurance had always imposed some order on the world. Now there was none.

"Kingfisher," Ridge boomed, right behind them. "I need to talk with you, son."

"Let him eat first," Fee cried, but Ridge took King's arm and drew him away to the opposite corner.

Celina caught snatches of his conversation: ''. . . give up the permits . . .'' and ''. . . half the Nation thinks . . .'' In a moment, King impatiently broke away, leaving Ridge glowering where he stood.

Fee and Lacey brought King to the table to fill his plate, clucking over his hardships, saying that he must be starved. He tried to be enthusiastic, but Celina could see his indifference to the food.

And to everything else except what was going on inside him. Both his tall, hard body and his rugged face were thinner, more finely drawn, from the fire that burned in his belly. Now it was eating him alive. He would go crazy if he had to stay in prison. How, how could she get him out?

Fee and Lacey sent plates to the men in the yard, and then made sure everyone else came forward to serve their own. They held them in their laps and ate sitting, scattered in chairs and on the steps all along the length of the porch, talking peacefully enough, although they couldn't seem to keep any conversation going except one relating to jail or court or what was likely to happen tomorrow.

The wind picked up steadily, bending and cracking the trees' branches and sending miniature tornadoes of dust twirling on their toes in the street. The thunder grew stronger by the minute and trembling-fast lightning shot back and forth from sky to earth.

Jessee almost burst into tears, and Laura did so, when somebody mentioned that King really ought to go back before the storm broke and drenched him to the skin. Fee started to send Dan, her oldest, to hitch up the gig, but King curtly countermanded the order.

He got up and tensed his long legs. "I'll need the walk tonight," he said.

"And the drenching," Ridge said to him irritably. "Maybe a good driving rain could drum some sense into you. All you have to do to stop this charade is to announce you're giving up building that confounded railroad."

King whirled on him like a stag at bay. "How do you know that?" he roared. "Because it's your old-fashioned friends who have framed me? Did you instigate this whole plot just to stop the railroad, the way everybody's saying you did?"

The blood drained out of Ridge's face as fast as if the word had been a knife stabbed into his vein. "No!" he choked. "No! How could you think . . ."

From the corner of the porch where Eli sat floated a tiny sound of amusement, but Ridge and King were too caught up in the moment to hear it. Lightning cracked, just outside the yard, etching rage into the two men's faces with one sickening yellow stroke. Then came the sullen thunder.

Lacey, her own face a ghastly white, appeared out of the shadows to stand beside Ridge. At the same time she reached out for King.

His face broke Celina's heart. The fury and frustration filling him struggled with his love for his father and hope. Hope that his father loved him, too.

Instinctively she moved toward him. *She* loved him. Would it help this misery if he knew that?

King turned and, in one long stride, was halfway down the steps.

Celina ran after him, clutching her skirts in her trembling fingers, stumbling, fighting the tears. "King!" she cried. "Wait!"

He stopped in the middle of the path. She caught his arm and he swung around to face her.

"King, I . . ." But she couldn't say it. How could she speak of love now?

He was looking right through her—his mind was on Ridge and jail and this horrible mess he was in.

"Ridge didn't do it, King!" she cried. "Look at his face and you'll know that it's true."

He tried to jerk away, but she held on, her feet lifting off the ground. "Listen to me! Think for a minute, just *think*. It isn't too late! Old Man Rabbit said that you mentioned the timber on Bald Knob Mountain where the marked logs came from—"

Lightning flashed again. This time it stripped King's face down to pure, naked rage. He grabbed her shoulders with both his huge hands. *"I* mentioned the timber on Bald Knob Mountain? Where the marked logs came from?" His eyes blazed a hole in her. "So. You've decided that I'm guilty!"

She stared back at him, robbed of her powers of speech by the shock of his accusation.

"I hate it when you don't trust me," he mimicked her.

"No!" The word burst out of her like a bullet.

"No, that's insane! I trust you. I love you! King, I love you!"

"You'll never find love," he said, his tone low and menacing. "Because you are totally incapable of it. If you don't trust me by now, you can't trust anybody enough to learn what love is." He turned her loose and spun on his heel.

She stood exactly where he left her, with her shoulders frozen still.

He whirled back to her. "You're not worth the fight I've had to make," he said. "I can see that now."

Then his head swung from side to side, his eyes flashing, trying to pierce the shadows. "All right!" he roared into the lowering night. "Ha! You flunkies of McKisick's! If you're going back to jail with me, get out here now!"

Chapter 19

The storm broke over their heads. Celina stood in the pelting rain until King had been gone for a long time, but she didn't see him go. She could see nothing but his accusing face in the baleful glare of the lightning.

Finally she let them lead her back up the steps and onto the porch. She walked into its corner and stood hugging the wooden post, holding her face up to the fierce onslaught of the wind as if begging it to take her and blow the world away.

"Honey, you've got to come in!" Aunt Fee shouted, her voice shrill beneath the sound of the thunder. "You'll catch your death out here!" She put her arms around her niece and tried to lead her away from the chill, driving rain, and Dolores, Jessee, and Lacey all begged her to come.

But Celina wouldn't move. Finally Dolores convinced the others to leave her alone.

It stormed all night. The huge elm and hackberry trees bent and swayed, old limbs thick as a man's waist cracked beneath the swirling force of the storm. Leaves lashed the yard and the house like tiny, slapping hands, and the earth shook under the wrathful thunder.

Thunder was her friend; the lightning and the wind and the roaring rain were her confederates. They would snatch her from this misery into the

whirling vortex of the storm and carry her, screaming, into another world.

But morning brought a lessening of the rain, and
then a stopping. It found Celina huddled into one
of the wide wicker armchairs, still on Aunt Fee's
side porch.

When the sun came up far enough to turn the
black of the wet tree trunks to a sleek, golden brown,
she got up and went to her room.

This was the day. The day of King's trial.

She opened one curtain, then stood in front of her
mirror and stared, amazed that her face looked the
same. For a long, long time she looked into her own
shadowy eyes. Then she tiptoed around the bed
where Jessee was sleeping and opened the armoire
to take out fresh clothes. She had no choice.

She would go to the courthouse now and go over
every word of the sworn depositions again. She
would find the key to make the liars tell the truth.

She would free King. She would clear his name.

And afterward she would tell him again that she
loved him. This time she would make him respond
to it. Then she would find out whether or not she
was forever too late.

As Celina hurried down the walk to Aunt Fee's
front gate, she heard the door behind her open and
close. She didn't turn around; company was exactly
what she didn't need right now.

"Celina!"

Reluctantly, she turned. Ridge strode toward her,
his bootheels ringing loud on the wooden planks.

"Are you ready?" he asked, only pausing beside
her, urging her with every line of his body to come
on, to move toward the courthouse and King.

"I have to be ready, don't I?" she said, bitterly.
Then she sighed and walked on beside him, trying
to match his long strides. "There's no more time."

He nodded brusquely, and they hurried along in

silence then, taking the east side of the road from Fee's downhill toward the square. Blue-black clouds were thickening again in the southwest, separating at the edges, then re-forming, stringing fast across the sky, whipped by the wind that changed every minute from north to south and back again.

"Mother and Lacey and the others had better bring their umbrellas," Celina said. "I don't see how it could rain any more, but I think it's going to."

Ridge gave her an absent smile, obviously trying to force his mind onto the spoken words. "You're becoming a weather prophet," he said. "Next you'll be studying to be a shaman."

Celina smiled, too, but she gave up trying to make conversation and let her mind rush back to the depositions. She and Ridge were crossing the street to the square before she realized they'd come that far, then a crush of people closed around them. The whole Nation must have turned out for the trial.

Ridge took her arm to guide her through the crowd. They were halfway up the walk to the door when he stopped short and looked around him.

"What is it?" Celina asked. "I'm in a hurry . . ."

"Wait a minute." He let go of her arm and smoothed a crumpled scrap of paper out in his palm.

"What's that? Where'd it come from?"

"Somebody just shoved it into my hand."

Celina looked around, too, but the dozen faces that surrounded her and Ridge all feigned polite disinterest as soon as their eyes met hers. Her gaze flew back to the paper.

It appeared to be a note, written in pencil, in Cherokee, the symbols from the syllabary smudged by rough treatment.

"Is it about King?" she asked, thoroughly frustrated that she couldn't read it. Ridge's eyes were racing from line to line. "Ridge!" she begged. "Is it about the trial?"

He took her arm again, in a grip so hard it hurt, and pulled her out of the knot of people around them, edging quickly to a spot against the building. Turning his back to the others, he read in a tone just above a whisper:

"Now! Friend Chekote, I just wrote you a few lines today. Do not trouble yourself. I know who marked the logs and I heard their talk.

"If need be, I will come out of the hills to tell it in court, for you have all the time called me friend.

"Now! If it has become necessary, send word to me. My lookouts cover the hills. The code word is wa-coo-lee.

"I, Ned Christie

"I greet you, Ridge Chekote."

Celina clapped her hand over her mouth to suppress a cry of joy. "That's wonderful!" she said, forcing herself to speak quietly. "Send word to him, quickly!"

Ridge was silent.

Celina touched his arm. "Ridge! Isn't Ned Christie an outlaw?"

"Yes," he said thoughtfully. He raised his eyes from the paper, but they looked right past her. "Ned is an outlaw, but he is also an old friend of mine; he used to serve on the National Council with me. He's the last person on earth I would've expected to hear from today."

"Would he really come if you asked him?"

"Of course he would, or he would never have sent this note. For his sake, though, I sure hate to ask it."

"Because he'd be putting his own freedom in danger?"

"He'd be putting his *life* in danger if anybody who arrested him took him to Fort Smith. He's wanted for killing a lawman from there, though I've never believed he did it." His words were solemn, but his face glowed with the same hope that had leapt to life in her heart.

"Are you going to send for him?" she asked.

"Can you free King without him?" he shot back.

Startled, she stared at him for a moment. Finally she said, honestly, "I don't know."

He reached into his pocket and took out a match. He struck it with his thumbnail and made sure the paper had started to burn before he looked at her again. His eyes held a flame like the one eating up the paper in his fingers, the twin of the one she felt burning in her own eyes.

"My legs ache to run, to find Ned Christie and bring him back here," he said. "But if King walks into that courtroom a few minutes from now, looks out at all those faces and doesn't find his father's among them . . ."

He stopped and swallowed hard. "I can't bear to think of how the boy would feel. He might even take my absence as proof that I had, indeed, conspired against him."

"Then send someone," she murmured.

"It would have to be someone I can trust with Ned's life," he said slowly. Then he dropped the burning ashes and ground them under his heel. "Jessee," he said. "I'll send Jessee."

Without another word he turned and left her. A sudden shaft of lightning slashed at the square.

Celina began King's defense with a review of his reputation, both business and personal, using character witnesses to testify to the truth of the claims she made.

The five-man jury seemed impressed in her favor, if one could judge by one smile, a couple of nods, and a stray wink. They listened to every word, and so did the audience, packed into the long oak benches so tightly they hardly could breathe. Except for her voice, there was no noise, no movement in the big room.

One reason for the extreme quiet inside was the intensity of the storm outside the room. It had unleashed itself against the windows before the judge was ushered to his bench, and throughout the presentation of the prosecution's case against King and the beginning of Celina's defense of him, the wind howled around the edges of the corner room and raindrops and hailstones hurled themselves at the tall, narrow panes of glass.

It was a good omen, Celina kept telling herself, remembering King's smile and his whispered, "Friends of Thunder" during that other, faraway trial that had seemed so fateful at the time. Little did they know then that it could be King's freedom at stake instead of merely his fortune—she wouldn't let herself even consider that it might be his life—and little did they know that their joking companionship of that time could turn into passion, and now, into sickening silence.

King sat sullen beside her at the table provided for the defense. He had barely acknowledged her presence when the guards brought him in from the jail and he hadn't met her gaze since. She had felt his eyes on her, though, when she was on her feet and speaking.

She took a drink of water and tried not to let his sullenness distract her. But her eyes strayed to his long, brown hands, rolling and then stopping a pencil on the polished top of the table. For one piercing instant she could feel that same deft touch on her skin.

Celina ducked her head and forced herself to look at the stack of depositions on the table between them. Choose one, any one, to begin the cross-examination of the prosecution's witnesses, she thought. All of them were lying.

Except perhaps for Old Man Rabbit and his hirelings, but his testimony would be damaging, too, if he mentioned King's interest in the Bald Knob Mountain timber. A racing despair chilled her veins.

She had to have proof, substantial proof, of King's innocence, and it was perfectly clear, as it had been since the very beginning, that the only way to get it was to force the guilty parties to confess. Ned Christie could never arrive in time to help her do that.

Celina picked up the whole stack of dog-eared depositions and stared, unseeing, at the judge's bench. Searching through the papers again, she found the one she wanted and brought it to the top of the stack, tapping the pages against the table to even them.

"Jack Gowan," she said.

She leaned close to King. "That bandy-legged little man knows you're innocent," she whispered. "And I'm going to make him tell it."

King shot her a surprised look.

She looked back, as surprised as he that she'd made such a brag. Maybe painting herself into such a corner would give her the inspiration she needed. She shrugged and stood up.

Jack Gowan took the stand and the oath, then sat down and looked at Celina with his usual secretive squint. The room became deathly silent again, as if everyone in it knew that Celina was desperate. The storm had stopped, probably for good this time. Sunlight poured in through the tall, arched windows and fell across Gowan's broad face.

Celina got up and walked out from behind the table, his deposition in her hand. "Mr. Gowan, I have here your sworn testimony, signed with your mark, that you hauled a load of logs to the construction site of the C and G Railroad on September twenty-nine, of this year. Is that correct?"

He stared at her for an age, then muttered, "Yes."

In that same, slow fashion they went back over every question in the deposition, questions she had already asked the man at least three times. This time, though, when she came to the subject of the marked logs, she had a sudden flash of inspiration; she knew what she should do: She would pretend that Ned could get here in time. Threatening Gowan with an unknown secret witness might break him down.

"Mr. Gowan, you realize you can be punished for not telling the truth under oath," she said. "If you knew that I had a witness to testify that he saw you drive directly from Old Man Rabbit's place to the timber cuttings up on Bald Knob Mountain, would you want to change anything you've told me earlier?"

She lifted the paper she held and tapped it thoughtfully against her other hand. "If this witness would testify that you and your men were seen stealing some logs from there and adding them to the ones Mr. Chekote bought from Mr. Rabbit, would you want to change the story you swore to in this paper?"

Gowan's slow gaze went to somewhere in the audience, then came back to Celina. He opened his mouth. He hesitated.

She stepped closer to him. "Under Cherokee Law, Mr. Gowan, you could be publicly whipped for lying in court."

There was still no response.

"Was this your plan to discredit Mr. Chekote and his railroad?" she asked sternly. "Have you begun stealing from your fellow Cherokee and lying to them in court so that you can keep out competition for your freight company?"

"No!"

"I think perhaps you have, Mr. Gowan. I think you're more worried about your own pocketbook than about the good of the Cherokee Nation."

He rose halfway out of his chair, one hand still clutching its arm. "No!" he shouted again. "He hired me to do it. Every bit of the plottin', he done it."

"Who did it, Mr. Gowan?"

"He never said his name," he declared, pointing into the audience. "But it's that old man right there!"

Celina whirled around. Gowan's shaking finger was leveled straight at Eli.

Eli's face lost its smugness fast, as if Gowan had wiped it away with a wet cloth. He leapt to his feet.

"That's a lie!" he shouted. "It's one old man's word against another's!"

"No, it ain't!" yelled the young, heavyset man who worked for Jack Gowan. "I'll back Jack up and I'll swear to it."

Someone else said, "Me, too. Jack ain't lying."

Eli shifted his gaze from Gowan to McKisick, who was on his feet now behind the prosecutor's table. "I paid you good money to take care of this," Eli said clearly, in that tone of barely suppressed hatred that Celina knew so well. "All of it. But I should've known better. Even as a boy, you always were too dumb to talk to, much less to trust with a scheme like this."

Pandemonium broke out. Half the audience was on its feet—everyone in the room, it seemed, was talking or laughing or calling to someone else. The judge lifted his gavel and brought it down with an earsplitting bang.

"Dismissed!" he shouted. "The case against Kingfisher Chekote is herewith dismissed!"

Celina stood rooted to the floor, looking from King's relieved face to Eli's sneering one. Could this actually be true? Had she really heard the words she thought she did? Was it Father who had done this? She should have known. This diabolical scheme to ruin King was typical of Eli. And he would never, ever be any different.

The tiny hope for love and acceptance in the deepest corner of her heart, battered and fragile, but still as old as she was, shattered into shards.

The double doors to the hallway flew open and children's frantic shrieks pierced, then quieted, the cacophony of the room.

"Mama! Papa!" The voice was Laura's.

Three or four other children, all with sweat pouring off their faces and fear darkening their eyes, came with her. The adults standing in the back of the room stepped apart to let them in.

A boy about Laura's age pushed into the room ahead of her. "The bad man sent me to say this," he shouted, gasping for breath. "He said, 'Send out Ned Christie from the courthouse or I'll drop the girl into the creek!'"

Laura climbed up on the back of the last bench, brushing her hair out of her huge hazel eyes so she could search the crowd. "Papa!" she cried. "Where are you? It's Jessee! The bad man has Jessee!"

"Here!" Ridge roared from his place at the front of the room. "Let me out of here!"

The crowd rolled before him like a wave of water; in an instant the room was empty. Celina ran behind and then beside Lacey—King and Ridge left them, somehow making headway through the mass of people. She had to hold on to Lacey, who could hardly see through the tears in her eyes. She was gasping for breath so she could shout questions at Celina. "How did some bad man get Jessee?" she demanded. "Jessee said she would come to the trial a few minutes after I did. Where did she go?"

Celina explained as they ran, keeping her eyes straight ahead, not only to find a safe path for them, but to avoid the horrified terror in Lacey's eyes.

The children led the whole crowd out of the square

and up the middle of the street, north along the hill. At the top of its first slope they veered to the left to run down again, toward the creek. Across the water, rushing over the rocky bed in a torrent after the storm, the rough cliffs gleamed wet in the new sunshine. The little boy in the lead stopped and pointed at them.

The sight drew a convulsive gasp from every throat. Celina stopped in her tracks. Lacey froze beside her.

Across the swollen stream, high on the stony bluff, Jessee dangled, helpless.

Her arms flailed, reaching desperately for a tree or an outcropping boulder to catch on to. But the only support within reach was a smooth, upthrusting rock and her burly captor had hold of it. He encircled it with one arm while he held her out over empty space with the other.

All he had to do was open his fingers from around her belt and she'd go crashing to the rocky creekbed below.

The man's massive head swung toward the crowd. He wore a battered hat, but he was much too far away for anyone to see his face. "Send out Ned Christie," he bellowed. "If you don't wanta see this little gal splatter at yore feet."

Sheriff Fourkiller shouted back, "Ned Christie's nowhere around here. What're you talking about? Who are you, anyway?"

"Red Flannery, bounty hunter out of Fort Smith!" the man yelled. "I aim to have the price that's on Christie's head."

"Christie's hid, up in the hills. Everybody knows that."

"Not right now, he ain't," the man replied. "This here young'un talked to one of his lookouts that I've been watchin'. The Injun said Christie was done gone to the courthouse."

"Well, he's not," the sheriff yelled.

"You think I won't drop her?"

"No need for that," the sheriff said, and Celina marveled at the calm tone of his voice. "Let her go safe and I'll give you an escort back to Fort Smith."

"No need for *that*," Flannery mocked him.

Jessee kicked. Her hair came loose and swayed back and forth like a shining black banner.

"Damn you!" Flannery shouted as he shook her.

Her whole body swung, high in the empty air. Fearful cries came from all over the crowd. Lacey gave an awful moan and clutched at Celina.

"Christie isn't here, I tell you!" the sheriff shouted.

"No, he isn't!" another voice confirmed. It was the captain of the Lighthorse who had arrested King. "The man's telling you the truth!"

"Then I reckon we'll jist wait here 'til Ned Christie shows up," Flannery shouted. "Likely he was delayed by the storm—high water, fallen trees—he may not know the country as good as this little buddy of mine." He gave Jessee another shake.

Lacey screamed. Celina turned and hugged her, pulling her into the shelter of a big oak tree, trying to shield her from a view of the creek. Ridge and King appeared out of the confusion.

"I'm sorry, Little One," Ridge said, taking Lacey from Celina. She went into his arms with a pitiful cry. "It's all my fault," he groaned. "I can't believe I was stupid enough to send Jess into such danger."

"Where'd you send her?" King demanded. "How'd that son of a bitch get hold of her?"

Ridge tucked Lacey's head beneath his chin and rocked her in his arms while his tortured gaze went from King to Celina to King. "I got a note from Ned Christie saying he could testify as to who stole those marked logs and why," he said. "So I sent Jessee to fetch him."

King stared into his father's ashen face. "Why didn't you go?"

"I couldn't leave *you*, son! There was no way I could."

Ridge's big hand circled comfort onto Lacey's back, but his eyes never left King's. "You'd have come into that courtroom and looked out to see your mother sitting there without me."

The cadence of his words quickened. "You'd have thought I believed you meant the things you said to me last night. You'd have thought they might even actually be true because it would've seemed I'd deserted you."

Lacey sobbed. Ridge held her closer to him, but still his gaze wouldn't let King's go.

"I was sick with fear," he said, "that Celina couldn't clear you without Ned's help."

King stared into the naked anguish in his father's eyes. Ridge stared back, not moving at all except for his absentminded caresses of Lacey.

His daughter was in terrible danger, where he had placed her, and Ridge Chekote was paralyzed by fear and guilt. He was human. He had made a stupid, unthinking mistake. The man was human. And he had made that mistake because he loved King so.

Ridge loved him.

Ridge had always loved him. Even his efforts to plan King's life for him were expressions of love. He had been trying to keep King at home, keep him close.

King took two steps toward Ridge and Lacey and threw his arms around them. He closed his eyes and hugged them to him.

"Don't worry," he said. "It'll be all right."

Tears choked Celina.

The bounty hunter shouted again. "Give me Ned Christie!"

King dropped his arms and turned. His eyes met

Celina's in a look she couldn't read, except to know that he was going after Jessee, no matter the danger.

He reached out and caressed Celina's hair in farewell, a touch as light as the brushing of a feather. Then he was gone, slipping away through the crowd. Celina watched him until he disappeared.

That ambiguous look and that touch had told her nothing more than farewell. Did he still believe she wasn't worth the fight he'd made?

A great sigh of fear swept over the crowd, interrupting her thoughts.

Ridge turned and, with Lacey clinging to his hand and to Celina's, pushed through to the bank of the creek. People left an open corridor where they had come and stood a little bit back from them, as if in respect for the bereaved. No! She would not think such things. They would be all right. Jessee and King both.

"Let her go!" the sheriff shouted. "We'll wait here for Christie anyway."

"My mama didn't raise no fools," Flannery yelled back. He began swinging Jessee back and forth, very slowly, as if he were building up momentum to throw her as far as he could.

Celina watched, mesmerized, every inch of the movement drawing her gaze to the left, then to the right. Jessee's red dress made a bleeding wound against the shining gray granite of the cliff.

Sunlight poured out over the whole, washed-clean world, the air smelled fresh—of mountain pines and crushed grass and flowers. The hills looked so innocent, the closer ones standing green and brown, the farther ones rolling purple against the soft line of the sky. How could such a day hold such ugliness?

King! Oh, Dear God, where was King? But what in the world could he do?

The authorities were obviously helpless. Several

members of the Lighthorse, along with the judge and the court bailiff, had gathered around the sheriff. They joined in shouting at Flannery, but the only result of their efforts was a slight speeding up of the rhythm with which he was swinging Jessee.

Dear Lord! How long could the man's arm hold out? What if it tired and gave way without warning?

Lacey and Ridge watched with their faces turned to the sky in raw despair. They stood a bit apart now, their hands joined in a stiff bridge between them as if they were trying for balance to walk out onto the water.

Celina put her arms around the trunk of the tree beside her and closed her eyes.

"Hey! Bounty Hunter!"

The cry came from the mountain. Celina's eyes flew open; she let go of the tree and took two steps toward the creek.

"You hear me?" It was King's voice, coming from above and behind the man holding Jessee.

Flannery went still. Jessee's small body swung almost to a stop, dangling high over the rocky creekbed.

"I'm Ned Christie," King shouted. "Let the girl go and I'll let you take me in to Forth Smith."

The man whirled to look behind him. Jessee grabbed the rock outcropping and hung on as he turned; it broke his grip on her belt.

"Damn it to hell!" he screamed. He drew a pistol from his belt and fired two shots in quick succession, one toward King and one back at Jessee, who was scrambling over the rocks downward toward the creek.

"Ha! Bounty Hunter!" King yelled. "Come and get me." He stepped out from behind a pine tree then, his shirt gleaming white between the dark green of the tree and the gray of the mountain. The fresh breeze caught his sleeve and whipped it once, like a flag.

Flannery fired again.

Celina's feet ran a couple of steps toward King before her mind insisted that it was impossible to reach him. He could be killed!

Oh, Dear God, King could die right here in front of her eyes and she'd never even told him she loved him in a way he could believe. And after all the changes he'd made for her and the way he'd loved her so!

What an idiotic coward she was!

All because she had let horrid Father, crazy Eli, warp her thinking for so long. Her eyes found Eli in the crowd in an instant—her subconscious, as always, must have been aware of him the whole time. He stood, not far from Lacey and Ridge, watching them and the drama unfolding on the side of the mountain with no trace of emotion whatsoever on his face.

She looked back at the Chekotes beside her. They had encircled each other's waists now to cling together, every straining line of their bodies telling the anguish of seeing their children in danger.

They had more feeling in one of their little fingers, she thought, than Eli had or ever would have in his entire being—body, soul, and spirit. If that were Celina out there it wouldn't make a bit of difference to him. He would still be watching with that same uncaring expression on his face. He wouldn't be feeling fear, even for her.

And he would never feel pride for her. Or understanding. Or anything else.

She stood stiff as a soldier, looking at his lifeless face, letting the realization soak into her consciousness and go all the way through her. A profound sadness rose to meet it, a sorrow that surged in her blood through all her veins.

But right behind it pulsed a winging sense of joy. She didn't care anymore whether Eli loved her or not. King had been right when he said that Eli was mad, that he couldn't love anyone. That was a fact and now she accepted it.

She was free. At last, for the first time in all her life, she was free.

Celina turned her back on her father and raised her eyes to the mountain. King wasn't there. And then he was.

He darted out from behind a fat cedar tree, throwing one quick glance over his shoulder to make sure that Flannery had seen him. The big man yelled and tore his way upward over the rocks after him.

King hid, but the minute Flannery stopped moving he showed himself again. His taunting words echoed across the heads of the muttering crowd.

"What's the matter, Bounty Hunter, trail too steep for you? How much do you *want* Ned Christie?" King turned his back and ran.

Flannery took out after him in earnest, his boots sending small rocks and dirt spiraling down through empty air into the creek.

Celina's heart plummeted. King wasn't very far ahead, and the barrel of Flannery's blue-black pistol stayed steadily pointed at him, gleaming like a wicked wand in the sun.

Her blood turned to water. Why, oh why hadn't she said yes to King that night in the honeysuckle bower? She had loved him then; her heart had known it even if her mind hadn't.

What if she never had another chance to tell him? The irony would be too cruel if now that she had found the courage to follow her heart, her man would die up there on the mountain.

King kept moving, dashing from tree to tree, leading Flannery steadily upward and away from the fleeing Jessee, who had almost reached the bottom of the bluff on the other side of the stream from the crowd. People began wading out into the creek toward her, but Celina couldn't watch them gather her in to safety. She had eyes only for King. Her King.

A gunshot cracked. For a heart-stopping instant Celina thought Flannery had fired at King, but instinctively she knew that that sound had been different from that of the pistol.

"Don't shoot!" Ridge's voice roared. "You might hit King!"

"Flannery'll fire again any minute!" the shooter called back. "And King isn't armed."

Celina looked to see a man with a rifle at the edge of the creek. She glanced at him, then stared. The man trying to save King was none other than Blue Hawk Deer-in-the-water.

Hawk fired again. The bullet hit close to Flannery, ricocheting off the granite boulder with a pinging sound that rang against the rocks.

It panicked the bounty hunter. He stopped in his tracks, turned around, and shot back at Hawk uselessly, firing again and again in quick succession, emptying his pistol in a matter of seconds.

King appeared on the rocks above him. He crouched, then leaped, like an avenging wildcat, down onto the bounty hunter's shoulders.

Flannery threw away his pistol and turned, reaching to defend himself with huge, hamlike hands.

Celina's breath stopped. The man was enormous, though shorter than King, and even from so far away she could see his face was red with fury.

He clawed at King even while he staggered backward under the attack. It hurt King—he winced—but he plowed straight on into Flannery without waiting to get his footing on the rough surface of the rocks.

They staggered dangerously close to the edge, then back toward the mountain, fighting on the broken ground of the cliff's outcropping with no regard at all for the open space yawning beneath them. Celina couldn't breathe, couldn't think, couldn't speak.

Except with her heart. I love you, Kingfisher Chekote. I love you, King. I love you. I love you.

He had to live. He had to live so that she could tell him that, whether he still loved her or not.

Flannery came at King again, forcing him backward toward yawning, empty air. But King stood, as if his heels were growing out of the rough rock, and waited until the man had reached just the right spot.

He drew back his right arm and landed a blow to Flannery's head that felled him, hard. King waited. The man didn't get up.

A great cheer rose from a hundred throats and went echoing through the long valley. Somewhere, back in the crowd, somebody started beating a drum.

Jessee came up out of the creek and onto the bank, water pouring from her clothes and the long, black cloak of her hair. She pushed it away from her eyes with both hands, straining to look up, back over her shoulder, to see King.

Celina couldn't take her eyes off him.

He strode to the edge of the jagged rock and planted one foot on a higher outcropping of the crag and raised both arms to the sky like a conquering warrior.

He could have been wearing wings of eagle feathers. He could have soared out into the sun-filled space and flown to the very tops of the farthest mountains. He could have swept far up into the blue sky to rule with Thunder.

The next instant, he disappeared.

Celina waited, her heart beating only until she could see him again. Even through the happy talk and confusion of hugs from Lacey and the wet Jessee and sympathetic Dolores and the rumbling relief in Ridge's voice, Celina was only waiting for King. He was alive. He had lived through it, unhurt.

Except for the terrible wounds she had given him. Were they too deep? Is that what he had meant by that look when he touched her hair? Or had he meant that he would come back to her?

The milling, chattering crowd grew noisier; King was moving toward her through the throng. She came to life again. She could breathe the storm-washed air once more, but only while she could fill her senses with him. A flap torn in his white shirt hung loose, the bronze muscles of his chest rippled there, where she used to stroke his skin. Would he ever let her do that again?

Slowly she let her gaze travel upward, over the naked column of his neck. Was he coming to her or to his family? Was it too late for her? Forever too late?

Her stare slipped up to his gorgeous, determined chin, to the sure set of his sensuous mouth. Would she ever kiss that mouth again? Her eyes flew to his. Their amber light pierced to the core of her.

"Well, Chekote!" somebody yelled. "Now you can go back to building your railroad!"

Without taking his eyes from Celina's, without missing a step in his journey to her, King shouted back. "Not now. Let's keep the Nation just the way it is for as long as we can!"

Celina felt a smile begin on her lips and spread over her face.

The approving shout that went up was deafening, and the cheering centered around his name, but King walked on, completely oblivious to everyone but her. His smile was as bright as the golden sunshine that had followed the storm.

He reached Celina and took her into his arms.

She went with a repentant sigh, reaching up to throw her arms around his neck as he crushed her body to his. Tears of happiness flooded into her eyes, and, at long, long last, she let them come.

She buried her face in the warm hollow of his throat for one precious instant, then pulled back just far enough to look up into his face.

His loving eyes were waiting. He cupped her chin in his hand. "This is the fourth time I've asked you," he said quietly, "and four is a sacred number to the Cherokee, so you must tell me the truth this time. Celina, will you marry me?"

"Yes!" she said, her voice strong and clear. "Yes, yes, yes!"

Chapter 20

K ing and Celina stood motionless, holding each other.

Finally Jessee called, "Are you all getting married? Is that what you said?"

Celina jumped, startled to be reminded that someone else existed. She turned her head to look at Jessee, but laid her cheek against King's bare chest and tightened her arms around him as if to make sure he didn't go away.

Jessee, her pretty face intensely curious beneath the wild, wet tangle of her hair, stood in the middle of the whole Chekote clan. All of them were waiting, with barely controlled impatience, to touch King, to know he was really safe. Celina could read that in the lines of their bodies because the same need was still filling hers.

Her own parents stood a short distance away, Eli frowning furiously, Dolores beaming at Celina and King. Her dark eyes asked the same question as Jessee's.

"Yes," Celina and King said at the same instant, their hold on each other tightening as they spoke. "Yes. We're getting married."

"No!" Ridge and Eli roared in unison, their voices booming over Jessee's squeals of delight. "No, you are not! I absolutely forbid it!"

They turned to stare at each other in absolute consternation. How could the two of them ever be in such agreement?

"You will do no such thing, Eli Hawthorne!" Dolores said into the stunned silence. "I *forbid* you to forbid it."

Eli's jaw dropped. He swung around to glare at her. "How dare you speak to me so?"

"I dare out of thirty years of enduring your tyranny," she said with her soft Spanish accent. "And out of twenty-one years of heartfelt pain every time you tried to kill the spirit of our daughter."

"Have you lost your mind?" he gasped.

"Not at all," she said, drawing herself up proudly. "I have found my mind and my new home."

"You're crazy," Eli insisted coldly. "Hush, woman. You're not making sense."

"Even if you can escape going to jail here in the Cherokee Nation," she said scornfully, "even if you go back to California, I'm not going back there. I'm going to ask to become a Cherokee so I can be near my grandchildren."

Her big brown eyes turned to Lacey, who immediately let go of Jessee to run to her.

"Of course you may stay in the Nation!" she said, through the joyful squeals and screams of Jessee and Laura and the other little girls swarming around.

King bent over to whisper in Celina's ear.

"Let's go back to the courthouse," he said, "and ask the judge to marry us before he goes home."

She couldn't take her eyes from the confusion of the happy family. She whispered back, "But what about them? They'll want to be there."

"Later," he said. "They can come to our church wedding."

"I want a traditional Cherokee wedding, too," Celina said. "And maybe an outdoor wedding right here on this spot."

King laughed and hugged her tighter.

"Four weddings! Celina, you've become a real Cherokee!"

She stood on tiptoe to slip her hands behind his neck. "No, King," she murmured, as she brought his lips down to hers. "Because of you I've become the real me."